A Publication Distributed by Heron Books

Jules Verne

Greatest Adventures

JULES VERNE
1828–1905

Jules Verne

Greatest Adventures

Journey to the centre of the earth

◆

Round the world in eighty days

DISTRIBUTED BY HERON BOOKS

Journey to the centre of the earth

Journey to the Centre of the Earth

CHAPTER I
MY UNCLE MAKES A GREAT DISCOVERY

OOKING back to all that has occurred to me since that eventful day, I am scarcely able to believe in the reality of my adventures. They were truly so wonderful that even now I am bewildered when I think of them.

My uncle was a German, though I am English, he having married my mother's sister. Being very much attached to his fatherless nephew, he invited me to study under him in his home in the fatherland. This home was in a large town, and my uncle a professor of philosophy, chemistry, geology, mineralogy, and many other ologies.

One day, after passing some hours in the laboratory— my uncle being absent at the time—I suddenly felt the necessity of renovating the tissues—*i. e.*, I was hungry, and was about to rouse up our old French cook, when my uncle, Professor Von Hardwigg, suddenly opened the street door, and came rushing upstairs.

Now, Professor Hardwigg, my worthy uncle, is by no means a bad sort of man; he is, however, choleric and original. To hear with him means to obey; and scarcely had his heavy feet resounded within our joint domicile than he shouted for me to attend upon him. " Harry— Harry—Harry——"

I hastened to obey, but before I could reach his room, jumping three steps at a time, he was stamping his right foot upon the landing. " Harry ! " he cried, in a frantic tone, " are you coming up ? "

To tell the truth, at that moment I was far more interested in the question as to what was to constitute our dinner than in any problem of science; to me soup was more interesting than soda, an omelette more tempting than arithmetic, and an artichoke of ten times more value than any amount of asbestos. But my uncle was not a man to be kept waiting; so adjourning all minor questions, I presented myself before him.

He was a very learned man. Now, most persons in this category supply themselves with information, as peddlers do with goods, for the benefit of others, and lay up stores in order to diffuse them abroad for the benefit of society in general. Not so my excellent uncle, Professor Hardwigg; he studied, he consumed the midnight oil, he pored over heavy tomes, and digested huge quartos and folios, in order to keep the knowledge acquired to himself. There was a reason, and it may be regarded as a good one, why my uncle objected to display his learning more than was absolutely necessary; he stammered, and when intent upon explaining the phenomena of the heavens, was apt to find himself at fault, and allude in such a vague way to sun, moon, and stars, that few were able to comprehend his meaning. To tell the honest truth, when the right word would not come, it was generally replaced by a very powerful adjective.

In connection with the sciences there are many almost unpronounceable names—names very much resembling those of Welsh villages; and my uncle being very fond of using them, his habit of stammering was not thereby improved. In fact, there were periods in his discourse when he would finally give up and swallow his discomfiture—in a glass of water.

As I said, my uncle, Professor Hardwigg, was a very learned man; and I now add a most kind relative. I was bound to him by the double ties of affection and interest. I took deep interest in all his doings, and hoped some day to be almost as learned myself. It was a rare thing for me to be absent from his lectures. Like him, I preferred mineralogy to all the other sciences. My anxiety was to gain *real knowledge of the earth.* Geology and mineralogy were to us the sole objects of life, and in connection with these studies many a fair specimen of stone, chalk, or metal did we break with our hammers.

But before I state the subject on which my uncle wished to confer with me, I must say a word about his personal

4

appearance. Alas! my readers will see a very different portrait of him at a future time, after he has gone through the fearful adventures yet to be related.

My uncle was fifty years old; tall, thin, and wiry. Large spectacles hid, to a certain extent, his vast, round and goggle eyes, while his nose was irreverently compared to a thin file. So much indeed did it resemble that useful article, that a compass was said in his presence to have made considerable deviation. The truth being told, however, the only article really attracted to my uncle's nose was tobacco.

Another peculiarity of his was, that he always stepped a yard at a time, clenched his fists as if he were going to hit you, and was, when in one of his peculiar humors, very far from a pleasant companion.

It is further necessary to observe, that he lived in a very nice house, in that very nice street, the Königstrasse at Hamburg. Though lying in the center of a town, it was perfectly rural in its aspect—half wood, half bricks, with old-fashioned gables—one of the few old houses spared by the great fire of 1842. When I say a nice house, I mean a handsome house—old, tottering, and not exactly comfortable to English notions: a house a little off the perpendicular and inclined to fall into the neighboring canal; exactly the house for a wandering artist to depict; all the more that you could scarcely see it for ivy and a magnificent old tree which grew over the door.

My uncle was rich; his house was his own property, and he had a considerable private income. To my notion the best part of his possessions was his god-daughter, Gretchen, who unfortunately was away upon a visit on that momentous day. The old cook, the young lady, the Professor and I were the sole inmates of his home.

I loved mineralogy, I loved geology. To me there was nothing like pebbles—and if my uncle had been in a little less of a fury, we should have been the happiest of families. To prove the excellent Hardwigg's impatience, I solemnly declare that when the flowers in the drawing-room pots began to grow, he rose every morning at four o'clock to make them grow quicker by pulling the leaves!

Having described my uncle, I will now give an account of our interview. He received me in his study; a perfect museum, containing every natural curiosity that can well be imagined—minerals, however, predominating. Every one was familiar to me, having been catalogued by my own hand. My uncle, apparently oblivious of the fact that he had summoned me to his presence, was absorbed in a book. He was particularly fond of early editions, tall copies, and unique works.

"Wonderful!" he cried, tapping his forehead. "Wonderful—wonderful!" It was one of those yellow-leaved volumes now rarely found on stalls, and to me it appeared to possess but little value. My uncle, however, was in raptures. He admired its binding, the clearness of its characters, the ease with which it opened in his hand, and repeated aloud, half-a-dozen times, that it was very, very old.

To my fancy he was making a great fuss about nothing, but it was not my province to say so. On the contrary, I professed considerable interest in the subject, and asked him what it was about.

"It is the Heims-Kringla of Snorre Tarleson," he said, "the celebrated Icelandic author of the tweifth century— it is a true and correct account of the Norwegian princes who reigned in Iceland."

My next question related to the language in which it was written. I hoped at all events it was translated into German. My uncle was indignant at the very thought, and declared he wouldn't give a penny for a translation. His delight was to have found the original work in the Icelandic tongue, which he declared to be one of the most magnificent and yet simple idioms in the world—while at the same time its grammatical combinations were the most varied known to students.

"About as easy as German?" was my insidious remark.

My uncle shrugged his shoulders.

"The letters at all events," I said, "are rather difficult of comprehension."

"It is a Runic manuscript, the language of the original population of Iceland, invented by Odin himself," cried my uncle, angry at my ignorance.

I was about to venture upon some misplaced joke on the subject, when a small scrap of parchment fell out of the leaves. Like a hungry man snatching at a morsel of bread the Professor seized it. It was about five inches by three and was scrawled over in the most extraordinary fashion.

The lines opening the next chapter are an exact facsimile of what was written on the venerable piece of parchment—and have wonderful importance, as they induced my uncle to undertake the most wonderful series of adventures which ever fell to the lot of human beings.

My uncle looked keenly at the document for some moments and then declared that it was Runic. The letters were similar to those in the book, but then what did they mean? This was exactly what I wanted to know.

Now, as I had a strong conviction that the Runic alphabet and dialect were simply an invention to mystify poor human nature, I was delighted to find that my uncle knew as much about the matter as I did—which was nothing. At all events, the tremulous motion of his fingers made me think so.

"And yet," he muttered to himself, "it is old Icelandic, I am sure of it."

My uncle ought to have known, for he was a perfect polyglot dictionary in himself. He did not pretend, like a certain learned pundit, to speak the two thousand languages and four thousand idioms made use of in different parts of the globe, but he did know all the more important ones.

It is a matter of great doubt to me now, to what violent measures my uncle's impetuosity might have led him, had not the clock struck two, and our old French cook called out to let us know that dinner was on the table.

"Bother the dinner!" cried my uncle. But I was hungry, I sallied forth to the dining-room, where I took up my usual quarters. Out of politeness I waited three minutes, but no sign of my uncle, the Professor. I was surprised. He was not usually so blind to the pleasure of a good dinner. It was the acme of German luxury—parsley soup, a ham omelette with sorrel trimmings, an oyster of veal stewed with prunes, delicious fruit, and sparkling Moselle. For the sake of poring over that musty old piece of parchment, my uncle forbore to share our meal. To satisfy my conscience, I ate for both.

The old cook and housekeeper was nearly out of her mind. After taking so much trouble, to find her master not appear at dinner was to her a sad disappointment—which, as she watched the havoc I was making on the viands, became also alarm. If my uncle were to come to table after all?

Suddenly, just as I had consumed the last apple and drank the last glass of wine, a terrible voice was heard at no great distance. It was my uncle roaring for me to come to him. I made very nearly one leap of it—so loud, so fierce was his tone.

CHAPTER II
THE MYSTERIOUS PARCHMENT

" I DECLARE," cried my uncle, striking the table fiercely with his fist, " I declare to you it is Runic—and contains some wonderful secret, which I must get at, at any price."

I was about to reply when he stopped me. " Sit down," he said, quite fiercely, " and write to my dictation."

I obeyed. " I will substitute," he said, " a letter of our alphabet for that of the Runic: we will then see what that will produce. Now, begin and make no mistakes."

The dictation commenced with the following incomprehensible result :—

m.rnlls	esruel	seecJde
sgtssmf	unteief	niedrke
kt,samn	atrateS	Saodrrn
emtnael	nuaect	rrilSa
Atvaar	.nscrc	ieaabs
ccdrmi	eeutul	frantu
dt,iac	oseibo	KediiI

Scarcely giving me time to finish, my uncle snatched the document from my hands and examined it with the most rapt and deep attention.

" I should like to know what it means," he said, after a long period.

I certainly could not tell him, nor did he expect me to— his conversation being uniformly answered by himself.

" I declare it puts me in mind of a cryptograph," he cried, " unless, indeed, the letters have been written without any real meaning; and yet why take so much trouble? Who knows but I may be on the verge of some great discovery? "

My candid opinion was that it was all rubbish! But this opinion I kept carefully to myself, as my uncle's choler was not pleasant to bear. All this time he was comparing the book with the parchment.

" The manuscript volume and the smaller document are written in different hands," he said, " the cryptograph is of much later date than the book; there is an undoubted proof of the correctness of my surmise. The first letter is a double M, which was only added to the Icelandic language in the twelfth century—this makes the parchment two hundred years posterior to the volume."

The circumstance appeared very probable and very logical, but it was all surmise to me.

" To me it appears probable that this sentence was written by some owner of the book. Now who was the owner, is the next important question. Perhaps by great good luck it may be written somewhere in the volume."

With these words Professor Hardwigg took off his spectacles, and, taking a powerful magnifying glass, examined the book carefully. On the fly leaf was what appeared to be a blot of ink, but on examination proved to be a line of writing almost effaced by time. This was what he sought and, after some considerable time, he made out these letters:

$$\text{ᛘᛣᚾᛐ ᚼᛠᚱᚾᚾᛂᛂᛐᚷ}$$

" Arne Saknussemm! " he cried in a joyous and triumphant tone, " that is not only an Icelandic name, but of a learned professor of the sixteenth century, a celebrated alchemist."

I bowed as a sign of respect.

" These alchemists," he continued, " Avicena, Bacon, Lully, Paracelsus, were the true, the only learned men of the day. They made surprising discoveries. May not this Saknussemm, nephew mine, have hidden on this bit of parchment some astounding invention? I believe the cryptograph to have a profound meaning—which I must make out."

My uncle walked about the room in a state of excitement almost impossible to describe.

"It may be so, sir," I timidly observed, "but why conceal it from posterity, if it be a useful, a worthy discovery?"

"Why—how should I know? Did not Galileo make a secret of his discoveries in connection with Saturn? But we shall see. Until I discover the meaning of this sentence I will neither eat nor sleep."

"My dear uncle——" I began.

"Nor you either," he added. It was lucky I had taken double allowance that day.

"In the first place," he continued, "there must be a clue to the meaning. If we could find that, the rest would be easy enough."

I began seriously to reflect. The prospect of going without food and sleep was not a promising one, so I determined to do my best to solve the mystery. My uncle, meanwhile, went on with his soliloquy.

"The way to discover it is easy enough. In this document there are one hundred and thirty-two letters, giving seventy-nine consonants to fifty-three vowels. This is about the proportion found in most southern languages, the idioms of the north being much more rich in consonants. We may confidently predict, therefore, that we have to deal with a southern dialect."

Nothing could be more logical.

"Now," said Professor Hardwigg "to trace the particular language."

"As Shakespeare says, 'that is the question,'" was my rather satirical reply.

"This man Saknussemm," he continued, "was a very learned man: now as he did not write in the language of his birth-place, he probably, like most learned men of the sixteenth century, wrote in Latin. If, however, I prove wrong in this guess, we must try Spanish, French, Italian, Greek, and even Hebrew. My own opinion, though, is decidedly in favor of Latin."

This proposition startled me. Latin was my favorite study, and it seemed sacrilege to believe this gibberish to belong to the country of Virgil.

"Barbarous Latin, in all probability," continued my uncle, "but still Latin."

"Very probably," I replied, not to contradict him.

"Let us see into the matter," continued my uncle; "here

you see we have a series of one hundred and thirty-two letters, apparently thrown pell-mell upon paper, without method or organization. There are words which are composed wholly of consonants, such as *m.rnlls,* others which are nearly all vowels, the fifth, for instance, which is *unteief,* and one of the last *oseibo.* This appears an extraordinary combination. Probably we shall find that the phrase is arranged according to some mathematical plan. No doubt a certain sentence has been written out and then jumbled up —some plan to which some figure is the clue. Now, Harry, to show your English wit—what is that figure?"

I could give him no hint. My thoughts were indeed far away. While he was speaking I had caught sight of the portrait of my cousin Gretchen, and was wondering when she would return. We were affianced, and loved one another very sincerely. But my uncle, who never thought of such sublunary matters, knew nothing of this. Without noticing my abstraction, the Professor began reading the puzzling cryptograph all sorts of ways, according to some theory of his own. Presently, rousing my wandering attention, he dictated one precious attempt to me.

I mildly handed it over to him. It read as follows:—

messunkaSenrA.icefdoK.segnittamurtn
ecertserrette,rotaivsadua,ednecsedsadne
lacartniiiluJsiratracSarbmutabiledmek
meretarcsilucoIsleffenSnI.

I could scarcely keep from laughing, while my uncle, on the contrary, got in a towering passion, struck the table with his fist, darted out of the room, out of the house, and then taking to his heels was presently lost to sight.

CHAPTER III
AN ASTOUNDING DISCOVERY

"WHAT is the matter?" cried the cook, entering the room; "when will master have his dinner?"

"Never."

"And, his supper?"

"I don't know. He says he will eat no more, neither shall I. My uncle has determined to fast and make me fast until he reads this abominable inscription," I replied.

" You will be starved to death," she said.

I was very much of the same opinion, but not liking to say so, sent her away, and began some of my usual work of classification. But busy as I made myself, nothing could keep me from thinking alternately of the stupid manuscript and of the pretty Gretchen.

Several times I was tempted to go out, but my uncle would have been angry at my absence. At the end of an hour, my allotted task was done. How to pass the time? I began by lighting my pipe. Like all other students, I delighted in tobacco; and, seating myself in the great armchair, I began to meditate.

Where was my uncle? I could easily imagine him tearing along some solitary road, gesticulating, talking to himself, cutting the air with his cane, and still thinking of the absurd bit of hieroglyphics. Would he hit upon some clue? Would he come home in better humor? While these thoughts were passing through my brain, I mechanically took up the execrable puzzle and tried every imaginable way of grouping the letters. I put them together by twos, by threes, fours, and fives—in vain. Nothing intelligible came out, except that the fourteenth, fifteenth and sixteenth made *ice* in English; the eighty-fourth, eighty-fifth and eighty-sixth, the word *sir;* then at last I seemed to find the Latin words *rota, mutabile, ira, nec, atra.*

" Ha! there seems to be some truth in my uncle's notion," thought I.

Then again I seemed to find the word *luco,* which means sacred wood. Then in the third line I appeared to make out *labiled,* a perfect Hebrew word, and at the last the syllables *mère, are, mer,* which were French. It was enough to drive one mad. Four different idioms in this absurd phrase. What connection could there be between ice, sir, anger, cruel, sacred wood, changing, mother, are and sea? The first and the last might, in a sentence connected with Iceland, mean sea of ice. But what of the rest of this monstrous cryptograph?

I was, in fact, fighting against an insurmountable difficulty; my brain was almost on fire; my eyes were strained with staring at the parchment; the whole absurd collection of letters appeared to dance before my vision in a number of black little groups. My mind was possessed with temporary hallucination—I was stifling. I wanted air. Mechanically I fanned myself with the document, of which now I saw the back and then the front.

Imagine my surprise when glancing at the back of the wearisome puzzle, the ink having gone through, I clearly made out Latin words, and among others *craterem* and *terrestre*.

I had discovered the secret! It came upon me like a flash of lightning. I had got the clue. All you had to do to understand the document was to read it backwards. All the ingenious ideas of the Professor were realized; he had dictated it rightly to me; by a mere accident I had discovered what he so much desired.

My delight, my emotion may be imagined, my eyes were dazzled and I trembled so that at first I could make nothing of it. One look, however, would tell me all I wished to know.

"Let me read," I said to myself, after drawing a long breath. I spread it before me on the table, I passed my finger over each letter, I spelt it through; in my excitement I read it out.

What horror and stupefaction took possession of my soul. I was like a man who had received a knock-down blow. Was it possible that I really read the terrible secret, and it had really been accomplished! A man had dared to do—what?

No living being should ever know "Never!" cried I, jumping up; "Never shall my uncle be made aware of the dread secret. He would be quite capable of undertaking the terrible journey. Nothing would check him, nothing stop him. Worse, he would compel me to accompany him, and we should be lost forever. But no; such folly and madness cannot be allowed."

I was almost beside myself with rage and fury. "My worthy uncle is already nearly mad," I cried aloud. "This would finish him. By some accident he may make the discovery; in which case, we are both lost. Perish the fearful secret—let the flames forever bury it in oblivion."

I snatched up book and parchment, and was about to cast them into the fire, when the door opened and my uncle entered. I had scarcely time to put down the wretched documents before my uncle was by my side. He was profoundly absorbed. His thoughts were evidently bent on the terrible parchment. Some new combination had probably struck him while taking his walk. He seated himself in his arm-chair, and with a pen began to make an algebraical calculation. I watched him with anxious eyes. My flesh crawled as it became probable that he would discover *the* secret. His combinations I knew were useless, I having discovered the one only clue. For three mortal hours he continued without speaking a word, without raising his head, scratching, re-writing, calculating over and over again. I knew that in time he must hit upon the right phrase. The letters of every alphabet have only a certain number of combinations. But then years might elapse before he would arrive at the correct solution.

Still time went on; night came, the sounds in the streets ceased—and still my uncle went on, not even answering our worthy cook when she called us to supper. I did not dare to leave him, so waved her away, and at last fell asleep on the sofa.

When I awoke my uncle was still at work. His red eyes, his pallid countenance, his matted hair, his feverish hands, his hecticly flushed cheeks, showed how terrible had been his struggle with the impossible, and what fearful fatigue he had undergone during that long sleepless night. It made me quite ill to look at him. Though he was rather severe with me, I loved him, and my heart ached at his sufferings. He was so overcome by one idea that he could not even get in a passion! All his energies were focussed on one point. And I knew that by speaking one little word all this suffering would cease. I could not speak it.

My heart was, nevertheless, inclining towards him. Why, then, did I remain silent? In the interest of my uncle himself. "Nothing shall make me speak," I muttered. "He will want to follow in the footsteps of the other! I know him well. His imagination is a perfect volcano, and to make discoveries in the interests of geology he would sacrifice his life. I will therefore be silent and strictly keep the secret I have discovered. To reveal it would be suicidal. He would not only rush, himself, to destruction, but drag me with him." I crossed my arms, looked another way and smoked—resolved never to speak.

AN ASTOUNDING DISCOVERY

When our cook wanted to go out to market, or on any
other errand, she found the front door locked and the key
taken away. Was this done purposely or not? Surely Professor Hardwigg did not intend the old woman and myself
to become martyrs to his obstinate will. Were we to be
starved to death? A frightful recollection came to my
mind. Once we had fed on bits and scraps for a week while
he sorted some curiosities. It gave me the cramp even to
think of it!

I wanted my breakfast, and I saw no way of getting it.
Still my resolution held good. I would starve rather than
yield. But the cook began to take me seriously to task.
What was to be done? She could not go out; and I dared
not.

My uncle continued counting and writing; his imagination seemed to have translated him to the skies. He
neither thought of eating nor drinking. In this way
twelve o'clock came round. I was hungry, and there was
nothing in the house. The cook had eaten the last bit of
bread. This could not go on. It did, however, until two,
when my sensations were terrible. After all, I began to
think the document very absurd. Perhaps it might only
be a gigantic hoax. Besides, some means would surely be
found to keep my uncle back from attempting any such
absurd expedition. On the other hand, if he did attempt
anything so Quixotic, I should not be compelled to accompany him. Another line of reasoning partially decided
me. Very likely he would make the discovery himself
when I should have suffered starvation for nothing. Under
the influence of hunger this reasoning appeared admirable.
I determined to tell all.

The question now arose as to how it was to be done. I
was still dwelling on the thought, when he rose and put on
his hat. What! go out and lock us in? Never!

" Uncle," I began.

He did not appear even to hear me.

" Professor Hardwigg," I cried.

" What," he retorted, " did you speak? "

" How about the key? "

" What key—the key of the door? "

" No—of these horrible hieroglyphics? "

He looked at me from under his spectacles, and started

TO THE CENTRE OF THE EARTH

at the odd expression of my face. Rushing forward, he clutched me by the arm and keenly examined my countenance. His very look was an interrogation. I simply nodded.

With an incredulous shrug of the shoulders, he turned upon his heel. Undoubtedly he thought I had gone mad.

"I have made a very important discovery."

His eyes flashed with excitement. His hand was lifted in a menacing attitude. For a moment neither of us spoke. It is hard to say which was most excited.

"You don't mean to say that you have any idea of the meaning of the scrawl?"

"I do," was my desperate reply. "Look at the sentence as dictated by you.

"Well, but it means nothing," was the angry answer.

"Nothing if you read from left to right, but mark, if from right to left——"

"Backwards!" cried my uncle, in wild amazement. "Oh most cunning Saknussemm; and I to be such a blockhead." He snatched up the document, gazed at it with haggard eye, and read it out as I had done. It read as follows:—

In Sneffels yoculis craterem kem delebat
Umbra Scartaris Julii intra calendas descende.
'Audas viator, et terrestre centrum attinges.
Kod feci. Arne Saknussemm.

Which dog-Latin being translated, reads as follows: "Descend into the crater of Yocul of Sneffels, which the shade of Scartaris caresses, before the kalends of July, audacious traveler, and you will reach the center of the earth. I did it. ARNE SAKNUSSEMM."

My uncle leaped three feet from the ground with joy. He looked radiant and handsome. He rushed about the room wild with delight and satisfaction. He knocked over tables and chairs. He threw his books about until at last utterly exhausted, he fell into his arm-chair. "What's o'clock?" he asked.

"About three."

"My dinner does not seem to have done me much good," he observed, "Let me have something to eat. We can then start at once. Get my portmanteau ready."

"What for?"

" And your own," he continued. " We start at once."

My horror may be conceived. I resolved however to show no fear. Scientific reasons were the only ones likely to influence my uncle. Now, there were many against this terrible journey. The very idea of going down to the center of the earth was simply absurd. I determined therefore to argue the point after dinner.

My uncle's rage was now directed against the cook for having no dinner ready. My explanation however satisfied him, and giving her the key she soon contrived to get sufficient to satisfy our voracious appetites.

During the repast my uncle was rather gay than otherwise. He made some of those peculiar jokes which belong exclusively to the learned. As soon however as dessert was over, he called me to his study. We each took a chair on opposite sides of the table.

" Henry," he said, in a soft and winning voice; " I have always believed you ingenious, and you have rendered me a service never to be forgotten. Without you, this great, this wondrous discovery would never have been made It is my duty, therefore, to insist on your sharing the glory."

" He is in a good humor," thought I; " I'll soon let him know my opinion of glory."

" In the first place," he continued, " you must keep the whole affair a profound secret. There is no more envious race of men than scientific discoverers. Many would start on the same journey. At all events, we will be the first in the field."

" I doubt your having many competitors," was my reply.

" A man of real scientific acquirements would be delighted at the chance. We should find a perfect stream of pilgrims on the traces of Arne Saknussemm, if this document were once made public."

" But my dear sir, is not this paper very likely to be a hoax?" I urged.

" The book in which we find it is sufficient proof of its authenticity," he replied.

" I thoroughly allow that the celebrated Professor wrote the lines, but only, I believe, as a kind of mystification," was my answer.

Scarcely were the words out of my mouth, when I was

sorry I had uttered them. My uncle looked at me with a dark and gloomy scowl, and I began to be alarmed for the results of our conversation. His mood soon changed, however, and a smile took the place of a frown. "We shall see," he remarked, with decisive emphasis.

"But see, what is all this about Yocul, and Sneffels, and this Scartaris? I have never heard anything about them."

"The very point to which I am coming. I lately received from my friend, Augustus Peterman, of Leipzig, a map. Take down the third atlas from the second shelf, series Z, plate 4."

I rose, went to the shelf, and presently returned with the volume indicated.

"This," said my uncle, "is one of the best maps of Iceland. I believe it will settle all your doubts, difficulties and objections."

With a grim hope to the contrary, I stooped over the map.

CHAPTER IV
WE START ON THE JOURNEY

"You see, the whole island is made up of volcanoes," said the Professor, "and note that they all bear the name of Yokul. The word is Icelandic, and means a glacier. In most of the lofty mountains of that region the volcanic eruptions come forth from ice-bound caverns. Hence the name applied to every volcano on this extraordinary island."

"But what does this word Sneffels mean?"

To this question I expected no rational answer. I was mistaken. "Follow my finger to the western coast of Iceland, there you see Reykjawik, its capital. Follow the direction of one of its innumerable fjords or arms of the sea, and what do you see below the sixty-fifth degree of latitude?"

"A peninsula—very like a thigh-bone in shape."

"And in the center of it——?"

"A mountain."

"Well, that's Sneffels."

I had nothing to say.

" That is Sneffels—a mountain about five thousand feet in height, one of the most remarkable in the whole island, and certainly doomed to be the most celebrated in the world, for through its crater we shall reach the Center of the Earth."

" Impossible! " cried I, startled and shocked at the thought.

" Why impossible? " said Professor Hardwigg in his severest tones.

" Because its crater is choked with lava, by burning rocks —by infinite dangers."

" But if it be extinct? "

" That would make a difference."

" Of course it would. There are about three hundred volcanoes on the whole surface of the globe—but the greater number are extinct. Of these Sneffels is one. No eruption has occurred since 1219—in fact it has ceased to be a volcano at all."

After this what more could I say? Yes—I thought of another objection. " But what is all this about Scartaris and the kalends of July——? "

My uncle reflected deeply. Presently he gave forth the result of his reflections in a sententious tone. " What appears obscure to you, to me is light. This very phrase shows how particular Saknussemm is in his directions. The Sneffels' mountain has many craters. He is careful therefore to point the exact one which is the highway into the Interior of the Earth. He lets us know, for this purpose, that about the end of the month of June, the shadow of Mount Scartaris falls upon the one crater. There can be no doubt about the matter."

My uncle had an answer for everything. " I accept all your explanations," I said, " and Saknussemm is right. He found out the entrance to the bowels of the earth, he has indicated correctly, but that he or anyone else ever followed up the discovery, is madness to suppose."

" Why so, young man? "

" All scientific teaching, theoretical and practical, shows it to be impossible."

" I care nothing for theories," retorted my uncle.

" But is it not well-known that heat increases one degree for every seventy feet you descend into the earth? which

19

gives a fine idea of the central heat. All the matters which compose the globe are in a state of incandescence; even gold, platinum, and the hardest rocks are in a state of fusion. What would become of us?"

"Don't be alarmed at the heat, my boy."

"How so?"

"Neither you nor anybody else knows anything about the real state of the earth's interior. All modern experiments tend to explode the older theories. Were any such heat to exist, the upper crust of the earth would be shattered to atoms, and the world would be at an end."

A long, learned and not uninteresting discussion followed, which ended in this: "I do not believe in the dangers and difficulties which you, Henry, seem to multiply; and the only way to learn, is like Arne Saknussemm, to go and see."

"Well," cried I, overcome at last, "let us go and see. Though how we can do that in the dark is another mystery."

"Fear nothing. We shall overcome these, and many other difficulties. Besides, as we approach the Center, I expect to find it luminous——"

"Nothing is impossible."

"And now that we have come to a thorough understanding, not a word to any living soul. Our success depends on secrecy and despatch."

Thus ended our memorable conference, which roused a perfect fever in me. Leaving my uncle, I went forth like one possessed. Reaching the banks of the Elbe, I began to think. Was all I had heard really and truly possible? Was my uncle in his sober senses, and could the interior of the earth be reached? Was I the victim of a madman, or was he a discoverer of rare courage and grandeur of conception?

To a certain extent I was anxious to be off. I was afraid my enthusiasm would cool. I determined to pack up at once. At the end of an hour, however, on my way home, I found that my feelings had very much changed. "I'm all abroad," I cried; "'tis a nightmare—I must have dreamed it."

At this moment I came face to face with Gretchen, whom I warmly embraced. "So you have come to meet me," she said; "how good of you. But what is the matter?"

Well, it was no use mincing the matter, I told her all. She listened with awe, and for some minutes she could not speak. " Well? " I at last asked, rather anxiously.

" What a magnificent journey. If I were only a man! A journey worthy of the nephew of Professor Hardwigg. I should look upon it as an honor to accompany him."

" My dear Gretchen, I thought you would be the first to cry out against this mad enterprise."

" No; on the contrary, I glory in it. It is magnificent, splendid—an idea worthy of my father. Henry Lawson, I envy you."

This was, as it were, conclusive. The final blow of all.

When we entered the house we found my uncle surrounded by workmen and porters, who were packing up. He was pulling and hauling at a bell. " Where have you been wasting your time? Your portmanteau is not packed —my papers are not in order—the precious tailor has not brought my clothes, nor my gaiters—the key of my carpet bag is gone! "

I looked at him stupefied. And still he tugged away at the bell. " We are really off, then? " I said.

" Yes—of course, and yet you go out for a stroll, unfortunate boy! "

" And when do we go? "

" The day after to-morrow, at daybreak."

I heard no more; but darted off to my little bedchamber and locked myself in. There was no doubt about it now. My uncle had been hard at work all the afternoon. The garden was full of ropes, rope-ladders, torches, gourds, iron clamps, crow-bars, alpenstocks, and pickaxes—enough to load ten men.

I passed a terrible night. I was called early the next day to learn that the resolution of my uncle was unchanged and irrevocable. I also found my cousin and affianced wife as warm on the subject as was her father.

Next day, at five o'clock in the morning, the post-chaise was at the door. Gretchen and the old cook received the keys of the house; and, scarcely pausing to wish anyone good-bye, we started on our adventurous journey into the Center of the Earth.

CHAPTER V
FIRST LESSONS IN CLIMBING

At Altona, a suburb of Hamburg, is the Chief Station of the Kiel railway, which was to take us to the shores of the Belt; and exactly at seven o'clock we were seated opposite each other in a first-class railway carriage. My uncle said nothing. He was too busy examining his papers, among which of course was the famous parchment, and some letters of introduction from the Danish consul, which were to pave the way to an introduction to the Governor of Iceland. In three hours we reached Kiel, and our baggage was at once transferred to the steamer.

We had now a day before us, a delay of about ten hours. Which fact put my uncle in a towering passion. We had nothing to do but to walk about the pretty town and bay. At length, however, we went on board, and at half past ten were steaming down the Great Belt. The next morning we reached Copenhagen, where, scarcely taking time for refreshment, my uncle hurried out to present one of his letters of introduction. It was to the director of the Museum of Antiquities, who having been informed that we were tourists bound for Iceland, did all he could to assist us. One wretched hope sustained me now. Perhaps no vessel was bound for such distant parts.

Alas! a little Danish schooner, the *Valkyrie,* was to sail on the second of June for Reykjawik. The captain, M. Bjarne, was on board, and was rather surprised at the energy and cordiality with which his future passenger shook him by the hand. To him a voyage to Iceland was merely a matter of course. My uncle, on the other hand, considered the event of sublime importance. The honest sailor took advantage of the Professor's enthusiasm to double the fare.

"On Tuesday morning at seven o'clock be on board," said M. Bjarne, handing us our receipts.

"Excellent! Capital! Glorious!" remarked my uncle as we sat down to a late breakfast; "refresh yourself, my boy, and we will take a run through the town."

Our meal concluded, we went to the Kongens-Nye-Torw; to the king's magnificent palace; to the beautiful bridge over the canal near the Museum; to the immense cenotaph of Thorwaldsen with its hideous naval groups; to the castle of Rosenberg; and to all the other lions of the place,—none of which my uncle even saw, so absorbed was he in his anticipated triumphs.

But one thing struck his fancy, and that was a certain singular church steeple situated on the Island of Amak, which is the south-east quarter of the city of Copenhagen. My uncle at once ordered me to turn my steps that way. This church exhibited nothing remarkable in itself; in fact, the worthy Professor had only been attracted to it by one circumstance, which was, that its rather elevated steeple started from a circular platform, after which there was an exterior staircase, which wound round to the very summit. "Let us ascend," said my uncle.

"But I never could climb church towers," I cried, "I am subject to dizziness in my head."

"The very reason why you should go up. I want to cure you of a bad habit."

"But my good sir——"

"I tell you to come. What is the use of wasting so much valuable time?"

It was impossible to dispute the dictatorial commands of my uncle. I yielded with a groan. On payment of a fee, a verger gave us the key. He, for one, was not partial to the ascent. My uncle at once showed me the way, running up the steps like a school-boy. I followed as well as I could, though no sooner was I outside the tower, than my head began to swim. There was nothing of the eagle about me. The earth was enough for me, and no ambitious desire to soar ever entered my mind. Still things did not go badly until I had ascended 150 steps, and was near the platform, when I began to feel the rush of cold air. I could scarcely stand, when clutching the railings, I looked upwards. The railing was frail enough, but nothing to those which skirted the terrible winding staircase, that appeared, from where I stood, to ascend to the skies.

"Now then, Henry."

"I can't do it!" I cried, in accents of despair.

"Are you, after all, a coward, sir?" said my uncle in a pitiless tone. "Go up, I say!"

To this there was no reply possible. And yet the keen air acted violently on my nervous system; sky, earth, all seemed to swim round; while the steeple rocked like a ship.

My legs gave way like those of a drunken man. I crawled upon my hands and knees; I hauled myself up slowly, crawling like a snake. Presently I closed my eyes, and allowed myself to be dragged upwards.

"Look around you," said my uncle, in a stern voice, "heaven knows what profound abysses you may have to look down. This is excellent practice."

Slowly, and shivering all the while with cold, I opened my eyes. What then did I see? My first glance was upwards at the cold fleecy clouds, which as by some optical delusion appeared to stand still, while the steeple, the weathercock, and our two selves were carried swiftly along. Far away on one side could be seen the grassy plain, while on the other lay the sea bathed in translucent light. The Sund, or Sound as we call it, could be discovered beyond the point of Elsinore, crowded with white sails, which, at that distance, looked like the wings of sea-gulls; while to the east could be made out the far-off coast of Sweden. The whole appeared a magic panorama.

Faint and bewildered as I was, there was no remedy for it. Rise and stand up I must. Despite my protestations my first lesson lasted quite an hour. When, nearly two hours later, I reached the bosom of mother earth, I was like a rheumatic old man bent double with pain. "Enough for one day," said my uncle, rubbing his hands, "we will begin again to-morrow."

There was no remedy. My lessons lasted five days, and at the end of that period, I ascended blithely enough, and found myself able to look down into the depths below without even winking, and with some degree of pleasure.

CHAPTER VI
OUR VOYAGE TO ICELAND

THE hour of departure came at last. The night before, the worthy Mr. Thompson brought us the most cordial letters of introduction for Count Trampe, Governor of Iceland, for M. Pictursson, coadjutor to the bishop, and for M. Finsen, mayor of the town of Reykjawik. In return, my uncle nearly crushed his hands, so warmly did he shake them.

24

OUR VOYAGE TO ICELAND

On the second of the month, at two in the morning, our precious cargo of luggage was taken on board the good ship *Valkyrie*. We followed, and were very politely introduced by the captain to a small cabin with two standing bed places, neither very well ventilated nor very comfortable. But in the cause of science men are expected to suffer.

" Well, and have we a fair wind? " cried my uncle, in his most mellifluous accents.

" An excellent wind! " replied Captain Bjarne; " we shall leave the Sound, going free with all sails set." A few minutes afterwards, the schooner started before the wind, under all the canvas she could carry, and entered the channel. An hour later, the capital of Denmark seemed to sink into the waves, and we were at no great distance from the coast of Elsinore. My uncle was delighted; for myself, moody and dissatisfied, I appeared almost to expect a glimpse of the ghost of Hamlet.

" Sublime madman," thought I, " you doubtless, would approve our proceedings. You might perhaps even follow us to the center of the earth, there to resolve your eternal doubts."

" How long will the voyage last? " asked my uncle.

" Well, I should think about ten days," replied the skipper, " unless, indeed, we meet with some north-east gales among the Faroe Islands."

" At all events, there will be no very considerable delay," cried the impatient Professor.

" No, Mr. Hardwigg," said the captain, " no fear of that. At all events, we shall get there some day."

The voyage offered no incident worthy of record. I bore it very well, but my uncle to his great annoyance, and even shame, was remarkably sea-sick! This *mal de mer* troubled him the more, that it prevented him from questioning Captain Bjarne as to the subject of Sneffels, as to the means of communication, and the facilities of transport. All these explanations he had to adjourn to the period of his arrival. His time meanwhile, was spent lying in bed groaning, and dwelling anxiously on the hoped-for termination of the voyage. I did not pity him.

On the eleventh day we sighted Cape Portland, over which towered Mount Myrdals Yokul, which, the weather being clear, we made out very readily. The cape itself is nothing but a huge mount of granite standing naked and alone to meet the Atlantic waves. The *Valkyrie* kept off the coast, steering to the westward. On all sides were to be seen whole "schools" of whales and sharks. After some hours we came in sight of a solitary rock in the ocean, forming a mighty vault, through which the foaming waves poured with intense fury. The islets of Westman appeared to leap from the ocean, being so low in the water as scarcely to be seen, until you were right upon them. From that moment the schooner was steered to the westward in order to round Cape Reykjaness, the western point of Iceland.

My uncle, to his great disgust, was unable even to crawl on deck, so heavy a sea was on, and thus lost the first view of the Land of Promise. Forty-eight hours later, after a storm which drove us far to sea under bare poles, we came once more in sight of land, and were boarded by a pilot, who, after three hours of dangerous navigation, brought the schooner safely to an anchor in the bay of Faxa before Reykjawik.

My uncle came out of his cabin pale, haggard, thin, but full of enthusiasm, his eyes dilated with pleasure and satisfaction. Nearly the whole population of the town was on foot to see us land. The fact was, that scarcely any one of them but expected some goods by the periodical vessel.

Professor Hardwigg was in haste to leave his prison, or rather as he called it, his hospital; but before he attempted to do so, he caught hold of my hand, led me to the quarter-deck of the schooner, took my arm with his left hand, and pointed inland with his right, over the northern part of the bay, to where rose a high two-peaked mountain—a double cone covered with eternal snow. "Behold," he whispered in an awe-stricken voice, "behold—Mount Sneffels!"

Without further remark, he put his finger to his lips, frowned darkly, and descended into the small boat which awaited us. I followed, and in a few minutes we stood upon the soil of mysterious Iceland!

Scarcely were we fairly on shore when there appeared before us a man of excellent appearance, wearing the costume of a military officer. He was, however, but a civil servant, a magistrate, the governor of the island—Baron Trampe. The Professor knew whom he had to deal with. He therefore handed him the letters from Copenhagen, and a brief conversation in Danish followed, to which I of course was a stranger, and for a very good reason, for I did not know the language in which they conversed. I afterwards heard, however, that Baron Trampe placed himself entirely at the beck and call of Professor Hardwigg.

My uncle was also most graciously received by M. Finsen, the mayor, who as far as costume went, was quite as military as the governor, but also from character and occupation quite as pacific. As for his coadjutor, M. Pictursson, he was absent on an episcopal visit to the northern portion of the diocese. We were therefore compelled to defer the pleasure of being presented to him. His absence was, however, compensated by the presence of M. Fridriksson, Professor of natural science in the college of Reykjawik, a man of invaluable ability. This modest scholar spoke no languages save Icelandic and Latin. When, therefore, he addressed himself to me in the language of Horace, we at once came to undertsand one another. He was, in fact, the only person that I did thoroughly understand during the whole period of my residence in this benighted island.

Out of three rooms of which his house was composed, two were placed at our service, and in a few hours we were installed with all our baggage, the amount of which rather astonished the simple inhabitants of Reykjawik.

"Now, Harry," said my uncle, rubbing his hands, "all goes well, the worst difficulty is now over."

"How the worst difficulty over?" I cried in fresh amazement.

"Doubtless. Here we are in Iceland. Nothing more remains but to descend into the bowels of the earth."

"Well, sir, to a certain extent you are right. We have only to go down—but, as far as am concerned, that is not the question. I want to know how we are to get up again."

"That is the least part of the business, and does not in any way trouble me. In the meantime, there is not an hour to lose. I am about to visit the public library. Very likely I may find there some manuscripts from the hand of Saknussemm. I shall be glad to consult them."

"In the meanwhile," I replied, "I will take a walk through the town. Will you not likewise do so?"

"I feel no interest in the subject," said my uncle. "What for me is curious in this island, is not what is above the surface, but what is below."

I bowed by way of reply, put on my hat and furred cloak, and went out.

It was not an easy matter to lose oneself in the two streets of Reykjawik; I had therefore no need to ask my way. The town lies on a flat and marshy plain, between two hills. A vast field of lava skirts it on one side, falling away in terraces towards the sea. On the other hand is the large bay of Faxa, bordered on the north by the enormous glacier of Sneffels. In the bay the *Valkyrie* was then the only vessel at anchor. Generally there were one or two English or French gunboats, to watch and protect the fisheries in the offing. They were now, however, absent on duty.

In three hours my tour was complete. The general impression upon my mind was sadness. No trees, no vegetation, so to speak—on all sides volcanic peaks—the huts of turf and earth—more like roofs than houses. Thanks to the heat of these residences, grass grows on the roof, which grass is carefully cut for hay. I saw but few inhabitants during my excursion, but I met a crowd on the beach, drying, salting and loading cod-fish, the principal article of exportation. The men appeared robust but heavy; fair-haired like Germans, but of pensive mien—exiles of a higher scale in the ladder of humanity than the Esquimaux, but, I thought, much more unhappy, since with superior perceptions they are compelled to live within the limits of the Polar Circle.

CHAPTER VII
CONVERSATION AND DISCOVERY

WHEN I returned, dinner was ready. This meal was devoured by my worthy relative with avidity and voracity. His shipboard diet had turned his interior into a perfect gulf. The repast, which was more Danish than Icelandic, was in itself nothing, but the excessive hospitality of our host made us enjoy it doubly. The conversation turned upon scientific matters, and M. Fridriksson asked my uncle what he thought of the public library.

"Library, sir?" cried my uncle; "it appears to me a collection of useless odd volumes, and a beggarly amount of empty shelves."

"What!" cried M. Fridriksson; "why, we have eight thousand volumes of most rare and valuable works—some in the Scandinavian language, besides all the new publications from Copenhagen."

"Eight thousand volumes, my dear sir—why, where are they?" cried my uncle.

"Scattered over the country, Professor Hardwigg. We are very studious, my dear sir, though we do live in Iceland. Every farmer, every laborer, every fisherman can both read and write—and we think that books instead of being locked up in cupboards, far from the sight of students, should be distributed as widely as possible. The books of our library are, therefore, passed from hand to hand without returning to the library shelves perhaps for years."

"Then when foreigners visit you, there is nothing for them to see?"

"Well, sir, foreigners have their own libraries, and our first consideration is, that our humbler classes should be highly educated. Fortunately, the love of study is innate in the Icelandic people. In 1816 we founded a Literary Society and Mechanics' Institute; many foreign scholars of eminence are honorary members; we publish books destined to educate our people, and these books have rendered valuable services to our country. Allow me to have the honor, Professor Hardwigg, to enrol you as an honorary member?"

My uncle, who already belonged to nearly every literary and scientific institution in Europe, immediately yielded to the amiable wishes of good M. Fridriksson. "And now," said the latter after many expressions of gratitude and goodwill, "if you will tell me what books you expected to find, perhaps I may be of some assistance to you."

I watched my uncle keenly. For a minute or two he hesitated, as if unwilling to speak; to speak openly was, perhaps, to unveil his projects. Nevertheless, after some reflection, he made up his mind. "Well, M. Fridriksson," he said in any easy, unconcerned kind of way, "I was desirous of ascertaining, if among other valuable works, you had any by the learned Arne Saknussemm."

"Arne Saknussemm!" cried the Professor of Reykja-wik; "you speak of one of the most distinguished scholars of the sixteenth century, of the great naturalist, the great alchemist, the great traveler."

"Exactly so."

"One of the most distinguished men connected with Ice-landic science and literature."

"As you say, sir——"

"A man illustrious above all."

"Yes, sir, all this is true, but his works?"

"We have none of them."

"Not in Iceland?"

"There are none in Iceland or elsewhere," answered the other, sadly.

"Why so?"

"Because Arne Saknussemm was persecuted for heresy, and in 1573 his works were publicly burnt at Copenhagen by the hands of the common hangman."

"Very good! capital!" murmured my uncle, to the great astonishment of the worthy Icelander.

"You said, sir——"

"Yes, yes, all is clear, I see the link in the chain; every-thing is explained, and I now understand why Arne Sak-nussemm, put out of court, forced to hide his magnificent discoveries, was compelled to conceal beneath the veil of an incomprehensible cryptograph, the secret——"

"What secret?"

"A secret—which," stammered my uncle.

"Have you discovered some wonderful manuscript?"

"No, no, I was carried away by my enthusiasm. A mere supposition."

"Very good, sir. But, really, to turn to another sub-ject, I hope you will not leave our island without examin-ing into its mineralogical riches."

"Well, the fact is, I am rather late. So many learned men have been here before me."

"Yes, yes, but there is still much to be done," cried M Fridriksson.

"You think so," said my uncle, his eyes twinkling with hidden satisfaction.

"Yes, you have no idea how many unknown mountains, glaciers, volcanoes there are which remain to be studied. Without moving from where we sit, I can show you one. Yonder on the edge of the horizon, you see Sneffels."

"Oh yes, Sneffels," said my uncle.

"One of the most curious volcanoes in existence, the crater of which has been rarely visited."

"Extinct?"

"Extinct, any time these five hundred years," was the ready reply.

"Well," said my uncle, who dug his nails into his flesh, and pressed his knees tightly together to prevent himself leaping up with joy. "I have a great mind to begin my studies with an examination of the geological mysteries of this Mount Seffel—Feisel—what do you call it?"

"Sneffels, my dear sir."

This portion of the conversation took place in Latin, and I therefore understood all that had been said. I could scarcely keep my countenance when I found my uncle so cunningly concealing his delight and satisfaction. I must confess that his artful grimaces, put on to conceal his happiness, made him look like a new Mephistopheles. "Yes, yes," he continued, "your proposition delights me. I will endeavor to climb to the summit of Sneffels, and, if possible, will descend into its crater."

"I very much regret," continued M. Fridriksson "that my occupation will entirely preclude the possibility of my accompanying you. It would have been both pleasurable and profitable if I could have spared the time."

"No, no, a thousand times no," cried my uncle. "I do not wish to disturb the serenity of any man. I thank you, however, with all my heart. The presence of one so learned as yourself, would no doubt have been most useful, but the duties of your office and profession before everything."

In the innocence of his simple heart, our host did not perceive the irony of these remarks. "I entirely approve your project," he continued after some further remarks. "It is a good idea to begin by examining this volcano. You will make a harvest of curious observations. In the first place, how do you propose to get to Sneffels?"

"By sea. I shall cross the bay. Of course that is the most rapid route."

" Of course.   But still it cannot be done."

" Why ? "

" We have not an available boat in all Reykjawik," replied the other.

" What is to be done ? "

" You must go by land along the coast.   It is longer, but much more interesting."

" Then I must have a guide."

" Of course; and I have your very man."

" Somebody on whom I can depend ? "

" Yes, an inhabitant of the peninsula on which Sneffels is situated.   He is a very shrewd and worthy man, with whom you will be pleased.   He speaks Danish like a Dane."

" When can I see him—to-day ? "

" No, to-morrow; he will not be here before."

" To-morrow be it," replied my uncle, with a deep sigh.

The conversation ended by compliments on both sides. During the dinner my uncle had learned much as to the history of Arne Saknussemm, the reasons for his mysterious and hieroglyphical document.   He also became aware that his host would not accompany him on his adventurous expedition, and that next day we should have a guide.

CHAPTER VIII

THE EIDER-DOWN HUNTER—OFF AT LAST

That evening I took a brief walk on the shore near Reykjawik, after which I returned to an early sleep on my bed of coarse planks, where I slept the sleep of the just. When I awoke I heard my uncle speaking loudly in the next room.   I rose hastily and joined him.   He was talking in Danish with a man of tall stature, and of perfectly Herculean build.   This man appeared to be possessed of very great strength.   His eyes, which started rather prominently from a very large head, the face belonging to which was simple and naive, appeared very quick and intelligent. Very long hair, which even in England would have been accounted exceedingly red, fell over his athletic shoulders. This native of Iceland was active and supple in appearance, though he scarcely moved his arms, being in fact one of

those men who despise the habit of gesticulation common
to southern people.

Everything in this man's manner revealed a calm and
phlegmatic temperament. There was nothing indolent
about him, but his appearance spoke of tranquility. He
was one of those who never seemed to expect anything
from anybody, who liked to work when he thought proper,
and whose philosophy nothing could astonish or trouble.

I began to comprehend his character, simply from the
way in which he listened to the wild and impassioned verbi-
age of my worthy uncle. While the excellent Professor
spoke sentence after sentence, he stood with folded arms,
utterly still, motionless to all my uncle's gesticulations.
When he wanted to say No he moved his head from left to
right; when he acquiesced he nodded, so slightly that you
could scarcely see the undulation of his head. This econ-
omy of motion was carried to the length of avarice.

Judging from his appearance I should have been a long
time before I had suspected him to be what he was, a mighty
hunter. Certainly his manner was not likely to frighten the
game. How, then, did he contrive to get at his prey? My
surprise was slightly modified when I knew that this tranquil and solemn personage, was only a hunter of the eider-
duck, the down of which is, after all, the greatest source of
the Icelanders' wealth.

This grave, sententious, silent person, as phlegmatic as an
Englishman on the French stage, was named Hans Bjelke.
He had called upon us in consequence of the recommendation of M. Fridriksson. He was, in fact, our future guide.
It struck me that had I sought the world over, I could not
have found a greater contradiction to my impulsive uncle.
They, however, readily understood one another. Neither
of them had any thought about money; one was ready to
take all that was offered him, the other ready to offer anything that was asked. It may readily be conceived, then,
that an understanding was soon come to between them.

The understanding was, that he was to take us to the
village of Stapi, situated on the southern slope of the peninsula of Sneffels, at the very foot of the volcano. Hans,
the guide, told us the distance was about twenty-two miles,
a journey which my uncle supposed would take about two
days. But when my uncle came to understand that they

were Danish miles, of eight thousand yards each, he was obliged to be more moderate in his ideas, and, considering the horrible roads we had to follow, to allow eight or ten days for the journey. Four horses were prepared for us, two to carry the baggage, and two to bear the important weight of myself and uncle. Hans declared that nothing ever would make him climb on the back of any animal. He knew every inch of that part of the coast, and promised to take us the very shortest way.

His engagement with my uncle was by no means to cease with our arrival at Stapi; he was further to remain in his service during the whole time required for the completion of his scientific investigations, at the fixed salary of three rix-dollars a week, being exactly fourteen shillings and two-pence, minus one farthing, English currency. One stipulation, however, was made by the guide—the money was to be paid to him every Saturday night, failing which, his engagement was at an end.

The day of our departure was fixed. My uncle wished to hand the eider-down hunter an advance, but he refused in one emphatic word—" *Efter.*"

Which being translated from Icelandic into plain English means—After.

The treaty concluded, our worthy guide retired without another word. " A splendid fellow," said my uncle; " only he little suspects the marvelous part he is about to play in the history of the world."

" You mean, then," I cried in amazement, " that he should accompany us? "

" To the Interior of the Earth, yes; " replied my uncle. " Why not? "

There were yet forty-eight hours to elapse before we made our final start. Our whole time was taken up in making preparations for our journey. All our industry and ability were devoted to packing every object in the most advantageous manner—the instruments on one side, the arms on the other, the tools here and the provisions there. There were, in fact, four distinct groups.

The instruments were of course of the best manufacture:—

1. A centigrade thermometer of Eizel, counting up to 150 degrees, which to me did not appear half enough—or

too much. Too hot by half, if the degree of heat was to ascend so high—in which case we should certainly be cooked —not enough, if we wanted to ascertain the exact temperature of springs or metal in a state of fusion.

2. A *manometer* worked by compressed air, an instrument used to ascertain the upper atmospheric pressure on the level of the ocean. Perhaps a common barometer would not have done as well, the atmospheric pressure being likely to increase in proportion as we descended below the surface of the earth.

3. A first-class chronometer made by Boissonnas, of Geneva, set at the meridian of Hamburg, from which Germans calculated as the English do from Greenwich.

4. Two compasses, one for horizontal guidance, the other to ascertain the dip.

5. A night glass.

6. Two Ruhmkorff's coils, which, by means of a current of electricity, would ensure us a very excellent, easily carried, and certain means of obtaining light.

7. A voltaic battery on the newest principle.

Our arms consisted of two rifles, with two revolving six-shooters. Why these arms were provided it was impossible for me to say. I had every reason to believe that we had neither wild beasts nor savage natives to fear. My uncle, on the other hand, was quite as devoted to his arsenal as to his collection of instruments, and above all was very careful with his provision of fulminating or gun cotton, warranted to keep in any climate, and of which the expansive force was known to be greater than that of ordinary gunpowder.

Our tools consisted of two pickaxes, two crowbars, a silken ladder, three iron-shod Alpine poles, a hatchet, a hammer, a dozen wedges, some pointed pieces of iron, and a quantity of strong rope. You may conceive that the whole made a tolerable parcel, especially when I mention that the ladder itself was three hundred feet long!

Then there came the important question of provisions. The hamper was not very large but tolerably satisfactory, for I knew that in concentrated essence of meat and biscuit there was enough to last six months. The only liquid provided by my uncle was scheidam. Of water, not a drop. We had, however, an ample supply of gourds, and my uncle counted on finding water, and enough to fill them, as soon as we commenced our downward journey.

My remarks as to the temperature and quality of such water, and even as to the possibility of none being found, remained wholly without effect.

To make up the exact list of our traveling gear—for the guidance of future travelers—I will add, that we carried a medicine and surgical chest with all apparatus necessary for wounds, fractures and blows; lint, scissors, lancets—in fact, a perfect collection of horrible-looking instruments; a number of phials containing ammonia, alcohol, ether, goulard water, aromatic vinegar, in fact, every possible and impossible drug—finally, all the materials for working the Ruhmkorff coil!

My uncle had also been careful to lay in a goodly supply of tobacco, several flasks of very fine gunpowder, boxes of tinder, besides a large belt crammed full of notes and gold. Good boots rendered water-tight were to be found to the number of six in the tool-box. " My boy, with such clothing, with such boots, and such general equipments," said my uncle, in a state of rapturous delight; " we may hope to travel far."

It took a whole day to put all these matters in order. In the evening we dined with Baron Trampe, in company with the Mayor of Reykjawik, and Doctor Hyaltalin, the great medical man of Iceland. M. Fridriksson was not present. Unfortunately, the consequence was, that I did not understand a word that was said at dinner—a kind of semi-official reception. One thing I can say, my uncle never left off speaking.

The next day our labor came to an end. Our worthy host delighted my uncle, Professor Hardwigg, by giving him a good map of Iceland, a most important and precious document for a mineralogist. Our last evening was spent in a long conversation with M. Fridriksson, whom I liked very much—the more that I never expected to see him or any one else again. After this agreeable way of spending an hour or so, I tried to sleep. In vain; with the exception of a few dozes, my night was miserable.

At five o'clock in the morning I was awakened from the only real half hour's sleep of the night, by the loud neighing of horses under my window. I hastily dressed myself and went down into the street. Hans was engaged in putting the finishing stroke to our baggage, which he did in a silent, quiet way that won my admiration, and yet he did it admirably well. My uncle wasted a great deal of breath in giving him directions, but worthy Hans took not the slightest notice of his words.

At six o'clock all our preparations were completed, and M. Fridriksson shook hands heartily with us. My uncle thanked him warmly, in the Icelandic language, for his kind hospitality, speaking truly from the heart. As for myself I put together a few of my best Latin phrases and paid him the highest compliments I could. This fraternal and friendly duty performed, we sallied forth and mounted our horses.

As soon as we were quite ready, M. Fridriksson advanced, and by way of farewell, called after me in the words of Virgil—words which appeared to have been made for us, travelers starting for an uncertain destination.

"*Et quacunque viam dederit fortuna sequamur.*"

("And whichsoever way thou goest, may fortune follow!")

CHAPTER IX
OUR START—WE MEET WITH ADVENTURES BY THE WAY

THE weather was overcast but settled, when we commenced our adventurous and perilous journey. We had neither to fear fatiguing heat nor drenching rain. It was, in fact, real tourist weather. As there is nothing I like better than horse exercise, the pleasure of riding through an unknown country, caused the early part of our enterprise to be particularly agreeable to me. I began to enjoy the exhilarating delight of traveling, a life of desire, gratification and liberty. The truth is, that my spirits rose so rapidly that I began to be indifferent to what had once appeared to be a terrible journey.

"After all," I said to myself, "what do I risk? Simply to take a journey through a curious country, to climb a remarkable mountain, and if the worst comes to the worst, to descend into the crater of an extinct volcano." There could be no doubt that this was all this terrible Saknussemm had done. As to the existence of a gallery or of subterraneous passages leading into the interior of the earth, the idea was simply absurd, the hallucination of a distempered imagination. All, then, that may be required of me I will do cheerfully, and will create no difficulty.

It was just before we left Reykjawik that I came to this decision. Hans, our extraordinary guide, went first, walking with a steady, rapid, and unvarying step. Our two horses with the luggage followed of their own accord, without requiring whip or spur. My uncle and I came behind, cutting a very tolerable figure upon our small but vigorous animals. Hans, on taking his departure from Reykjawik, had followed the line of the sea. We took our way through poor and sparse meadows, which made a desperate effort every year to show a little green. They very rarely succeed in a good show of yellow. Every now and then a spur of rock came down through the arid ground, leaving us scarcely room to pass. Our horses, however, appeared not only well acquainted with the country, but by a kind of instinct, knew which was the best road. My uncle had not even the satisfaction of urging forward his steed by whip, spur, or voice. It was utterly useless to show any signs of impatience. I could not help smiling to see him look so big on his little horse; his long legs now and then touching the ground made him look like a six-footed centaur.

" Good beast, good beast," he would cry. " I assure you, Henry, that I begin to think no animal is more intelligent than an Icelandic horse. Snow, tempest, impracticable roads, rocks, icebergs—nothing stops him. He is brave; he is sober; he is safe; he never makes a false step; never glides or slips from his path. I dare to say that if any river, any ford has to be crossed—and I have no doubt there will be many—you will see him enter the water without hesitation like an amphibious animal, and reach the opposite side in safety. We must not, however, attempt to hurry him; we must allow him to have his own way, and I will undertake to say that between us we shall do our ten leagues a day."

" We may do so," was my reply, " but what about our worthy guide?"

" I have not the slightest anxiety about him; that sort of people go ahead without knowing even what they are about. Look at Hans. He moves so little that it is impossible for him to become fatigued. Besides, if he were to complain of weariness, he could have the loan of my horse. I should have a violent attack of the cramp if I were not to have some sort of exercise. My arms are right—but my legs are getting a little stiff."

All this while we were advancing at a rapid pace. The country we had reached was already nearly a desert. Here and there could be seen an isolated farm, some solitary boër, or Icelandic house, built of wood, earth, fragments of lava —looking like beggars on the highway of life. These wretched and miserable huts excited in us such pity that we felt half disposed to leave alms at every door. In this country there are no roads, paths are nearly unknown, and vegetation, poor as it was, slowly as it reached perfection, soon obliterated all traces of the few travelers who passed from place to place.

A few stray cows and sheep were only seen occasionally. What, then, must we expect when we come to the up-heaved regions—to the districts broken and roughened from volcanic eruptions and subterraneous commotions?

We were to learn this all in good time. I saw, however, on consulting the map, that we avoided a good deal of this rough country, by following the winding and desolate shores of the sea. In reality, the great volcanic movement of the island, and all its attendant phenomena, is concentrated in the interior of the island; there, horizontal layers or strata of rocks, piled one upon the other, eruptions of basaltic origin, and streams of lava, have given this country a kind of supernatural reputation.

Little did I expect, however, the spectacle which awaited us when we reached the peninsula of Sneffels, where agglomerations of nature's ruins form a kind of terrible chaos.

Some two hours or more after we had left the city of Reykjawik, we reached the little town called Aoalkirkja, or the principal church. It consists simply of a few houses —not what in England or Germany we should call a hamlet. Hans stopped here one-half hour. He shared our frugal breakfast, answered *yes* and *no* to my uncle's questions as to the nature of the road, and at last when asked where we were to pass the night was as laconic as usual. " Gardar ! " was his one-worded reply.

I took occasion to consult the map, to see where Gardar was to be found. After looking keenly I found a small town of that name on the borders of the Hvalfjord, about four miles from Reykjawik. I pointed this out to my uncle, who made a very energetic grimace.

"Only four miles out of twenty-two? Why it is only a little walk."

He was about to make some energetic observation to the guide, but Hans, without taking the slightest notice of him, went in front of the horses, and walked ahead with the same imperturbable phlegm he had always exhibited.

Still traveling over those apparently interminable and sandy prairies, we were compelled to go round the Kollafjord, then following a narrow strip of shore between high rocks and the sea, we came to the " aoalkirkja " of Brantar, and after another mile to " Saurboer Annexia," a chapel of ease, situated on the southern bank of the Hvalfjord. It was four o'clock in the evening and we had traveled four Danish miles, about equal to twenty English.

The fjord was in this place about half-a-mile in width. The sweeping and broken waves came rolling in úpon the pointed rocks; the gulf was surrounded by rocky walls—a mighty cliff, three thousand feet in height, remarkable for its brown strata, separated here and there by beds of tufa of a reddish hue. Now, whatever may have been the intelligence of our horses, I had not the slightest reliance upon them, as a means of crossing a stormy arm of the sea. To ride over salt water upon the back of a little horse seemed to me absurd.

"If they are really intelligent," I said to myself, "they will certainly not make the attempt. In any case, I shall trust rather to my own intelligence than theirs."

But my uncle was in no humor to wait. He dug his heels into the sides of his steed, and made for the shore. His horse went to the very edge of the water, sniffed at the approaching wave and retreated.

My uncle, who was, sooth to say, quite as obstinate as the beast he bestrode, insisted on his making the desired advance. This attempt was followed by a new refusal on the part of the horse which quietly shook his head. This demonstration of rebellion was followed by a volley of words and a stout application of whipcord; also followed by kicks on the part of the horse, which threw its head and heels upwards and tried to throw his rider. At length the sturdy little pony, spreading out his legs, in a stiff and ludicrous attitude, got from under the professor's legs, and left him standing, with both feet on a separate stone, like the Colossus of Rhodes.

" Wretched animal!" cried my uncle, suddenly transformed into a foot passenger—and as angry and ashamed as a dismounted cavalry officer on the field of battle.

" *Farja,*" said the guide, tapping him familiarly on the shoulder.

" What, a ferry boat!"

" *Der,*" answered Hans, pointing to where lay the boat in question—" there."

" Well," I cried, much relieved by the information; " so it is."

" Why did you not say so before," cried my uncle; " why not start at once?"

" Tidvatten," said the guide.

" What does he say?" I asked, considerably puzzled by the delay and the dialogue.

" He says tide," replied my uncle, translating the Danish word for my information.

"Of course, I understand—we must wait till the tide serves."

" *For bida?* " asked my uncle.

" *Ja,*" replied Hans.

My uncle frowned, stamped his feet and then followed the horses to where the boat lay. I thoroughly understood and appreciated the necessity for waiting, before crossing the fjord, for that moment when the sea at its highest point is in a state of slack water. As neither the ebb nor flow can then be felt, the ferry boat was in no danger of being carried out to sea, or dashed upon the rocky coast.

The favorable moment did not come until six o'clock in the evening. Then my uncle, myself, and guide, two boatmen and the four horses got into a very awkward flat-bottom boat. Accustomed as I had been to the steam ferryboats of the Elbe, I found the long oars of the boatmen but sorry means of locomotion. We were more than an hour in crossing the fjord; but at length the passage was concluded without accident. Half-an-hour later we reached Gardar.

CHAPTER X
TRAVELING IN ICELAND

It ought, one would have thought, to have been night, even in the sixty-fifth parallel of latitude; but still the nocturnal illumination did not surprise me. For in Iceland, during the months of June and July, the sun never sets. The temperature, however, was very much lower than I expected. I was cold, but even that did not affect me so much as ravenous hunger. Welcome indeed, therefore, was the hut which hospitably opened its doors to us.

It was merely the house of a peasant, but in the matter of hospitality, it was worthy of being the palace of a king. As we alighted at the door the master of the house came forward, held out his hand, and without any further ceremony, signaled to us to follow him. We followed him, for to accompany him was impossible. A long, narrow, gloomy passage led into the interior of this habitation, made from beams roughly squared by the ax. This passage gave ingress to every room. The chambers were four in number— the kitchen, the work-shop, where the weaving was carried on, the general sleeping-chamber of the family, and the best room, to which strangers were especially invited. My uncle, whose lofty stature had not been taken into consideration when the house was built, contrived to knock his head against the beams of the roof.

As soon as we had freed ourselves from our heavy traveling costume, the voice of our host was heard calling to us to come into the kitchen, the only room in which the Icelanders ever make any fire, no matter how cold it may be. My uncle, nothing loth, hastened to obey this hospitable and friendly invitation. I followed.

On our entrance, our worthy host, as if he had not seen us before, advanced ceremoniously, uttered a word which means " be happy," and then kissed both of us on the cheek. His wife followed, pronounced the same word, with the same ceremonial, then the husband and wife, placing their right hands upon their hearts, bowed profoundly.

This excellent Icelandic woman was the mother of nineteen children, who, little and big, rolled, crawled, and walked about in the midst of volumes of smoke arising from the angular fire-place in the middle of the room. Every now and then I could see a fresh white head, and a slightly melancholy expression of countenance, peering at me through the vapor. · Both my uncle and myself, however, were very friendly with the whole party, and before we were aware of it, there were three or four of these little ones on our shoulders, as many on our boxes, and the rest hanging about our legs. Those who could speak kept crying out *saellvertu* in every possible and impossible key. Those who did not speak only made all the more noise.

This concert was interrupted by the announcement of supper. At this moment our worthy guide, the eider-duck hunter, came in after seeing to the feeding and stabling of the horses—which consisted in letting them loose to browse on the stunted green of the Icelandic prairies. There was little for them to eat, but moss and some very dry and innutritious grass; next day they were ready before the door, some time before we were.

"Welcome," said Hans. Then tranquilly, with the air of an automaton, without any more expression in one kiss than another, he embraced the host and hostess and their nineteen children.

This ceremony concluded to the satisfaction of all parties, we all sat down to table, that is twenty-four of us, somewhat crowded. Those who were best off had only two juveniles on their knees. As soon, however, as the inevitable soup was placed on the table, natural taciturnity common even to Icelandic babies, prevailed over all else. Our host filled our plates with a portion of *Lichen* soup of Iceland moss, of by no means disagreeable flavor, an enormous lump of fish floating in sour butter. After that there came some " skyr," a kind of curds and whey, served with biscuits and juniper-berry juice. To drink, we had blanda, skimmed milk with water. I was hungry, so hungry, that by way of dessert I finished up with a basin of thick oaten porridge.

As soon as the meal was over, the children disappeared, whilst the grown people sat around the fire-place, on which was placed turf, heather, cow dung and dried fish-bones. As soon as everybody was sufficiently warm, a general dispersion took place, all retiring to their respective couches.

Our hostess offered to pull off our stockings and trousers, according to the custom of the country, but as we graciously declined to be so honored, she left us to our bed of dry fodder.

Next day, at five in the morning, we took our leave of these hospitable peasants. My uncle had great difficulty in making them accept a sufficient and proper remuneration. That evening, after fording the Alfa and the Heta, two rivers rich in trout and pike, we were compelled to pass the night in a deserted house, worthy of being haunted by all the fays of Scandinavian mythology. The King of Cold had taken up his residence there, and made us feel his presence all night.

The two following days were remarkable by their lack of any particular incidents. Always the same damp and swampy soil; the same dreary uniformity; the same sad and monotonous aspect of scenery. I confess that fatigue began to tell severely upon me; but my uncle was as firm and as hard as he had been on the first day. I could not help admiring both the excellent Professor and the worthy guide; for they appeared to regard this rugged expedition as a mere walk!

On Saturday, the 20th of June, at six o'clock in the evening, we reached Budir, a small town picturesquely situated on the shore of the ocean; and here the guide asked for his money. My uncle settled with him immediately. It was now the family of Hans himself, that is to say, his uncles, his cousins-german, who offered us hospitality. We were exceedingly well received, and without taking too much advantage of the goodness of these worthy people, I should have liked very much to have rested with them after the fatigues of the journey. But my uncle, who did not require rest, had no idea of anything of the kind; and despite the fact that next day was Sunday, I was compelled once more to mount my steed.

The soil was again affected by the neighborhood of the mountains, whose granite peered out of the ground like tops of an old oak. We were skirting the enormous base of the mighty volcano. My uncle never took his eyes from off it; he could not keep from gesticulating, and looking at it with a kind of sullen defiance as much as to say " That is the giant I have made up my mind to conquer."

44

After four hours of steady traveling, the horses stopped of themselves before the door of the presbytery of Stapi. We had reached the foot of the volcano.

CHAPTER XI
WE REACH MOUNT SNEFFELS—THE " REYKIR "

STAPI is a town consisting of thirty huts, built on a large plain of lava, exposed to the rays of the sun, reflected from the volcano. It stretches its humble tenements along the end of a little fjord, surrounded by a basaltic wall of the most singular character. Here we found Nature proceeding geometrically, and working quite after a human fashion, as if she had employed the plummet line, the compass and the rule. If elsewhere she produces grand artistic effects by piling up huge masses without order or connection—if elsewhere we see truncated cones, imperfect pyramids, with an odd succession of lines; here, as if wishing to give a lesson in regularity, and preceding the architects of the early ages, she has erected a severe order of architecture, which neither the splendors of Babylon nor the marvels of Greece ever surpassed. The walls of the fjord, like nearly the whole of the peninsula, consisted of a series of vertical columns, in height about thirty feet. These upright pillars of stone, of the finest proportions, supported an archivault of horizontal columns which formed a kind of half-vaulted roof above the sea. At certain intervals, and below this natural basin, the eye was pleased and surprised by the sight of oval openings through which the outward waves came thundering in volleys of foam. Some banks of basalt, torn from their fastenings by the fury of the waves, lay scattered on the ground like the ruins of an ancient temple—ruins eternally young, over which the storms of ages swept without producing any perceptible effect!

This was the last stage of our journey. Hans had brought us along with fidelity and intelligence, and I began to feel somewhat more comfortable when I reflected that he was to accompany us still farther on our way.

When we halted before the house of the Rector, a small and incommodious cabin, neither handsome nor more comfortable than those of his neighbors, I saw a man in the act of shoeing a horse, a hammer in his hand, and a leathern apron tied around his waist.

"Be happy," said the eider-down hunter, using his national salutation in his own language.

"*Good-dag*—good-day!" replied the former, in excellent Danish.

"Kyrkoherde," cried Hans, turning round and introducing him to my uncle.

"The Rector," repeated the worthy Professor; "it appears, my dear Harry, that this worthy man is the Rector, and is not above doing his own work."

During the speaking of these few words the guide intimated to the Kyrkoherde what was the true state of the case. The good man, ceasing from his occupation, gave a kind of halloo, upon which a tall woman, almost a giantess, came out of the hut. She was at least six feet high, which in that region is something considerable. My first impression was one of horror. I thought she had come to give us the Icelandic kiss. I had, however, nothing to fear, for she did not even show much inclination to receive us into her house.

The room devoted to strangers appeared to me to be by far the worst in the presbytery; it was narrow, dirty and offensive. There was, however, no choice about the matter. The Rector had no notion of practicing the usual cordial and antique hospitality. My uncle soon became aware of the kind of man he had to deal with. Instead of a worthy and learned scholar, he found a dull, ill-mannered peasant. He therefore resolved to start on his great expedition as soon as possible. He did not care about fatigue, and resolved to spend a few days in the mountains.

The preparations for our departure were made the very next day after our arrival at Stapi; Hans now hired three Icelanders to take the place of the horses—which could no longer carry our luggage. When, however, these worthy islanders had reached the bottom of the crater, they were to go back and leave us to ourselves. This point was settled before they would agree to start. On this occasion, my uncle partially confided in Hans, the eider-duck hunter, and gave him to understand that it was his intention to continue his exploration of the volcano to the last possible limits.

WE REACH MOUNT SNEFFELS

Hans listened calmly, and then nodded his head. To go there, or elsewhere, to bury himself in the bowels of the earth, or to travel over its summit, was all the same to him! As for me, amused and occupied by the incidents of travel, I had begun to forget the inevitable future; but now I was once more destined to realize the actual state of affairs. What was to be done? Run away? But if I really had intended to leave Professor Hardwigg to his fate, it should have been at Hamburg and not at the foot of Sneffels.

One idea above all others, began to trouble me: a very terrible idea, and one calculated to shake the nerves of a man even less sensitive than myself. " Let us consider the matter," I said to myself; " we are going to ascend the Sneffels mountain. Well and good. We are about to pay a visit to the very bottom of the crater. Good, still. Others have done it and did not perish from that course.

" That, however, is not the whole matter to be considered. If a road does really present itself by which to descend into the dark and subterraneous bowels of Mother Earth, if this thrice unhappy Saknussemm has really told the truth, we shall be most certainly lost in the midst of the labyrinth of subterraneous galleries of the volcano. Now, we have no evidence to prove that Sneffels is really extinct. What proof have we that an eruption is not shortly about to take place? Because the monster has slept soundly since 1229, does it follow that he is never to wake? If he does wake what is to become of us? "

These were questions worth thinking about, and upon them I reflected long and deeply. I could not lie down in search of sleep without dreaming of eruptions. The more I thought, the more I objected to be reduced to the state of dross and ashes. I could stand it no longer; so I determined at last to submit the whole case to my uncle, in the most adroit manner possible, and under the form of some totally irreconcilable hypothesis.

I sought him. I laid before him my fears, and then drew back in order to let him get his passion over at his ease.

" I have been thinking about the matter," he said, in the quietest tone in the world.

What did he mean? Was he at last about to listen to the voice of reason? Did he think of suspending his projects?

It was almost too much happiness to be true. I however made no remark. In fact, I was only too anxious not to interrupt him, and allowed him to reflect at his leisure. After some moments he spoke out.

"I have been thinking about the matter," he resumed. "Ever since we have been at Stapi, my mind has been almost solely occupied with the grave question which has been submitted to me by yourself—for nothing would be unwiser and more inconsistent than to act with imprudence."

"I heartily agree with you, my dear uncle," was my somewhat hopeful rejoinder.

"It is now six hundred years since Sneffels has spoken, but though now reduced to a state of utter silence, he may speak again. New volcanic eruptions are always preceded by perfectly well-known phenomena. I have closely examined the inhabitants of this region; I have carefully studied the soil, and I beg to tell you emphatically, my dear Harry, there will be no eruption at present."

As I listened to his positive affirmations, I was stupefied and could say nothing.

"I see you doubt my word," said my uncle; "follow me."

I obeyed mechanically. Leaving the presbytery, the Professor took a road through an opening in the basaltic rock, which led far away from the sea. We were soon in open country, if we could give such a name to a place all covered with volcanic deposits. The whole land seemed crushed under the weight of enormous stones—of trap, of basalt, of granite, of lava, and of all other volcanic substances.

I could see many spouts of steam rising in the air. These white vapors, called in the Icelandic language "reykir," come from hot water fountains, and indicate by their violence the volcanic activity of the soil. Now the sight of these appeared to justify my apprehension. I was, therefore, all the more surprised and mortified when my uncle thus addressed me. "You see all this smoke, Harry, my boy?"

"Yes, sir."

"Well, as long as you see them thus, you have nothing to fear from the volcano."

"How can that be?"

"Be careful to remember this," continued the Professor.

" At the approach of an eruption these spouts of vapor redouble their activity—to disappear altogether during the period of volcanic eruption; for the elastic fluids, no longer having the necessary tension, seek refuge in the interior of the crater, instead of escaping through the fissures of the earth. If, then, the steam remains in its normal or habitual state, if their energy does not increase, and if you add to this, the remark, that the wind is not replaced by heavy atmospheric pressure and dead calm, you may be quite sure that there is no fear of any immediate eruption."

" But——"

" Enough, my boy. When science has sent forth her fiat—it is only to hear and obey."

I came back to the house quite downcast and disappointed. My uncle had completely defeated me with his scientific arguments. Nevertheless, I had still one hope, and that was, when once we were at the bottom of the crater, that it would be impossible in default of a gallery or tunnel, to descend any deeper; and this, despite all the learned Saknussemms in the world.

I passed the whole of the following night with a nightmare on my chest! and, after unheard-of miseries and tortures, found myself in the very depths of the earth, from which I was suddenly launched into planetary space, under the form of an eruptive rock!

Next day, the 23d June, Hans calmly awaited us outside the presbytery with his two companions loaded with provisions, tools, and instruments. Two iron-shod poles, two guns, and two large game bags, were reserved for my uncle and myself. Hans, who was a man who never forgot even the minutest precautions, had added to our baggage a large skin full of water, as an addition to our gourds. This assured us water for eight days.

It was nine o'clock in the morning when we were quite ready. The rector and his huge wife or servant, I never knew which, stood at the door to see us off. They appeared to be about to inflict on us the usual final kiss of the Icelanders. To our supreme astonishment their adieu took the shape of a formidable bill, in which they even counted the use of the pastoral house, really and truly the most abominable and dirty place I ever was in. The worthy couple cheated and robbed us like a Swiss innkeeper, and made us feel, by the sum we had to pay, the splendors of their hospitality. My uncle, however, paid without bargaining. A man who had made up his mind to undertake a voyage into the Interior of the Earth, is not the man to haggle over a few miserable rix-dollars.

This important matter settled, Hans gave the signal for departure, and some few moments later we had left Stapi.

CHAPTER XII
THE ASCENT OF MOUNT SNEFFELS

THE huge volcano which was the first stage of our daring experiment, is above five thousand feet high. Sneffels is the termination of a long range of volcanic mountains, of a different character to the system of the island itself. One of its peculiarities is its two huge pointed summits. From where we started it was impossible to make out the real outlines of the peak against the gray field of sky. All we could distinguish was a vast dome of white, which fell downwards from the head of the giant. The commencement of the great undertaking filled me with awe. Now that we had actually started, I began to believe in the reality of the undertaking!

Our party formed quite a procession. We walked in single file, preceded by Hans, the imperturbable eider-duck hunter. He calmly led us by narrow paths where two persons could by no possibility walk abreast. Conversation was wholly impossible. We had all the more opportunity to reflect, and to admire the awful grandeur of the scene around.

As we advanced, the road became every moment more difficult. The soil was broken and dangerous. The rocks broke and gave way under our feet, and we had to be scrupulously careful in order to avoid dangerous and constant falls. Hans advanced as calmly as if he had been walking over Salisbury Plain; sometimes he would disappear behind huge blocks of stone, and we momentarily lost sight of him. There was a little period of anxiety and then there was a shrill whistle, just to tell us where to look for him.

Occasionally he would take it into his head to stop to

pick up lumps of rock, and silently pile them up into small heaps, *in order that we might not lose our way on our return.* He had no idea of the journey we were about to undertake. At all events, the precaution was a good one; though how utterly useless and unnecessary—but I must not anticipate.

Three hours of terrible fatigue, walking incessantly, had only brought us to the foot of the great mountain. This will give some notion of what we had still to undergo.

Suddenly, however, Hans cried a halt—that is, he made signs to that effect—and a summary kind of breakfast was laid out on the lava before us. My uncle, who now was simply Professor Hardwigg, was so eager to advance, that he bolted his food like a greedy clown. This halt for refreshment was also a halt for repose. The Professor was therefore compelled to wait the good pleasure of his imperturbable guide, who did not give the signal for departure for a good hour. The three Icelanders, who were as taciturn as their comrade, did not say a word; but went on eating and drinking very quietly and soberly.

From this, our first real stage, we began to ascend the slopes of the Sneffels volcano. Its magnificent snowy night-cap, as we began to call it, by an optical delusion very common in mountains, appeared to me to be close at hand; and yet how many long weary hours must elapse before we reached its summit. What unheard-of fatigue must we endure!

The stones on the mountain side, held together by no cement of soil, bound together by no roots or creeping herbs, gave way continually under our feet, and went rushing below into the plains, like a series of small avalanches. In certain places the sides of this stupendous mountain were at an angle so steep that it was impossible to climb upwards, and we were compelled to get round these obstacles as best we might. Those who understand Alpine climbing will comprehend our difficutlies. Often we were obliged to help each other along by means of our climbing poles.

I must say this for my uncle, that he stuck as close to me as possible. He never lost sight of me, and on many occasions his arm supplied me with firm and solid support. He was strong, wiry, and apparently insensible to fatigue. Another great advantage with him was that he had the innate sentiment of equilibrium—for he never slipped or failed in his steps. The Icelanders, though heavily loaded, climbed with the agility of mountaineers.

Looking up, every now and then, at the height of the great volcano of Sneffels, it appeared to me wholly impossible to reach to the summit on that side; at all events, if the angle of inclination did not speedily change.

Fortunately, after an hour of unheard-of fatigues, and of gymnastic exercises that would have been trying to an acrobat, we came to a vast field of ice, which wholly surrounded the bottom of the cone of the volcano. The natives called it the table-cloth, probably from some such reason as the dwellers in the Cape of Good Hope call their mountain Table Mountain, and their roads Table Bay.

Here, to our mutual surprise, we found an actual flight of stone steps, which wonderfully assisted our ascent. This singular flight of stairs was, like everything else, volcanic. It had been formed by one of those torrents of stones cast up by the eruptions, and of which the Icelandic name is stinâ. If this singular torrent had not been checked in its descent by the peculiar shape of the flanks of the mountain, it would have swept into the sea, and would have formed new islands. Such as it was, it served us admirably. The abrupt character of the slopes momentarily increased, but these remarkable stone steps, a little less difficult than those of the Egyptian pyramids, were the one simple natural means by which we were enabled to proceed.

About seven in the evening of that day, after having clambered up two thousand of these rough steps, we found ourselves overlooking a kind of spur or projection of the mountain—a sort of buttress upon which the cone-like crater, properly so called, leaned for support.

The ocean lay beneath us at a depth of more than three thousand two hundred feet—a grand and mighty spectacle. We had reached the region of eternal snows. The cold was keen, searching and intense. The wind blew with extraordinary violence. I was utterly exhausted.

My worthy uncle, the Professor, saw clearly that my legs refused further service, and that, in fact, I was utterly exhausted. Despite his hot and feverish impatience, he decided, with a sigh, upon a halt. He called the eider-duck hunter to his side. That worthy, however, shook his head.

"Ofvanfor," was his sole spoken reply.

"It appears," says my uncle with a woe-begone look, "that we must go higher."

He then turned to Hans, and asked him to give some reason for this decisive response.

"Mistour," replied the guide.

"*Ja mistour*—yes, the mistour," cried one of the Icelandic guides in a terrified tone.

It was the first time he had spoken.

"What does this mysterious word signify?" I anxiously inquired.

"Look," said my uncle.

I looked down upon the plain below, and I saw a vast, a prodigious volume of pulverized pumice-stone, of sand, of dust, rising to the heavens in the form of a mighty waterspout. It resembled the fearful phenomenon of a similar character known to the travelers in the desert of the great Sahara.

The wind was driving it directly towards that side of Sneffels on which we were perched. This opaque veil standing up between us and the sun projected a deep shadow on the flanks of the mountain. If this sand-spout broke over us, we must all be infallibly destroyed, crushed in its fearful embraces. This extraordinary phenomenon, very common when the wind shakes the glaciers, and sweeps over the arid plains, is in the Icelandic tongue called *mistour*.

"Hastigt, Hastigt!" cried our guide.

Now I certainly knew nothing of Danish, but I thoroughly understood that his gestures were meant to quicken us. The guide turned rapidly in a direction which would take us to the back of the crater, all the while ascending slightly. We followed rapidly, despite our excessive fatigue.

A quarter of an hour later Hans paused to enable us to look back. The mighty whirlwind of sand was spreading up the slope of the mountain to the very spot where we had proposed to halt. Huge stones were caught up, cast into the air, and thrown about as during an eruption. We were happily a little out of the direction of the wind, and therefore out of reach of danger. But for the precaution and knowledge of our guide, our dislocated bodies, our crushed and broken limbs, would have been cast to the wind, like dust from some unknown meteor.

Hans, however, did not think it prudent to pass the night on the bare side of the cone. We therefore continued our journey in a zigzag direction. The fifteen hundred feet which remained to be accomplished took us at least five hours. The turnings and windings, the no-thoroughfares, the marches and marches, turned that insignificant distance into at least three leagues. I never felt such misery, fatigue and exhaustion in my life. I was ready to faint from hunger and cold. The rarefied air at the same time painfully acted upon my lungs.

At last, when I thought myself at my last gasp, about eleven at night, it being in that region quite dark, we reached the summit of Mount Sneffels! it was in an awful mood of mind, that despite my fatigue, before I descended into the crater which was to shelter us for the night, I paused to behold the sun rise at midnight on the very day of its lowest declension, and enjoyed the spectacle of its ghastly pale rays cast upon the isle which lay sleeping at our feet!

I no longer wondered at people traveling all the way from England to Norway, to behold this magical and wondrous spectacle.

CHAPTER XIII
THE SHADOW OF SCARTARIS

OUR supper was eaten with ease and rapidity, after which everybody did the best he could for himself within the hollow of the crater. The bed was hard, the shelter unsatisfactory, the situation painful—lying in the open air, five thousand feet above the level of the sea! Nevertheless, it has seldom happened to me to sleep so well as I did on that particular night. I did not even dream. So much for the effects of what my uncle called " wholesome fatigue."

Next day, when we awoke under the rays of a bright and glorious sun, we were nearly frozen by the keen air. I left my granite couch and made one of the party to enjoy a view of the magnificent spectacle which developed itself, panorama-like, at our feet.

THE SHADOW OF SCARTARIS

I stood upon the lofty summit of Mount Sneffels' southern peak.   Thence I was able to obtain a view of the greater part of the island.   The optical delusion, common to all lofty heights, raised the shores of the island, while the central portions appeared depressed.   It was by no means too great a flight of fancy to believe that a giant picture was stretched out before me.   I could see the deep valleys that crossed each other in every direction.   I could see precipices looking like sides of wells, lakes that seemed to be changed into ponds, ponds that looked like puddles, and rivers that were transformed into petty brooks.   To my right were glaciers upon glaciers, and multiplied peaks, topped with light clouds of smoke.

The undulation of these infinite numbers of mountains, whose snowy summits make them look as if covered by foam, recalled to my remembrance the surface of a stormbeaten ocean.   If I looked towards the west, the ocean lay before me in all its majestic grandeur, a continuation as it were, of these fleecy hill-tops.   Where the earth ended and the sea began it was impossible for the eye to distinguish.

I soon felt that strange and mysterious sensation which is awakened in the mind when looking down from lofty hill tops, and now I was able to do so without any feeling of nervousness, having fortunately hardened myself to that kind of sublime contemplation.   I wholly forgot who I was, and where I was.   I became intoxicated with a sense of lofty sublimity, without thought of the abysses into which my daring was soon about to plunge me.   I was presently, however, brought back to the realities of life by the arrival of the Professor and Hans, who joined me upon the lofty summit of the peak.

My uncle, turning in a westerly direction, pointed out to me a light cloud of vapor, a kind of haze, with a faint outline of land rising out of the waters.   " Greenland! " said he.

" Greenland? " cried I in reply.

" Yes," continued my uncle, who always when explaining anything spoke as if he were in a Professor's chair; " we are not more than thirty-five leagues distant from that wonderful land.   When the great annual break up of the ice takes place, white bears come over to Iceland, carried

by the floating masses of ice from the north. This, however, is a matter of little consequence. We are now on the
summit of the great, the transcendent Sneffels, and here are
its two peaks, north and south. Hans will tell you the
name by which the people of Iceland call that on which
we stand."

My uncle turned to the imperturbable guide, who
nodded, and spoke as usual—one word. " *Scartaris.*"

My uncle looked at me with a proud and triumphant
glance. " A crater," he said, " you hear? "

I did hear, but I was totally unable to make reply.

The crater of Mount Sneffels represented an inverted
cone, the gaping orifice apparently half a mile across; the
depth indefinite feet. Conceive what this *hole* must have
been like when full of flame and thunder and lightning.
The bottom of the funnel-shaped hollow was about five
hundred feet in circumference, by which it will be seen
that the slope from the summit to the bottom was very
gradual, and we were therefore clearly able to get there
without much fatigue or difficulty. Involuntarily, I compared this crater to an enormous loaded cannon; and the
comparison completely terrified me.

" To descend into the interior of a cannon," I thought
to myself, " when perhaps it is loaded, and will go off at
the least shock, is the act of a madman."

But there was no longer any opportunity for me to hesitate. Hans, with a perfectly calm and indifferent air, took
his usual post at the head of the adventurous little band.
I followed without uttering a syllable. I felt like the lamb
led to the slaughter.

In order to render the descent less difficult, Hans took
his way down the interior of the cone in rather a zigzag
fashion, making, as the sailors say, long tacks to the eastward, followed by equally long ones to the west. It was
necessary to walk through the midst of eruptive rocks, some
of which, shaken in their balance, went rolling down with
thundering clamor to the bottom of the abyss. These continual falls awoke echoes of singular power and effect.

Many portions of the cone consisted of inferior glaciers.
Hans, whenever he met with one of these obstacles advanced
with a great show of precaution, sounding the soil with his
long iron pole in order to discover fissures and layers of

deep soft snow.   In many doubtful or dangerous places, it became necessary for us to be tied together by a long rope in order that should any one of us be unfortunate enough to slip, he would be supported by his companions.   This connecting link was doubtless a prudent precaution, but not by any means unattended with danger.

Nevertheless, despite all the manifold difficulties of the descent, along slopes with which our guide was wholly unacquainted, we made considerable progress without accident.   One of our great parcels of rope slipped from one of the Iceland porters, and rushed by a short cut to the bottom of the abyss.

By mid-day we were at the end of our journey.   I looked upwards, and saw only the upper orifice of the cone, which served as a circular frame to a very small portion of the sky—a portion which seemed to me singularly beautiful. Should I ever again gaze on that lovely sunlit sky!

The only exception to this extraordinary landscape, was the Peak of Scartaris, which seemed lost in the great void of the heavens.

The bottom of the crater was composed of three separate shafts, through which, during periods of eruption, when Sneffels was in action, the great central furnace sent forth its burning lava and poisonous vapors.   Each of these chimneys or shafts gaped open-mouthed in our path.   I kept as far away from them as possible, not even venturing to take the faintest peep downwards.

As for the Professor, after a rapid examination of their disposition and characteristics, he became breathless and panting.   He ran from one to the other like a delighted school-boy, gesticulating wildly, and uttering incomprehensible and disjointed phrases in all sorts of languages. Hans, the guide, and his humbler companions seated themselves on some piles of lava and looked silently on.   They clearly took my uncle for a lunatic; and—waited the result.

Suddenly the Professor uttered a wild, unearthly cry. At first I imagined he had lost his footing, and was falling headlong into one of the yawning gulfs.   Nothing of the kind.   I saw him, his arms spread out to their widest extent, his legs stretched apart, standing upright before an enormous pedestal, high enough and black enough to bear a gigantic statue of Pluto. His attitude and mien were that of a man utterly stupefied. But his stupefaction was speedily changed to the wildest joy. "Harry! Harry! come here!" he cried; "make haste—wonderful—wonderful!"

Unable to understand what he meant, I turned to obey his commands. Neither Hans, nor the other Icelanders moved a step.

"Look!" said the Professor, in something of the manner of the French general, pointing out the pyramids to his army. And fully partaking his stupefaction, if not his joy, I read on the eastern side of the huge block of stone, the same characters, half eaten away by the corrosive action of time, the name, to me a thousand times accursed—

ᛁᛆᚾᛏ ᛋᛁᛏᚴᚾᛋᛋᛏᚠ

"'Arne Saknussemm!'" cried my uncle, "now, unbeliever, do you begin to have faith?"

It was totally impossible for me to answer a single word. I went back to my pile of lava, in a state of silent awe. The evidence was unanswerable, overwhelming!

In a few moments, however, my thoughts were far away, back in my German home, with Gretchen and the old cook. What would I have given for one of my cousin's smiles, for one of the ancient domestic's omelettes, and for my own feather bed! How long I remained in this state I know not. All I can say is, that when at last I raised my head from between my hands, there remained at the bottom of the crater only myself, my uncle and Hans. The Icelandic porters had been dismissed and were now descending the exterior slopes of Mount Sneffels, on their way to Stapi. How heartily did I wish myself with them!

Hans slept tranquilly at the foot of a rock in a kind of rill of lava, where he had made himself a rough and ready bed. My uncle was walking about the bottom of the crater like a wild beast in a cage. I had no desire, neither had I the strength, to move from my recumbent position. Taking example by the guide, I gave way to a kind of painful somnolency, during which I seemed both to hear and feel continual heavings and shudderings in the mountain. In this way we passed our first night in the interior of a crater.

THE SHADOW OF SCARTARIS

Next morning, a gray, cloudy, heavy sky hung like a funeral-pall over the summit of the volcanic cone. I did not notice it so much from the obscurity that reigned around us, as from the rage with which my uncle was devoured.

I fully understood the reason, and again a glimpse of hope made my heart leap with joy. I will briefly explain the cause. Of the three openings which yawned beneath our steps, only one could have been followed by the adventurous Saknussemm. According to the words of the learned Icelander, it was only to be known by that one particular mentioned in the cryptograph, that the shadow of Scartaris fell upon it, just touching its mouth in the last days of the month of June. We were, in fact, to consider the pointed peak as the *stylus* of an immense sun-dial, the shadow of which pointed on one given day, like the inexorable finger of fate, to the yawning chasm which led into the interior of the earth.

Now, as often happens in these regions, should the sun fail to burst through the clouds, no shadow. Consequently, no chance of discovering the right aperture. We had already reached the 25th June. If the kindly heavens would only remain densely clouded for six more days, we should have to put off our voyage of discovery for another year, when certainly there would be one person fewer in the party. I already had sufficient of the mad and monstrous enterprise.

It would be utterly impossible to depict the impotent rage of Professor Hardwigg. The day passed away, and not the faintest outline of a shadow could be seen at the bottom of the crater. Hans the guide never moved from his place. He must have been curious to know what we were about, if indeed he could believe we were about anything. As for my uncle, he never addressed a word to me. He was nursing his wrath to keep it warm! His eyes fixed on the black and foggy atmosphere, his complexion hideous with suppressed passion. Never had his eyes appeared so fierce, his nose so aquiline, his mouth so hard and firm.

On the 26th no change for the better. A mixture of rain and snow fell during the whole day. Hans very quietly built himself a hut of lava into which he retired like Diogenes into his tub. I took a malicious delight in watching the thousand little cascades that flowed down the side of the cone, carrying with them at times a stream of stones into the " vasty deep " below.

My uncle was almost frantic: to be sure it was enough to make even a patient man angry. He had reached to a certain extent the goal of his desires, and yet he was likely to be wrecked in port.

But if the heavens and the elements are capable of causing us much pain and sorrow, there are two sides to a medal. And there was reserved for Professor Hardwigg a brilliant and sudden surprise which was to compensate him for all his sufferings. Next day the sky was still overcast, but on Sunday, the 26th, the last day but one of the month, with a sudden change of wind and a new moon there came a change of weather. The sun poured its beaming rays to the very bottom of the crater.

Each hillock, every rock, every stone, every asperity of the soil had its share of the luminous effulgence, and its shadow fell heavily on the soil. Among others, to his insane delight, the shadow of Scartaris was marked and clear, and moved slowly with the radiant star of day.

My uncle moved with it in a state of mental ecstasy. At twelve o'clock exactly, when the sun had attained its highest altitude for the day, the shadow fell upon the edge of the central pit!

" Here it is," gasped the Professor in an agony of joy, " here it is—we have found it. Forward, my friends, into the Interior of the Earth."

I looked curiously at Hans to see what reply he would make to this terrific announcement. " Forut," said the guide tranquilly.

" Forward it is," answered my uncle, who was now in the seventh heaven of delight.

When we were quite ready, our watches indicated thirteen minutes past one!

CHAPTER XIV
THE REAL JOURNEY COMMENCES

OUR real journey now commenced. Hitherto our courage and determination had overcome all difficulties. We were fatigued at times; and that was all. Now, unknown and fearful dangers were to be encountered.

I had not as yet ventured to take a glimpse down the horrible abyss into which in a few minutes more I was about to plunge. The fatal moment had, however, at last arrived. I had still the option of refusing or accepting a share in this foolish and audacious enterprise. But I was ashamed to show more fear than the eider-duck hunter. Hans seemed to accept the difficulties of the journey so tranquilly, with such calm indifference, with such perfect recklessness of all danger, that I actually blushed to appear less of a man than he! Had I been alone with my uncle, I should certaily have sat down and argued the point fully; but in the presence of the guide I held my tongue. I gave one moment to the thought of my charming cousin, and then I advanced to the mouth of the central shaft.

It measured about a hundred feet in diameter, which made about three hundred in circumference. I leaned over a rock which stood on its edge, and looked down. My hair stood on end, my teeth chattered, my limbs trembled. I seemed utterly to lose my center of gravity, while my head was in a sort of whirl, like that of a drunken man. There is nothing more powerful than this attraction towards an abyss. I was about to fall headlong into the gaping well, when I was drawn back by a firm and powerful hand. It was that of Hans. I had not taken lessons enough at the Frelser's-kirk of Copenhagen in the art of looking down from lofty eminences without blinking!

However, few as the minutes were during which I gazed down this tremendous and even wondrous shaft, I had a sufficient glimpse of it to give me some idea of its physical conformation. Its sides, which were almost as perpendicular as those of a well, presented numerous projections which doubtless would assist our descent.

It was a sort of wild and savage staircase, without bannister or fence. A rope fastened above, near the surface, would certainly support our weight and enable us to reach the bottom, but how, when we had arrived at its utmost depth, were we to loosen it above? This was, I thought, a question of some importance.

My uncle, however, was one of those men who are nearly always prepared with expedients. He hit upon a very simple method of obviating this difficulty. He unrolled a cord about as thick as my thumb, and at least four hundred feet in length. He allowed about half of it to go down the pit and catch in a hitch over a great block of lava which stood on the edge of the precipice. This done, he threw the second half after the first.

Each of us could now descend by catching the two cords in one hand. When about two hundred feet below, all the explorer had to do was to let go one end and pull away at the other, when the cord would come falling at his feet. In order to go down farther, all that was necessary was to continue the same operation. Going down thus appeared to me easy enough, it was the coming up again that now occupied my thoughts.

"Now," said my uncle, as soon as he had completed this important preparation, "let us see about the baggage. It must be divided into three separate parcels, and each of us must carry one on his back. I allude to the more important and fragile articles." My worthy and ingenious uncle did not appear to consider that we came under that denominations. "Hans," he continued, "you will take charge of the tools and some of the provisions; you, Harry, must take possession of another third of the provisions and of the arms. I will load myself with the rest of the eatables, and with the more delicate instruments."

"But," I exclaimed, "our clothes, this mass of cord and ladders—who will undertake to carry them down?"

"They will go down of themselves."

"And how so?" I asked.

"You shall see." My uncle was not fond of half measures, nor did he like anything in the way of hesitation. Giving his orders to Hans he had the whole of the non-fragile articles made up into one bundle; and the packet firmly and solidly fastened, was simply pitched over the edge of the gulf.

I heard the moaning of the suddenly displaced air, and the noise of falling stones. My uncle leaning over the abyss followed the descent of his luggage with a perfectly self-satisfied air, and did not rise until it had completely disappeared from sight. "Now then," he cried, "it is our turn."

I put it in good faith to any man of common sense—was it possible to hear this energetic cry without a shudder? The Professor fastened his case of instruments on his back. Hans took charge of the tools, I of the arms. The descent then commenced in the following order: Hans went first, my uncle followed, and I went last. Our progress was made in profound silence—a silence only troubled by the fall of pieces of rock, which breaking from the jagged sides, fell with a roar into the depths below.

I allowed myself to slide, so to speak, holding frantically on the double cord with one hand and with the other keeping myself off the rocks by the assistance of my iron-shod pole. One idea was all the time impressed upon my brain. I feared that the upper support would fail me. The cord appeared to me far too fragile to bear the weight of three such persons as we were, with our luggage. I made as little use of it as possible, trusting to my own agility and doing miracles in the way of feats of dexterity and strength upon the projecting shelves and spurs of lava which my feet seemed to clutch as strongly as my hands.

The guide went first as I have said, and when one of the slippery and frail supports broke from under his feet he had recourse to his usual monosyllabic way of speaking. "Gifakt——"

"Attention—look out," repeated my uncle.

In about half an hour we reached a kind of small terrace formed by a fragment of rock projecting some distance from the sides of the shaft. Hans now began to haul upon the cord on one side only, the other going as quietly upward as the other came down. It fell at last, bringing with it a shower of small stones, lava and dust, a disagreeable kind of rain or hail.

While we were seated on this extraordinary bench I ventured once more to look downwards. With a sigh I discovered that the bottom was still wholly invisible. Were we, then, going direct to the interior of the earth?

The performance with the cord recommenced, and a quarter of an hour later we had descended another two hundred feet.

I have very strong doubts if the most determined geologist would, during that descent have studied the nature of the different layers of earth around him. I did not trouble my head much about the matter; whether we were among the combustible carbon, silurians, or primitive soil, I neither knew nor cared to know.

Not so the inveterate Professor. He must have taken notes all the way down, for, at one of our halts, he began a brief lecture. " The farther we advance," said he, " the greater is my confidence in the result. The disposition of these volcana strata absolutely confirms the theories of Sir Humphrey Davy. We are still within the region of the primordial soil, the soil in which took place the chemical operation of metals becoming inflamed by coming in contact with the air and water. I at once regret the old and now for ever exploded theory of a central fire. At all events, we shall soon know the truth."

Such was the conclusion to which he came. I, however, was very far from being in humor to discuss the matter. I had something else to think of. My silence was taken for consent; and still we continued to go down.

At the expiration of three hours, we were, to all appearance, as far off as ever from the bottom of the well. When I looked upwards, however, I could see that the upper orifice was every minute decreasing in size. The sides of the shaft were getting closer and closer together, we were approaching the regions of eternal night!

And still we continued to descend! At length, I noticed that when pieces of stone were detached from the sides of this stupendous precipice, they were swallowed up with less noise than before. The final sound was sooner heard. We were approaching the bottom of the abyss!

As I had been very careful to keep account of all the changes of cord which took place, I was able to tell exactly what was the depth we had reached, as well as the time it had taken. We had shifted the rope twenty-eight times, each operation taking a quarter of an hour, which in all made seven hours. To this had to be added twenty-eight pauses; in all ten hours and a half. We started at one, it was now, therefore, about eleven o'clock at night.

It does not require great knowledge of arithmetic to know that twenty-eight times two hundred feet makes five thousand six hundred feet in all (more than an English mile).

While I was making this mental calculation a voice broke the silence. It was the voice of Hans. " Halt! " he cried.

I checked myself very suddenly, just at the moment when I was about to kick my uncle on the head.

" We have reached the end of our journey," said the worthy Professor in a satisfied tone.

" What, the interior of the earth? " said I, slipping down to his side.

" No, you stupid fellow! but we have reached the bottom of the well."

" And I suppose there is no farther progress to be made? " I hopefully exclaimed.

" Oh, yes, I can dimly see a sort of tunnel, which turns off obliquely to the right. At all events, we must see about that to-morrow. Let us sup now, and seek slumber as best we may."

I thought it time, but made no observations on that point. I was fairly launched on a desperate course, and all I had to do was to go forward hopefully and trustingly.

It was not even now quite dark, the light filtering down in a most extraordinary manner. We opened the provision bag, ate a frugal supper, and each did his best to find a bed amid the pile of stones, dirt, and lava which had accumulated for ages at the bottom of the shaft. I happened to grope out the pile of ropes, ladders, and clothes which we had thrown down; and upon them I stretched myself. After such a day's labor, my rough bed seemed as soft as down!

For a while I lay in a sort of pleasant trance. Presently, after lying quietly for some minutes, I opened my eyes and looked upwards. As I did so I made out a brilliant little dot, at the extremity of this long, gigantic telescope.

It was a star without scintillating rays. According to my calculation, it must be in the constellation of the Little Bear. After this little bit of astronomical recreation, I dropped into a sound sleep.

AT eight o'clock the next morning, a faint kind of dawn awoke us. The thousand and one prisms of the lava collected the light as it passed and brought it to us like a shower of sparks. We were able with ease to see objects around us.

"Well, Harry, my boy," cried the delighted Professor, rubbing his hands together, "what say you now? Did you ever pass a more tranquil night in our house in the König Strasse? No deafening sounds of cart-wheels, no cries of hawkers, no bad language from boatmen or watermen!"

"Well, uncle, we are quiet at the bottom of this well—but to me there is something terrible in this calm."

"Why," said the Professor, hotly, "one would say you were already beginning to be afraid. How will you get on presently? Do you know, that as yet, we have not penetrated one inch into the bowels of the earth."

"What can you mean, sir?" was my bewildered and astonished reply.

"I mean to say that we have only just reached the soil of the island itself. This long vertical tube, which ends at the bottom of the crater of Sneffels, ceases here just about on a level with the sea."

"Are you sure, sir?"

"Quite sure. Consult the barometer."

It was quite true that the mercury, after rising gradually in the instrument, as long as our descent was taking place, had stopped precisely at twenty-nine degrees. "You perceive," said the Professor, "we have as yet only to endure the pressure of air. I am curious to replace the barometer by the manometer." The barometer, in fact, was about to become useless—as soon as the weight of the air was greater than what was calculated as above the level of the ocean.

"But," said I, "is it not very much to be feared that this ever-increasing pressure may not in the end turn out very painful and inconvenient?"

"No," said he. "We shall descend very slowly, and our lungs will be gradually accustomed to breathe compressed air. It is well known that aëronauts have gone so high as to be nearly without air at all—why, then, should we not accustom ourselves to breathe when we have, say, a little too much of it? For myself, I am certain I shall prefer it. Let us not lose a moment. Where is the packet which preceded us in our descent?"

I smilingly pointed it out to my uncle. Hans had not seen it, and believed it caught somewhere above us; "huppe" as he phrased it.

"Now," said my uncle, "let us breakfast, and breakfast like people who have a long day's work before them."

Biscuit and dried meat, washed down by some mouthfuls of water flavored with schiedam, was the material of our luxurious meal. As soon as it was finished, my uncle took from his pocket a note-book destined to be filled by memoranda of our travels. He had already placed his instruments in order, and this is what he wrote:—Monday, July 1st. Chronometer, 8h. 17m. morning. Barometer, 29 degrees. Thermometer, 43 degrees Fahr. Direction, E. S. E.

This last observation referred to the obscure gallery, and was indicated to us by the compass.

"Now, Harry," cried the Professor, in an enthusiastic tone of voice, "we are truly about to take our first step into the Interior of the Earth; never before visited by man since the first creation of the world. You may consider, therefore, that at this precise moment our travels really commence."

As my uncle made this remark, he took in one hand the Ruhmkorff coil apparatus, which hung round his neck, and with the other he put the electric current into communication with the worm of the lantern. And a bright light at once illumined that dark and gloomy tunnel! The effect was magical!

Hans, who carried the second apparatus, had it also put into operation. This ingenious application of electricity to practical purposes enabled us to move along by the light of an artificial day, amid even the flow of the most inflammable and combustible gases.

"Forward!" cried my uncle. Each took up his burden. Hans went first, my uncle followed, and I going third, we entered the somber gallery! Just as we were about to engulf ourselves in this dismal passage, I lifted up my head, and through the tubelike shaft I saw that Iceland sky I was never to see again! Was it the last I should ever see of any sky?

The stream of lava flowing from the bowels of the earth in 1229, had forced itself a passage through the tunnel. It lined the whole of the inside with its thick and brilliant coating. The electric light added very greatly to the brilliancy of the effect. The great difficulty of our journey now began. How were we to prevent ourselves from slipping down the steeply-inclined plane? Happily some cracks, abrasures of the soil, and other irregularities, served the place of steps; and we descended slowly; allowing our heavy luggage to slip on before, at the end of a long cord.

But that which served as steps under our feet, became in other places stalactites. The lava, very porous in certain places, took the form of little round blisters. Crystals of opaque quartz, adorned with limpid drops of natural glass suspended to the roof like lusters, seemed to take fire as we passed beneath them. One would have fancied that the genii of romance were illuminating their underground palaces to receive the sons of men.

"Magnificent, glorious!" I cried in a moment of involuntary enthusiasm, "what a spectacle, uncle! Do you not admire these variegated shades of lava, which run through a whole series of colors, from reddish brown to pale yellow —by the most insensible degrees? And these crystals, they appear like luminous globes."

"You are beginning to see the charms of travel, Master Harry," cried my uncle. "Wait a bit, until we advance farther. What we have as yet discovered is nothing—onwards, my boy, onwards!"

It would have been a far more correct and appropriate expression, had he said, "let us slide," for we were going down an inclined plane with perfect ease. The compass indicated that we were moving in a south-easterly direction. The flow of lava had never turned to the right or the left. It had the inflexibility of a straight line.

Nevertheless, to my surprise, we found no perceptible increase in heat. This proved the theories of Humphrey Davy to be founded on truth, and more than once I found myself examining the thermometer in silent astonishment. Two hours after my departure it only marked 54 degrees Fahrenheit. I had every reason to believe from this that our descent was far more horizontal than vertical. As for discovering the exact depth to which we had attained, nothing could be easier. The Professor, as he advanced measured the angles of deviation and inclination; but he kept the result of his observations to himself.

About eight o'clock in the evening, my uncle gave the signal for the night's rest. Hans seated himself on the ground. The lamps were hung to fissures in the lava rock. We were now in a large cavern where air was not wanting. On the contrary, it abounded. What could be the cause of this—to what atmospheric agitation could be ascribed this draught? But this was a question which I did not care to discuss just then. Fatigue and hunger made me incapable of reasoning. An almost unceasing march of twelve hours had not been kept up without great exhaustion. I was really and truly worn out; and delighted enough I was to hear the word Halt.

Hans laid out some provisions on a lump of lava, and we each supped with keen relish. One thing, however, caused us great uneasiness—our water reserve was already half exhausted. My uncle had full confidence in finding subterranean resources, but hitherto we had completely failed in so doing. I could not help calling my uncle's attention to the circumstance. "And you are surprised at this total absence of springs?" he said.

"Doubtless—I am very uneasy on the point. We have certainly not enough water to last us five days."

"Be quite easy on that matter," continued my uncle. "I answer for it we shall find plenty of water—in fact, far more than we shall want."

"But when?"

"When we once get through this crust of lava. How can you expect springs to force their way through these solid stone walls?"

"But what is there to prove that this concrete mass of lava does not extend to the center of the earth? I don't think we have as yet done much in a vertical way."

"What puts that into your head, my boy?" asked my uncle, mildly.

"Well, it appears to me that if we had descended very far below the level of the sea—we should find it rather hotter than we have."

"According to your system," said my uncle; "but what does the thermometer say?"

"Scarcely 15 degrees by Reaumur, which is only an increase of 9 since our departure."

"Well, and what conclusion does that bring you to?" inquired the Professor.

"The deduction I draw from this is very simple. According to the most exact observations, the augmentation of the temperature of the interior of the earth is 1 degree for every hundred feet. But certain local causes may considerably modify this figure. The difference evidently depends on the conductibility of certain rocks. In the neighborhood of an extinct volcano, it has been remarked that the elevation of temperature was only 1 degree in every 125 feet. Let us, then, go upon this calculation—which is the most favorable—and calculate."

"Calculate away, my boy."

"Nothing easier," said I, pulling out my note-book and pencil. "Nine times one hundred and twenty-five feet, make a depth of eleven hundred and twenty-five feet."

"Archimedes could not have spoken more· geometrically."

"Well?"

"Well, according to my observations, we are at least ten thousand feet below the level of the sea."

"Can it be possible?"

"Either my calculation is correct, or there is no truth in figures."

The calculations of the Professor were perfectly correct. We were already six thousand feet deeper down in the bowels of the earth than anyone had ever been before. The lowest known depth to which man had hitherto penetrated was in the mines of Kitz-Bahl, on the Tyrol, and those of Württemburg in Bohemia.

The temperature, which should have been eighty-one, was in this place only fifteen. This was a matter for serious consideration.

CHAPTER XVI
THE EASTERN TUNNEL

THE next day was Tuesday, the 2d of July—and at six o'clock in the morning we resumed our journey. We still continued to follow the gallery of lava, a perfect natural pathway, as easy of descent as some of those inclined planes which, in very old German houses, serve the purpose of staircases. This went on until seventeen minutes past twelve, the precise instant at which we rejoined Hans, who having been somewhat in advance, had suddenly stopped.

"At last," cried my uncle, "we have reached the end of the shaft."

I looked wonderingly about me. We were in the center of four cross paths—somber and narrow tunnels. The question now arose as to which it was wise to take; and this of itself was no small difficulty. My uncle, who did not wish to appear to have any hesitation about the matter before myself or the guide, at once made up his mind. He pointed quietly to the eastern tunnel; and, without delay, we entered within its gloomy recesses.

Besides, had he entertained any feeling of hesitation it might have been prolonged indefinitely, for there was no indication by which to determine on a choice. It was absolutely necessary to trust to chance and good fortune!

The descent of this obscure and narrow gallery was very gradual and winding. Sometimes we gazed through a succession of arches, its course very like the aisles of a Gothic cathedral. The great artistic sculptors and builders of the middle ages might have here completed their studies with advantage. Many most beautiful and suggestive ideas of architectural beauty would have been discovered by them. After passing through this phase of the cavernous way, we suddenly came, about a mile farther on, upon a square system of arch, such as that adopted by the early Romans, projecting from the solid rock, and keeping up the weight of the roof. Suddenly we would come upon a series of low subterranean tunnels which looked like beaver holes, or the work of foxes. Through these narrow and winding ways we had literally to crawl!

The heat still remained at quite a supportable degree. With an involuntary shudder, I reflected on what the heat must have been when the volcano of Sneffels was pouring its smoke, flames, and streams of boiling lava—all of which must have come up by the road we were now following. I could imagine the torrents of hot seething stone darting on, bubbling up with accompaniments of smoke, steam, and sulphurous stench! "Only to think of the consequences," I mused, "if the old volcano were once more to set to work."

I did not communicate these rather unpleasant reflections to my uncle. His only idea was to go ahead. He walked, he slid, he clambered over piles of fragments, he rolled down heaps of broken lava, with an earnestness and conviction it was impossible not to admire.

At six o'clock in the evening, after a very wearisome journey, but one not so fatiguing as before, we had made six miles towards the southward, but had not gone more than a mile downwards.

My uncle, as usual, gave the signal to halt. We ate our meal in thoughtful silence, and then retired to sleep. Our arrangements for the night were very primitive and simple. A traveling rug, in which each rolled himself, was all our bedding. We had no necessity to fear cold or any unpleasant visit. Travelers who bury themselves in the wilds and depths of the African desert, who seek profit and pleasure in the forests of the New World, are compelled to take it in turn to watch during the hours of sleep; but in this region of the earth absolute solitude and complete security reigned supreme.

After a night's sweet repose, we awoke fresh and ready for action. There being nothing to detain us, we started on our journey. We continued to burrow through the lava tunnel as before. It was impossible to make out through what soil we were making way. The tunnel, moreover, instead of going down into the bowels of the earth, became absolutely horizontal. I even thought, after some examination, that we were actually tending upwards. About ten o'clock in the day this state of things became so clear, that finding the change very fatiguing I was obliged to slacken my pace and finally to come to a halt. "Well," said the Professor quickly, "what is the matter?"

"The fact is, I am dreadfully tired," was my earnest reply.

"What," cried my uncle, "tired after a three hours' walk, and by so easy a road?"

"Easy enough, I dare say, but very fatiguing."

"But how can that be, when all we have to do is to go downwards."

"I beg your pardon, sir. For some time I have noticed that we are going upwards."

"Upwards," cried my uncle, shrugging his shoulders, "how can that be?"

"There can be no doubt about it. For the last half hour the slopes have been upward—and if we go on in this way much longer we shall find ourselves back in Iceland."

My uncle shook his head with the air of a man who does not want to be convinced. I tried to continue the conversation. He would not answer me, but once more gave the signal for departure. His silence I thought was only caused by concentrated ill-temper.

However this might be, I once more took up my load, and resolutely followed Hans, who was now in advance of my uncle. I did not like to be beaten or even distanced. The very idea of being left behind, lost in that terrible labyrinth, made me shiver as with the ague. Besides, if the ascending path was more arduous and painful to clamber, I had one source of secret consolation and delight. It was to all appearance taking us back to the surface of the earth. That of itself was hopeful. Every step I took confirmed me in my belief, and I began already to build castles in the air in relation to my marriage with my pretty little cousin.

About twelve o'clock there was a great and sudden change in the aspect of the rocky sides of the gallery. I first noticed it from the diminution of the rays of light which cast back the reflection of the lamp. From being coated with shining and resplendent lava, it became living rock. The sides were sloping walls, which sometimes became quite vertical. We were now in what the geological professors call a state of transition, in the period of Silurian stones. "I can see, clearly now," I cried; "the sediment from the waters which once covered the whole earth, formed during the second period of its existence, these schists and these calcareous rocks. We are turning our backs on the granite rocks."

I might just as well have kept my observations to myself. My geological enthusiasm got the better, however, of my cooler judgment, and Professor Hardwigg heard my observations. "What is the matter now?" he said, in a tone of great gravity.

"Well," cried I, "do you not see these different layers of calcareous rocks and the first indication of slate strata?"

"Well; what then?"

"We have arrived at that period of the world's existence when the first plants and the first animals made their appearance."

"You think so?"

"Yes, look; examine and judge for yourself."

I induced the Professor with some difficulty to cast the light of his lamp on the sides of the long winding gallery. I expected some exclamation to burst from his lips. I was very much mistaken. The worthy Professor never spoke a word.

It was impossible to say whether he understood me or not. Perhaps it was possible that in his pride—my uncle and a learned professor—he did not like to own that he was wrong in having chosen the eastern tunnel, or was he determined at any price to go to the end of it? It was quite evident we had left the region of lava, and that the road by which we were going could not take us back to the great crater of Mount Sneffels. "At all events, if I am right," I thought to myself, "I must certainly find some remains of primitive plants ,and it will be absolutely necessary to give way to such indubitable evidence. Let us have a good search."

I accordingly lost no opportunity of searching, and had not gone more than about a hundred yards, when the evidence I sought for cropped up in the most incontestable manner before my eyes. It was quite natural that I should expect to find these signs, for during the Silurian period the seas contained no fewer than fifteen hundred different animal and vegetable species. My feet so long accustomed to the hard and arid lava soil, suddenly found themselves treading on a kind of soft dust, the remains of plants and shells. Upon the walls themselves I could clearly make out the outline, as plain as a sun picture, of the fucus and the lycopodes. The worthy and excellent Professor Hardwigg could not of course make any mistake about the matter; but

I believe he deliberately closed his eyes, and continued on his way with a firm and unalterable step.

I began to think that he was carrying his obstinacy a great deal too far. I could no longer act with prudence or composure. I stooped on a sudden and picked up an almost perfect shell, which had undoubtedly belonged to some animal very much resembling some of the present day. Having secured the prize, I followed in the wake of my uncle. "Do you see this?" I said.

"Well," said the Professor, with the most imperturbable tranquillity, "it is the shell of a crustaceous animal of the extinct order of the trilobites; nothing more I assure you."

"But," cried I, much troubled at his coolness, "do you draw no conclusion from it?"

"Well, if I may ask, what conclusion do you draw from it yourself?"

"Well, I thought——"

"I know, my boy, what you would say, and you are right, perfectly and incontestably right. We have finally abandoned the crust of lava and the road by which the lava ascended. It is quite possible that I may have been mistaken, but I shall be unable to discover my error until I get to the end of this gallery."

"You are quite right as far as that is concerned," I replied, "and I should highly approve of your decision, if we had not to fear the greatest of all dangers."

"And what is that?"

"Want of water."

"Well, my dear Henry, it can't be helped. We must put ourselves on rations."

And on he went.

CHAPTER XVII
DEEPER AND DEEPER—THE COAL MINE

IN truth, we were compelled to put ourselves upon rations. Our supply would certainly last not more than three days. I found this out about supper time. The worst part of the matter was, that in what is called the transition rocks, it was hardly to be expected we should meet with water! I had read of the horrors of thirst, and

I knew that where we were, a brief trial of its sufferings would put an end to our adventures—and our lives! But it was utterly useless to discuss the matter with my uncle. He would have answered by some axiom from Plato.

During the whole of the next day we proceeded on our journey through this interminable gallery, arch after arch, tunnel after tunnel. We journeyed without exchanging a word. We had become as mute and reticent as Hans our guide. The road had no longer an upward tendency; at all events, if it had, it was not to be made out very clearly. Sometimes there could be no doubt that we were going downwards. But this inclination was scarcely to be distinguished, and was by no means reassuring to the Professor, because the character of the strata was in no wise modified, and the transition character of the rocks became more and more marked.

It was a glorious sight to see how the electric light brought out the sparkles in the walls of the calcareous rocks, and the old red sandstone. One might have fancied oneself in one of those deep cuttings in Devonshire, which have given their name to this kind of soil. Some magnificent specimens of marble projected from the sides of the gallery; some of an agate gray with white veins of variegated character, others of a yellow spotted color, with red veins; farther off might be seen samples of color in which cherry-tinted seams were to be found in all their brightest shades.

The greater number of these marbles were stamped with the marks of primitive animals. Since the previous evening, nature and creation had made considerable progress. Instead of the rudimentary trilobites, I perceived the remains of a more perfect order. Among others, the fish in which the eye of a geologist has been able to discover the first form of the reptile. It was quite evident to me that we were ascending the scale of animal life of which man forms the summit. My excellent uncle, the Professor, appeared not to take notice of these warnings. He was determined at any risk to proceed.

He must have been in expectation of one of two things; either that a vertical well was about to open under his feet, and thus allow him to continue his descent, or that some insurmountable obstacle would compel us to stop and go back by the road we had so long traveled. But evening came again, and, to my horror, neither hope was doomed to be realized!

On Friday, after a night when I began to feel the gnawing agony of thirst, and when in consequence appetite decreased, our little band rose and once more followed the turnings and windings, the ascents and descents, of this interminable gallery. All were silent and gloomy. I could see that even my uncle felt we had ventured too far.

After about ten hours of further progress,—a progress dull and monotonous to the last degree—I remarked that the reverberation, and reflection of our lamps upon the sides of the tunnel had singularly diminished. The marble, the schist, the calcareous rocks, the red sandstone, had disappeared, leaving in their places a dark and gloomy wall, sombre and without brightness. When we reached a remarkably narrow part of the tunnel, I leaned my left hand against the rock. When I took my hand away, and happened to glance at it, it was quite black. We had reached the coal strata of the Central Earth. "A coal mine!" I cried.

"A coal mine without miners," responded my uncle, a little severely.

"How can we tell?"

"I can tell," replied my uncle, in a sharp and doctorial tone. "I am perfectly certain that this gallery through successive layers of coal, was not cut by the hand of man. But whether it is the work of nature or not is of little concern to us. The hour for our evening meal has come —let us sup."

Hans, the guide, occupied himself in preparing food. I had come to that point when I could no longer eat. All I cared about were the few drops of water which fell to my share. What I suffered it is useless to record. The guide's gourd, not quite half full, was all that was left for us three! Having finished their repast, my two companions laid themselves down upon their rugs, and found in sleep a remedy for their fatigue and sufferings. As for me, I could not sleep, I lay counting the hours until morning.

The next morning, Saturday, at six o'clock, we started again. Twenty minutes later we suddenly came upon a vast excavation. From its mighty extent I saw at once that the hand of man could have had nothing to do with this coal mine; the vault above would have fallen in; as it was, it was only held together by some miracle of nature. This mighty natural cavern was about a hundred feet wide, by about a hundred and fifty high. The earth had evidently been cast apart by some violent subterranean commotion. The mass, giving way to some prodigious upheaving of nature, had split in two, leaving the vast gap into which we inhabitants of the earth had penetrated for the first time.

The whole singular history of the coal period was written on those dark and gloomy walls. A geologist would have been able easily to follow the different phases of its formation. The seams of coal were separated by strata of sandstone, a compact clay, which appeared to be crushed down by the weight from above.

While we still continued our journey, I forgot the length of the road, by giving myself up wholly to these geological considerations. The temperature continued to be very much the same as while we were traveling amid the lava and the schists. On the other hand my sense of smell was much affected by a very powerful odor. I immediately knew that the gallery was filled to overflowing with that dangerous gas the miners call fire-damp, the explosion of which has caused such fearful and terrible accidents, making a hundred widows, and hundreds of orphans in a single hour.

Happily, we were able to illume our progress by means of the Ruhmkorff apparatus. If we had been so rash and imprudent as to explore this gallery, torch in hand, a terrible explosion would have put an end to our travels, simply because no travelers would be left.

Our excursion through this wondrous coal mine in the very bowels of the earth lasted until evening. My uncle was scarcely able to conceal his impatience and dissatisfaction at the road continuing still to advance in a horizontal direction. The darkness, dense and opaque, a few yards in advance and in the rear, rendered it impossible to make out what was the length of the gallery. For myself, I began to believe that it was simply interminable, and would go on in the same manner for months.

Suddenly, however, at six o'clock, we stood in front of a

wall. To the right, to the left, above, below, nowhere was there any passage. We had reached a spot where the rocks said in unmistakable accents—No Thoroughfare. I stood stupefied. The guide simply folded his arms. My uncle was silent.

"Well, well, so much the better," cried my uncle, at last, " I now know what we are about. We are decidedly not upon the road followed by Saknussemm. All we have to do is to go back. Let us take one night's good rest, and before three days are over, I promise you we shall have regained the point where the galleries divided."

"Yes, we may, if our strength lasts as long," I cried, in a lamentable voice.

" And why not? "

" To-morrow, among us three, there will not be a drop of water. It is just gone."

"And your courage with it," said my uncle, speaking in a severe tone.

What could I say? I turned round on my side, and from sheer exhaustion fell into a heavy but troubled sleep. Dreams of water! And I awoke unrefreshed. I would have bartered a diamond mine for a glass of pure spring water!

CHAPTER XVIII
THE WRONG ROAD

NEXT day, our departure took place at a very early hour. There was no time for the least delay. According to my account, we had five days' hard work to get back to the place where the galleries divided.

I can never tell all the sufferings we endured upon our return. My uncle bore them like a man who has been in the wrong—that is, with concentrated and suppressed anger; Hans, with all the resignation of his pacific character; and I—I confess that I did nothing but complain, and despair. I had no heart for this bad fortune. But there was one consolation. Defeat at the outset would probably upset the whole journey!

As I had expected from the first, our supply of water gave completely out on our first day's march. Our provision of liquids was reduced to our supply of schiedam;

but this horrible—nay, I will say it—this infernal liquor burnt the throat, and I could not even bear the sight of it. I found the temperature to be stifling. I was paralyzed with fatigue. More than once I was about to fall insensible to the ground. The whole party then halted, and the worthy Icelander and my excellent uncle did their best to console and comfort me. I could, however, plainly see that my uncle was contending painfully against the extreme fatigues of our journey, and the awful torture generated by the absence of water. At length a time came when I ceased to recollect anything—when all was one awful, hideous, fantastic dream!

At last, on Tuesday, the eighth of the month of July, after crawling on our hands and knees for many hours, more dead than alive, we reached the point of junction between the galleries. I lay like a log, an inert mass of human flesh on the arid lava soil. It was then ten in the morning.

Hans and my uncle, leaning against the wall, tried to nibble away at some pieces of biscuit, while deep groans and sighs escaped from my scorched and swollen lips. Then I fell off into a kind of deep lethargy. Presently I felt my uncle approach, and lift me up tenderly in his arms. "Poor boy," I heard him say in a tone of deep commiseration.

I was profoundly touched by these words, being by no means accustomed to signs of womanly weakness in the Professor. I caught his trembling hands in mine and gave them a gentle pressure. He allowed me to do so without resistance, looking at me kindly all the time. His eyes were wet with tears. I then saw him take the gourd which he wore at his side. To my surprise, or rather to my stupefaction, he placed it to my lips.

"Drink, my boy," he said.

Was it possible my ears had not deceived me? Was my uncle mad? I looked at him, with, I am sure, quite an idiotic expression. I would not understand him. I too much feared the counteraction of disappointment.

"Drink," he said again.

Had I hear aright? Before, however, I could ask myself the question a second time, a mouthful of water cooled my parched lips and throat—one mouthful, but I do believe it brought me back to life. I thanked my uncle by clasping my hands. My heart was too full to speak.

"Yes," said he, "one mouthful of water, the very last—do you hear, my boy—the very last! I have taken care of it at the bottom of my bottle as the apple of my eye. Twenty times, a hundred times, I have resisted the fearful desire to drink it. But—no—no, Harry, I saved it for you."

"My dear uncle," I exclaimed, and the big tears rolled down my hot and feverish cheeks.

"Yes, my poor boy, I knew that when you reached this place, this cross road in the earth, you would fall down half dead, and I saved my last drop of water in order to restore you."

"Thanks," I cried; "thanks from my heart."

As little as my thirst was really quenched, I had nevertheless partially recovered my strength. The contracted muscles of my throat relaxed—and the inflammation of my lips in some measure subsided. At all events, I was able to speak. "Well," I said, "there can be no doubt now as to what we have to do. Water has utterly failed us; our journey is therefore at an end. Let us return."

While I spoke thus, my uncle evidently avoided my face: he held down his head; his eyes were turned in every possible direction but the right one.

"Yes," I continued, getting excited by my own words, "we must go back to Sneffels. May heaven give us strength to enable us once more to revisit the light of day. Would that we now stood on the summit of the crater."

"Go back," said my uncle speaking to himself—"and must it be so?"

"Go back—yes, and without losing a single moment," I vehemently cried.

For some moments there was silence under that dark and gloomy vault. "So, my dear Harry," said the Professor in a very singular tone of voice, "those few drops of water have not sufficed to restore your energy and courage."

"Courage!" I cried.

"I see that you are quite as downcast as before—and still give way to discouragement and despair.

What, then, was the man made of, and what other projects were entering his fertile and audacious brain! "You are not discouraged, sir?"

"What! give up just as we are on the verge of success," he cried, "never, never shall it be said that Professor Hardwigg retreated."

"Then we must make up our minds to perish," I cried with a helpless sigh.

"No, Harry, my boy, certainly not. Go, leave me, I am very far from desiring your death. Take Hans with you, *I will go on alone.*"

"You ask us to leave you?"

"Leave me, I say. I have undertaken this dangerous and perilous adventure. I will carry it to the end—or I will never return to the surface of Mother Earth. Go— Harry—once more I say to you—go!"

My uncle as he spoke was terribly excited. His voice, which before had been tender, almost womanly, became harsh and menacing. He appeared to be struggling with desperate energy against the impossible. I did not wish to abandon him at the bottom of that abyss, while, on the other hand, the instinct of preservation told me to fly.

Meanwhile, our guide was looking on with profound calmness and indifference. He appeared to be an unconcerned party, and yet he perfectly well knew what was going on between us. Our gestures sufficiently indicated the different roads each wished to follow—and which each tried to influence the other to undertake. But Hans appeared not to take the slightest interest in what was really a question of life and death for us all, but waited quite ready to obey the signal which should say go aloft, or to resume his desperate journey into the interior of the earth.

How then I wished with all my heart and soul that I could make him understand my words. My representations, my sighs and groans, the earnest accents in which I should have spoken would have convinced that cold hard nature. Those fearful dangers and perils of which the stolid guide had no idea, I would have pointed them out to him—I would have, as it were, made him see and feel. Between us, we might have convinced the obstinate Professor. If the worst had come to the worst, we could have compelled him to return to the summit of Sneffels. I approached Hans. I caught his hand in mine. He never moved a muscle. I indicated to him the road to the top of the crater. He remained motionless. My panting form, my haggard countenance, must have indicated the extent of my sufferings. The Icelander gently shook his head and pointed to my uncle. *"Master,"* he said.

"The master!" I cried, beside myself with fury—"madman! no—I tell you he is not the master of our lives; we must fly! we must drag him with us! do you hear me? Do you understand me, I say?"

I have already explained that I held Hans by the arm. I tried to make him rise from his seat. I struggled with him and tried to force him away. My uncle now interposed. "My good Henry, be calm," he said. "You will obtain nothing from my devoted follower; therefore, listen to what I have to say."

I folded my arms, as well as I could, and looked my uncle full in the face.

"This wretched want of water," he said, "is the sole obstacle to the success of my project. In the entire gallery, composed of lava, schist, and coal, it is true we found not one liquid molecule. It is quite possible that we may be more fortunate in the western tunnel."

My sole reply was to shake my head with an air of incredulity.

"Listen to me to the end," said the Professor in his well known lecturing voice. "While you lay yonder without life or motion, I undertook a reconnoitering journey into the conformation of this other gallery. I have discovered that it goes directly downwards into the bowels of the earth, and in a few hours will take us to the old granitic formation. In this we shall undoubtedly find innumerable springs. The nature of the rock makes this a mathematical certainty, and instinct agrees with logic to say that it is so. Now, this is the serious proposition which I have to make to you. When Christopher Columbus asked of his men three days to discover the land of promise, his men ill, terrified, and hopeless, yet gave him three days—and the New World was discovered. Now I, the Christopher Columbus of this subterranean region, only ask of you one more day. If, when that time is expired, I have not found the water of which we are in search, I swear to you, I will give up my mighty enterprise and return to the earth's surface."

Despite my irritation and despair, I knew how much it cost my uncle to make this proposition, and to hold such conciliatory language. Under the circumstances, what could I do, but yield?

" Well," I cried, " let it be as you wish, and may heaven reward your superhuman energy. But as, unless we discover water, our hours are numbered, let us lose no time, but go ahead."

CHAPTER XIX
THE WESTERN GALLERY—A NEW ROUTE

OUR descent was now resumed by means of the second gallery. Hans took up his post in front as usual. We had not gone more than a hundred yards when the Professor carefully examined the walls. " This is the primitive formation—we are on the right road—onwards is our hope!"

When the whole earth got cool in the first hours of the world's morning, the diminution of the volume of the earth produced a state of dislocation in its upper crust, followed by ruptures, crevasses and fissures. The passage was a fissure of this kind, through which, ages ago, had flowed the eruptive granite. The thousand windings and turnings formed an inextricable labyrinth through the ancient soil. As we descended, successions of layers composing the primitive soil appeared with the utmost fidelity of detail.

No mineralogists had ever found themselves placed in such a marvelous position to study nature in all her real and naked beauty. The sounding rod, a mere machine, could not bring to the surface of the earth the objects of value for the study of its internal structure, which we were about to see with our own eyes, to touch with our own hands. Remember that I am writing this *after* the journey.

Across the streak of the rocks, colored by beautiful green tints, wound metallic threads of copper, of manganese, with traces of platinum and gold. I could not help gazing at these riches buried in the entrails of mother earth, and of which no man would have the enjoyment to the end of time! These treasures—mighty and inexhaustible, were buried in the morning of the earth's history, at such awful depths, that no crowbar or pickax will ever drag them from their tomb! The light of our Ruhmkorf's coil, increased tenfold by the myriad of prismatic masses of rock, sent their jets of fire in every direction, and I could fancy myself traveling through a huge hollow diamond, the rays of which produced myriads of extraordinary effects. Towards six o'clock, this festival of light began sensibly and visibly to decrease, and soon almost ceased. The sides of the gallery assumed a crystallized tint, with a somber hue; white mica began to commingle more freely with feldspar and quartz, to form what may be called the true rock—the stone which is hard above all, that supports, without being crushed, the four stories of the earth's soil. We were walled by an immense prison of granite!

It was now eight o'clock, and still there was no sign of water. The sufferings I endured were horrible. My uncle now kept at the head of our little column. Nothing could induce him to stop. I, meanwhile, had but one real thought. My ear was keenly on the watch to catch the sound of a spring. But no pleasant sound of falling water fell upon my listening ear.

At last the time came when my limbs refused to longer carry me. I contended heroically against the terrible tortures I endured, because I did not wish to compel my uncle to halt. To him I knew this would be the last fatal stroke. Suddenly I felt a deadly faintness come over me. My eyes could no longer see; my knees shook. I gave one despairing cry—and fell!

" Help, help, I am dying! "

My uncle turned and slowly retraced his steps. He looked at me with folded arms, and then allowed one sentence to escape, in hollow accents, from his lips—" All is over."

The last thing I saw was a face fearfully distorted with pain and sorrow; and then my eyes closed.

When I again opened them, I saw my companions lying near me, motionless, wrapped in their huge traveling rugs. Were they asleep or dead? For myself, sleep was wholly out of the question. My fainting fit over, I was wakeful as the lark. I suffered too much for sleep to visit my eye-

lids—the more, that I thought myself sick unto death—
dying. The last words spoken by my uncle seemed to be
buzzing in my ears—*all is over!* It was probable that he
was right. In the state of prostration to which I was reduced, it was madness to think of ever again seeing the light
of day. Above were miles upon miles of the earth's crust.
As I thought of it, I could fancy the whole weight
resting on my shoulders. I was crushed, annihilated! and
exhausted myself in vain attempts to turn in my granite
bed.

Hours upon hours passed away. A profound and terrible silence reigned around us—a silence of the tomb.
Nothing could make itself heard through these gigantic
walls of granite. The very thought was stupendous.

Presently, despite my apathy, despite the kind of deadly
calm into which I was cast, something aroused me. It
was a slight but peculiar noise. While I was watching
intently, I observed that the tunnel was becoming dark.
Then gazing through the dim light that remained, I thought
I saw the Icelander taking his departure, lamp in hand.

Why had he acted thus? Did Hans the guide mean to
abandon us? My uncle lay fast asleep—or dead. I tried
to cry out, and arouse him. My voice, feebly issuing from
my parched and fevered lips, found no echo in that fearful
place. My throat was dry, my tongue stuck to the roof of
my mouth. The obscurity had by this time become intense,
and at last even the faint sound of the guide's footsteps was
lost in the blank distance. My soul seemed filled with
anguish, and death appeared welcome, only let it come
quickly.

"Hans is leaving us," I cried. "Hans—Hans, if you
are a man, come back."

These words were spoken to myself. They could not be
heard aloud. Moreover, a moment's reflection re-assured
me. Hans's departure could not be a flight. Instead of
ascending the gallery, he was going deeper down into the
gulf. Had he had any bad design, his way would have
been upwards.

This reasoning calmed me a little and I began to hope!
The good, and peaceful, and imperturbable Hans would
certainly not have arisen from his sleep without some serious and grave motive. Was he bent on a voyage of dis-

covery? During the deep, still silence of the night had he at last heard that sweet murmur about which we were all so anxious?

CHAPTER XX
WATER, WHERE IS IT? A BITTER DISAPPOINTMENT

DURING a long, long, weary hour, there crossed my wildly delirious brain all sorts of reasons as to what could have aroused our quiet and faithful guide. The most absurd and ridiculous ideas passed through my head, each more impossible than the other. I believe I was either half or wholly mad. Suddenly, however, there arose, as it were from the depths of the earth, a voice of comfort. It was the sound of footsteps! Hans was returning. Presently the uncertain light began to shine upon the walls of the passage, and then it came in view far down the sloping tunnel. At length Hans himself appeared.

He approached my uncle, placed his hand upon his shoulder, and gently awakened him. My uncle, as soon as he saw who it was, instantly rose. " Well! " exclaimed the Professor.

" *Vatten,*" said the hunter.

I did not know a single word of the Danish language, and yet by a sort of mysterious instinct I understood what the guide had said.

"Water, water!" I cried, in a wild and frantic tone, clapping my hands, and gesticulating like a madman.

" Water! " murmured my uncle, in a voice of deep emotion and gratitude. " *Hvar?* "

" *Nedat.*"

"Where? below!" I understood every word. I had caught the hunter by the hands, and I shook them heartily, while he looked on with perfect calmness.

The preparations for our departure did not take long, and we were soon making a rapid descent into the tunnel. An hour later we had advanced a thousand yards, and descended two thousand feet. At this moment I heard an accustomed and well-known sound running along the floors of the granite rock—a kind of dull and sullen roar, like that of a distant waterfall.

During the first half-hour of our advance, not finding the discovered spring, my feelings of intense suffering returned. Once more I began to lose all hope. My uncle, however, observing how down-hearted I was again becoming, took up the conversation. " Hans was right," he exclaimed, enthusiastically; " that is the dull roaring of a torrent."

" A torrent," I cried, delighted at even hearing the welcome words.

" There's not the slightest doubt about it," he replied, " a subterranean river is flowing beside us."

I made no reply, but hastened on, once more animated by hope. I did not even feel the deep fatigue which hitherto had overpowered me. The very sound of this glorious murmuring water already refreshed me. We could hear it increasing in volume every moment. The torrent, which for a long time could be heard flowing over our heads, now ran distinctly along the left wall, roaring, rushing, spluttering, and still falling.

Several times I passed my hand across the rock hoping to find some trace of humidity—of the slightest percolation. Alas! in vain. Again a half hour passed in the same weary toil. Again we advanced.

It now became evident that the hunter, during his absence, had not been able to carry his researches any farther. Guided by an instinct peculiar to the dwellers in mountain regions and water finders, he " smelt " the living spring through the rock. Still he had not seen the precious liquid. He had neither quenched his own thirst nor brought us one drop in his gourd.

Moreover, we soon made the disastrous discovery, that if our progress continued, we should soon be moving away from the torrent, the sound of which gradually diminished. We turned back. Hans halted at the precise spot where the sound of the torrent appeared nearest.

I could bear the suspense and suffering no longer, and seated myself against the wall, behind which I could hear the water seething and effervescing not two feet away. But a solid wall of granite still separated us from it!

Hans looked keenly at me, and, strange enough, for once I thought I saw a smile on his imperturbable face. He rose from a stone on which he had been seated, and took up the lamp. I could not help rising and following. He moved slowly along the firm and solid granite wall. I watched him with mingled curiosity and eagerness. Presently he halted and placed his ear against the dry stone, moving slowly along and listening with the most extreme care and attention. I understood at once that he was searching for the exact spot where the torrent's roar was most plainly heard. This point he soon found in the lateral wall on the left side, about three feet above the level of the tunnel floor.

I was in a state of intense excitement. I scarcely dared believe what the eider-duck hunter was about to do. It was, however, impossible in a moment more not to both understand and applaud, and even to smother him in my embraces, when I saw him raise the heavy crowbar and commence an attack upon the rock itself.

" Saved," I cried.

" Yes," cried my uncle, even more excited and delighted than myself; " Hans is quite right. Oh, the worthy, excellent man! We should never have thought of such an idea."

And nobody else, I think, would have done so. Such a process, simple as it seemed, would most certainly not have entered our heads. Nothing could be more dangerous than to begin to work with pickaxes in that particular part of the globe. Supposing while he was at work a break-up were to take place, and supposing the torrent once having gained an inch were to take an ell, and come pouring bodily through the broken rock!

Not one of these dangers was chimerical. They were only too real. But at that moment no fear of falling in of roof, or even of inundation was capable of stopping us. Our thirst was so intense, that to quench it we would have dug below the bed of old Ocean itself.

Hans went quietly to work—a work which neither my uncle nor I could have undertaken. Our impatience was so great, that if we had once begun with pickax and crowbar, the rock would soon have split into a hundred fragments. The guide, on the contrary, calm, ready, moderate, wore away the hard rock by little steady blows of his instrument, making no attempt at a larger hole than about six inches. As I stood, I heard, or I thought I heard, the roar of the torrent momentarily increasing in loudness, and at times

89

I almost felt the pleasant sensation of water upon my parched lips.

At the end of what appeared an age, Hans had made a hole, which enabled his crowbar to enter two feet into the solid rock. He had been at work exactly an hour. It appeared a dozen. I was getting wild with impatience. My uncle began to think of using more violent measures. I had the greatest difficulty in checking him. He had indeed just got hold of his crowbar when a loud and welcome hiss was heard. Then a stream, or rather a jet of water burst through the wall and came out with such force as to hit the opposite side!

Hans, the guide, who was half upset by the shock, was scarcely able to keep down a cry of pain and grief. I understood his meaning when plunging my hands into the sparkling jet I myself gave a wild and frantic cry. The water was scalding hot! "Boiling," I cried, in bitter disappointment.

"Well, never mind," said my uncle, "it will soon get cool."

The tunnel began to be filled by clouds of vapor, while a small stream ran away into the interior of the earth. In a short time we had some sufficiently cool to drink. We swallowed it in huge mouthfuls.

Oh what exalted delight—what rich and incomparable luxury! What was this water, whence did it come? To us what was that? The simple fact was—it was water; and, though still with a tinge of warmth about it, it brought back to the heart, that life which, but for it, must surely have faded away. I drank greedily, almost without tasting it.

When, however, I had almost quenched my ravenous thirst, I made a discovery. "Why, it is ferruginous water."

"Most excellent stomachic," replied my uncle, "and highly mineralized. Here is a journey worth twenty to Spa."

"It's very good," I replied.

"I should think so. Water found six miles under ground. There is a peculiarly inky flavor about it, which is by no means disagreeable. Hans may congratulate himself on having made a rare discovery. What do you say, nephew, according to the usual custom of travelers, to name the stream after him?"

"Good," said I. And the name of "Hans-bach" was at once agreed upon.

Hans was not a bit more proud after hearing our determination than he was before. After having taken a very small modicum of the welcome refreshment, he had seated himself in a corner with his usual imperturbable gravity.

"Now," said I, "it is not worth while letting this water run to waste."

"What is the use," replied my uncle, "the source from which this river rises is inexhaustible."

"Never mind," I continued, "let us fill our goat skin and gourds, and then try to stop the opening up."

My plan, after some hesitation, was followed or attempted. Hans picked up all the broken pieces of granite he had knocked out, and using some tow he happened to have about him, tried to shut up the fissure he had made in the wall. All he did was to scald his hands. The pressure was too great, and all our attempts were utter failures.

"It is evident," I remarked, "that the upper surface of these springs is situated at a very great height above—as we may fairly infer from the great pressure of the jet."

"That is by no means doubtful," replied my uncle, "if this column of water is about thirty-two thousand feet high, the atmospheric pressure must be something enormous. But a new idea has just struck me."

"And what is that?"

"Why be at so much trouble to close this aperture?"

"Because——" I hesitated and stammered, having no real reason.

"When our water bottles are empty, we are not at all sure that we shall be able to fill them," observed my uncle.

"I think that is very probable."

"Well, then, let this water run. It will, of course, naturally follow in our track, and will serve to guide and refresh us."

"I think the idea a good one," I cried, in reply, "and with this rivulet as a companion, there is no further reason why we should not succeed in our marvellous project."

"Ah, my boy," said the professor, laughing, "after all, you are coming round."

"More than that, I am now confident of ultimate success. Forward."

"One moment, nephew mine. Let us begin by taking some hours of repose."

I had utterly forgotten that it was night. The chronometer, however, informed me of the fact. Soon we were sufficiently restored and refreshed, and had all fallen into a profound sleep.

CHAPTER XXI
UNDER THE OCEAN

By the next day we had nearly forgotten our past sufferings. The first sensation I experienced was surprise at not being thirsty, and I actually asked myself the reason. The running stream, which flowed in rippling wavelets at my feet, was the satisfactory reply.

We breakfasted with a good appetite, and then drank our fill of the excellent water. I felt myself quite a new man, ready to go anywhere my uncle chose to lead. I began to think. Why should not a man as seriously convinced as my uncle, succeed, with so excellent a guide as worthy Hans, and so devoted a nephew as myself? These were the brilliant ideas which now invaded my brain. Had the proposition now been made to go back to the summit of Mount Sneffels, I should have declined the offer in a most indignant manner. But fortunately there was no question of going up. We were about to descend farther into the interior of the earth. "Let us be moving," I cried, awakening the echoes of the old world.

We resumed our march on Thursday at eight o'clock in the morning. The great granite tunnel went round by sinuous and winding ways, presenting every now and then sharp turns, and in fact had all the appearance of a labyrinth. Its direction, however, was in general towards the southwest. My uncle made several pauses in order to consult his compass. The gallery now began to trend downwards in a horizontal direction, with about two inches of fall in every furlong. The murmuring stream flowed quietly at our feet. I could not but compare it to some familiar spirit, guiding us through the earth, and I dabbled my fingers in its tepid water, which sang like a naiad as we progressed. My good humor began to assume a mythological character.

As for my uncle he began to complain of the horizontal character of the road. His route he found began to be indefinitely prolonged, instead of " sliding down the celestial ray," according to his expression.

But we had no choice; and as long as our road led towards the center—however little progress we made, there was no reason to complain. Moreover, from time to time the slopes were much greater; the naiad sang more loudly, and we began to dip downwards in earnest. I felt, however, no further painful sensation. I had not got over the excitement of the discovery of water.

That day and the next we did a considerable amount of horizontal, and relatively very little vertical, traveling. On Friday evening, the tenth of July, according to our estimation, we ought to have been thirty leagues to the southeast of Reykjawik, and about two leagues and a half deep. We now received a rather startling surprise.

Under our feet there opened a horrible well. My uncle was so delighted that he actually clapped his hands—as he saw how steep and sharp was the descent. " Ah, ah!" he cried, in rapturous delight; " this will take us a long way. Look at the projections of the rock. Hah!" he exclaimed, " it's a fearful staircase!"

Hans, however, who in all our troubles had never given up the ropes, took care so to dispose of them as to prevent any accidents. Our descent then began. I dare not call it a perilous descent, for I was already too familiar with that sort of work to look upon it as anything but a very ordinary affair. This well was a kind of narrow opening in the massive granite of the kind known as a fissure. The contraction of the terrestrial scaffolding, when it suddenly cooled, had been evidently the cause. If it had ever served in former times as a kind of funnel through which passed the eruptive masses vomited by Sneffels, I was at a loss to explain how it had left no mark. We were, in fact, descending a spiral, something like those winding staircases in use in modern houses.

We were compelled every quarter of an hour or thereabouts to sit down in order to rest our legs. Our calves ached. We then seated ourselves on some projecting rock with our legs hanging over, and gossiped while we ate a mouthful—drinking still from the pleasantly warm running stream which had not deserted us.

It is scarcely necessary to say, that in this curiously shaped fissure the Hansbach had become a cascade to the detriment of its size. It was still, however, sufficient, and more, for our wants. Besides we knew that, as soon as the declivity ceased to be so abrupt, the stream must resume its peaceful course. At this moment it reminded me of my uncle, his impatience and rage, while when it flowed more peacefully, I pictured to myself the placidity of the Icelandic guide.

During the whole of two days, the sixth and seventh of July, we followed the extraordinary spiral staircase of the fissure, penetrating two leagues farther into the crust of the earth, which placed us five leagues below the level of the sea. On the eighth, however, at twelve o'clock in the day, the fissure suddenly assumed a much more gentle slope still trending in a southeast direction. The road now became comparatively easy, and at the same time dreadfully monotonous. It would have been difficult for matters to have turned out otherwise. Our peculiar journey had no chance of being diversified by landscape and scenery. At all events, such was then my idea.

At length, on Wednesday the fifteenth, we were actually seven leagues (twenty-one miles) below the surface of the earth, and fifty leagues distant from the mountain of Sneffels. Though, if the truth be told, we were very tired, our health had resisted all suffering, and was in a most satisfactory state. Our traveler's box of medicaments had not even been opened. My uncle was careful to note every hour the indications of the compass, of the manometer, and of the thermometer, all which he afterwards published in his elaborate philosophical and scientific account of our remarkable voyage. He was therefore able to give an exact relation of the situation. When, therefore, he informed me that we were fifty leagues in a horizontal direction distant from our starting-point, I could not suppress a loud exclamation.

" What is the matter now? " cried my uncle.

" Nothing very important, only an idea has entered my head," was my reply.

" Well, out with it, my boy."

" It is my opinion that if your calculations are correct we are no longer under Iceland."

" Do you think so? "

" We can very easily find out," I replied, pulling out the map and compasses.

" You see," I said, after careful measurement, " that I am not mistaken. We are far beyond Cape Portland; and those fifty leagues to the southeast will take us into the open sea."

" Under the open sea," cried my uncle, rubbing his hands with a delighted air.

" Yes," I cried, " no doubt old ocean flows over our heads."

" Well, my dear boy, what can be more natural. Do you not know that in the neighborhood of Newcastle there are coal mines which have been worked far out under the sea? "

Now my worthy uncle, the Professor, no doubt regarded this discovery as a very simple fact, but to me the idea was by no means a pleasant one. And yet when one came to think the matter over seriously, what mattered it whether the plains and mountains of Iceland were suspended over our devoted heads, or the mighty billows of the Atlantic Ocean? The whole question rested on the solidity of the granite roof above us. However, I soon got used to the idea, for the passage now level, now running down, and still always to the southeast, kept going deeper and deeper into the profound abysses of Mother Earth.

Three days later, on the eighteenth day of July, on a Saturday, we reached a kind of vast grotto. My uncle here paid Hans his usual rix-dollars, and it was decided that the next day should be a day of rest.

CHAPTER XXII
SUNDAY BELOW GROUND

I AWOKE on Sunday morning without any sense of hurry and bustle attendant on an immediate departure. Though the day to be devoted to repose and reflection was spent under such strange circumstances, and in so wonderful a place, the idea was a pleasant one. Besides, we all began to get used to this kind of existence. I had almost ceased to think of the sun, of the moon, of the stars, of the trees, houses, and towns; in fact, about any terrestrial necessities. In our peculiar position we were far above such reflections.

The grotto was a vast and magnificent hall. Along its granitic soil the stream flowed placidly and pleasantly. So great a distance was it now from its fiery source, that its water was scarcely lukewarm, and could be drank without delay or difficulty.

After a frugal breakfast, the Professor made up his mind to devote some hours to putting his notes and calculations in order. "In the first place," he said, "I have a good many to verify and prove, in order that we may know our exact position. I wish to be able on our return to the upper regions, to make a map of our journey, a kind of vertical section of the globe, which will be as it were the profile of the expedition."

"That would indeed be a curious work, uncle; but can you make your observations with anything like certainty and precision?"

"I can. I have never on one occasion failed to note with great care the angles and slopes. I am certain as to having made no mistake. Take the compass and examine how she points."

I looked at the instrument with care. "East one-quarter southeast."

"Very good," resumed the Professor, noting the observation, and going through some rapid calculations. "I make out that we have journeyed two hundred and fifty miles from the point of our departure."

"Then the mighty waves of the Atlantic are rolling over our heads?"

"Certainly."

"And at this very moment it is possible that fierce

tempests are raging above, and that men and ships are battling against the angry blasts just over our heads?"

"It is quite within the range of possibility," rejoined my uncle, smiling.

"And that whales are playing in shoals, thrashing the bottom of the sea, the roof of our adamantine prison?"

"Be quite at rest on that point; there is no danger of their breaking through. But to return to our calculations. We are to the southeast, two hundred and fifty miles from the base of Sneffels, and, according to my preceding notes, I think we have gone sixteen leagues in a downward direction."

"Sixteen leagues—fifty miles!" I cried.

"I am sure of it."

"But that is the extreme limit allowed by science for the thickness of the earth's crust," I replied, referring to my geological studies.

"I do not contravene that assertion," was his quiet answer.

"And at this stage of our journey, according to all known laws on the increase of heat, there should be here a temperature of *fifteen hundred* degrees of Reaumur."

"There should be—you say, my boy."

"In which case this granite would not exist, but be in a state of fusion."

"But you perceive, my boy, that it is not so, and that facts, as usual, are very stubborn things, overruling all theories."

"I am forced to yield to the evidence of my senses, but I am nevertheless very much surprised."

"What heat does the thermometer really indicate?" continued the philosopher.

"Twenty-seven six-tenths."

"So that science is wrong by fourteen hundred and seventy-four degrees and four-tenths. According to which, it is demonstrated that the proportional increase in temperature is an exploded error. Humphrey Davy here shines forth in all his glory. He is right, and I have acted wisely to believe him. Have you any answer to make to this statement?"

Had I chosen to have spoken, I might have said a great deal. I in no way admitted the theory of Humphrey

Davy—I still held out for the theory of proportional increase of heat, though I did not feel it. I was far more willing to allow that this chimney of an extinct volcano was covered by lava of a kind refractory to heat—in fact a bad conductor—which did not allow the great increase of temperature to percolate through its sides. The hot water jet supported my view of the matter.

But without entering on a long and useless discussion, or seeking for new arguments to controvert my uncle, I contented myself with taking up facts as they were. " Well, sir, I take for granted that all your calculations are correct, but allow me to draw from them a rigorous and definite conclusion."

" Go on, my boy—have your say," cried my uncle, good-humoredly.

" At the place where we now are, under the latitude of Iceland, the terrestrial depth is about fifteen hundred and eighty-three leagues."

" Fifteen hundred, eighty-three and a quarter."

" Well, suppose we say sixteen hundred in round numbers. Now, out of a voyage of sixteen hundred leagues we have completed sixteen."

" As you say, what then? "

" At the expense of a diagonal journey of no less than eighty-five leagues."

" Exactly."

" We have been twenty days about it."

" Exactly twenty days."

" Now sixteen is the hundredth part of our contemplated expedition. If we go on in this way we shall be two thousand days, that is about five years and a half, going down."

The Professor folded his arms, listened, but did not speak.

" Without counting that if a vertical descent of sixteen leagues costs us a horizontal of eighty-five, we shall have to go about eight thousand leagues to the southeast, and we must therefore come out somewhere in the circumference long before we can hope to reach the center."

" Bother your calculations," cried my uncle in one of his old rages. " On what basis do they rest? How do you know that this passage does not take us direct to the end we require? Moreover, I have in my favor, fortunately, a precedent. What I have undertaken to do, another has done, and he having succeeded, why should I not be equally successful?"

"I hope, indeed, you will, but still, I suppose I may be allowed to——"

"You are allowed to hold your tongue," cried Professor Hardwigg, "when you talk so unreasonably as this."

I saw at once that the old doctorial Professor was still alive in my uncle—and fearful to rouse his angry passions, I dropped the unpleasant subject.

"Now, then," he explained, "consult the manometer. What does that indicate?"

"A considerable amount of pressure."

"Very good. You see, then, that by descending slowly, and by gradually accustoming ourselves to the density of this lower atmosphere, we shall not suffer.

"Well, I suppose not, except it may be a certain amount of pain in the ears," was my rather grim reply.

"That, my dear boy, is nothing, and you will easily get rid of that source of discomfort by bringing the exterior air in communication with the air contained in your lungs."

"Perfectly," said I, for I had quite made up my mind in no wise to contradict my uncle. "I should fancy almost that I should experience a certain amount of satisfaction in making a plunge into this dense atmosphere. Have you taken note of how wonderfully sound is propagated?"

"Of course I have. There can be no doubt that a journey into the interior of the earth would be an excellent cure for deafness."

"But then, uncle," I ventured mildly to observe, "this density will continue to increase."

"Yes—according to a law which, however, is scarcely defined. It is true that the intensity of weight will diminish just in proportion to the depth to which we go. You know very well that it is on the surface of the earth that its action is most powerfully felt, while on the contrary, in the very center of the earth bodies cease to have any weight at all."

"I know that is the case, but as we progress will not the atmosphere finally assume the density of water?"

"I know it; when placed under the pressure of seven hundred and ten atmospheres," cried my uncle with imperturbable gravity."

"And when we are still lower down?" I asked with natural anxiety."

"Well, lower down, the density will become even greater still."

"Then how shall we be able to make our way through this atmospheric fog?"

"Well, my worthy nephew, we must ballast ourselves by filling our pockets with stones," said Professor Hardwigg.

"Faith, uncle, you have an answer for everything," was my only reply. I began to feel that it was unwise in me to go any farther into the wide field of hypotheses, for I should certainly have revived some difficulty, or rather impossibility that would have enraged the Professor.

It was evident, nevertheless, that the air under a pressure which might be multiplied by thousands of atmospheres, would end by becoming perfectly solid, and that then admitting our bodies resisted the pressure, we should have to stop, in spite of all the reasonings in the world. Facts overcome all arguments.

But I thought it best not to urge this argument. My uncle would simply have quoted the example of Saknussemm. Supposing the learned Icelander's journey ever really to have taken place—there was one simple answer to be made:—In the sixteenth century neither the barometer nor the manometer had been invented—how, then, could Saknussemm have been able to discover when he did reach the center of the earth? This unanswerable and learned objection I, however, kept to myself, and bracing up my courage awaited the course of events—little aware of how adventurous yet were to be the incidents of our remarkable journey.

The rest of this day of leisure and repose was spent in calculation and conversation. I made it a point to agree with the Professor in everything; but I envied the perfect indifference of Hans, who without taking any such trouble about the cause and effect, went blindly onwards wherever destiny chose to lead.

CHAPTER XXIII
ALONE

It must in all truth be confessed, things as yet had gone on well, and I should have acted in bad taste to have complained. If our difficulties did not increase, it was within the range of possibility that we might ultimately reach the end of our journey. Then what glory would be ours! I began in the newly aroused ardor of my soul to speak enthusiastically to the Professor. Was I serious? The whole state in which we existed was a mystery—and it was impossible to know whether or not I was in earnest.

For several days after our memorable halt, the slopes became more rapid—some were even of a most frightful character—almost vertical, so that we were for ever going down into the solid interior mass. During some days, we actually descended a league and a half, even two leagues towards the center of the earth. The descents were sufficiently perilous, and while we were engaged in them we learned fully to appreciate the marvelous coolness of our guide, Hans. Without him we should have been wholly lost. The grave and impassible Icelander devoted himself to us with the most incomprehensible *sang froid* and ease; and, thanks to him, many a dangerous pass was got over, where, but for him, we should inevitably have stuck fast.

His silence increased every day. I think that we began to be influenced by this peculiar trait in his character. It is certain that the inanimate objects by which you are surrounded have a direct action on the brain. It must be that a man who shuts himself up between four walls must lose the faculty of associating ideas and words. How many persons condemned to the horrors of solitary confinement have gone mad—simply because the thinking faculties have lain dormant!

During the two weeks that followed our last interesting conversation, there occurred nothing worthy of being especially recorded. I have, while writing these memoirs, taxed my memory in vain for one incident of travel during this particular period.

But the next event to be related is terrible indeed. Its very memory, even now, makes my soul shudder, and my blood run cold. It was on the seventh of August. Our constant and successive descents had taken us quite thirty leagues into the interior of the earth, that is to say that there were above us thirty leagues, nearly a hundred miles, of rocks, and oceans, and continents, and towns, to say nothing of living inhabitants. We were in a southeasterly direction, about two hundred leagues from Iceland.

On that memorable day the tunnel had begun to assume an almost horizontal course. I was on this occasion walking on in front. My uncle had charge of one of the Ruhmkorf coils, I had possession of the other. By means of its light I was busy examining the different layers of granite. I was completely absorbed in my work. Suddenly halting and turning round, I found that I was alone!

"Well," thought I to myself, "I have certainly been walking too fast—or else Hans and my uncle have stopped to rest. The best thing I can do is to go back and find them. Luckily, there is very little ascent to tire me."

I accordingly retraced my steps, and while doing so, walked for at least a quarter of an hour. Rather uneasy, I paused and looked eagerly around. Not a living soul. I called aloud. No reply. My voice was lost amid the myriad cavernous echoes it aroused!

I began for the first time to feel seriously uneasy. A cold shiver shook my whole body, and perspiration, chill and terrible, burst upon my skin.

"I must be calm," I said, speaking aloud, as boys whistle to drive away fear. "There can be no doubt that I shall find my companions. There cannot be two roads. It is certain that I was considerably ahead; all I have to do is to go back."

Having come to this determination I ascended the tunnel for at least half an hour, unable to decide if I had ever seen certain landmarks before. Every now and then I paused to discover if any loud appeal was made to me, well knowing that in that dense and intensified atmosphere I should hear it a long way off. But no. The most extraordinary silence reigned in this immense gallery. Only the echoes of my own footsteps could be heard.

At last I stopped. I could scarcely realize the fact of my isolation. I was quite willing to think that I had made a mistake, but not that I was lost. If I had made a mistake, I might find my way: if lost—I shuddered to think of it.

"Come, come," said I to myself, "since there is only one road, and they must come by it, we shall at last meet. All I have to do is still to go upwards. Perhaps, however, not seeing me, and forgetting I was ahead, they may have gone back in search of me. Still even in this case, if I make haste, I shall get up to them. There can be no doubt about the matter."

But as I spoke these last words aloud, it would have been quite clear to any listener—had there been one—that I was by no means convinced of the fact. Moreover, in order to associate together these simple ideas and to reunite them under the form of reasoning, required some time. I could not all at once bring my brain to think.

Then another dread doubt fell upon my soul. After all, was I ahead. Of course I was. Hans was no doubt following behind, preceded by my uncle. I perfectly recollected his having stopped for a moment to strap his baggage on his shoulder. I now remembered this trifling detail. It was, I believed, just at that very moment that I had determined to continue my route.

"Again," thought I, reasoning as calmly as was possible, "there is another sure means of not losing my way, a thread to guide me through the labyrinthine subterraneous retreat—one which I had forgotten—my faithful river."

This course of reasoning roused my drooping spirits, and I resolved to resume my journey without further delay. No time was to be lost. It was at this moment that I had reason to bless the thoughtfulness of my uncle, when he refused to allow the eider hunter to close the orifices of the hot spring—that small fissure in the great mass of granite. This beneficent spring after having saved us from thirst during so many days would now enable me to regain the right road. Having come to this mental decision, I made up my mind, before I started upwards, that ablution would certainly do me a great deal of good.

I stopped to plunge my hands and forehead in the pleasant water of the Hansbach stream, blessing its presence as a certain consolation.

Conceive my horror and stupefaction!—I was treading a hard, dusty, shingly road of granite. The stream on which I reckoned had wholly disappeared!

CHAPTER XXIV
LOST!

No words in any human language can depict my utter despair. I was literally buried alive; with no other expectation before me but to die in all the slow horrible torture of hunger and thirst. Mechanically I crawled about, feeling the dry and arid rock. Never to my fancy had I ever felt anything so dry.

But, I frantically asked myself, how had I lost the course of the flowing stream? There could be no doubt it had ceased to flow in the gallery in which I now was. Now I began to understand the cause of the strange silence which prevailed when last I tried if any appeal from my companions might perchance reach my ear.

It so happened that when I first took an imprudent step in the wrong direction, I did not perceive the absence of the all-important stream. It was now quite evident that when we halted, another tunnel must have received the waters of the little torrent, and that I had unconsciously entered a different gallery. To what unknown depths had my companions gone? Where was I?

How to get back! Clue or landmark there was absolutely none! My feet left no signs on the granite and shingle. My brain throbbed with agony as I tried to discover the solution of this terrible problem. My situation, after all sophistry and reflection, had finally to be summed up in three awful words—*Lost!* LOST!! LOST!!!

Lost at a depth which, to my infinite understanding, appeared to be immeasurable. These thirty leagues of the crust of the earth weighed upon my shoulders like the globe on the shoulders of Atlas. I felt myself crushed by the awful weight. It was indeed a position to drive the sanest man to madness.

I tried to bring my thoughts back to the things of the world so long forgotten. It was with the greatest difficulty that I succeeded in doing so. Hamburg, the house on

LOST!

the Königstrasse, my dear cousin Gretchen—all that world which had before vanished like a shadow floated before my now vivid imagination. There they were before me, but how unreal. Under the influence of a terrible hallucination I saw the whole incidents of our journey pass before me like the scenes of a panorama. The ship and its inmates, Iceland, M. Fridriksson, and the great summit of Mount Sneffels! I said to myself that if in my position, I retained the most faint and shadowy outline of a hope it would be a sure sign of approaching delirium. It were better to give way wholly to despair!

In fact, if I reasoned with calmness and philosophy, what human power was there in existence able to take me back to the surface of the earth, and ready too, to split asunder those huge and mighty vaults which stood above my head? Who could enable me to find my road—and regain my companions? Insensate folly and madness to entertain even a shadow of hope!

"Oh, uncle!" was my despairing cry. This was the only word of reproach which came to my lips; for I thoroughly understood how deeply and sorrowfully the worthy Professor would regret my loss, and how in his turn he would patiently seek for me.

When I at last began to resign myself to the fact that no further aid was to be expected from man, and knowing that I was utterly powerless to do anything for my own salvation, I kneeled with earnest fervor and asked assistance from Heaven. The remembrance of my innocent childhood, the memory of my mother, known only in my infancy, came welling forth from my heart. I had recourse to prayer. And little as I had right to be remembered by Him whom I had forgotten in the hour of prosperity, and whom I so tardily invoked, I prayed earnestly and sincerely.

This renewal of my youthful faith brought about a much greater amount of calm, and I was enabled to concentrate all my strength and intelligence on the terrible realities of my unprecedented situation. I had about me that which I had at first wholly forgotten—three days' provisions. Moreover, my water bottle was quite full. Nevertheless, the one thing which it was impossible to do was to remain alone. Try to find my companions I must, at any price. But which course should I take? Should I go upwards, or again descend? Doubtless it was right to retrace my steps in an upward direction.

By doing this with care and coolness, I must reach the point where I had turned away from the rippling stream. I must find the fatal bifurcation or fork. Once at this spot, once the river at my feet, I could, at all events, regain the awful crater of Mount Sneffels. Why had I not thought of this before? This, at last, was a reasonable hope of safety. The most important thing, then, to be done was to discover the bed of the Hansbach.

After a slight meal and a draught of water, I rose like a giant refreshed. Leaning heavily on my pole, I began the ascent of the gallery. The slope was very rapid and rather difficult. But I advanced hopefully and carefully, like a man who at last is making his way out of a forest, and knows there is only one road to follow.

During one whole hour nothing happened to check my progress. As I advanced I tried to recollect the shape of the tunnel—to recall to my memory certain projections of rocks—to persuade myself that I had followed certain winding routes before. But no one particular sign could I bring to mind, and I was soon forced to allow that this gallery would never take me back to the point at which I had separated myself from my companions. It was absolutely without issue—a mere blind alley in the earth.

The moment at length came when, facing the solid rock, I knew my fate, and fell inanimate on the arid floor!

To describe the horrible state of despair and fear into which I then fell would now be vain and impossible. My last hope, the courage which had sustained me, drooped before the sight of this pitiless granite rock! Lost in a vast labyrinth, the sinuosities of which spread in every direction, without guide, clue or compass, it was a vain and useless task to attempt flight. All that remained to me was to lie down and die. To lie down and die the most cruel and horrible of deaths!

In my state of mind, the idea came into my head that one day perhaps, when my fossil bones were found, their discovery so far below the level of the earth might give rise to solemn and interesting scientific discussions. I tried to cry aloud, but hoarse, hollow and inarticulate sounds alone could make themselves heard through my parched lips. I literally panted for breath.

In the midst of all these horrible sources of anguish and despair, a new horror took possession of my soul. My lamp, by falling down, had got out of order. I had no means of repairing it. Its light was already becoming paler and paler, and soon would expire. With a strange sense of resignation and despair, I watched the luminous current in the coil getting less and less. A procession of shadows moved flashing along the granite wall. I scarcely dared to lower my eyelids, fearing to lose the last spark of this fugutive light. Every instant it seemed to me that it was about to vanish and to leave me forever—in utter darkness!

At last, one final trembling flame remained in the lamp; I followed it with all my power of vision; I gasped for breath; I concentrated upon it all the power of my soul, as upon the last scintillation of light I was ever destined to see; and then I was to be lost forever in Cimmerian and tenebrous shades.

A wild and plaintive cry escaped my lips. On earth during the most profound and comparatively complete darkness, light never allows a complete destruction and extinction of its power. Light is so diffuse, so subtle, that it permeates everywhere, and whatever little may remain, the retina of the eye will succeed in finding it. In this place nothing—not the faintest ray of light. It mazed me!

My head was now wholly lost. I raised my arms, trying the effects of the feeling in getting against the cold stone wall. It was painful in the extreme. Madness must have taken possession of me. I knew not what I did. I began to run, to fly, rushing at haphazard in this inextricable labyrinth, always going downwards, running wildly underneath the terrestrial crust, like an inhabitant of the subterranean furnaces, screaming, roaring, howling, until bruised by the pointed rocks, falling and picking myself up all covered with blood, seeking madly to drink the blood which dripped from my torn features, mad because this blood trickled over my face, and watching always for this horrid wall which ever presented to me the fearful obstacle against which I could not dash my head.

Where was I going? It was impossible to say. Several hours passed in this way. After a long time, having utterly exhausted my strength, I fell a heavy inert mass along the side of the tunnel, and lost all consciousness of existence!

CHAPTER XXV
THE WHISPERING GALLERY

WHEN at last I came back to a sense of life and being, my face was wet; but wet as I soon knew with tears. How long this state of insensibility lasted, it is quite impossible for me now to say. I had no means left to me of taking any account of time. Never since the creation of the world, had such a solitude as mine existed. I was completely abandoned.

After my fall I had lost much blood. I had felt myself flooded with the life-giving liquid. My first sensation was perhaps a natural one. Why was I not dead? Because I was alive, there was something left to do. I tried to make up my mind to think no longer. As far as I was able, I drove away all ideas, and utterly overcome by pain and grief, crouched against the granite wall.

I commenced to feel the fainting coming on again, with the sensation that this was the last struggle before complete annihilation,—when, on a sudden, a violent uproar reached my ears. It had some resemblance to the prolonged rumbling voice of thunder, and I clearly distinguished sonorous voices, lost one after the other, in the distant depths of the gulf.

Whence came this noise? Again I listened with deep attention. I was extremely anxious to hear if the strange and inexplicable sound was likely to be renewed! A whole quarter of an hour elapsed in painful expectation. Deep and solemn silence reigned in the tunnel. So still that I could hear the beatings of my own heart! I waited, waited, waited with a strange kind of hopefulness.

Suddenly my ear, which leant accidentally against the wall, appeared to catch as it were the faintest echo of a sound. I thought that I heard vague, incoherent and distant voices. I quivered all over with excitement and hope!

"It must be hallucination," I cried. "It cannot be! it is not true!"

But no! By listening more attentively, I really did convince myself that what I heard was truly the sound of human voices. To make any meaning out of the sound, however, was beyond my power. I was too weak even to hear distinctly. Still it was a positive fact that some one was speaking. Of that I was quite certain.

There was a moment of fear. A dread fell upon my soul that it might be my own words brought back to me by a distant echo. Perhaps without knowing it, I might have been crying aloud. I resolutely closed my lips, and once more placed my ear to the huge granite wall. Yes, for certain. It was in truth the sound of human voices.

I now by the exercise of great determination dragged myself along the sides of the cavern, until I reached a point where I could hear more distinctly. But though I could detect the sound, I could only make out uncertain, strange, and incomprehensible words. They reached my ear as if they had been spoken in a low tone—murmured, as it were, afar off. At last, I made out the word *förlorad* repeated several times in a tone betokening great mental anguish and sorrow.

What could this word mean, and who was speaking it? It must be either my uncle or the guide Hans! If, therefore, I could hear them, they must surely be able to hear me. "Help," I cried at the top of my voice; "help, I am dying!"

I then listened with scarcely a breath; I panted for the slightest sound in the darkness—a cry, a sigh, a question! But silence reigned supreme. No answer came! In this way some minutes passed. A whole flood of ideas flashed through my mind. I began to fear that my voice weakened by sickness and suffering could not reach my companions who were in search of me.

"It must be them," I cried; "what other men can by possibility be buried a hundred miles below the level of the earth?" The mere supposition was preposterous. I began, therefore, to listen again with the most breathless attention. As I moved my ears along the side of the place I was in, I found a mathematical point as it were, where the voices appeared to attain their maximum of intensity. The word *förlorad* again distinctly reached my ear. Then came again that rolling noise like thunder which had awakened me out of torpor.

" I begin to understand," I said to myself, after some little time devoted to reflection; " it is not through the solid mass that the sound reaches my ears. The walls of my cavernous retreat are of solid granite, and the most fearful explosion would not make uproar enough to penetrate them. The sound must come along the gallery itself. The place I was in must possess some peculiar acoustic properties of its own."

Again I listened; and this time—yes, this time—I heard my name distinctly pronounced: cast as it were into space. It was my uncle the Professor who was speaking. He was in conversation with the guide, and the word which had so often reached my ears, *förlorad,* was a Danish expression.

Then I understood it all. In order to make myself heard, I too must speak as it were along the side of the gallery, which would carry the sound of my voice just as the wire carries the electric fluid from point to point. But there was no time to lose. If my companions were only to remove a few feet from where they stood, the acoustic effect would be over, my Whispering Gallery would be destroyed. I again therefore crawled towards the wall, and said as clearly and distinctly as I could—" Uncle Hardwigg."

I then awaited a reply.

Sound does not possess the property of traveling with such extreme rapidity. Besides the density of the air at that depth from light and motion, was very far from adding to the rapidity of circulation. Several seconds elapsed, which, to my excited imagination, appeared ages; and these words reached my eager ears, and moved my wildly beating heart—" Harry, my boy, is that you? "

A short delay between question and answer.

" Yes—yes."

" Where are you? "

" Lost! "

" And your lamp? "

" Out."

" But the guiding stream? "

" Is lost ! "

" Keep your courage, Harry. We will do our best."

" One moment, my uncle," I cried; " I have no longer strength to answer your questions. But—for heaven's sake—do you—continue—to speak—to me ! "

Absolute silence, I felt, would be annihilation.

" Keep up your courage," said my uncle. " As you are so weak do not speak. We have been searching for you in all directions, both by going upwards and downwards in the gallery. My dear boy, I had begun to give over all hope—and you can never know what bitter tears of sorrow and regret I have shed. At last, supposing you to be still on the road beside the Hansbach we again descended, firing off guns as signals. Now, however, that we have found you, and that our voices reach each other, it may be a long time before we actually meet. We are conversing by means of some extraordinary acoustic arrangement of the labyrinth. But do not despair, my dear boy. It is something gained even to hear each other."

While he was speaking my brain was at work reflecting. A certain undefined hope, vague and shapeless as yet, made my heart beat wildly. In the first place, it was absolutely necessary for me to know one thing. I once more therefore leaned my head against the wall, which I almost touched with my lips, and again spoke.

" Uncle."

" My boy," was his ready answer.

" It is of the utmost consequence that we should know how far we are asunder."

" That is not difficult."

" You have your chronometer at hand? " I asked.

" Certainly."

" Well, take it into your hand. Pronounce my name, noting exactly the second at which you speak. I will reply as soon as I hear your words—and you will then note exactly the moment at which my reply reaches you."

" Very good; and the time between my question and your answer will be the time occupied by my voice in reaching you."

" That is exactly what I mean, uncle," was my eager reply.

" Are you ready? "

" Yes."

" Well, make ready, I am about to pronounce your name," said the Professor.

I applied my ear close to the sides of the cavernous gallery, and as soon as the word Harry reached my ear, I turned round, and placing my lips to the wall, repeated the sound.

" Forty seconds," said my uncle. " There has elapsed forty seconds between the two words. The sound, therefore, takes twenty seconds to ascend. Now, allowing a thousand and twenty feet for every second—we have twenty thousand four hundred feet—a league and a half and one-eighth."

These words fell on my soul like a kind of death-knell. " A league and a-half," I muttered in a low and despairing voice.

" It shall be got over, my boy," cried my uncle in a cheery tone; " depend on us."

" But do you know whether to ascend or descend? " I asked faintly enough.

" You have to descend, and I will tell you why. We have reached a vast open space, a kind of bare cross road, from which galleries diverge in every direction. That in which you are now lying, must necessarily bring you to this point, for it appears that all these mighty fissures, these fractures of the globe's interior radiate from the vast cavern which we at this moment occupy. Rouse yourself, then, have courage and continue your route. Walk if you can, if not drag yourself along—slide, if nothing else is possible. The slope must be rather rapid—and you will find strong arms to receive you at the end of your journey. Make a start, like a good fellow."

These words served to rouse some kind of courage in my sinking frame. " Farewell for the present, good uncle, I am about to take my departure. As soon as I start, our voices will cease to commingle. Farewell, then, until we meet again."

" Adieu, Harry—until we say Welcome." Such were the last words which reached my anxious ears, before I commenced my weary and almost hopeless journey.

This wonderful and surprising conversation which took place through the vast mass of the earth's labyrinth, these words exchanged, the speakers being about five miles apart —ended with hopeful and pleasant expressions. I breathed one more prayer to Heaven, I sent up words of thanksgiving—believing in my inmost heart that He had led me to the only place where the voices of my friends could reach my ears.

I accordingly rose to my feet. I soon found, however, that I could not walk; that I must drag myself along. The slope, as I expected, was very rapid; but I allowed myself to slip down.

Soon the rapidity of the descent began to assume frightful proportions; and menaced a fearful fall. I clutched at the sides; I grasped at projections of rocks; I threw myself backwards. All in vain. My weakness was so great I could do nothing to save myself.

Suddenly earth failed me. I was first launched into a dark, and gloomy void. I then struck against the projecting asperities of a vertical gallery, a perfect well. My head bounded against a pointed rock, and I lost all knowledge of existence. As far as I was concerned, death had claimed me for his own.

CHAPTER XXVI
A RAPID RECOVERY

When I returned to the consciousness of existence, I found myself surrounded by a kind of semi-obscurity, lying on some thick and soft coverlids. My uncle was watching—his eyes fixed intently on my countenance, a grave expression on his face; a tear in his eye. At the first sigh which struggled from my bosom he took hold of my hand. When he saw my eyes open and fix themselves upon his, he uttered a loud cry of joy. "He lives! he lives!"

"Yes, my good uncle," I whispered.

"My dear boy," continued the grim Professor, clasping me to his heart, "you are saved!"

I was deeply and unaffectedly touched by the tone in which these words were uttered, and even more by the kindly care which accompanied them. The Professor was one of those men who must be severely tried in order to

113

induce any display of affection or gentle emotion. At
this moment our friend Hans, the guide, joined us. He
saw my hand in that of my uncle, and I venture to say,
that, taciturn as he was, his eyes beamed with lively satisfaction. *" God dag,"* he said.

" Good day, Hans, good day," I replied, in as hearty a
tone as I could assume, " and now, uncle, that we are together, tell me where we are. I have lost all idea of our
position, as of everything else."

" To-morrow, Harry, to-morrow," he replied. " To-day
you are far too weak. Your head is surrounded with
bandages and poultices that must not be touched. Sleep,
my boy, sleep, and to-morrow you will know all that you
require."

" But " I cried, " let me know what o'clock it is—what
day it is? "

" It is now eleven o'clock at night, and this is once more
Sunday. It is now the ninth of the month of August.
And I distinctly prohibit you from asking any more ques-
tions until the tenth of the same."

I was, if the truth were told, very weak indeed, and my
eyes soon closed involuntarily. I did require a good
night's rest, and I went off reflecting at the last moment
that my perilous adventure in the interior of the earth, in
total darkness, had lasted four days!

On the morning of the next day, at my awakening, I
began to look around me. My sleeping-place, made of all
our traveling bedding, was in a charming grotto, adorned
with magnificent stalagmites, glittering in all the colors of
the rainbow, the floor of soft and silvery sand. A dim obscurity prevailed. No torch, no lamp was lighted, and yet
certain unexplained beams of light penetrated from without,
and made their way through the opening of the beautiful
grotto.

I, moreover, heard a vague and indefinite murmur, like
the ebb and flow of waves upon a strand, and sometimes I
verily believed I could hear the sighing of the wind. I
began to believe that, instead of being awake, I must be
dreaming. Surely my brain had not been affected by my
fall, and all that occurred during the last twenty-four hours
was not the frenzied visions of madness? And yet after
some reflection, a trial of my faculties, I came to the con-

clusion that I could not be mistaken. Eyes and ears could not surely both deceive me.

"It is a ray of the blessed daylight," I said to myself, "which has penetrated through some mighty fissure in the rocks. But what is the meaning of this murmur of waves, this unmistakable moaning of the salt sea billows? I can hear, too, plainly enough, the whistling of the wind. But can I be altogether mistaken? If my uncle, during my illness, has but carried me back to the surface of the earth! Has he, on my account, given up his wondrous expedition, or in some strange manner has it come to an end?"

I was puzzling my brain over these and other questions, when the Professor joined me. "Good-day, Harry," he cried in a joyous tone. "I fancy you are quite well."

"I am very much better," I replied, actually sitting up in my bed.

"I knew that would be the end of it, as you slept both soundly and tranquilly. Hans and I have each taken turn to watch, and every hour we have seen visible signs of amelioration."

"You must be right, uncle," was my reply, "for I feel as if I could do justice to any meal you could put before me. I am really hungry."

"You shall eat, my boy, you shall eat. The fever has left you. Our excellent friend Hans has rubbed your wounds and bruises, with I know not what ointment, of which the Icelanders alone possess the secret. And they have healed your bruises in the most marvelous manner. Ah, he's a wise fellow, is Master Hans."

While he was speaking, my uncle was placing before me several articles of food, which despite his earnest injunctions, I readily devoured. As soon as the first rage of hunger was appeased, I overwhelmed him with questions, to which he now no longer hesitated to give answers. I then learned, for the first time, that my providential fall had brought me to the bottom of an almost perpendicular gallery. As I came down, amidst a perfect shower of stones, the least of which falling on me would have crushed me to death, they came to the conclusion that I had carried with me an entire dislocated rock. Riding as it were on this terrible chariot, I was cast headlong into my uncle's arms. And into them I fell, insensible and covered with blood. " It is indeed a miracle," was the Professor's final remark, " that you were not killed a thousand times over. But let us take care never to separate; for surely we should risk never meeting again."

" Let us take care never again to separate." These words fell with a sort of chill upon my heart. The journey, then, was not over. I looked at my uncle with surprise and astonishment.

My uncle, after an instant's examination of my countenance, said—" What is the matter, Harry? "

" I want to ask you a very serious question. You say that I am all right in health? "

" Certainly you are."

" And all my limbs are sound and capable of new exertion? " I asked.

" Most undoubtedly."

" But what about my head? " was my next anxious question.

" Well, your head, except that you have one or two contusions, is exactly where it ought to be—on your shoulder," said my uncle, laughing.

" Well, my own opinion is that my head is not exactly right. In fact, I believe myself slightly delirious."

" What makes you think so? "

" I will explain why I fancy I have lost my senses," I cried, " have we not returned to the surface of mother earth? "

" Certainly not."

" Then truly I must be mad, for do I not see the light of day? do I not hear the whistling of the wind? and can I not distinguish the wash of a great sea? "

" And that is all that makes you uneasy? " said my uncle, with a smile.

" Can you explain? "

" I will not make any attempt to explain; for the whole matter is utterly inexplicable. But you shall see and judge for yourself. You will then find that geological science is as yet in its infancy—and that we are doomed to enlighten the world."

" Let us advance, then," I cried eagerly, no longer able to restrain my curiosity.

" Wait a moment, my dear Harry," he responded; " you

must take precautions after your illness before going into the open air."

"The open air?"

"Yes, my boy. I have to warn you that the wind is rather violent—and I have no wish for you to expose yourself without necessary precautions."

"But I beg to assure you that I am perfectly recovered from my illness."

"Have just a little patience, my boy. A relapse would be inconvenient to all parties. We have no time to lose— as our approaching sea voyage may be of long duration."

"Sea voyage?" I cried, more bewildered than ever.

"Yes. You must take another day's rest, and we shall be ready to go on board by to-morrow," replied my uncle, with a peculiar smile.

Go on board! The words utterly astonished me. Go on board—what? and how? Had we come upon a river, a lake, had we discovered some inland sea? Was a vessel lying at anchor in some part of the interior of the earth?

My curiosity was worked up to the very highest pitch. My uncle made vain attempts to restrain me. When at last, however, he discovered that my feverish impatience would do more harm than good—and that the satisfaction of my wishes could alone restore me to a calm state of mind, he gave way.

I dressed myself rapidly—and then taking the precaution, to please my uncle, of wrapping myself in one of the coverlets, I rushed out of the grotto.

CHAPTER XXVII
THE CENTRAL SEA

AT first I saw absolutely nothing. My eyes, wholly unused to the effulgence of light, could not bear the sudden brightness; and I was compelled to close them. When I was able to re-open them, I stood still, far more stupefied than astonished. Not all the wildest effects of imagination could have conjured up such a scene! "The sea—the sea," I cried.

"Yes," replied my uncle, in a tone of pardonable pride; "The Central Sea. No future navigator will deny the fact of my having discovered it; and hence of acquiring a right of giving it a name."

It was quite true. A vast, limitless expanse of water, the end of a lake if not of an ocean, spread before us, until it was lost in the distance. The shore, which was very much indented, consisted of a beautiful soft golden sand, mixed with small shells, the long deserted homes of some of the creatures of a past age. The waves broke incessantly, and with a peculiarly sonorous murmur—to be found in underground localities. A slight frothy flake arose as the wind blew along the pellucid waters; and many a dash of spray was blown into my face. The mighty superstructure of rock which rose above to an inconceivable height, left only a narrow margin—but where we stood, there was a long beach of strand. On all sides were capes and promontories and enormous cliffs, partially worn by the eternal breaking of the waves, through countless ages! And as I gazed from side to side, the mighty rocks faded in the distance like a fleecy film of cloud.

It was in reality an ocean, with all the usual characteristics of an inland sea, only horribly wild—so rigid, cold and savage.

One thing startled and puzzled me greatly. How was it that I was able to look upon that vast sheet of water instead of being plunged in utter darkness? The vast landscape before me was lit up like day. But there was wanting the dazzling brilliancy, the splendid irradiation of the sun; the pale cold illumination of the moon; the brightness of the stars. The illuminating power in this subterraneous region, from its trembling and flickering character, its clear dry whiteness, the very slight elevation of its temperature, its great superiority to that of the moon, was evidently electric; something in the nature of the aurora borealis, only that its phenomena were constant, and able to light up the whole of the ocean cavern.

The tremendous vault above our heads, the sky, so to speak, appeared to be composed of a conglomeration of nebulous vapors, in constant motion. I should originally have supposed, that under such an atmospheric pressure as must exist in that place, the evaporation of water could not really take place; yet there were heavy and dense clouds rolling along that mighty vault, partially concealing the roof. Electric currents produced astonishing play of light and shade in the distance, especially around the heavier clouds. Deep shadows were cast beneath, and then suddenly, between two clouds, there would come a ray of unusual beauty, and remarkable intensity. Yet it was not like the sun, for it gave no heat.

The effect was sad and excruciatingly melancholy. Instead of a noble firmament of blue, studded with stars, there was above me a heavy roof of granite, which seemed to crush me. Gazing around, I began to think of the theory of the English captain, who compared the earth to a vast hollow sphere in the interior of which the air is retained in a luminous state by means of atmospheric pressure, while two stars, Pluto and Proserpine, circled there in their mysterious orbits. After all, suppose the old fellow was right!

In truth, we were imprisoned—bound as it were, in a vast excavation. Its width it was impossible to make out; the shore, on either hand, widening rapidly until lost to sight; while its length was equally uncertain. A haze on the distant horizon bounded our view. As to its height we could see that it must be many miles to the roof. Looking upward, it was impossible to discover where the stupendous roof began. The lowest of the clouds must have been floating at an elevation of two thousand yards, a height greater than that of terrestrial vapors, which circumstance was doubtless owing to the extreme density of the air.

I use the word cavern in order to give an idea of the place. I cannot describe its awful grandeur; human language fails to convey an idea of its savage sublimity. Whether this singular vacuum had or had not been caused by the sudden cooling of the earth when in a state of fusion, I could not say. I had read of most wonderful and gigantic caverns—but none in any way like this.

The great grotto of Guachara, in Colombia, visited by the learned Humboldt; the vast and partially explored Mammoth Cave in Kentucky; what were these holes in the earth to that in which I stood in speechless admiration! with its vapory clouds, its electric light, and the mighty ocean slumbering in its bosom! Imagination, not description, can alone give an idea of the splendor and vastness of the cave.

I gazed at these marvels in profound silence. Words were utterly wanting to indicate the sensations of wonder I experienced. I seemed, as I stood upon that mysterious shore, as if I were some wandering inhabitant of a distant planet, present for the first time at the spectacle of some terrestrial phenomena belonging to another existence. To give body and existence to such new sensations, would have required the coinage of new words—and here my feeble brain found itself wholly at fault. I looked on, I thought, I reflected, I admired, in a state of stupefaction not altogether unmingled with fear!

The unexpected spectacle restored some color to my pallid cheeks. I seemed to be actually getting better under the influence of this novelty. Moreover, the vivacity of the dense atmosphere reanimated my body, by inflating my lungs with unaccustomed oxygen.

It will be readily conceived that after an imprisonment of forty-seven days, in a dark and miserable tunnel, it was with infinite delight that I breathed this saline air. It was like the genial, reviving influence of the salt sea waves. My uncle had already got over the first surprise. With the Latin poet Horace his idea was that—

> "Not to admire, is all the art I know
> To make man happy and to keep him so."

" Well," he said, after giving me time thoroughly to appreciate the marvels of this underground sea, " do you feel strong enough to walk up and down? "

" Certainly," was my ready answer, " nothing would give me greater pleasure."

" Well, then, my boy," he said, " lean on my arm, and we will stroll along the beach."

I accepted his offer eagerly, and we began to walk along the shores of this extraordinary lake. To our left were abrupt rocks, piled one upon the other,—a stupendous titanic pile; down their sides leapt innumerable cascades, which at last, becoming limpid and murmuring streams, were lost in the waters of the lake. Light vapors, which rose here and there, and floated in fleecy clouds from rock to rock, indicated hot springs, which also poured their superfluity into the vast reservoir at our feet.

Among them I recognized our old and faithful stream,

the Hansbach, which, lost in that wild basin, seemed as if it had been flowing since the creation of the world.

"We shall miss our excellent friend," I remarked, with a deep sigh.

"Bah!" said my uncle, testily, "what matters it. That or another, it is all the same."

I thought the remark ungrateful, and felt almost inclined to say so; but I forbore. At this moment my attention was attracted by an unexpected spectacle. After we had gone about five hundred yards, we suddenly turned a steep promontory, and found ourselves close to a lofty forest! It consisted of straight trunks with tufted tops, in shape like parasols. The air seemed to have no effect upon these trees—which in spite of a tolerable breeze remained as still and motionless as if they had been petrified.

I hastened forward. I could find no name for these singular formations. Did they belong to the two thousand and more known trees—or were we to make the discovery of a new growth? When we at last reached the forest, and stood beneath the trees, my surprise gave way to admiration. In truth, I was simply in the presence of a very ordinary product of the earth, of singular and gigantic proportions. My uncle unhesitatingly called them by their real names. "It is only," he said, in his coolest manner, "a forest of mushrooms."

On close examination I found that he was not mistaken. Judge of the development attained by this product of damp hot soils. I had heard that the *lycoperdon giganteum* reaches nine feet in circumference, but here were white mushrooms, nearly forty feet high, and with tops of equal dimensions. They grew in countless thousands—the light could not make its way through their massive substance, and beneath them reigned a gloomy and mystic darkness.

Still I wished to go forward. The cold in the shades of this singular forest was intense. For nearly an hour we wandered about in this darkness visible. At length I left the spot, and once more returned to the shores of the lake, to light and comparative warmth.

The amazing vegetation of this subterranean land was not confined to gigantic mushrooms. New wonders awaited us at every step. We had not gone many hundred yards, when we came upon a mighty group of other trees with discolored leaves—the common humble trees of mother earth, of an exorbitant and phenomenal size; mosses a hundred feet high; flowering ferns as tall as pines; gigantic grasses!

"Astonishing, magnificent, splendid!" cried my uncle; "here we have before us the whole Flora of the second period of the world, that of transition. Behold the humble plants of our gardens, which in the first ages of the world were mighty trees. Look around you, my dear Harry. No botanist ever before gazed on such a sight!"

My uncle's enthusiasm, usually a little more than was required, was now excusable. "You are right, uncle," I remarked. "Providence appears to have designed the preservation in this vast and mysterious hot-house of antediluvian plants, to prove the sagacity of learned men in figuring them so marvelously on paper."

"Well said, my boy—very well said; it is indeed a mighty hot-house;—but you would also be within the bounds of reason and common sense, if you also added—a vast menagerie."

I looked rather anxiously around. If the animals were as exaggerated as the plants, the matter would certainly be serious. "A menagerie?"

"Doubtless. Look at the dust we are treading under foot—behold the bones with which the whole soil of the seashore is covered——"

"Bones," I replied, "yes, certainly, the bones of antediluvian animals." I stooped down as I spoke, and picked up one or two singular remains, relics of a by-gone age. It was easy to give a name to these gigantic bones, in some instances as big as trunks of trees.

"Here is, clearly, the lower jaw-bone of a mastodon," I cried, almost as warmly and enthusiastically as my uncle, "here are the molars of the dinotherium; here is a leg-bone which belonged to the megatherium. You are right, uncle, it is indeed a menagerie; for the mighty animals to which these bones once belonged, have lived and died on the shores of this subterranean sea, under the shadow of these plants. Look, yonder are whole skeletons—and yet——"

"And yet, nephew?" said my uncle, noticing that I suddenly came to a full stop.

"I do not understand the presence of such beasts in granite caverns, however vast and prodigious," was my reply.

"Why not?" said my uncle, with very much of his old professional impatience.

"Because it is well known that animal life only existed on earth during the secondary period, when the sedimentary soil was formed by the alluviums, and thus replaced the hot and burning rocks of the primitive age."

"I have listened to you earnestly and with patience, Harry, and I have a simple and clear answer to your objections: and that is, that this itself is a sedimentary soil."

"How can that be at such enormous depth from the surface of the earth?"

"The fact can be explained both simply and geologically. At a certain period, the earth consisted only of an elastic crust, liable to alternative upward and downward movements in virtue of the law of attraction. It is very probable that many a landslip took place in those days, and that large portions of sedimentary soil were cast into huge and mighty chasms."

"Quite possible," I dryly remarked. "But, uncle, if these antediluvian animals formerly lived in these subterranean regions, what more likely than that one of these huge monsters may at this moment be concealed behind one of yonder mighty rocks."

As I spoke, I looked keenly around, examining with care every point of the horizon; but nothing alive appeared to exist on these deserted shores.

I now felt rather fatigued, and told my uncle so. The walk and excitement were too much for me in my weak state. I therefore seated myself at the end of a promontory, at the foot of which the waves broke in incessant rolls. I looked round a bay formed by projections of vast granitic rocks. At the extreme end was a little port protected by huge pyramids of stones. A brig and three or four schooners might have lain there with perfect ease. So natural did it seem, that every minute my imagination induced me to expect a vessel coming out under all sail and making for the open sea under the influence of a warm southerly breeze.

TO THE CENTRE OF THE EARTH

But the fantastic illusion never lasted more than a minute. We were the only living creatures in this subterranean world!

During certain periods there was an utter cessation of wind, when a silence deeper, more terrible than the silence of the desert fell upon these solitary and arid rocks—and seemed to hang like a leaden weight upon the waters of this singular ocean. I sought, amid the awful stillness, to penetrate through the distant fog, to tear down the veil which concealed the mysterious distance. What unspoken words were murmured by my trembling lips—what questions did I wish to ask and did not! Where did this sea end—to what did it lead? Should we ever be able to examine its distant shores?

But my uncle had no doubts about the matter. He was convinced that our enterprise would in the end be successful. For my part, I was in a state of painful indecision—I desired to embark on the journey and to succeed, and still I feared the result.

After we had passed an hour or more in silent contemplation of the wondrous spectacle, we rose and went down towards the bank on our way to the grotto, which I was not sorry to gain. After a slight repast, I sought refuge in slumber, and at length, after many and tedious struggles, sleep came over my weary eyes.

CHAPTER XXVIII
LAUNCHING THE RAFT

On the morning of the next day, to my great surprise, I awoke completely restored. I thought a bath would be delightful after my long illness and sufferings. So, soon after rising, I went and plunged into the waters of this new Mediterranean. The bath was cool, fresh and invigorating.

I came back to breakfast with an excellent appetite. Hans, our worthy guide, thoroughly understood how to cook such eatables as we were able to provide; he had both fire and water at discretion, so that he was enabled slightly to vary the weary monotony of our ordinary repast. Our morning meal was like a capital English breakfast, with coffee by way of a wind-up. And never had this delicious beverage been so welcome and refreshing.

My uncle had sufficient regard for my state of health not to interrupt me in the enjoyment of the meal, but he was evidently delighted when I had finished. "Now then," said he, "come with me. It is the height of the tide, and I am anxious to study its curious phenomena."

"What," I cried, rising in astonishment, "did you say the tide, uncle?"

"Certainly I did."

"You do not mean to say," I replied, in a tone of respectful doubt, "that the influence of the sun and moon is felt here below."

"And pray why not? Are not all bodies influenced by the law of universal attraction? Why should this vast underground sea be exempt from the general law, the rule of the universe? Besides, there is nothing like that which is proved and demonstrated. Despite the great atmospheric pressure down here, you will notice that this inland sea rises and falls with as much regularity as the Atlantic itself."

As my uncle spoke, we reached the sandy shore, and saw and heard the waves breaking monotonously on the beach. They were evidently rising.

"This is truly the flood," I cried, looking at the water at my feet.

"Yes, my excellent nephew," replied my uncle, rubbing his hands with the gusto of a philosopher, "and you see by these several streaks of foam, that the tide rises at least ten or twelve feet."

"It is indeed marvelous."

"By no means," he responded; "on the contrary, it is quite natural."

"It may appear so in your eyes, my dear uncle," was my reply, "but the whole phenomena of the place appear to me to partake of the marvelous. It is almost impossible to believe that which I see. Who in his wildest dreams could have imagined that, beneath the crust of our earth, there could exist a real ocean, with ebbing and flowing tides, with its changes of winds, and even its storms. I for one should have laughed the suggestion to scorn."

"But, Harry, my boy, why not?" inquired my uncle, with a pitying smile, "is there any physical reason in opposition to it?"

"Not if we give up the great theory of the central heat of the earth. That point once granted, I certainly can see no reason for doubting the existence of seas and other wonders, even countries, in the interior of the globe."

"That is so—but of course these varied countries are uninhabited?"

"Well, I grant that it is more likely than not: still, I do not see why this sea should not have given shelter to some species of unknown fish."

"Hitherto we have not discovered any, and the probabilities are rather against our ever doing so," observed the Professor.

I was losing my skepticism in the presence of these wonders. "Well, I am determined to solve the question. It is my intention to try my luck with my fishing line and hook."

"Certainly; make the experiment," said my uncle, pleased with my enthusiasm. "While we are about it, it will certainly be only proper to discover all the secrets of this extraordinary region."

"But, after all, where are we now?" I asked; "all this time I have quite forgotten to ask you a question, which, doubtless, your philosophical instruments have long since answered."

"Well," replied the Professor, "examining the situation from only one point of view, we are now distant three hundred and fifty leagues from Iceland."

"So much?" was my exclamation.

"I have gone over the matter several times, and am sure not to have made a mistake of five hundred yards," replied my uncle positively.

"And as to the direction—are we still going to the southeast?"

"Yes, with a western declination of nineteen degrees, forty-two minutes, just as it is above. As for the inclination I have discovered a very curious fact."

"What may that be, uncle? Your information interests me."

"Why that the needle, instead of dipping towards the

pole as it does on earth, in the northern hemisphere, has an upward tendency."

"This proves," I cried, "that the great point of magnetic attraction lies somewhere between the surface of the earth and the spot we have succeeded in reaching."

"Exactly, my observant nephew," exclaimed my uncle, elated and delighted, "and it is quite probable that if we succeed in getting toward the polar regions—somewhere near the seventy-third degree of latitude, where Sir James Ross discovered the magnetic pole, we shall behold the needle point directly upward. We have therefore discovered that this great center of attraction is not situated at a very great depth."

"Well," said I, rather surprised, "this discovery will astonish experimental philosophers. It was never suspected."

"Science, great, mighty and in the end unerring," replied my uncle dogmatically, "science has fallen into many errors—errors which have been fortunate and useful rather than otherwise, for they have been the stepping-stones to truth."

After some further discussion, I turned to another matter. "Have you any idea of the depth we have reached?"

"We are now," continued the Professor, "exactly thirty-five leagues—above a hundred miles—down into the interior of the earth."

"So," said I, after measuring the distance on the map, "we are now beneath the Scottish Highlands, and have over our heads the lofty Grampian hills."

"You are quite right," said the Professor, laughing, "it sounds very alarming, the weight being heavy—but the vault which supports this vast mass of earth and rock is solid and safe—the mighty Architect of the Universe has constructed it of solid materials. Man, even in his highest flights of vivid and poetic imagination, never thought of such things! What are the finest arches of our bridges, what the vaulted roofs of our cathedrals, to that mighty dome above us, and beneath which floats an ocean with its storms and calms and tides!"

"I admire it all as much as you can, uncle, and have no fear that our granite sky will fall upon our heads. But now that we have discussed matters of science and discovery, what are your future intentions? Are you not thinking of getting back to the surface of our beautiful earth?" This was said more as a feeler than with any hope of success.

"Go back, nephew," cried my uncle in a tone of alarm, "you are not surely thinking of anything so absurd or cowardly. No, my intention is to advance and continue our journey. We have as yet been singularly fortunate, and henceforth I hope we shall be more so."

"But," said I, "how are we to cross yonder liquid plain?"

"It is not my intention to leap into it head foremost, or even to swim across it, like Leander over the Hellespont. But as oceans are, after all, only great lakes, inasmuch as they are surrounded by land, so does it stand to reason, that this central sea is circumscribed by granite surroundings."

"Doubtless," was my natural reply.

"Well, then, do you not think that when once we reach the other end, we shall find some means of continuing our journey?"

"Probably, but what extent do you allow to this internal ocean?"

"I should fancy it to extend about forty or fifty leagues —more or less."

"But even supposing this approximation to be a correct one—what then?" I asked.

"My dear boy, we have no time for further discussion. We shall embark to-morrow."

I looked around with surprise and incredulity. I could see nothing in the shape of boat or vessel. "What!" I cried, "we are about to launch out upon an unknown sea; and where, if I may ask, is the vessel to carry us?"

"Well, my dear boy, it will not be exactly what you would call a vessel. For the present we must be content with a good and solid raft."

"A raft," I cried, incredulously, "but down here a raft is as impossible of construction as a vessel—and I am at a loss to imagine——"

"My good Harry—if you were to listen instead of talking so much, you would hear," said my uncle, waxing a little impatient.

"I should hear?"

"Yes—certain knocks with the hammer, which Hans is now employing to make the raft. He has been at work for many hours."

"But where has he found trees suitable for such a construction?"

"He found the trees all ready to his hand. Come, and you shall see our excellent guide at work."

More and more amazed at what I heard and saw, I followed my uncle like one in a dream. After a walk of about a quarter of an hour, I saw Hans at work on the other side of the promonotory which formed our natural port. A few minutes more and I was beside him. To my great surprise, on the sandy shore lay a half-finished raft. It was made from beams of a very peculiar wood, and a great number of limbs, joints, boughs, and pieces lay about, sufficient to have constructed a fleet of ships and boats.

I turned to my uncle, silent with astonishment and awe. "Where did all this wood come from?" I cried; "what wood is it?"

"Well, there is pine-wood, fir, and the palms of the northern regions, mineralized by the action of the sea," he replied, sententiously.

"Can it be possible?"

"Yes," said the learned Professor, "what you see is called fossil wood."

"But then," cried I, after reflecting for a moment, "like the lignites, it must be as hard and as heavy as iron, and therefore will certainly not float."

"Sometimes that is the case. Many of these woods have become true anthracites, but others again, like those you see before you, have only undergone one phase of fossil transformation. But there is no proof like demonstration," added my uncle, picking one or two of these precious waifs and casting them into the sea.

The piece of wood, after having disappeared for a moment, came to the surface, and floated about with the oscillation produced by wind and tide. "Are you convinced?" said my uncle, with a self-satisfied smile.

"I am convinced," I cried, "that what I see is incredible."

The fact was that my journey into the interior of the earth was rapidly changing all preconceived notions, and day by day preparing me for the marvelous. I should not have been surprised to have seen a fleet of native canoes afloat upon that silent sea.

The very next evening, thanks to the industry and ability of Hans, the raft was finished. It was about ten feet long and five feet wide. The beams bound together with stout ropes, were solid and firm, and once launched by our united efforts, the improvised vessel floated tranquilly upon the waters of what the Professor had well named the Central Sea.

CHAPTER XXIX
ON THE WATERS.—A RÁFT VOYAGE

On the 13th of August we were up betimes. There was no time to be lost. We now had to inaugurate a new kind of locomotion, which would have the advantage of being rapid and not fatiguing. A mast, made of two pieces of wood fastened together, to give additional strength, a yard made from another one, the sail a linen sheet from our bed. We were fortunately in no want of cordage, and the whole on trial appeared solid and seaworthy.

At six o'clock in the morning, when the eager and enthusiastic Professor gave the signal to embark, the victuals, the luggage, all our instruments, our weapons, and a goodly supply of sweet water, which we had collected from springs in the rocks, were placed on the raft. Hans had, with considerable ingenuity, contrived a rudder, which enabled him to guide the floating apparatus with ease. He took the tiller, as a matter of course. The worthy man was as good a sailor as he was a guide and duck-hunter. I then let go the painter which held us to the shore, the sail was brought to the wind, and we made a rapid offing. Our sea voyage had at length commenced; and once more we were making for distant and unknown regions.

Just as we were about to leave the little port where the raft had been constructed, my uncle, who was very strong as to geographic nomenclature, wanted to give it a name, and among others, suggested mine.

" Well," said I, " before you decide I have another to propose."

"Well; out with it."

"I should like to call it Gretchen. Port Gretchen will sound very well on our future map."

"Well, then, Port Gretchen let it be," said the Professor. And thus it was that the memory of my dear girl was attached to our adventurous and memorable expedition.

When we left the shore the wind was blowing from the northward and eastward. We went directly before the wind at a much greater speed than might have been expected from a raft. The dense layers of atmosphere at that depth had great propelling power and acted upon the sail with considerable force. At the end of an hour, my uncle, who had been taking careful observations, was enabled to judge of the rapidity with which we moved. It was far beyond anything seen in the upper world.

"If," he said, "we continue to advance at our present rate, we shall have traveled at least thirty leagues in twenty-four hours. With a mere raft this is an almost incredible velocity."

I certainly was surprised, and without making any reply went forward upon the raft. Already the northern shore was fading away on the edge of the horizon. The two shores appeared to separate more and more, leaving a wide and open space for our departure. Before me I could see nothing but the vast and apparently limitless sea—upon which we floated—the only living objects in sight.

Huge and dark clouds cast their gray shadows below—shadows which seemed to crush that colorless and sullen water by their weight. Anything more suggestive of gloom and of regions of nether darkness I never beheld. Silvery rays of electric light, reflected here and there upon some small spots of water, brought up luminous sparkles in the long wake of our cumbrous bark. Presently we were wholly out of sight of land, not a vestige could be seen, nor any indication of where we were going. So still and motionless did we seem without any distant point to fix our eyes on, that but for the phosphoric light at the wake of the raft I should have fancied that we were still and motionless.

But I knew that we were advancing at a very rapid rate. About twelve o'clock in the day, vast collections of seaweed were discovered surrounding us on all sides. I was aware of the extraordinary vegetative power of these plants, which have been known to creep along the bottom of the great ocean, and stop the advance of large ships. But never were seaweeds ever seen, so gigantic and wonderful as those of the Central Sea. I could well imagine how, seen at a distance, tossing and heaving on the summit of the billows, the long lines of Algæ have been taken for living things, and thus have been the fertile sources of the belief in sea serpents.

Our raft swept past great specimens of fucæ or seawrack, from three to four thousand feet in length, immense, incredibly long, looking like snakes that stretched out far beyond our horizon. It afforded me great amusement to gaze on their variegated ribbon-like endless lengths. Hour after hour passed without our coming to the termination of these floating weeds. If my astonishment increased, my patience was well-nigh exhausted.

What natural force could possibly have produced such abnormal and extraordinary plants? What must have been the aspect of the globe, during the first centuries of its formation, when under the combined action of heat and humidity, the vegetable kingdom occupied its vast surface to the exclusion of everything else? These were considerations of never-ending interest for the geologist and the philosopher.

All this while we were advancing on our journey; and at length night came; but as I had remarked the evening before, the luminous state of the atmosphere was in nothing diminished. Whatever was the cause, it was a phenomenon upon the duration of which we could calculate with certainty.

As soon as our supper had been disposed of, and some little speculative conversation indulged in, I stretched myself at the foot of the mast and presently went to sleep. Hans remained motionless at the tiller, allowing the raft to rise and fall on the waves. The wind being aft, and the sail square, all he had to do was to keep his oar in the center.

Ever since we had taken our departure from the newly named Port Gretchen, my worthy uncle had directed me to keep a regular log of our day's navigation, with instructions to put down even the most minute particulars, every interesting and curious phenomenon, the direction of the wind, our rate of sailing, the distance we went; in a word, every incident of our extraordinary voyage. From our log, therefore, I tell the story of our voyage on the Central Sea.

Friday, August 14th. A steady breeze from the north-west. Raft progressing with extreme rapidity, and going perfectly straight. Coast still dimly visible about thirty miles to leeward. Nothing to be seen beyond the horizon in front. The extraordinary intensity of the light neither increases nor diminishes. It is singularly stationary. The weather remarkably fine; that is to say, the clouds have ascended very high, and are light and fleecy, and surrounded by an atmosphere resembling silver in fusion. Thermometer + 32 degrees centigrade.

About twelve o'clock in the day our guide, Hans, having prepared and baited a hook, cast his line into the subterranean waters. The bait he used was a small piece of meat, by means of which he concealed his hook. Anxious as I was, I was for a long time doomed to disappointment. Were these waters supplied with fish or not? That was the important question. No—was my decided answer. Then there came a sudden and rather hard tug. Hans coolly drew it in, and with it a fish, which struggled violently to escape.

" A fish," cried my uncle, putting on his spectacles to examine it.

" It is a sturgeon!" I cried, " certainly a small sturgeon."

The Professor examined the fish carefully, noting every characteristic; and he did not coincide in my opinion. The fish had a flat head, round body, and the lower extremities covered with bony scales; its mouth was wholly without teeth, the pectoral fins, which were highly developed, sprouted direct from the body, which properly speaking had no tail. The animal certainly belonged to the order in which naturalists class the sturgeon, but it differed from that fish in many essential particulars. My uncle, after all, was not mistaken. After a long and patient examination, he said: " This fish, my dear boy, belongs to a family which has been extinct for ages, and of which no trace has ever been found on earth, except fossil remains in the Devonian strata."

"You do not mean to say," I cried, "that we have captured a live specimen of a fish belonging to the primitive stock that existed before the deluge?"

"We have," said the Professor, who all this time was continuing his observations, "and you may see by careful examination that these fossil fish have no identity with existing species. To hold in one's hand, therefore, a living specimen of the order, is enough to make a naturalist happy for life. Moreover this fish offers to our notice a remarkable peculiarity, never known to exist in any other fish but those which are the natives of subterranean waters, wells, lakes, in caverns, and such like hidden pools."

"And what may that be?"

"It is blind."

"Blind!" I cried, much surprised.

"Not only blind," continued the Professor, "but absolutely without organs of sight."

I now examined our discovery for myself. It was singular, to be sure, but it was really a fact. This, however, might be a solitary instance, I suggested. The hook was baited again and once more thrown into the water. This subterranean ocean must have been tolerably well supplied with fish, for in two hours we took a large number of similar fish. All, without exception, however, were blind. This unexpected capture enabled us to renew our stock of provisions in a very satisfactory way.

We were now convinced that this Subterranean Sea contained only fish known to us as fossil specimens—and fish and reptiles alike, were all the more perfect the farther back they dated their origin. We began to hope that we should find some of those Saurians which science has succeeded in reconstructing from bits of bone or cartilage. I took up the telescope and carefully examined the horizon —looked over the whole sea; it was utterly and entirely deserted. Doubtless we were still too near the coast.

After an examination of the ocean, I looked upward, towards the strange and mysterious sky. Why should not one of the birds, reconstructed by the immortal Cuvier, flap his stupendous wings aloft in the dull strata of subterranean air? It would, of course, find quite sufficient food from the fish in the sea. I gazed for some time upon the void above. It was as silent and as deserted as the shores we had but lately left.

Nevertheless, though I could neither see nor discover anything, my imagination carried me away into wild hypotheses. I was in a kind of waking dream. I thought I saw on the surface of the water those enormous antediluvian turtles as big as floating islands. Upon those dull and somber shores passed a spectral row of the mammifers of early days, the great Leptotherium found in the cavernous hollow of the Brazilian hills, the Mesicotherium, a native of the glacial regions of Siberia. Farther on, the pachydermatous Lophrodon, that gigantic tapir, which concealed itself behind rocks, ready to do battle for its prey with the Anoplotherium, a singular animal partaking of the nature of the rhinoceros, the horse, the hippopotamus and the camel.

I thought, such was the effect of my imagination, that I saw this whole tribe of antediluvian creatures. I carried myself back to far ages, long before man existed—when, in fact, the earth was in too imperfect a state for him to live upon it. The whole panorama of the world's life before the historic period, seemed to be born over again, and mine was the only human heart that beat in this unpeopled world! There were no more seasons; there were no more climates; the natural heat of the world increased unceasingly, and neutralized that of the great radiant Sun.

Next, unrolled before me like a panorama, came the great and wondrous series of terrestrial transformations. Plants disappeared; the granitic rocks lost all trace of solidity; the liquid state was suddenly substituted for that which had before existed. This was caused by intense heat acting on the organic matter of the earth. The waters flowed over the whole surface of the globe; they boiled; they were volatilized, or turned into vapor; a kind of steam-cloud wrapped the whole earth, the globe itself becoming at last nothing but one huge sphere of gas, indescribable in color, between white heat and red, as big and as brilliant as the sun.

What an extraordinary dream! Where would it finally take me? My feverish hand began to write down the marvelous details—details more like the imaginings of a lunatic than anything sober and real. I had during this period of hallucination forgotten everything—the Professor, the guide, and the raft on which we were floating. My mind was in a state of semi-oblivion.

"What is the matter, Harry?" said my uncle, suddenly.

My eyes, which were wide opened like those of a somnambulist, were fixed upon him, but I did not see him, nor could I clearly make out anything around me.

"Take care, my boy," again cried my uncle, "you will fall into the sea."

As he uttered these words, I felt myself seized on the other side by the firm hand of our devoted guide. Had it not been for the presence of mind of Hans, I must infallibly have fallen into the waves and been drowned.

"Have you gone mad?" cried my uncle, shaking me on the other side.

"What—what is the matter?" I said at last, coming to myself.

"Are you ill, Henry?" continued the Professor in an anxious tone.

"No—no; but I have had an extraordinary dream. It, however, has passed away. All now seems well," I added, looking around me with strangely puzzled eyes.

"All right," said my uncle; "a beautiful breeze, a splendid sea. We are going along at a rapid rate, and if I am not out in my calculations we shall soon see land. I shall not be sorry to exchange the narrow limits of our raft for the mysterious strand of the Subterranean Ocean."

As my uncle uttered these words, I rose and carefully scanned the horizon. But the line of water was still confounded with the lowering clouds that hung aloft, and in the distance appeared to touch the edge of the water.

CHAPTER XXX
TERRIFIC SAURIAN COMBAT

SATURDAY, August 15. The sea still retains its uniform monotony. The same leaden hue, the same eternal glare from above. No indication of land being in sight. The horizon appears to retreat before us, more and more as we advance.

TERRIFIC SAURIAN COMBAT

My head is still dull and heavy from the effects of my extraordinary dream, which I cannot as yet banish from my mind. The Professor, who has not dreamed, is, however, in one of his morose and unaccountable humors. Spends his time in scanning the horizon, at every point of the compass. His telescope is raised every moment to his eyes, and when he finds nothing to give any clew to our whereabouts, he assumes a Napoleonic attitude and walks anxiously.

I remarked that my uncle, the Professor, had a strong tendency to resume his old impatient character, and I could not but make a note of this disagreeable circumstance. I saw clearly that it had required all the influence of my danger and suffering, to extract from him one scintillation of humane feeling. Now that I was quite recovered, his original nature had conquered and obtained the upper hand.

"You seem uneasy, uncle," said I, when for about the hundredth time he put down his telescope and walked up and down, muttering to himself.

"No, I am not uneasy," he replied in a dry harsh tone, "by no means."

"Perhaps I should have said impatient," I replied, softening the force of my remark.

"Enough to make me so, I think."

"And yet we are advancing at a rate seldom attained by a raft," I remarked.

"What matters that?" cried my uncle. "I am not vexed at the rate we go at, but I am annoyed to find the sea so much vaster than I expected."

I then recollected that the Professor, before our departure, had estimated the length of this Subterranean Ocean, as at most about fifty leagues. Now we had traveled at least over thrice that distance without discovering any trace of the distant shore. I began to understand my uncle's anger.

"We are not going down," suddenly exclaimed the Professor. "We are not progressing with our great discoveries. All this is utter loss of time. After all, I did not come from home to undertake a party of pleasure. This voyage on a raft over a pond annoys and wearies me."

He called this adventurous journey a party of pleasure, and this great Inland Sea a pond! "But," argued I, "if we have followed the route indicated by the great Saknussemm, we cannot be going far wrong."

"'That is the question,' as the great, the immortal Shakespeare, has it. Are we following the route indicated by that wondrous sage? Did Saknussemm ever fall in with this great sheet of water? If he did, did he cross it? I begin to fear that the rivulet we adopted for a guide has led us wrong."

"In any case, we can never regret having come thus far. It is worth the whole journey to have enjoyed this magnificent spectacle—it is something to have seen."

"I care nothing about seeing, nor about magnificent spectacles. I came down into the interior of the earth with an object, and that object I mean to attain. Don't talk to me about admiring scenery, or any other sentimental trash."

After this I thought it well to hold my tongue, and allow the Professor to bite his lips until the blood came, without further remark.

At six o'clock in the evening, our matter-of-fact guide, Hans, asked for his week's salary, and receiving his three rix-dollars, put them carefully in his pocket. He was perfectly contented and satisfied.

Sunday, 16th August. Nothing new to record. The same weather as before. The wind has a slight tendency to freshen up, with signs of an approaching gale. When I awoke, my first observation was in regard to the intensity of the light. I keep on fearing, day after day, that the extraordinary electric phenomenon should become first obscured, and then go wholly out, leaving us in total darkness. Nothing, however, of the kind occurs. The shadow of the raft, its mast and sails, is clearly distinguished on the surface of the water.

This wondrous sea is, after all, infinite in its extent. It must be quite as wide as the Mediterranean—or perhaps even as the great Atlantic Ocean. Why, after all, should it not be so? My uncle has on more than one occasion, tried deep sea soundings. He tied the cross of one of our heaviest crowbars to the extremity of a cord, which he allowed to run out to the extent of two hundred fathoms.

We had the greatest difficulty in hoisting in our novel kind of lead.

When the crowbar was finally dragged on board, Hans called my attention to some singular marks upon its surface. The piece of iron looked as if it had been crushed between two very hard substances. I looked at our worthy guide with an inquiring glance. "Tander," said he.

Of course I was at a loss to understand. I turned round towards my uncle, absorbed in gloomy reflections. I had little wish to disturb him from his reverie. I accordingly turned once more toward our worthy Icelander. Hans very quietly and significantly opened his mouth once or twice, as if in the act of biting, and in this way made me understand his meaning.

"Teeth!" cried I, with stupefaction, as I examined the bar of iron with more attention.

Yes. There can be no doubt about the matter. The indentations on the bar of iron are the marks of teeth! What jaws must the owner of such molars be possessed of! Have we, then, come upon a monster of unknown species, which still exists within the vast waste of waters —a monster more voracious than a shark, more terrible and bulky than the whale. I am unable to withdraw my eyes from the bar of iron, actually half-crushed!

Is, then, my dream about to come true—a dread and terrible reality? All day my thoughts were bent upon these speculations, and my imagination scarcely regained a degree of calmness and power of reflection until after a sleep of many hours. This day, as on other Sundays, we observed as a day of rest and pious meditation.

Monday, August 17th. I have been trying to realize from memory the particular instincts of those antediluvian animals of the secondary period, which succeeding to the mollusca, to the crustacea, and to the fish, preceded the appearance of the race of mammifers. The generation of reptiles then reigned supreme upon the earth. These hideous monsters ruled everything in the seas of the secondary period, which formed the strata of which the Jura mountains are composed. What a gigantic structure was theirs; what vast and prodigious strength they possessed! The existing Saurians, which include all such reptiles as lizards, crocodiles, and alligators, even the largest and most formidable of their class, are but feeble imitations of their mighty sires, the animals of ages long ago. If there were giants in the days of old, there were also gigantic animals.

I shuddered as I evolved from my mind the idea and recollection of these awful monsters. No eye of man had seen them in the flesh. They took their walks abroad upon the face of the earth thousands of ages before man came into existence, and their fossil bones, discovered in the limestone, have allowed us to reconstruct them anatomically, and thus to get some faint idea of their colossal formation.

I recollect once seeing in the great Museum of Hamburg the skeleton of one of these wonderful Saurians. It measured no less than thirty feet from the nose to the tail. Am I, then, an inhabitant of the earth of the present day, destined to find myself face to face with a representative of this antediluvian family? I can scarcely believe it possible; can hardly believe it true. And yet these marks of powerful teeth upon the bar of iron! can there be a doubt from their shape that the bite is the bite of a crocodile?

My eyes stare wildly and with terror upon the subterranean sea. Every moment I expect one of these monsters to rise from its vast cavernous depths. I fancy that the worthy Professor in some measure shares my notions, if not my fears, for, after an attentive examination of the crowbar, he cast his eyes rapidly over the mighty and mysterious ocean.

" What could possess him to leave the land," I thought, " as if the depth of this water was of any importance to us. No doubt he has disturbed some terrible monster in his watery home, and perhaps we may pay dearly for our temerity." Anxious to be prepared for the worst, I examined our weapons, and saw that they were in a fit state for use. My uncle looked on at me and nodded his head approvingly. He, too, had noticed what we had to fear.

Already the uplifting of the waters on the surface indicates that something is in motion below. The danger approaches. It comes nearer and nearer. It behooves us to be on the watch.

Tuesday, August 18. Evening came at last, the hour, when the desire for sleep caused our eyelids to be heavy. Night there is not, properly speaking, in this place, any more than there is in summer in the arctic regions. Hans, however, is immovable at the rudder. When he snatches a moment of rest I really cannot say. I took advantage of his vigilance to take some little repose.

Two hours after, I was awakened from a heavy sleep by an awful shock. The raft appeared to have struck upon a sunken rock. It was lifted right out of the water by some wondrous and mysterious power, and then started off twenty fathoms distant.

"Eh, what is it?" cried my uncle, starting up, "are we shipwrecked, or what?"

Hans raised his hand and pointed to where, about two hundred yards off, a huge black mass was moving up and down. I looked with awe. My worst fears were realized. "It is a colossal monster!" I cried, clasping my hands.

"Yes," cried the agitated Professor, "there yonder is a huge sea lizard of terrible size and shape."

"And farther on behold a prodigious crocodile. Look at his hideous jaws, and that row of monstrous teeth. Ha! he has gone."

"A whale! a whale!" shouted the Professor, "I can see her enormous fins. See, see, how she blows air and water!"

Two liquid columns rose to a vast height above the level of the sea, into which they fell with a terrific crash, waking up the echoes of that awful place. We stood still —surprised, stupefied, terror-stricken at the sight of what seemed a group of fearful marine monsters, more hideous in the reality than in my dream. They were of supernatural dimensions; the very smallest of the whole party could with ease have crushed our raft and ourselves with a single bite.

Hans, seizing the rudder which had flown out of his hand, puts it hard a-weather in order to escape from such dangerous vicinity; but no sooner does he do so, than he finds he is flying from Scylla to Charybdis. To leeward is a turtle about forty feet wide, and a serpent quite as long, with an enormous and hideous head peering from out the waters. Look which way we will, it is impossible for us to fly. The fearful reptiles advanced upon us; they turned and twisted about the raft with awful rapidity. They formed around our devoted vessel a series of concentric circles. I took up my rifle in desperation. But what effect can a rifle-ball produce upon the armor scales with which the bodies of these horrid monsters are covered?

We remain still and dumb from utter horror. They advance upon us, nearer and nearer. Our fate appears certain, fearful and terrible. On one side the mighty crocodile, on the other the great sea serpent. The rest of the fearful crowd of marine prodigies have plunged beneath the briny waves and disappeared!

I was about at all risks to fire, and try the effect of a shot. Hans, the guide, however, interfered by a sign to check me. The two hideous and ravenous monsters passed within fifty fathoms of the raft, and then made a rush at one another—their fury and rage preventing them from seeing us.

The combat commenced. We distinctly made out every action of the two hideous monsters. To my excited imagination the other animals appeared about to take part in the fierce and deadly struggle—the monster, the whale, the lizard, and the turtle. I distinctly saw them every moment. I pointed them out to the Icelander. But he only shook his head. "Tva," he said.

"What—two only does he say. Surely he is mistaken," I cried, in a tone of wonder.

"He is quite right," replied my uncle coolly and philosophically, examining the terrible duel with his telescope and speaking as if he were in a lecture room.

"How can that be?"

"Yes, it is so. The first of these hideous monsters has the snout of a porpoise, the head of a lizard, the teeth of a crocodile; and it is this that has deceived us. It is the most fearful of all antediluvian reptiles, the world-renowned Ichthyosaurus or Great Fish Lizard."

"And the other?"

"The other is a monstrous serpent, concealed under the hard vaulted shell of the turtle, the terrible enemy of its fearful rival, the Plesiosaurus, or Sea Crocodile."

Hans was quite right. The two monsters only, disturbed the surface of the sea! At last have mortal eyes gazed upon two reptiles of the great primitive ocean! I saw the flaming red eyes of the Ichthyosaurus, each as big, or bigger than a man's head. Nature in its infinite wisdom had gifted this wondrous marine animal with an optical apparatus of extreme power, capable of resisting the pressure of the heavy layers of water which rolled over him in the depth of the ocean where he usually fed. It has by some authors truly been called the whale of the Saurian race, for it is as big and quick in its motions as our king of the seas. This one measured not less than a hundred feet in length, and I could form some idea of his girth, when I saw him lift his prodigious tail out of the waters. His jaw is of awful size and strength, and according to the best-informed naturalists, it does not contain less than a hundred and eighty-two teeth.

The other was the mighty Plesiosaurus, a serpent with a cylindrical trunk, with a shorty stumpy tail, with fins like a bank of oars in a Roman galley. Its whole body was covered by a carapace or shell; and its neck, as flexible as that of a swan, rose more than thirty feet above the waves, a tower of animated flesh!

These animals attacked one another with inconceivable fury. Such a combat was never seen before by mortal eyes, and to us who did see it, it appeared more like the phantasmagoric creation of a dream than anything else. They raised mountains of water, which dashed in spray over the raft, already tossed to and fro by the waves. Twenty times we seemed on the point of being upset and hurled headlong into the waves. Hideous hisses appeared to shake the gloomy granite roof of that mighty cavern—hisses which carried terror to our hearts. The awful combatants held each other in a tight embrace. I could not make out one from the other. Still the combat could not last for ever; and woe unto us, whichsoever became the victor.

One hour, two hours, three hours passed away, without any decisive result. The struggle continued with the same deadly tenacity, but without apparent result. The deadly opponents now approached, now drew away from the raft. Once or twice we fancied they were about to leave us altogether, but instead of that, they came nearer and nearer. We crouched on the raft ready to fire at them at a moment's notice, poor as the prospect of hurting or terrifying them was. Still we were determined not to perish without a struggle.

Suddenly the Ichthyosaurus and the Plesiosaurus disappeared beneath the waves, leaving behind them a maelstrom in the midst of the sea. We were very nearly drawn down by the indraught of the water!

Several minutes elapsed before anything was again seen. Was this wonderful combat to end in the depths of the ocean? Was the last act of this terrible drama to take place without spectators? It was impossible for us to say.

Suddenly, at no great distance from us, an enormous mass rose out of the waters—the head of the great Plesiosaurus. The terrible monster was wounded unto death. I could see nothing of his enormous body. All that could be distinguished was his serpent-like neck, which he twisted and curled in all the agonies of death. Now he struck the waters with it as if it had been a gigantic whip, and then again wriggled like a worm cut in two. The water was spurted up to a great distance in all directions. A great portion of it swept over our raft and nearly blinded us. But soon the end of the beast approached nearer and nearer; his movements slackened visibly; his contortions almost ceased; and at last the body of the mighty snake lay an inert, dead mass on the surface of the now calm and placid waters.

As for the Ichthyosaurus, has he gone down to his mighty cavern under the sea to rest, or will he reappear to destroy us? This question remained unanswered. And we had breathing time.

CHAPTER XXXI
THE SEA MONSTER

WEDNESDAY, August 19. Fortunately the wind, which at the present blows with great violence, allowed us to escape from the scene of the unparalleled and extraordinary struggle. Hans with his usual imperturbable calm remained at the helm. My uncle, who for a short time had been withdrawn from his absorbing reverie by the novel incidents of this sea-fight, fell back again apparently into a brown study. All this time, however, his eyes were fixed impatiently on the wide-spread ocean.

Our voyage now became monotonous and uniform. Dull

as it has become, I have no desire to have it broken by any repetition of the perils and adventures of yesterday.

Thursday, August 20. The wind is now N. N. E., and blows very irregularly. It has changed to fitful gusts. The temperature is exceedingly high. We are now progressing at the average rate of about ten miles and a half per hour. About twelve o'clock a distant sound as of thunder fell upon our ears. I make a note of the fact without even venturing a suggestion as to its cause. It was one continuous roar as of a sea falling over mighty rocks.

"Far off in the distance," said the Professor dogmatically, "there is some rock or some island against which the sea, lashed to fury by the wind, is breaking violently."

Hans, without saying a word, clambered to the top of the mast, but could make out nothing. The ocean was level in every direction as far as the eye could reach.

Three hours passed away without any sign to, indicate what might be before us. The sound began to assume that of a mighty cataract. I expressed my opinion on this point strongly to my uncle. He merely shook his head. Are we advancing towards some mighty waterfall which shall cast us into the abyss? Probably this mode of descending into the abyss may be agreeable to the Professor, because it would be something like the vertical descent he is so eager to make. I entertain a very different view. Whatever be the truth, it is certain that not many leagues distant there must be some very extraordinary phenomenon, for as we advance the roar becomes something mighty and stupendous. Is it in the water, or in the air?

I cast hasty glances aloft at the suspended vapors, and I seek to penetrate their mighty depths. But the vault above is tranquil. The clouds, which are now elevated to the very summit, appear utterly still and motionless, and completely lost in the irradiation of electric light. It is necessary, therefore, to seek for the cause of this phenomenon elsewhere.

I examine the horizon, now perfectly calm, pure and free from all haze. Its aspect still remains unchanged. But if this awful noise proceeds from a cataract—if, so to speak in plain English, this vast interior ocean is precipitated into a lower basin—if these tremendous roars are produced by the noise of falling waters, the current would increase in activity, and its increasing swiftness would give me some idea of the extent of the peril with which we are menaced. I consult the current. It simply does not exist: there is no such thing. An empty bottle cast into the water lies to leeward without motion.

About four o'clock Hans rises, clambers up the mast and reaches the truck itself. From this elevated position his looks are cast around. They take in a vast circumference of the ocean. At last, his eyes remain fixed. His face expresses no astonishment, but his eyes slightly dilate.

" He has seen something at last," cried my uncle.

" I think so," I replied.

Hans came down, stood beside us and pointed with his right hand to the south. " *Der nere,*" he said.

" There," replied my uncle. And seizing his telescope he looked at it with great attention for about a minute, which to me appeared an age. I knew not what to think or expect.

" Yes, yes," he cried in a tone of considerable surprise, " there it is."

" What? " I asked.

" A tremendous spurt of water rising out of the waves."

" Some other marine monster," I cried, already alarmed.

" Perhaps."

" Then let us steer more to the westward, for we know what we have to expect from antediluvian animals," was my eager reply.

" Go ahead," said my uncle.

I turned towards Hans. Hans was at the tiller steering with his usual imperturbable calm. Nevertheless, if from the distance which separated us from this creature, a distance which must be estimated at not less than a dozen leagues, and this spurting of water proceeded from the pranks of some antediluvian animal, his dimensions must be something preternatural. To fly is, therefore, the course to be suggested by ordinary prudence. But we have not come into that part of the world to be prudent. Such is my uncle's determination.

We, accordingly, continued to advance. The nearer we come, the loftier is the spouting water. What monster can fill himself with such huge volumes of water, and then unceasingly spout them out in such lofty jets?

At eight o'clock in the evening, reckoning as above

ground, where there is day and night, we are not more than two leagues from the mighty beast. Its long, black, enormous, mountainous body, lies on the top of the water like an island. But then sailors have been said to have gone ashore on sleeping whales, mistaking them for land. Is it illusion, or is it fear? Its length cannot be less than a thousand fathoms. What, then, is this cetaceous monster of which no Cuvier ever thought? It is quite motionless and presents the appearance of sleep. The sea seems unable to lift him upwards; it is rather the waves which break on his huge and gigantic frame. The water-spout, rising to a height of five hundred feet, breaks in spray with a dull, sullen roar. We advance, like senseless lunatics, towards this mighty mass.

I honestly confess that I was abjectly afraid. I declared that I would go no farther. I threatened in my terror to cut the sheet of the sail. I attacked the Professor with considerable acrimony, calling him foolhardy, mad, I know not what. He made no answer. Suddenly the imperturbable Hans once more pointed his finger to the menacing object. *"Holme!"*

"An island!" cried my uncle.

"An island?" I replied, shrugging my shoulders at this poor attempt at deception.

"Of course it is," cried my uncle, bursting into a loud and joyous laugh.

"But the water spout?"

"Geyser," said Hans.

"Yes, of course—a geyser," replied my uncle, still laughing, "a geyser like those common in Iceland. Jets like this are the great wonders of the country."

At first I would not allow that I had been so grossly deceived. What could be more ridiculous than to have taken an island for a marine monster? But kick as one may, one must yield to evidence, and I was finally convinced of my error. It was nothing, after all, but a natural phenomenon.

As we approached nearer and nearer, the dimensions of the liquid sheaf of waters became truly grand and stupendous. The island had, at a distance, presented the appearance of an enormous whale, whose head rose high above the waters. The geyser, a word which signifies fury, rose majestically from its summit. Dull detonations are heard every now and then, and the enormous jet, taken as it were with sudden fury, shakes its plume of vapor, and bounds into the first layer of the clouds. It is alone. Neither spurts of vapor nor hot springs surround it, and the whole volcanic power of that region is concentrated in one sublime column. The rays of electric light mix with this dazzling sheaf, every drop as it falls assuming the prismatic colors of the rainbow.

"Let us go on shore," said the Professor, after some minutes of silence. It was necessary, however, to take great precaution, in order to avoid the weight of falling waters, which would cause the raft to founder in an instant. Hans, however, steered admirably, and brought us to the other extremity of the island.

I was the first to leap on the rock. My uncle followed, while the eider-duck hunter remained still, like a man above any childish sources of astonishment. We were now walking on granite mixed with silicious sandstone; the soil shivered under our feet like the sides of boilers in which over-heated steam is forcibly confined. It was burning. We soon came in sight of the little central basin from which rose the geyser. I plunged a thermometer into the water which ran bubbling from the center, and it marked a heat of a hundred and sixty-three degrees! This water, therefore, came from some place where the heat was intense. This was singularly in contradiction with the theories of Professor Hardwigg. I could not help telling him my opinion on the subject.

"Well," said he sharply, "and what does this prove against my doctrine?"

"Nothing," replied I dryly, seeing that I was running my head against a foregone conclusion. I am compelled to confess that until now we have been most remarkably fortunate, and that this voyage is being accomplished in most favorable conditions of temperature; but it appears evident, in fact, certain, that we shall sooner or later arrive at one of those regions, where the central heat will reach its utmost limits, and will go far beyond all the possible gradations of thermometers. Visions of the Hades of the ancients, believed to be in the center of the earth, floated through my imagination.

We shall, however, see what we shall see. That is the Professor's favorite phrase now. Having christened the volcanic island by the name of his nephew, the leader of the expedition turned away and gave the signal for embarkation. We went carefully round the projecting, and rather dangerous, rocks of the southern side. Hans had taken advantage of this brief halt to repair the raft. Not before it was required.

Before we took our final departure from the island, however, I made some observations to calculate the distance we had gone over, and I put them down in my Journal. Since we left Port Gretchen, we had traveled two hundred and seventy leagues—more than eight hundred miles—on this great inland sea; we were, therefore, six hundred and twenty leagues from Iceland, and exactly under England.

CHAPTER XXXII
THE BATTLE OF THE ELEMENTS

FRIDAY, August 21st. This morning the magnificent geyser had wholly disappeared. The wind had freshened up, and we were fast leaving the neighborhood of Henry's Island. Even the roaring sound of the mighty column was lost to the ear.

The weather, if, under the circumstances, we may use such an expression, is about to change very suddenly. The atmosphere is being gradually loaded with vapors, which carry with them the electricity formed by the constant evaporation of the saline waters; the clouds are slowly but sensibly falling towards the sea, and are assuming a dark olive texture; the electric rays can scarcely pierce through the opaque curtain which has fallen like a drop-scene before this wondrous theater, on the stage of which another and terrible drama is soon to be enacted. This time it is no fight of animals; it is the fearful battle of the elements.

In the distance, the clouds have assumed the appearance of enormous balls of cotton, or rather pods, piled one above the other in picturesque confusion. By degrees, they appear to swell out, break, and gain in number what they lose in grandeur; their heaviness is so great that they are unable to lift themselves from the horizon; but under the influence of the upper currents of air, they are gradually broken up, become much darker, and then present the appearance of one single layer of a formidable character; now and then a lighter cloud, still lit up from above, rebounds upon this gray carpet, and is lost in the opaque mass.

There can be no doubt that the entire atmosphere is saturated with electric fluid; I am myself wholly impregnated; my hairs literally stand on end as if under the influence of a galvanic battery. If one of my companions ventured to touch me, I think he would receive rather a violent and unpleasant shock.

About ten o'clock in the morning, the symptoms of the storm became more thorough and decisive; the wind appeared to soften down as if to take breath for a renewed attack; the vast funereal pall above us looked like a huge bag—like the cave of Æolus, in which the storm was collecting its forces for the attack. I tried all I could not to believe in the menacing signs of the sky, and yet I could not avoid saying, as it were involuntarily—" I believe we are going to have bad weather."

The Professor made me no answer. He was in a horrible, in a detestable humor—to see the ocean stretching interminably before his eyes. On hearing my words he simply shrugged his shoulders.

" We shall have a tremendous storm," I said again, pointing to the horizon. " These clouds are falling lower and lower upon the sea, as if to crush it."

A great silence prevailed. The wind wholly ceased. Nature assumed a dead calm, and ceased to breathe. Upon the mast, where I noticed a sort of slight *ignis fatuus,* the sail hung in loose heavy folds. The raft lay motionless in the midst of a dark heavy sea—without undulation, without motion. It was as still as glass. " Let us lower the sail," I said, " it is only an act of common prudence."

" No—no," cried my uncle, in an exasperated tone, " a hundred times, no. Let the wind strike us and do its worst, let the storm sweep us away where it will—only let me see the glimmer of some coast—of some rocky cliffs, even if they dash our raft into a thousand pieces. No! keep up the sail—no matter what happens."

These words were scarcely uttered, when the southern

horizon underwent a sudden and violent change. The long accumulated vapors were resolved into water, and the air required to fill up the void produced became a wild and raging tempest. It came from the most distant corners of the mighty cavern. It raged from every point of the compass. It roared; it yelled; it shrieked with glee as of demons let loose. The darkness increased and became indeed darkness visible.

The raft rose and fell with the storm, and bounded over the waves. My uncle was cast headlong upon the deck. I with great difficulty dragged myself towards him. He was holding on with might and main to the end of a cable, and appeared to gaze with pleasure and delight at the spectacle of the unchained elements.

Hans never moved a muscle. His long hair driven hither and thither by the tempest and scattered wildly over his motionless face, gave him a most extraordinary appearance—for every single hair was illuminated by little sparkling sprigs. His countenance presented the extraordinary appearance of an antediluvian man, a true contemporary of the megatherium.

Still the mast holds good against the storm. The sail spreads out and fills like a soap bubble about to burst. The raft rushes on at a pace impossible to estimate.

"The sail, the sail!" I cried, making a trumpet of my hands, and then endeavoring to lower it.

"Let it alone!" said my uncle, more exasperated than ever.

"*Nej,*" said Hans, gently shaking his head.

The rain formed a roaring cataract before this horizon of which we were in search, and to which we were rushing like madmen. But before this wilderness of waters reached us, the mighty veil of cloud was torn in twain; the sea began to foam wildly. To the fearful claps of thunder were added dazzling flashes of lightning, such as I had never seen. The flashes crossed one another, hurled from every side; while the thunder came pealing like an echo.

The mass of vapor becomes incandescent; the hail-stones which strike the metal of our boots and our weapons, are actually luminous; the waves as they rise appear to be fire-eating monsters, beneath which seethes an intense fire, their crests surmounted by combs of flame. My eyes are dazzled, blinded by the intensity of light, my ears are deafened by the awful roar of the elements. I am compelled to hold on to the mast, which bends like a reed beneath the violence of the storm, to which none ever before seen by mariners bore any resemblance.

.   .   .   .   .

Here my traveling notes become very incomplete, loose and vague. I have only been able to make out one or two fugitive observations, dotted down in a mere mechanical way. But even their brevity, even their obscurity, show the emotions which overcame me.

.   .   .   .   .

Sunday, August 23d. Where have we got to? In what region are we wandering? We are still carried forward with inconceivable rapidity. The night has been fearful, something not to be described. The storm shows no signs of cessation. We exist in the midst of an uproar which has no name. The detonations as of artillery are incessant. Our ears literally bleed. We are unable to exchange a word, or hear each other speak. The lightning never ceases to flash for a single instant. I can see the zigzags after a rapid dart, strike the arched roof of this mightiest of mighty vaults. If it were to give way and fall upon us! Other lightnings plunge their forked streaks in every direction, and take the form of globes of fire, which explode like bomb-shells over a beleaguered city. The general crash and roar do not apparently increase; it has already gone far beyond what human ear can appreciate. If all the powder-magazines in the world were to explode together, it would be impossible for us to hear worse noise.

There is a constant emission of light from the storm-clouds; the electric matter is incessantly released; innumerable columns of water rush up like waterspouts, and fall back upon the surface of the ocean in foam. Whither are we going? My uncle still lies at full length upon the raft, without speaking—without taking any note of time.

Monday, August 24. This terrible storm will never end. Why should not this state of the atmosphere, so dense and murky, once modified, again remain definitive?

We are utterly broken and harassed by fatigue. Hans remains just as usual. The raft runs to the south-east invariably. We have now already run two hundred leagues from the newly-discovered island.

About twelve o'clock the storm becomes worse than ever. We are obliged to fasten every bit of cargo tightly on the deck of the raft, or everything would be swept away. We tie ourselves to the mast, each man lashing the other. The waves drive over us, so that several times we are actually under water.

We had been under the painful necessity of abstaining from speech for three days and three nights. We opened our mouths, we moved our lips, but no sound came. Even when we placed our mouths to each other's ears it was the same. The wind carried the voice away. My uncle once contrived to get his head close to mine after several almost vain endeavors. He appeared to my nearly exhausted senses to articulate some word. I had a notion, more from intuition than anything else, that he said to me, " we are lost."

I took out my note book, from which under the most desperate circumstances I never parted, and wrote a few words as legibly as I could—" Take in sail." With a deep sigh he nodded his head and acquiesced.

His head had scarcely time to fall back in the position from which he had momentarily raised it, than a disc or ball of fire appeared on the very edge of the raft—our devoted, our doomed craft. The mast and sail were carried away bodily, and I saw them swept away to a prodigious height like a kite.

We were frozen, actually shivered with terror. The ball of fire, half white, half azure-colored, about the size of a ten-inch bomb-shell, moved along, turning with prodigious rapidity to leeward of the storm. It ran about here, there and everywhere, it clambered up one of the bulwarks of the raft, it leaped upon the sack of provisions, and then finally descended lightly, fell like a foot ball and landed on our powder barrel.

Horrible situation. An explosion of course seemed now inevitable. The dazzling disc moved to one side, it approached Hans, who looked at it with singular fixity; then it approached my uncle, who cast himself on his knees to avoid it; it came towards me, as I stood pale and shuddering in the dazzling light and heat; it pirouetted round my feet, which I endeavored to withdraw. An odor of nitrous gas filled the whole air; it penetrated to the throat, to the lungs. I felt ready to choke.

Why is it that I cannot withdraw my feet? Are they riveted to the flooring of the raft? No. The fall of the electric globe has turned all the iron on board into loadstones —the instruments, the tools, the arms are clanging together with awful and horrible noise; the nails of my heavy boots adhere closely to the plate of iron incrustated in the wood. I cannot withdraw my foot.

'At last, by a violent and almost superhuman effort, I tear it away just as the ball which is still executing its gyratory motions is about to run round it and drag me with it—if——

O what intense stupendous light! The globe of fire bursts—we are enveloped in cascades of living fire, which flood the space around with luminous matter.

Then all went out and darkness once more fell upon the deep! I had just time to see my uncle once more cast apparently senseless on the flooring of the raft, Hans at the helm, " spitting fire " under the influence of the electricity which seemed to have gone through him.

Tuesday, August 25. I have just come out of a long fainting fit. The awful and hideous storm still continues; the lightning has increased in vividness, and pours out its fiery wrath like a brood of serpents let loose in the atmosphere.

Are we still upon the sea? Yes, and being carried along with incredible velocity. We have passed under England, under the Channel, under France, probably under the whole extent of Europe.

.   .   .   .   .

Another awful clamor in the distance. This time it is certain that the sea is breaking upon the rocks at no great distance. Then——

CHAPTER XXXIII
OUR ROUTE REVERSED

HERE ends what I call My Journal of our voyage on board the raft, which Journal was happily saved from the wreck. I proceed with my narrative as I did before I commenced my daily notes.

What happened when the terrible shock took place, when the raft was cast upon the rocky shore, it would be impossible for me now to say. I felt myself precipitated violently into the boiling waves, and if I escaped from a certain and cruel death, it was wholly owing to the determination of the faithful Hans, who clutching me by the arm, saved me from the yawning abyss.

The courageous Icelander then carried me in his powerful arms, far out of the reach of the waves, and laid me down upon a burning expanse of sand, where I found myself some time afterwards in the company of my uncle the Professor. Then Hans quietly returned towards the fatal rocks, against which the furious waves were beating, in order to save any stray waifs from the wreck. This man was always practical and thoughtful.

I could not utter a word; I was quite overcome with emotion; my whole body was broken and bruised with fatigue; it took hours before I was anything like myself. Meanwhile, there fell a fearful deluge of rain, drenching us to the skin. Its very violence, however, proclaimed the approaching end of the storm. Some overhanging rocks afforded us a slight protection from the torrents.

Under this shelter, Hans prepared some food, which, however, I was unable to touch; and, exhausted by the three weary days and nights of watching, we fell into a deep and painful sleep. My dreams were fearful, but at last exhausted nature asserted her supremacy, and I slumbered.

Next day when I awoke the change was magical. The weather was magnificent. Air and sea, as if by mutual consent, had regained their serenity. Every trace of the storm, even the faintest, had disappeared. I was saluted on my awakening by the first joyous tones I had heard from the Professor for many a day. His gayety, indeed, was something terrible. "Well, my lad," he cried, rubbing his hands together, "have you slept soundly?"

155

Might it not have been supposed that we were in the old house on the Königstrasse; that I had just come down quietly to my breakfast, and that my marriage with Gretchen was to take place that very day? My uncle's coolness was exasperating.

Alas, considering how the tempest had driven us in an easterly direction, we had passed under the whole of Germany, under the city of Hamburg where I had been so happy, under the very street which contained all I loved and cared for in the world. It was a positive fact that I was only separated from her by a distance of forty leagues. But these forty leagues were of hard impenetrable granite! All these dreary and miserable reflections passed through my mind, before I attempted to answer my uncle's question.

" Why, what is the matter? " he cried, " cannot you say whether you have slept well or not? "

" I have slept very well," was my reply, " but every bone in my body aches. I suppose that will lead to nothing."

" Nothing at all, my boy. It is only the result of the fatigue of the last few days—that is all."

" You appear—if I may be allowed to say so—to be very jolly this morning," I said.

" Delighted, my dear boy, delighted. Was never happier in my life. We have at last reached the wished-for port."

" The end of our expedition? " cried I, in a tone of considerable surprise.

" No; but to the confines of that sea which I began to fear would never end, but go round the whole world. We will now tranquilly resume our journey by land, and once again endeavor to dive into the center of the Earth."

" My dear uncle," I began, in a hesitating kind of way, " allow me to ask you one question? "

" Certainly, Harry; a dozen if you think proper."

" One will suffice. How about getting back? " I asked.

" How about getting back? What a question to ask. We have not as yet reached the end of our journey."

" I know that. All I want to know is, how you propose we shall manage the return voyage? "

" In the most simple manner in the world," said the imperturbable Professor. " Once we reach the exact center of this sphere, either we shall find a new road by which to ascend to the surface, or we shall simply turn round and go back by the way we came. I have every reason to believe that while we are traveling forward, it will not close behind us."

" Then one of the first matters to see to will be to repair the raft," was my rather melancholy response.

" Of course. We must attend to that above all things," continued the Professor.

" Then comes the all-important question of provisions," I urged. " Have we anything like enough left to enable us to accomplish such great, such amazing, designs as you contemplate carrying out? "

" I have seen into the matter, and my answer is in the affirmative. Hans is a very clever fellow, and has saved the greater part of the cargo. But the best way to satisfy your scruples, is to come and judge for yourself." Saying which, he led the way out of the kind of open grotto in which we had taken shelter. I had almost begun to hope that which I should rather have feared, the impossibility of such a shipwreck leaving even the slightest signs of what it had carried as freight.

As soon as I reached the shores of this inland sea, I found Hans standing gravely in the midst of a large number of things laid out in complete order. My uncle wrung his hands with deep and silent gratitude. His heart was too full for speech. This man, whose superhuman devotion to his employers, I never saw surpassed, nor even equaled, had been hard at work all the time we slept, and at the risk of his life had succeeded in saving the most precious articles of our cargo.

Of course, under the circumstances, we necessarily experienced several severe losses. Our weapons had wholly vanished. But experience had taught us to do without them. The provision of powder had, however, remained intact, after having narrowly escaped blowing us all to atoms in the storm.

" Well," said the Professor, who was now ready to make the best of everything, " as we have no guns, all we have to do is to give up all idea of hunting."

" Yes, my dear sir, we can do without them, but what about all our instruments? "

" Here is the manometer, the most useful of all, which

I gladly accept in lieu of the rest. With it alone I can calculate the depth as we proceed; by its means alone I shall be able to decide when we have reached the center of the earth. Ha, ha! but for this little instrument we might make a mistake, and run the risk of coming out at the antipodes!" All this was said amid bursts of unnatural laughter.

"But the compass," I cried, "without that what can we do?"

"Here it is safe and sound!" he cried, with real joy, "ah, ah, and here we have the chronometer and the thermometers. Hans the hunter is indeed an invaluable man!"

It was impossible to deny this fact. As far as the nautical and other instruments were concerned, nothing was wanting. Then on further examination, I found ladders, cords, pickaxes, crowbars, and shovels, all scattered about on the shore. "But what are we to do for food?" I asked.

"Let us see to the commissariat department," replied my uncle gravely. The boxes which contained our supply of food for the voyage were placed in a row along the strand, and proved in a capital state of preservation; the sea had in every case respected their contents. Taking into consideration, biscuits, salt meat, schiedam and dried fish, we could still calculate on having about four months' supply, if used with prudence and caution.

"Four months," cried the sanguine Professor, in high glee, "then we shall have plenty of time both to go and to come, and with what remains I undertake to give a grand dinner to my colleagues of the Johanneum."

I sighed. I should by this time have used myself to the temperament of my uncle, and yet this man astonished me more and more every day. He was the greatest human enigma I ever had known.

"Now," said he, "before we do anything else we must lay in a stock of fresh water. The rain has fallen in abundance, and filled the hollows of the granite. There is a rich supply of water, and we have no fear of suffering from thirst, which in our circumstances is of the last importance. As for the raft, I shall recommend Hans to repair it to the best of his abilities; though I have every reason to believe we shall not require it again."

" How is that? " I cried, more amazed than ever at my uncle's style of reasoning.

" I have an idea, my dear boy; it is none other than this simple fact: we shall not come out by the same opening as that by which we entered."

I began to look at my uncle with vague suspicion. An idea had more than once taken possession of me; and this was, that he was going mad. Little did I think how true and prophetic his words were doomed to be.

" And now," he said, " having seen to all these matters of detail, to breakfast." I followed him to a sort of projecting cape, after he had given his last instructions to our guide. In this original position, with dried meat, biscuit, and a delicious cup of tea, we made a satisfactory meal— I may say one of the most welcome and pleasant I ever remember. Exhaustion, the keen atmosphere, the state of calm after so much agitation, all contributed to give me an excellent appetite. Indeed, it contributed very much to producing a pleasant and cheerful state of mind.

While breakfast was in hand, and between the sips of warm tea, I asked my uncle if he had any idea of how we now stood in relation to the world above. " For my part," I added, " I think it will be rather difficult to determine."

" Well, if we were compelled to fix the exact spot," said my uncle, " it might be difficult, since during the three days of that awful tempest I could keep no account either of the quickness of our pace, or of the direction in which the raft was going. Still, we will endeavor to approximate to the truth. We shall not, I believe, be so very far out."

" Well, if I recollect rightly," I replied, " out last observation was made at the Geyser island."

" Harry's Island, my boy! Harry's Island. Do not decline the honor of having named it; given your name to an island discovered by us, the first human beings who trod it since the creation of the world! "

" Let it be so, then. At Harry's Island we had already gone over two hundred and seventy leagues of sea, and we were, I believe, about six hundred leagues, more or less, from Iceland."

" Good. I am glad to see that you remember so well. Let us start from that point, and let us count four days of storm, during which our rate of traveling must have been very great. I should say that our velocity must have been about eighty leagues to the twenty-four hours."

I agreed that I thought this a fair calculation. There were then three hundred leagues to be added to the grand total.

" Yes, and the Central Sea must extend at least six hundred leagues from side to side. Do you know, my boy, Harry, that we have discovered an inland lake larger than the Mediterranean? "

" Certainly, and we only know of its extent in one way. It may be hundreds of miles in length."

" Very likely."

" Then," said I, after calculating for some minutes, " if your previsions are right, we are at this moment exactly under the Mediterranean itself."

" Do you think so? "

" Yes, I am almost certain of it. Are we not nine hundred leagues distant from Reykjawik? "

" That is perfectly true, and a famous bit of road we have traveled, my boy. But why we should be under the Mediterranean more than under Turkey or the Atlantic Ocean can only be known when we are sure of not having deviated from our course; and of this we know nothing."

" I do not think we were driven very far from our course: the wind appears to me to have been always about the same. My opinion is that this shore must be situated to the southeast of Port Gretchen."

" Good—I hope so. It will, however, be easy to decide the matter by taking the bearings from our departure by means of the compass. Come along, and we will consult that invaluable invention." The Professor now walked eagerly in the direction of the rock where the indefatigable Hans had placed the instruments in safety. My uncle was gay and light-hearted; he rubbed his hands, and assumed all sorts of attitudes. He was to all appearance once more a young man. Since I had known him never had he been so amiable and pleasant. I followed him, rather curious to know whether I had made any mistake in my estimation of our position. As soon as we had reached the rock, my uncle took the compass, placed it horizontally before him and looked keenly at the needle. As he had at first shaken it to give it vivacity, it oscillated considerably, and then slowly assumed its right position under the influence of the magnetic power.

The Professor bent his eyes curiously over the wondrous instrument. A violent start immediately showed the extent of his emotion. He closed his eyes, rubbed them, and took another and a keener survey. Then he turned slowly round to me, stupefaction depicted on his countenance.

" What is the matter? " said I, beginning to be alarmed.

He could not speak. He was too overwhelmed for words. He simply pointed to the instrument. I examined it eagerly according to his mute directions, and a loud cry of surprise escaped my lips. The needle of the compass pointed due north, in the direction we expected was the south! It pointed to the shore instead of to the high seas.

I shook the compass; I examined it with a curious and anxious eye. It was in a state of perfection. No blemish in any way explained the phenomenon. Whatever position we forced the needle into, it returned invariably to the same unexpected point.

It was useless attempting to conceal from ourselves the fatal truth. There could be no doubt, unwelcome as was the fact, that during the tempest, there had been a sudden slant of wind, of which we had been unable to take any account, and thus the raft had carried us back to the shores we had left, apparently for ever, so many days before!

CHAPTER XXXIV
A VOYAGE OF DISCOVERY

It would be altogether impossible for me to give any idea of the utter astonishment which overcame the Professor on making this extraordinary discovery. Amazement, incredulity, and rage were blended in such a way as to alarm me. During the whole course of my life I had never seen a man at first so chapfallen; and then so furiously indignant.

The terrible fatigues of our sea voyage, the fearful dangers we had passed through, had all, all, gone for nothing. We had to begin them all over again. Instead of progressing, as we fondly expected, during a voyage of so many days, we had retreated. Every hour of our expedition on the raft had been so much lost time!

Presently, however, the indomitable energy of my uncle overcame every other consideration. " So," he said, between his set teeth, " fatality will play me these terrible tricks. The elements themselves conspire to overwhelm me with mortification. Air, fire, and water combine their united efforts to oppose my passage. Well, they shall see what the earnest will of a determined man can do. I will not yield, I will not retreat even one inch; and we shall see who shall triumph in this great contest—man or nature."

Standing upright on a rock, irritated and menacing, Professor Hardwigg, like the ferocious Ajax, seemed to defy the fates. I, however, took upon myself to interfere, and to impose some sort of check upon such insensate enthusiasm.

" Listen to me, uncle," I said, in a firm but temperate tone of voice, " there must be some limit to ambition here below. It is utterly useless to struggle against the impossible. Pray listen to reason. We are utterly unprepared for a sea voyage; it is simple madness to think of performing a second journey of five hundred leagues upon a wretched pile of beams, with a counterpane for a sail, a paltry stick for a mast, and a tempest to contend with. As we are totally incapable of steering our frail craft, we shall become the mere plaything of the storm, and it is acting the part of madmen if we, a second time, run any risk upon this dangerous and treacherous Central Sea."

These are only a few of the reasons and arguments I put together—reasons and arguments which to me appeared unanswerable. I was allowed to go on without interruption for about ten minutes. The explanation to this I soon discovered. The Professor was not even listening, and did not hear a word of all my eloquence.

" To the raft! " he cried, in a hoarse voice, when I paused for a reply.

Such was the result of my strenuous effort to resist his iron will. I tried again; I begged and implored him; I got into a passion; but I had to deal with a will more determined than my own. I seemed to feel like the waves which fought and battled against the huge mass of granite at our feet, which had smiled grimly for so many ages at their puny efforts.

Hans, meanwhile, without taking part in our discussion, had been repairing the raft. One would have supposed that he instinctively guessed at the further projects of my uncle. By means of some fragments of cordage, he had again made the raft sea-worthy. While I had been speaking he had hoisted a new mast and sail, the latter already fluttering and waving in the breeze.

The worthy Professor spoke a few words to our imperturbable guide, who immediately began to put our baggage on board, and to prepare for our departure. The atmosphere was now tolerably clear and pure, and the north-east wind blew steadily and serenely. It appeared likely to last for some time.

What, then, could I do? Could I undertake to resist the iron will of two men? It was simply impossible; if even I could have hoped for the support of Hans. This, however, was out of the question. It appeared to me that the Icelander had set aside all personal will and identity. He was a picture of abnegation. I could hope for nothing from one so infatuated with and devoted to his master. All I could do, therefore, was to swim with the stream. In a mood of stolid and sullen resignation, I was about to take my accustomed place on the raft, when my uncle placed his hand upon my shoulder. " There is no hurry, my boy," he said, " we shall not start until to-morrow."

I looked the picture of resignation to the dire will of fate. " Under the circumstances," he said, " I ought to neglect no precautions. As fate has cast me upon these shores, I shall not leave without having completely examined them."

In order to understand this remark, I must explain that though we had been driven back to the northern shore, we had landed at a very different spot from that which had been our starting point. Port Gretchen must, we calculated, be very much to the westward. Nothing, therefore, was more natural and reasonable than that we should reconnoiter this new shore upon which we had so unexpectedly landed. " Let us go on a journey of discovery," I cried.

And leaving Hans to his important operation, we started on our expedition. As we trudged along, our feet crushed innumerable shells of every shape and size—once the dwelling place of animals of every period of creation. I particularly noticed some enormous shells—carapaces (turtle and tortoise species) the diameter of which exceeded fifteen feet.

They had in past ages belonged to those gigantic glyptodons of the pliocene period, of which the modern turtle is but a minute specimen. In addition, the whole soil was covered by a vast quantity of stony relics, having the appearance of flints worn by the action of the waves, and lying in successive layers one above the other. It appeared clear that we were walking upon a kind of sediment, formed like all the soils of that period, so frequent on the surface of the globe, by the subsidence of the waters. The Professor, who was now in his element, carefully examined every rocky fissure. Let him only find an opening and it directly became important to him to examine its depth.

For a whole mile we followed the windings of the Central Sea, when suddenly an important change took place in the aspect of the soil. It seemed to have been rudely cast up, convulsionized, as it were, by a violent upheaving of the lower strata. In many places, hollows here, and hillocks there, attested great dislocations at some other period of the terrestrial mass. We advanced with great difficulty over the broken masses of granite mixed with flint, quartz and alluvial deposits, when a large field, more even than a field, a plain of bones, appeared suddenly before our eyes! It looked like an immense cemetery, where generation after generation had mingled their mortal dust.

Lofty barrows of early remains rose at intervals. They undulated away to the limits of the distant horizon and were lost in a thick and brown fog. On that spot, some three square miles in extent, was accumulated the whole history of animal life—scarcely one creature still a habitant of the comparatively modern soil of the upper and inhabited world, had there existed.

We were drawn forward by an all-absorbing and impatient curiosity. Our feet crushed with a dry and crackling sound the remains of those prehistoric fossils, for which the museums of great cities quarrel, even when they obtain only rare and curious morsels. I was utterly confounded. My uncle stood for some minutes with his arms raised on high towards the thick granite vault which served us for a sky. His mouth was wide open; his eyes sparkled wildly behind his spectacles (which he had fortunately saved), his head bobbed up and down and from side to side, while his whole attitude and mien expressed unbounded astonishment.

He stood in the presence of an endless, wondrous and inexhaustibly rich collection of antediluvian monsters, piled up for his own private and peculiar satisfaction. Fancy an enthusiastic lover of books carried suddenly into the very midst of the famous library of Alexandria burned by the sacrilegious Omar, and which some miracle had restored to its pristine splendor! Such was something of the state of mind in which uncle Hardwigg was now placed.

For some time he stood thus, literally aghast at the magnitude of his discovery.

But it was even a greater excitement when, darting wildly over this mass of organic dust, he caught up a naked skull and addressed me in a quivering voice—" Harry, my boy—Harry—this is a human head!"

CHAPTER XXXV
DISCOVERY UPON DISCOVERY

It will be easy to understand the Professor's mingled astonishment and joy when, on advancing about twenty yards further, he found himself in the presence of, I may say face to face with an entire fossil of the human race, actually belonging to the quarternary period!

The human skull was perfectly recognizable. Had a soil of very peculiar nature, like that of the cemetery of St. Michel at Bordeaux, preserved it during countless ages? This was the question I asked myself, but which I was wholly unable to answer. This head with stretched and parchmenty skin, with the teeth whole, the hair abundant, was before our eyes as in life!

I stood mute, almost paralyzed with wonder and awe before this dread apparition of another age. My uncle, who on almost every occasion was a great talker, remained for a time completely dumbfounded. He was too full of emotion for speech to be possible. After a while, however, we raised up the body to which the skull belonged. We stood it on end. It seemed, to our excited imaginations, to look at us with its terrible hollow eyes.

After some minutes of silence, the man was vanquished by the Professor. Human instincts succumbed to scientific pride and exultation. Professor Hardwigg, carried away by his enthusiasm, forgot all the circumstances of our journey, the extraordinary position in which we were placed, the immense cavern which stretched far away over our heads. There can be no doubt that he thought himself at the institution addressing his attentive pupils, for he put on his most doctorial style, waved his hand, and began——

" Gentlemen, I have the honor on this auspicious occasion to present to you a man of the quartenary period of our globe. Many learned men have denied his very existence, while other able persons, perhaps of even higher authority, have affirmed their belief in the reality of his life. If the St. Thomases of palæontology were present, they would reverentially touch him with their fingers and believe in his existence, thus acknowledging their obstinate heresy. I know that science should be careful in relation to all discoveries of this nature. I am not without having heard of the many Barnums and other quacks who have made a trade of such like pretended discoveries. I have, of course, heard of the discovery of the knee-bones of Ajax, of the pretended finding of the body of Orestes by the Spartiates, and of the body of Asterius, ten spans long, fifteen feet—of which we read in Pausanias.

" I have read everything in relation to the skeleton of Trapani, discovered in the fourteenth century, and which many persons chose to regard as that of Polyphemus, and the history of the giant dug up during the sixteenth century in the environs of Palmyra. You are as well aware as I am, gentlemen, of the existence of the celebrated analysis made near Lucerne, in 1577, of the great bones which the celebrated Doctor Felix Plater declared belonged to a giant about nineteen feet high. I have devoured all the treatises of Cassanion, and all those memoirs, pamphlets, speeches, and replies, published in reference to the skeleton of Teutobochus, king of the Cimbri, the invader of Gaul, dug out of a gravel pit in Dauphiny, in 1613. In the eighteenth century I should have denied, with Peter Campet, the existence of the preadamites of Scheuchzer. I have had in my hands the writing called Gigans——"

Here my uncle was afflicted by the natural infirmity which prevented him from pronouncing difficult words in public. It was not exactly stuttering, but a strange sort of constitutional hesitation. "The writing named Gigans——" he repeated.

He, however, could get no further. "*Giganteo*——"

Impossible! The unfortunate word would not come out. There would have been great laughter at the Institution, had the mistake happened there. "Gigantosteology!" at last exclaimed Professor Hardwigg, between two savage growls.

"Yes, gentlemen, I am well acquainted with all these matters, and know, also, that Cuvier and Blumenbach fully recognized in these bones, the undeniable remains of mammoths of the quaternary period. But after what we now see, to allow a doubt is to insult scientific inquiry. There is the body; you can see it; you can touch it. It is not a skeleton, it is a complete and uninjured body, preserved with an anthropological object." I did not attempt to controvert this singular and astounding assertion.

"If I could but wash this corpse in a solution of sulphuric acid," continued my uncle, "I would undertake to remove all the earthy particles, and these resplendent shells, which are incrusted all over this body. But I am without this precious dissolving medium. Nevertheless, such as it is, this body will tell its own history."

Here the Professor held up the fossil body, and exhibited it with rare dexterity. No professional showman could have shown more activity.

"As on examination you will see," my uncle continued, "it is only about six feet in length, which is a long way from the pretended giants of early days. As to the particular race to which it belonged, it is incontestably Caucasian. It is of the white race, that is, of our own. The skull of this fossil being is a perfect ovoid without any remarkable or prominent development of the cheek bones, and without any projection of the jaw. But I will advance still farther on the road of inquiry and deduction, and I dare venture to say that this human sample or specimen belongs to the Japhetic family, which spread over the

167

world from India to the uttermost limits of western Europe. There is no occasion, gentlemen, to smile at my remarks."

Of course nobody smiled. But the excellent Professor was so accustomed to beaming countenances at his lectures, that he believed he saw all his audience laughing during the delivery of his learned dissertation.

"Yes," he continued, with renewed animation, "this is a fossil man, a contemporary of the mastodons, with the bones of which this whole amphitheater is covered. But if I am called on to explain how he came to this place, how these various strata by which he is covered have fallen into this vast cavity, I can undertake to give you no explanation. But there is the man, surrounded by the works of his hands, his hatchets, and his carved flints, which belong to the stone period; and the only rational supposition is, that, like myself, he visited the center of the earth as a traveling tourist, a pioneer of science. At all events, there can be no doubt of his great age, and of his being one of the oldest race of human beings."

The Professor with these words ceased his oration, and I burst forth into loud and "unanimous" applause. Besides, after all, my uncle was right. Much more learned men than his nephew would have found it rather hard to refute his facts and arguments.

Another circumstance soon presented itself. This fossilized body was not the only one in this vast plain of bones —the cemetery of an extinct world. Other bodies were found, as we trod the dusty plain, and my uncle was able to choose the most marvelous of these specimens in order to convince the most incredulous.

In truth, it was a surprising spectacle, the successive remains of generations and generations of men and animals confounded together in one vast cemetery. But a great question now presented itself to our notice, and one we were actually afraid to contemplate in all its bearings. Had these once animated beings been buried so far beneath the soil by some tremendous convulsion of nature, after they had been earth to earth and ashes to ashes, or had they lived here below, in this subterranean world, under this factitious sky, born, married, and given in marriage, and dying at last, just like ordinary inhabitants of the earth?

DISCOVERY UPON DISCOVERY

Up to the present moment, marine monsters, fish, and such like animals, had alone been seen alive! The question which rendered us rather uneasy, was a pertinent one. Were any of these men of the abyss wandering about the deserted shores of this wondrous sea of the center of the earth? This was a question which rendered me very uneasy and uncomfortable. How, should they really be in existence, would they receive us men from above?

CHAPTER XXXVI

WHAT IS IT?

FOR a long and weary hour we tramped over this great bed of bones. We advanced regardless of everything, drawn on by ardent curiosity. What other marvels did this great cavern contain—what other wondrous treasures for the scientific man? My eyes were quite prepared for any number of surprises, my imagination lived in expectation of something new and wonderful.

The borders of the great Central Ocean had for some time disappeared behind the hills that were scattered over the ground occupied by the plane of bones. The imprudent and enthusiastic Professor, who did not care whether he lost himself or not, hurried me forward. We advanced silently, bathed in waves of electric fluid. The light illumined equally the sides of every hill and rock. The appearance presented was that of a tropical country at mid-day in summer—in the midst of the equatorial regions and under the vertical rays of the sun. The rocks, the distant mountains, some confused masses of far-off forests, assumed a weird and mysterious aspect under this equal distribution of the luminous fluid! We resembled, to a certain extent, the mysterious personage in one of Hoffmann's fantastic tales—the man who lost his shadow.

After we had walked about a mile farther, we came to the edge of a vast forest, not, however, one of the vast mushroom forests we had discovered near Port Gretchen. It was the glorious and wild vegetation of the tertiary period, in all its superb magnificence. Huge palms, of a

169

species now unknown, superb palmacites—a genus of fossil palms from the coal formation—pines, yews, cypress, and conifers or cone-bearing trees, the whole bound together by an inextricable and complicated mass of creeping plants. A beautiful carpet of mosses and ferns grew beneath the trees. Pleasant brooks murmured beneath umbrageous boughs, little worthy of this name, for no shade did they give. Upon their borders grew small tree-like shrubs, such as are seen in the hot countries on our own inhabited globe.

The one thing wanted to these plants, these shrubs, these trees—was color! Forever deprived of the vivifying warmth of the sun, they were vapid and colorless. All shade was lost in one uniform tint, of a brown and faded character. The leaves were wholly devoid of green, and the flowers, so numerous during the tertiary period which gave them birth, were without color and without perfume, something like paper discolored by long exposure to the atmosphere.

My uncle ventured beneath the gigantic groves. I followed him, though not without a certain amount of apprehension. Since nature had shown herself capable of producing such stupendous vegetable productions, why might we not meet with animals as large, and therefore dangerous.

Suddenly I stopped short and restrained my uncle. The extreme diffuseness of the light enabled me to see the smallest objects in the distant copse. I thought I saw— no, I really did see with my own eyes,—immense, gigantic animals moving about under the mighty trees. Yes, they were truly gigantic animals, a whole herd of mastodons, not fossils, but living.

Yes, I could see these enormous elephants, whose trunks were tearing down large boughs, and working in and out the trees like a legion of serpents. I could hear the sounds of the mighty tusks uprooting huge trees! The boughs crackled, and the whole masses of leaves and green branches went down the capacious throats of these terrible monsters!

That wondrous dream, when I saw the ante-historical times revivified, when the tertiary and quaternary periods passed before me, was now realized! And there we were alone, far down in the bowels of the earth, at the mercy of its ferocious inhabitants!

My uncle paused, full of wonder and astonishment. "Come," he said at last, when his first surprise was over, "come along, my boy, and let us see them nearer."

"No," replied I, restraining his efforts to drag me forward, "we are wholly without arms. What should we do in the midst of that flock of gigantic quadrupeds? Come away, uncle, I implore you. No human creature can with impunity brave the ferocious anger of these monsters."

"No human creature," said my uncle, suddenly lowering his voice to a mysterious whisper, "you are mistaken, my dear Henry. Look! look yonder! It seems to me that I behold a human being—a being like ourselves—a man!"

I looked, shrugging my shoulders, decided to push incredulity to its very last limits. But whatever might have been my wish, I was compelled to yield to the weight of ocular demonstration. Yes—not more than a quarter of a mile off, leaning against the trunk of an enormous tree, was a human being—a Proteus of these subterranean regions, a new son of Neptune keeping this innumerable herd of mastodons. *Immanis, pecoris custos, immanis ipse!* (The keeper of gigantic cattle, himself a giant!) Yes—it was no longer a fossil whose corpse we had raised from the ground in the great cemetery, but a giant capable of guiding and driving these prodigious monsters. His height was above twelve feet. His head, as big as the head of a buffalo, was lost in a mane of matted hair. It was indeed a huge mane, like those which belonged to the elephants of the earlier ages of the world. In his hand was a branch of a tree, which served as a crook for this antediluvian shepherd.

We remained profoundly still, speechless with surprise. But we might at any moment be seen by him. Nothing remained for us but instant flight. "Come, come!" I cried, dragging my uncle along; and, for the first time, he made no resistance to my wishes.

A quarter of an hour later we were far away from that terrible monster! Now that I think of the matter calmly, and that I reflect upon it dispassionately; now that months, years, have passed since this strange and unnatural adventure befell us,—what am I to think, what am I to believe?

No, it is utterly impossible! Our ears must have deceived us, and our eyes have cheated us! we have not seen what we believed we had seen. No human being could by any possibility have existed in that subterranean world! No generation of men could inhabit the lower caverns of the globe without taking note of those who peopled the surface, without communication with them. It was folly, folly, folly! nothing else!

I am rather inclined to admit the existence of some animal resembling in structure the human race—of some monkey of the first geological epochs, like that discovered by M. Lartet in the ossiferous deposits of Sansan. But this animal, or being, whichsoever it was, surpassed in height all things known to modern science. Never mind. However unlikely it may be, it might have been a monkey —but a man, a living man, and with him a whole generation of gigantic animals, buried in the entrails of the earth —it was too monstrous to be believed!

CHAPTER XXXVII
THE MYSTERIOUS DAGGER

DURING this time, we had left the bright and transparent forest far behind us. We were mute with astonishment, overcome by a kind of feeling which was next door to apathy. We kept running in spite of ourselves. It was a perfect flight, which resembled one of those horrible sensations we sometimes meet with in our dreams.

Instinctively we made our way towards the Central Sea, and I cannot now tell what wild thoughts passed through my mind, nor of what follies I might have been guilty, but for a very serious pre-occupation which brought me back to practical life. Though I was aware that we were treading on a soil quite new to us, I, every now and then noticed certain aggregations of rock, the shape of which forcibly reminded me of those near Port Gretchen.

This confirmed, moreover, the indications of the compass and our extraordinary and unlooked-for, as well as involuntary, return to the north of this great Central Sea. It was so like our starting point, that I could scarcely doubt the reality of our position. Streams and cascades, fell in hundreds over the numerous projections of the rocks. I actually thought I could see our faithful and monotonous Hans and the wonderful grotto in which I had come back to life after my tremendous fall.

Then, as we advanced still farther, the position of the cliffs, the appearance of a stream, the unexpected profile of a rock, would throw me again into a state of bewildering doubt. After some time, I explained my state of mental indecision to my uncle. He confessed to a similar feeling of hesitation. He was totally unable to make up his mind in the midst of this extraordinary but uniform panorama.

"There can be no doubt," I insisted, "that we have not landed exactly at the place whence we first took our departure; but the tempest has brought us above our starting point. I think, therefore, that if we follow the coast we shall once more find Port Gretchen."

"In that case," cried my uncle, "it is useless to continue our exploration. The very best thing we can do is to make our way back to the raft. Are you quite sure, Harry, that you are not mistaken?"

"It is difficult," was my reply, "to come to any decision, for all these rocks are exactly alike. There is no marked difference between them. At the same time, the impression on my mind is, that I recognize the promontory at the foot of which our worthy Hans constructed the raft. We are, I am nearly convinced, near the little port; if this be not it," I added, carefully examining a creek which appeared singularly familiar to my mind.

"My dear Harry—if this were the case, we should find traces of our own footsteps, some signs of our passage; and I can really see nothing to indicate our having passed this way."

"But I see something," I cried, in an impetuous tone of voice, as I rushed forward and eagerly picked up something which shone in the sand under my feet.

"What is it?" cried the astonished and bewildered Professor.

"This," was my reply. And I handed to my startled relative a rusty dagger, of singular shape.

173

" What made you bring with you so useless a weapon? "
he exclaimed. "It was needlessly hampering yourself."

"I bring it?—it is quite new to me. I never saw it before—are you sure it is not out of your collection? "

" Not that I know of," said the Professor, puzzled.
" I have no recollection of the circumstance. It was never
my property."

" This is very extraordinary," I said, musing over the
novel and singular incident.

" Not at all. There is a very simple explanation, Harry.
The Icelanders are known to keep up the use of these an-
tiquated weapons, and this must have belonged to Hans,
who has let it fall without knowing it."

I shook my head. That dagger had never been in the
possession of the pacific and taciturn Hans. I knew him
and his habits too well. " What can it be—unless it be
the weapon of some antediluvian warrior," I continued,
" of some living man, a contemporary of that mighty
shepherd from whom we have just escaped? But no—
mystery upon mystery—this is no weapon of the stone
epoch, nor even of the bronze period. It is made of excellent steel——"

Ere I could finish my sentence, my uncle stopped me
short from entering upon a whole train of theories, and
spoke in his most cold and decided tone of voice. " Calm
yourself, my dear boy, and endeavor to use your reason.
This weapon, upon which we have fallen so unexpectedly,
is a true *dague,* one of those worn by gentlemen in their
belts during the sixteenth century. Its use was to give
the *coup de grâce,* the final blow, to the foe who would not
surrender. It is clearly of Spanish workmanship. It belongs neither to you, nor to me, nor the eiderdown hunter,
nor to any of the living beings who may still exist so
marvelously in the interior of the earth."

" What can you mean, uncle? " I said, now lost in a
host of surmises.

" Look closely at it," he continued; " these jagged edges
were never made by the resistance of human blood and
bone. The blade is covered with a regular coating of
iron-mould and rust, which is not a day old, not a year old
not a century old, but much more——"

The Professor began to get quite excited, according to

custom, and was allowing himself to be carried away by his fertile imagination. I could have said something. He stopped me. "Harry," he cried, "we are now on the verge of a great discovery. This blade of a dagger you have so marvelously discovered, after being abandoned upon the sand for more than a hundred, two hundred, even three hundred years, has been indented by someone endeavoring to carve an inscription on these rocks."

"But this poignard never got here of itself," I exclaimed, "it could not have twisted itself. Someone, therefore, must have preceded us upon the shores of this extraordinary sea."

"Yes, a man."

"But what man has been sufficiently desperate to do such a thing."

"A man who has somewhere written his name with this very dagger—a man who has endeavored once more to indicate the right road to the interior of the earth. Let us look around, my boy. You know not the importance of your singular and happy discovery."

Prodigiously interested, we walked along the wall of rock, examining the smallest fissures, which might finally expand into the much wished for gully or shaft. We at last reached a spot where the shore became extremely narrow. The sea almost bathed the foot of the rocks, which were here very lofty and steep. There was scarcely a path wider than two yards at any point. At last, under a huge overhanging rock, we discovered the entrance of a dark and gloomy tunnel.

There, on a square tablet of granite, which had been smoothed by rubbing it with another stone, we could see two mysterious, and much worn letters, the two initials of the bold and extraordinary traveler who had preceded us on our adventurous journey.

$$\cdot \ \mathcal{A} \cdot \mathcal{H} \cdot$$

"A. S.," cried my uncle; "you see I was right. Arne Saknussemm, always Arne Saknussemm!"

EVER since the commencement of our marvelous journey, I had experienced many surprises, had suffered from many illusions. I thought that I was case-hardened against all surprises and could neither see nor hear anything to amaze me again. When, however, I saw these two letters, which had been engraven three hundred years before, I stood fixed in an attitude of mute surprise.

Not only was there the signature of the learned and enterprising alchemist written in the rock, but I held in my hand the identical instrument with which he had laboriously engraved it. It was impossible, without showing an amount of incredulity scarcely becoming a sane man, to deny the existence of the traveler, and the reality of that voyage which I believed all along to have been a myth—the mystification of some fertile brain.

While these reflections were passing through my mind, my uncle, the Professor, gave way to an access of feverish and poetical excitement. "Wonderful and glorious Genius, great Saknussemm," he cried, "you have left no resource omitted to show to other mortals the way into the interior of our mighty globe, and your fellow-creatures can find the trail left by your illustrious footsteps, three hundred years ago. You have been careful to secure for others the contemplation of these wonders and marvels of creation. Your name engraved at every important stage of your glorious journey, leads the hopeful traveler direct to the mighty discovery to which you devoted such energy and courage. The audacious traveler, who shall follow your footsteps to the last, will doubtless find your initials engraved with your own hand upon the center of the earth. *I* will be that audacious traveler—*I*, too, will sign my name upon the very same spot, upon the central granite stone of this wondrous work of the Creator. But in justice to your devotion, and to your being the first to indicate the road, let this Cape, seen by you upon the shores of this sea discovered by you, be called of all time, Cape Saknussemm."

This is what I heard, and I began to be roused to the pitch of enthusiasm indicated by those words. A fierce excitement roused me. I forgot everything. The dangers of the voyage, and the perils of the return journey, were now as nothing! What another man had done in ages past, could I felt be done again; I was determined to do it myself, and now nothing that man had accomplished appeared to me impossible. "Forward—forward," I cried in a burst of genuine and hearty enthusiasm.

I had already started in the direction of the somber and gloomy gallery, when the Professor stopped me; he, the man so rash and hasty, he, the man so easily roused to the highest pitch of enthusiasm, checked me, and asked me to be patient and show more calm. "Let us return to our good friend, Hans," he said; "we will then bring the raft down to this place."

I must say that though I at once yielded to my uncle's request, it was not without dissatisfaction, and I hastened along the rocks of that wonderful coast. "Do you know, my dear uncle," I said, as we walked along, "that we have been singularly helped by a concurrence of circumstances, right up to this very moment."

"So you begin to see it, do you, Harry?" said the Professor, with a smile.

"Doubtless," I responded, "and strangely enough, even the tempest has been the means of putting us on the right road. Blessings on the tempest! It brought us safely back to the very spot from which fine weather would have driven us forever. Supposing we had succeeded in reaching the southern and distant shores of this extraordinary sea, what would have become of us? The name of Saknussemm would never have appeared to us, and at this moment we should have been cast away upon an inhospitable coast, probably without an outlet."

"Yes, Harry, my boy, there is certainly something providential in that wandering at the mercy of wind and waves towards the south: we have come back exactly north; and what is better still, we fall upon this great discovery. There is something in it which is far beyond my comprehension. The coincidence is unheard-of, marvelous!"

"What matter! It is not our duty to explain facts, but to make the best possible use of them."

"Doubtless, my boy; but if you will allow me——" said the really-delighted Professor.

"Excuse me, sir, but I see exactly how it will be; we shall take the northern route; we shall pass under the northern regions of Europe, under Sweden, under Russia, under Siberia, and who knows where—instead of burying ourselves under the burning plains and deserts of Africa, or beneath the mighty waves of the ocean; and that is all, at this stage of our journey, that I care to know. Let us advance, and Heaven will be our guide!"

"Yes, Harry, you are right, quite right; all is for the best. Let us abandon this horizontal sea, which could never have led to anything satisfactory. We shall descend, descend, and everlastingly descend. Do you know, my dear boy, that to reach the interior of the earth we have only five thousand miles to travel!"

"Bah!" I cried, carried away by a burst of enthusiasm, "the distance is scarcely worth speaking about. The thing is to make a start."

My wild, mad, and incoherent speeches continued until we rejoined our patient and phlegmatic guide. All was, we found, prepared for an immediate departure. There was not a single parcel but what was in its proper place. We all took up our posts on the raft, and the sail being hoisted, Hans received his directions, and guided the frail barque towards Cape Saknussemm, as we had definitely named it.

The wind was very unfavorable to a craft that was unable to sail close to the wind. We were continually reduced to pushing ourselves forward by means of poles. On several occasions the rocks ran far out into deep water and we were compelled to make a long round. At last, after three long and weary hours of navigation, that is to say, about six o'clock in the evening, we found a place at which we could land.

I jumped on shore first. In my present state of excitement and enthusiasm, I was always first. My uncle and the Icelander followed. The voyage from the port to this point of the sea had by no means calmed me. It had rather produced the opposite effect. I even proposed to burn our vessel, that is to destroy our raft, in order to completely cut off our retreat. But my uncle sternly opposed this wild project. I began to think him particularly lukewarm and unenthusiastic. "At any rate, my dear uncle," I said, "let us start without delay."

"Yes, my boy, I am quite as eager to do so as you can

be. But, in the first place, let us examine this mysterious gallery, in order to find if we shall need to prepare and mend our ladders."

My uncle now began to see to the efficiency of our Ruhmkorff's coil, which would doubtless soon be needed; the raft, securely fastened to a rock, was left alone. The opening into the new gallery was not twenty paces distant from the spot. Our little troop, with myself at the head, advanced.

The orifice, which was almost circular, presented a diameter of about five feet; the somber tunnel was cut in the living rock, and coated on the inside by the different material which had once passed through it in a state of fusion. The lower part was about level with the water, so that we were able to penetrate to the interior without difficulty. We followed an almost horizontal direction; when, at the end of about a dozen paces, our further advance was checked by the interposition of an enormous block of granite rock.

"Accursed stone!" I cried, furiously, on perceiving that we were stopped by what seemed an insurmountable obstacle.

In vain we looked to the right, in vain we looked to the left; in vain examined it above and below. There existed no passage, no sign of any other tunnel. I experienced the most bitter and painful disappointment. So enraged was I that I would not admit the reality of any obstacle. I stooped to my knees; I looked under the mass of stone. No hole, no interstice. I then looked above. The same barrier of granite! Hans, with the lamp, examined the sides of the tunnel in every direction. But all in vain! It was necessary to renounce all hope of passing through.

I had seated myself upon the ground. My uncle walked angrily and hopelessly up and down. He was evidently desperate. "But," I cried, after some moments' thought, "what about Arne Saknussemm?"

"You are right," replied my uncle, "he can never have been checked by a lump of rock."

"No—ten thousand times no," I cried, with extreme vivacity. "This huge lump of rock, in consequence of some concussion, has in some unexpected way closed up

179

the passage. Many and many years have passed away since the return of Saknussemm, and the fall of this huge block of granite. Is it not quite evident that this gallery was formerly the outlet for the pent-up lava in the interior of the earth, and that these eruptive matters then circulated freely? Look at these recent fissures in the granite roof; it is evidently formed of pieces of enormous stone, placed here as if by the hand of a giant, who had worked to make a strong and substantial arch. One day, after an unusually heavy shock, the vast rock which stands in our way, fell through to a level with the soil and has barred our further progress. We are right, then, in thinking that this is an unexpected obstacle, with which Saknussemm did not meet; and if we do not upset it in some way, we are unworthy of following in the footsteps of the great discoverer, and incapable of finding our way to the Center of the Earth!"

In this wild way I addressed my uncle. The zeal of the Professor, his earnest longing for success, had become part and parcel of my being. I wholly forgot the past; I utterly despised the future. Nothing existed for me upon the surface of this spheroid in the bosom of which I was engulfed, no towns, no country, no Hamburg, no Königstrasse, not even my poor Gretchen, who by this time would believe me utterly lost in the interior of the earth!

" Well," cried my uncle, roused to enthusiasm by my words, " let us go to work with pick-axes, with crowbars, with anything that comes to hand—but down with these terrible walls."

" It is far too tough and too big to be destroyed by a pick-ax or crowbar," I replied.

" What then?"

" As I said, it is useless to think of overcoming such a difficulty by means of ordinary tools."

" What then?"

" What else but gunpowder, a subterranean mine? Let us blow up the obstacle that stands in our way."

" Gunpowder!"

" Yes; all we have to do is to get rid of this paltry obstacle."

" To work, Hans, to work!" cried the Professor. The Icelander went back to the raft, and soon returned with a huge crowbar, with which he began to dig a hole in the rock, which was to serve as a mine. It was by no means a slight task. It was necessary for our purpose to make a cavity large enough to hold fifty pounds of fulminating gun cotton, the expansive power of which is four times as great as that of ordinary gunpowder.

I had now roused myself to an almost miraculous state of excitement. While Hans was at work, I actively assisted my uncle to prepare a long wick, made from damp gunpowder, the mass of which we finally enclosed in a bag of linen. " We are bound to go through," I cried enthusiastically.

" We are bound to go through," responded the Professor, tapping me on the back.

At midnight, our work as miners was completely finished; the charge of fulminating cotton was thrust into the hollow, and the match, which we had made of considerable length, was ready. A spark was now sufficient to ignite this formidable engine, and to blow the rock to atoms!

" We will now rest until to-morrow."

It was absolutely necessary to resign myself to my fate, and to consent to wait for the explosion for six weary hours!

CHAPTER XXXIX
THE EXPLOSION AND ITS RESULTS

THE next day, which was the twenty-seventh of August, was a date celebrated in our wondrous, subterranean journey.

I never think of it even now, but I shudder with horror. My heart beats wildly at the very memory of that awful day. From this time forward, our reason, our judgment, our human ingenuity, had nothing to do with the course of events. We were about to become the plaything of the great phenomena of the earth!

At six o'clock we were all up and ready. The dreaded moment was arriving when we were about to seek an opening into the interior of the earth by means of gunpowder. What would be the consequences of breaking through the crust of the earth.

181

I begged that it might be my duty to set fire to the mine. I looked upon it as an honor. This task once performed, I could rejoin my friends upon the raft, which had not been unloaded. As soon as we were all ready, we were to sail away to some distance to avoid the consequences of the explosion, the effects of which would certainly not be concentrated in the interior of the earth. The slow match we calculated to burn for about ten minutes, more or less, before it reached the chamber in which the great body of powder was confined. I should therefore have plenty of time to reach the raft and put off to a safe distance.

After a hearty repast, my uncle and the hunter-guide embarked on board the raft, while I remained alone upon the desolate shore. I was provided with a lantern which was to enable me to set fire to the wick of the infernal machine. " Go, my boy," said my uncle, " and Heaven be with you. But come back as soon as you can. I shall be all impatience."

" Be easy on that matter," I replied, " there is no fear of my delaying on the road." Having said this, I advanced toward the opening of the somber gallery. My heart beat wildly. I opened my lantern and seized the extremity of the wick.

The Professor, who was looking on, held his chronometer in his hand. " Are you ready?" cried he.

" Quite ready."

" Well, then, fire away!" I hastened to put the light to the wick, which crackled and sparkled, hissing and spitting like a serpent; then, running as fast as I could, I returned to the shore.

" Get on board my lad, and you, Hans, shove off!" cried my uncle. By a vigorous application of his pole Hans sent us flying over the water. The raft was quite twenty fathoms distant.

It was a moment of palpitating interest, of deep anxiety. My uncle, the Professor, never took his eyes off the chronometer. " Only five minutes more," he said in a low tone, " only four, only three."

My pulse went a hundred to the minute. I could hear my heart beating.

"Only two, one! Now, then, mountains of granite, crumble beneath the power of man!"

THE EXPLOSION AND ITS RESULTS

What happened after that? As to the terrific roar of the explosion, I do not think I heard it. But the form of the rocks completely changed in my eyes—they seemed to be drawn aside like a curtain. I saw a fathomless, a bottomless abyss, which yawned beneath the turgid waves. The sea, which seemed suddenly to have gone mad, then became one great mountainous mass, upon the top of which the raft rose perpendicularly.

We were all thrown down. The light gave place to the most profound obscurity. Then I felt all solid support give way not to my feet, but to the raft itself. I thought it was going bodily down a tremendous well. I tried to speak, to question my uncle. Nothing could be heard but the roaring of the mighty waves. We clung together in utter silence.

Despite the awful darkness, despite the noise, the surprise, the emotion, I thoroughly understood what had happened. Beyond the rock which had been blown up, there existed a mighty abyss. The explosion had caused a kind of earthquake in this soil, broken by fissures and rents. The gulf, thus suddenly thrown open, was about to swallow the inland sea, which, transformed into a mighty torrent, was dragging us with it. One only idea filled my mind. We were utterly and completely lost!

One hour, two hours—what more I cannot say, passed in this manner. We sat close together, elbow touching elbow, knee touching knee! We held one another's hands not to be thrown off the raft. We were subjected to the most violent shocks, whenever our sole dependence, a frail wooden raft, struck against the rocky sides of the channel. Fortunately for us, these concussions became less and less frequent, which made me fancy that the gallery was getting wider and wider. There could be now no doubt that we had chanced upon the road once followed by Saknussemm, but instead of going down in a proper manner, we had, through our own imprudence, drawn a whole sea with us!

These ideas presented themselves to my mind in a very vague and obscure manner. I felt rather than reasoned. I put my ideas together only confusedly, while spinning along like a man going down a waterfall. To judge by the air which, as it were, whipped my face, we must have been rushing at a perfectly lightning rate.

To attempt under these circumstances to light a torch was simply impossible, and the last remains of our electric machine, of our Ruhmkorf's coil, had been destroyed during the fearful explosion. I was therefore very much confused to see at last a bright light shining close to me. The calm countenance of the guide seemed to gleam upon me. The clever and patient hunter had succeeded in lighting the lantern; and though, in the keen and thorough draught, the flame flickered and vacillated and was very nearly put out, it served partially to dissipate the awful obscurity.

The gallery into which we had entered was very wide. I was, therefore, quite right in that part of my conjecture. The insufficient light did not allow us to see both of the walls at the same time. The slope of waters, which was carrying us away, was far greater than that of the most rapid river. The whole surface of the stream seemed to be composed of liquid arrows, darted forward with extreme violence and power. I can give no idea of the impression it made upon me.

The raft, at times, caught in certain whirlpools, and rushed forward, yet turned on itself all the time. How it did not upset I shall never be able to understand. When it approached the sides of the gallery, I took care to throw upon them the light of the lantern, and I was able to judge of the rapidity of motion by looking at the projecting masses of rock, which as soon as seen were again invisible. I believe we were going at a rate of not less than a hundred miles an hour.

My uncle and I looked at one another with wild and haggard eyes; we clung convulsively to the stump of the mast, which, at the moment when the catastrophe took place, had snapped short off. We turned our backs as much as possible to the wind, in order not to be stifled by a rapidity of motion which nothing human could face and live.

And still the long monotonous hours went on. The situation did not change in the least, though a discovery I suddenly made seemed to complicate it very much. When we had slightly recovered our equilibrium, I proceeded to examine our cargo. I then made the unsatisfactory discovery that the greater part of it had utterly disappeared. I became alarmed, and determined to discover what were our resources. My heart beat at the idea, but it was absolutely necessary to know on what we had to depend. With this in view, I took the lantern and looked around.

Of all our former collection of nautical and philosophical instruments there remained only the chronometer and the compass. The ladders and ropes were reduced to a small piece of rope fastened to the stump of the mast. Not a pickax, not a crowbar, not a hammer, and, far worse than all, no food—not enough for one day!

This discovery was a prelude to a certain and horrible death. Seated gloomily on the raft, clasping the stump of the mast mechanically, I thought of all I had read as to sufferings from starvation. I remembered everything that history had taught me on the subject, and I shuddered at the remembrance of the agonies to be endured. Maddened at the prospect, I persuaded myself that I must be mistaken. I examined the cracks in the raft; I poked between the joints and beams; I examined every possible hole and corner. The result was—simply nothing! Our stock of provisions consisted of nothing but a piece of dry meat and some soaked and half-mouldy biscuits.

I gazed around me scared and frightened. I could not understand the awful truth. And yet of what consequence was it in regard to any new danger? Supposing that we had had provisions for months, and even for years, how could we ever get out of the awful abyss into which we were being hurled by the irresistible torrent we had let loose? Why should we trouble ourselves about the sufferings and tortures to be endured from hunger, when death stared us in the face under so many other swifter and perhaps even more horrid forms?

I had the greatest mind to reveal all to my uncle, to explain to him the extraordinary and wretched position to which we were reduced, in order that, between the two, we might make a calculation as to the exact space of time which remained for us to live. It was, it appeared to me, the only thing to be done. But I had the courage to hold my tongue, to gnaw at my entrails like the Spartan boy. I wished to leave him all his coolness.

At this moment, the light of the lantern slowly fell, and at last went out! The wick had wholly burnt to an end. The obscurity became absolute. It was no longer possible to see through the impenetrable darkness! There was one torch left, but it was impossible to keep it alight. Then, like a child, I shut my eyes, that I might not see the darkness.

After a great lapse of time, the rapidity of our journey increased. I could feel it by the rush of air upon my face. The slope of the waters was excessive. I began to feel that we were no longer going down a slope; we were falling. I felt as one does in a dream, going down bodily— falling; falling; falling!

I felt that the hands of my uncle and Hans were vigorously clasping my arms. Suddenly, after a lapse of time scarcely appreciable, I felt something like a shock. The raft had not struck a hard body, but had suddenly been checked in its course. A waterspout, a liquid column of water, fell upon us. I felt suffocating. I was being drowned. Still the sudden inundation did not last. In a few seconds I felt myself once more able to breathe. My uncle and Hans pressed my arms, and the raft carried us all three away.

CHAPTER XL
THE APE GIGANS

It is difficult for me to determine what was the real time, but I should suppose, by after calculation, that it must have been ten at night.

I lay in a stupor, a half dream, during which I saw visions of astounding character. Monsters of the deep were side by side with the mighty elephantine shepherd. Gigantic fish and animals formed strange conjunctions. It seemed in my vision that the raft took a sudden turn, whirled round; entered another tunnel; this time illumined in a most singular manner. The roof was formed of porous stalactite, through which a moon-lit vapor appeared to pass, casting its brilliant light upon our gaunt and haggard figures. The light increased as we advanced, while the roof ascended; until at last, we were once more in a kind of water cavern, the lofty dome of which disappeared in a luminous cloud! My uncle and the guide moved as men in a dream. I was afraid to waken them, knowing the danger of such a sudden start. I seated myself beside them to watch.

As I did so, I became aware of something moving in the distance, which at once fascinated my eyes. It was floating, apparently, upon the surface of the water, advancing by means of what at first appeared paddles. I looked with glaring eyes. One glance told me that it was something monstrous.

But what? It was the great *Shark Crocodile* of the early writers on geology. About the size of an ordinary whale, with hideous jaws and two gigantic eyes, it advanced. Its eyes fixed on me with terrible sternness. Some indefinite warning told me that it had marked me for its own.

I attempted to rise—to escape, no matter where, but my knees shook under me; my limbs trembled violently; I almost lost my senses. And still the mighty monster advanced. My uncle and the guide made no effort to save themselves. With a strange noise, like none other I had ever heard, the beast came on. His jaws were at least seven feet apart, and his distended mouth looked large enough to have swallowed a boatful of men.

We were about ten feet distant, when I discovered that much as his body resembled that of a crocodile, his mouth was wholly that of a shark. His twofold nature now became apparent. To snatch us up at a mouthful it was necessary for him to turn on his back, which motion necessarily caused his legs to kick up helplessly in the air. I actually laughed even in the very jaws of death!

But next minute, with a wild cry, I darted away into the interior of the cavern, leaving my unhappy comrades to their fate! This cavern was deep and dreary. After about a hundred yards, I paused and looked around. The whole floor, composed of sand and malachite, was strewn with bones, freshly-gnawed bones of reptiles and fish, with a mixture of mammalia. My very soul grew sick as my body shuddered with horror. I had truly, according to the old proverb, fallen out of the frying-pan into the fire. Some beast larger and more ferocious even than the Shark-Crocodile inhabited this den.

What could I do? The mouth of the cave was guarded by one ferocious monster, the interior was inhabited by something too hideous to contemplate. Flight was impossible! Suddenly a groaning, as of fifty bears in a fight, fell upon my ears—hisses, spitting, moaning, hideous to hear—and then I saw—

Never, were ages to pass over my head, shall I forget the horrible apparition. It was the Ape Gigans, the antediluvian Gorilla! Fourteen feet high, covered with coarse hair, of a blackish brown, it advanced. Its arms were as long as its body, while its legs were prodigious. It had thick, long, and sharply-pointed teeth—like a mammoth saw. It struck its breast as it came on smelling and sniffing, reminding me of the stories we read in our early childhood of giants who ate the flesh of men and little boys!

Suddenly it stopped. My heart beat wildly, for I was conscious that, somehow or other, the fearful monster had smelt me out and was peering about with his hideous eyes to try and discover my whereabouts. I gave myself up for lost. No hope of safety or escape seemed to remain.

At this moment, just as my eyes appeared to close in death, there came a strange noise from the entrance of the cave; and turning, the Gorilla evidently recognized some enemy more worthy his prodigious size and strength. It was the huge Shark-Crocodile, which perhaps having disposed of my friends, was coming in search of further prey.

The Gorilla placed himself on the defensive, and clutching a bone some seven or eight feet in length, a perfect club, aimed a deadly blow at the hideous beast, which reared upwards and fell with all its weight upon its adversary. A terrible combat ensued. The struggle was awful and ferocious. I, however, did not wait to witness the result. Regarding myself as the object of contention, I determined to remove from the presence of the victor. I slid down from my hiding-place, reached the ground, and gliding against the wall, strove to gain the open mouth of the cavern. But I had not taken many steps when the fearful clamor ceased, to be followed by a mumbling and groaning which appeared to be indicative of victory.

I looked back and saw the huge ape, gory with blood, coming after me with glaring eyes, with dilated nostrils · that gave forth two columns of heated vapor. I could feel his hot and fetid breath on my neck; and with a horrid jump—awoke from my nightmare sleep.

Yes—it was all a dream. I was still on the raft with my uncle and the guide.

The relief was not instantaneous, for under the influence of the hideous nightmare my senses had become numbed. After a while, however, my feelings were tranquilized. The first of my perceptions which returned in full force was that of hearing. I listened with acute and attentive ears. All was still as death. All I comprehended was silence. To the roaring of the waters, which had filled the gallery with awful reverberations, succeeded perfect peace.

After some little time my uncle spoke, in a low and scarcely audible tone—" Harry, boy, where are you? "

" I am here," was my faint rejoinder.

" Well, don't you see what has happened? We are going upwards."

" My dear uncle, what can you mean? " was my half delirious reply.

" Yes, I tell you we are ascending rapidly. Our downward journey is quite checked."

I held out my hand, and, after some little difficulty, succeeded in touching the wall. My hand was in an instant covered with blood. The skin was torn from the flesh. We were ascending with extraordinary rapidity.

" The torch—the torch! " cried the Professor, wildly; " it must be lighted." Hans, the guide, after many vain efforts, at last succeeded in lighting it, and the flame, having now nothing to prevent its burning, shed a tolerably clear light. We were enabled to form an approximate idea of the truth.

" It is just as I thought," said my uncle, after a moment or two of silent attention. " We are in a narrow well about four fathoms square. The waters of the great inland sea, having reached the bottom of the gulf, are now forcing themselves up the mighty shaft. As a natural consequence, we are being cast up on the summit of the waters."

" That I can see," was my lugubrious reply; " but where will this shaft end, and to what fall are we likely to be exposed? "

" Of that I am as ignorant as yourself. All I know is, that we should be prepared for the worst. We are going up at a fearfully rapid rate. As far as I can judge, we are ascending at the rate of two fathoms a second, of a hundred and twenty fathoms a minute, or rather more than three and a half leagues an hour. At this rate, our fate will soon be a matter of certainty."

"No doubt of it," was my reply. "The great concern I have now, however, is to know whether this shaft has any issue. It may end in a granite roof—in which case we shall be suffocated by compressed air, or dashed to atoms against the top. I fancy, already, that the air is beginning to be close and condensed. I have a difficulty in breathing." This might be fancy, or it might be the effect of our rapid motion, but I certainly felt a great oppression of the chest.

"Henry," said the Professor, "I do believe that the situation is to a certain extent desperate. There remain, however, many chances of ultimate safety, and I have, in my own mind, been revolving them over, during your heavy but agitated sleep. I have come to this logical conclusion—whereas we may at any moment perish, so at any moment we may be saved! We need, therefore, to prepare ourselves for whatever may turn up in the great chapter of accidents."

"But what would you have us do?" I cried; "are we not utterly helpless?"

"No! While there is life there is hope. At all events, there is one thing we can do—eat, and thus obtain strength to face victory or death."

As he spoke, I looked at my uncle with a haggard glance. I had put off the fatal communication as long as possible. It was now forced upon me, and I must tell him the truth. Still I hesitated. "Eat," I said, in a deprecating tone as if there were no hurry.

"Yes, and at once. I feel like a starving prisoner," he said, rubbing his yellow and shivering hands together. And, turning round to the guide, he spoke some hearty, cheering words, as I judged from his tone, in Danish. Hans shook his head in a terribly significant manner. I tried to look unconcerned.

"What!" cried the Professor, "you do not mean to say that all our provisions are lost?"

"Yes," was my lowly spoken reply, as I held out something in my hand, "this morsel of dried meat is all that remains for us three."

My uncle gazed at me as if he could not fully appreciate the meaning of my words. The blow seemed to stun him by its severity. I allowed him to reflect for some moments.

"Well," said I, after a short pause, "what do you think now? Is there any chance of our escaping from our horrible subterranean dangers? Are we not doomed to perish in the great hollows of the Center of the Earth?"

But my pertinent questions brought no answer. My uncle either heard me not, or appeared not to do so. And in this way a whole hour passed. Neither of us cared to speak. For myself, I began to feel the most fearful and devouring hunger. My companions, doubtless, felt the same horrible tortures, but neither of them would touch the wretched morsel of meat that remained. It lay there a last remnant of all our great preparations for the mad and senseless journey!

I looked back, with wonderment, to my own folly. Fully was I aware that, despite his enthusiasm, and the ever-to-be-hated scroll of Saknussemm, my uncle should never have started on his perilous voyage. What memories of the happy past, what previsions of the horrible future, now filled my brain!

CHAPTER XLI
HUNGER

HUNGER, prolonged, is temporary madness! The brain is at work without its required food, and the most fantastic notions fill the mind. Hitherto I had never known what hunger realy meant. I was likely to understand it now only too well.

After dreaming for some time, and thinking of this and other matters, I once more looked around me. We were still ascending with fearful rapidity. Every now and then the air appeared to check our respiration as it does that of aëronauts when the ascension of the balloon is too rapid. But if they feel a degree of cold in proportion to the elevation they attain in the atmosphere, we experienced quite a contrary effect. The heat began to increase in a most threatening and exceptional manner. I cannot tell exactly the mean, but I think it must have reached 122 degrees of Fahrenheit.

What was the meaning of this extraordinary change in the temperature? As far as we had hitherto gone, facts had proved the theories of Davy and of Lidenbrock to be correct. Until now, all the peculiar conditions of refractory rocks, of electricity of magnetism, had modified the general laws of nature, and had created for us a moderate temperature; for the theory of the central fire, remained, in my eyes, the only explainable one.

Were we, then, going to reach a position in which these phenomena were to be carried out in all their rigor, and in which the heat would reduce the rocks to a state of fusion? Such was my not unnatural fear, and I did not conceal the fact from my uncle. My way of doing so might be cold and heartless, but I could not help it. "If we are not drowned, or smashed into pancakes, and if we do not die of starvation, we have the satisfaction of knowing that we must be burned alive."

My uncle, in presence of this brusque attack, simply shrugged his shoulders, and resumed his reflections—whatever they might be.

An hour passed away, and except that there was a slight increase in the temperature no incident modified the situation. My uncle at last, of his own accord, broke silence. "Well, Henry, my boy," he said, in a cheerful way, "we must make up our minds."

"Make up our minds to what?" I asked, in considerable surprise.

"Well—to something. We must at whatever risk recruit our physical strength. If we make the fatal mistake of husbanding our little remnant of food, we may probably prolong our wretched existence a few hours—but we shall remain weak to the end."

"Yes," I growled, "to the end. That, however, will not keep us long waiting."

"Well, only let a chance of safety present itself,—only allow that a moment of action be necessary,—where shall we find the means of action if we allow ourselves to be reduced to physical weakness by inanition?"

"When this piece of meat is devoured, uncle, what hope will there remain unto us?"

"None, my dear Henry, none. But will it do you any good to devour it with your eyes? You appear to me to reason like one without will or decision, like a being without energy."

"Then," cried I, exasperated to a degree which is scarcely to be explained, "you do not mean to tell me—that you—that you—have not lost all hope."

"Certainly not," replied the Professor, with consummate coolness.

"You mean to tell me, uncle, that we shall get out of this monstrous subterranean shaft?"

"While there is life there is hope. I beg to assert, Henry, that as long as a man's heart beats, as long as a man's flesh quivers, I do not allow that a being gifted with thought and will can allow himself to despair."

What a resolution! The man placed in a position like that we occupied must have been very brave to speak like this. "Well," I cried, "what do you mean to do?"

"Eat what remains of the food we have in our hands; let us swallow the last crumb. It will be, heaven willing, our last repast. Well, never mind—instead of being exhausted skeletons, we shall be men."

"True," muttered I in a despairing tone, "let us take our fill."

"We must," replied my uncle, with a deep sigh—"call it what you will." My uncle took a piece of the meat that remained, and some crusts of biscuit which had escaped the wreck. He divided the whole into three parts. Each had one pound of food to last him as long as he remained in the interior of the earth.

Each now acted in accordance with his own private character. My uncle, the Professor, ate greedily, but evidently without appetite, eating simply from some mechanical motion. I put the food inside my lips, and hungry as I was, chewed my morsel without pleasure, and without satisfaction. Hans the guide, just as if he had been eider-down hunting, swallowed every mouthful, as though it were a usual affair. He looked like a man equally prepared to enjoy superfluity or total want. Hans, in all probability, was no more used to starvation than ourselves, but his hardy

Icelandic nature had prepared him for many sufferings. As long as he received his three rix-dollars every Saturday night, he was prepared for anything. The fact was, Hans never troubled himself about much except his money. He had undertaken to serve a certain man at so much per week, and no matter what evils befell his employer or himself, he never found fault or grumbled, so long as his wages were duly paid.

Suddenly my uncle roused himself. He had seen a smile on the face of our guide. I could not make it out. " What is the matter? " said my uncle.

" Schiedam," said the guide, producing a bottle of this precious fluid.

We drank. My uncle and myself will own to our dying day that hence we derived strength to exist until the last bitter moment. That precious bottle of Hollands was in reality only half-full; but, under the circumstances, it was nectar. The worthy Professor swallowed about half a pint and did not seem able to drink any more. " *Fortrafflig*," said Hans, swallowing nearly all that was left.

" Excellent—very good," said my uncle, with as much gusto as if he had just left the steps of the club at Hamburg.

I had begun to feel as if there had been one gleam of hope. Now all thought of the future vanished! We had consumed our last ounce of food, and it was five o'clock in the morning!

CHAPTER XLII
THE VOLCANIC SHAFT

MAN'S constitution is so peculiar, that his health is purely a negative matter. No sooner is the rage of hunger appeased, than it becomes difficult to comprehend the meaning of starvation. It is only when you suffer that you really understand. As to anyone who has not endured privation having any notion of the matter, it is simply absurd. With us, after a long fast, some mouthfuls of bread and meat, a little mouldy biscuit and salt beef triumphed over all our previous saturnine thoughts.

Nevertheless, after this repast each gave way to his own

reflections. I wondered what were those of Hans—the man of the extreme north, who was yet gifted with the fatalistic resignation of Oriental character. But the utmost stretch of the imagination would not allow me to realize the truth. As for my individual self, my thoughts had ceased to be anything but memories of the past, and were all connected with that upper world which I never should have left. I saw it all now, the beautiful house in the Königstrasse, my poor Gretchen, the good Martha; they all passed before my mind like visions of the past. Every time any of the lugubrious groanings which were to be distinguished in the hollows around fell upon my ears, I fancied I heard the distant murmur of the great cities above my head.

As for my uncle, always thinking of his science, he examined the nature of the shaft by means of a torch. He closely examined the different strata one above the other, in order to recognize his situation by geological theory. This calculation, or rather this estimation, could by no means be anything but approximate. •But a learned man, a philosopher, is nothing if not a philosopher, when he keeps his ideas calm and collected; and certainly the Professor possessed this quality to perfection.

I heard him, as I sat in silence, murmuring words of geological science. As I understood his object and his meaning, I could not but interest myself despite my preoccupation in that terrible hour. "Eruptive granite," he said to himself, "we are still in the primitive epoch. But we are going up—going up, still going up. But who knows? Who knows?"

Then he still hoped. He felt along the vertical sides of the shaft with his hand, and some few minutes later, he would go on again in the following style—"This is gniess. This is mocashites—silicious mineral. Good again; this is the epoch of transition, at all events, we are close to them —and then, and then——"

What could the Professer mean? Could he, by any conceivable means, measure the thickness of the crust of the earth suspended above our heads? Did he possess any possible means of making any approximation to this calculation? No. The manometer was wanting, and no summary estimation could take the place of it.

TO THE CENTRE OF THE EARTH

As we progressed, the temperature increased in the most extraordinary degree, and I began to feel as if I were bathed in a hot and burning atmosphere. Never before had I felt anything like it. I could only compare it to the hot vapor from an iron foundry, when the liquid iron is in a state of ebullition and runs over. By degrees, and one after the other, Hans, my uncle, and myself had taken off our coats and waistcoats. They were unbearable. Even the slightest garment was the cause of extreme suffering.

"Are we ascending to a living fire?" I cried; when, to my horror and astonishment, the heat became greater than before.

"No, no," said my uncle, "it is simply impossible, quite impossible."

"And yet," said I, touching the side of the shaft with my naked hand, "this wall is literally burning."

At this moment, feeling as I did that the sides of this extraordinary wall were red hot, I plunged my hands into the water to cool them. I drew them back with a cry of despair. "The water is boiling!" I cried.

My uncle, the Professor, made no reply other than a gesture of rage and despair. Something very like the truth had probably struck his imagination.

An invincible dread took possession of my brain and soul. I could only look forward to an immediate catastrophe, such a catastrophe as not even the most vivid imagination could have thought of. An idea, at first vague and uncertain, was gradually being changed into certainty. It was so terrible an idea that I scarcely dared to whisper it to myself. Yet all the while certain, and as it were, involuntary observations determined my convictions. By the doubtful glare of the torch, I could make out some singular changes in the granitic strata; a strange and terrible phenomenon was about to be produced, in which electricity played a part. Then this boiling water, this terrible and excessive heat? I determined as a last resource to examine the compass.

The compass had gone mad! Yes, wholly stark, staring mad. The needle jumped from pole to pole with sudden and surprising jerks, ran round, or as it is said, boxed the compass, and then ran suddenly back again as if it had the vertigo.

196

THE VOLCANIC SHAFT

Terrible detonations, like heaven's artillery, began to multiply themselves with fearful intensity. I could only compare them with the noise made by hundreds of heavily-laden chariots being madly driven over a stone pavement. It was a continuous roll of heavy thunder.

And then the mad compass, shaken by the wild electric phenomena, confirmed me in my rapidly-formed opinion. The mineral crust was about to burst, the heavy granite masses were about to rejoin, the fissure was about to close, the void was about to be filled up, and we poor atoms to be crushed in its awful embrace! "Uncle, uncle!" I cried, "we are wholly, irretrievably lost!"

"What, then my young friend, is your new cause of terror and alarm?" he said, in his calmest manner. "What fear you now?"

"What do I fear now!" I cried, in fierce and angry tones. "Do you not see that the walls of the shaft are in motion? do you not see that the solid granite masses are cracking? do you not feel the terrible, torrid heat? do you not observe the awful boiling water on which we float? do you not remark this mad needle? every sign and portent of an awful earthquake?"

My uncle coolly shook his head. "An earthquake?" he questioned in the most calm and provoking tone.

"Yes."

"My nephew, I tell you that you are utterly mistaken," he continued.

"Do you not, can you not, recognize all the well-known symptoms——"

"Of an earthquake? by no means. I am expecting something far more important."

"My brain is strained beyond endurance—what, what do you mean?" I cried.

"An eruption, Harry."

"An eruption," I gasped. "We are, then, in the volcanic shaft of a crater in full action and vigor."

"I have every reason to think so," said the Professor in a smiling tone, "and I beg to tell you that it is the most fortunate thing that could happen to us."

The most fortunate thing! Had my uncle really and truly gone mad? What did he mean by these awful words —what did he mean by this terrible calm, this solemn smile?

"What!" cried I, in the height of my exasperation, "we are on the way to an eruption, are we? Fatality has cast us into a well of burning and boiling lava, of rocks on fire, of boiling water, in a word, filled with every kind of eruptive matter? We are about to be expelled, thrown up, vomited, spit out of the interior of the earth, in common with huge blocks of granite, with showers of cinders and scoriæ, in a wild whirlwind of flame, and you say—the most fortunate thing which could happen to us."

"Yes," replied the Professor, looking at me calmly from under his spectacles, "it is the only chance which remains to us of ever escaping from the interior of the earth to the light of day."

It is quite impossible that I can put on paper the thousand strange, wild thoughts which followed this extraordinary announcement. But my uncle was right, quite right, and never had he appeared to me so audacious and so convinced as when he looked me calmly in the face and spoke of the chances of an eruption—of our being cast upon mother earth once more through the gaping crater of a volcano!

While we were speaking we were still ascending; we passed the whole night going up, or to speak more scientifically, in an ascensional motion. The fearful noise redoubled; I was ready to suffocate. I seriously believed that my last hour was approaching, and yet, so strange is imagination, all I thought of was some childish hypothesis or other. In such circumstances you do not choose your own thoughts. They overcome you.

It was quite evident that we were being cast upwards by eruptive matter; under the raft there was a mass of boiling water, and under this was a heaving mass of lava, and an aggregate of rocks which on reaching the summit of the water would be dispersed in every direction. That we were inside the chimney of a volcano there could no longer be the shadow of a doubt. Nothing more terrible could be conceived!

But on this occasion, instead of Sneffels, an old and extinct volcano, we were inside a mountain of fire in full activity. Several times I found myself asking, what mountain was it, and on what part of the world we should be shot out. As if it were of any consequence! In the northern regions, there could be no reasonable doubt about that. Before it went decidedly mad, the compass had never made the slightest mistake. From the cape of Saknussemm, we had been swept away to the northward many hundreds of leagues. Now the question was, were we once more under Iceland—should we be belched forth on to the earth through the crater of Mount Hecla, or should we reappear through one of the other seven fire-funnels of the island? Taking in my mental vision a radius of five hundred leagues to the westward, I could see under this parallel only the little-known volcanoes of the northwest coasts of America. ⹁ To the east one only existed somewhere about the eightieth degree of latitude, the Esk, upon the island of Jean Mayen, not far from the frozen regions of Spitzbergen. It was not craters that were wanting, and many of them were big enough to vomit a whole army; all I wished to know was the particular one towards which we were making with such fearful velocity. I often think now of my folly; as if I should have expected to escape!

Towards morning, the ascending motion became greater and greater. If the degree of heat increased instead of decreasing, as we approached the surface of the earth, it was simply because the causes were local and wholly due to volcanic influence. Our very style of locomotion left in my mind no doubt upon the subject. An enormous force, a force of some hundred of combined atmospheres produced by vapors accumulated and long compressed in the interior of the earth, were hoisting us upwards with irresistible power.

But though we were approaching the light of day, to what fearful dangers were we about to be exposed? Instant death appeared the only fate which we could expect or contemplate.

Soon a dim, sepulchral light penetrated the vertical gallery, which became wider and wider. I could make out to the right and left long dark corridors like immense tunnels, from which awful and horrid vapors poured out. Tongues of fire, sparkling and crackling, appeared about to lick us up. The hour had come!

"Look, uncle, look!" I cried.

"Well, what you see are the great sulphurous flames. Nothing more common in connection with an eruption."

" But if they lap us round! " I angrily replied.

" They will not lap us round," was his quiet and serene answer.

" But it will be all the same in the end if they stifle us," I cried.

" We shall not be stifled. The gallery is rapidly becoming wider and wider, and if it be necessary, we will presently leave the raft and take refuge in some fissure in the rock."

" But the water, the water, which is continually ascending? " I despairingly replied.

" There is no longer any water, Harry," he answered, " but a kind of lava paste, which is heaving us up, in company with itself, to the mouth of the crater."

In truth, the liquid column of water had wholly disappeared to give place to dense masses of boiling eruptive matter. The temperature was becoming utterly insupportable, and a thermometer exposed to this atmosphere would have marked between 189 and 190 degrees Fahrenheit. Perspiration rushed from every pore. But for the extraordinary rapidity of our ascent we should have been stifled.

Nevertheless, the Professor did not carry out his proposition of abandoning the raft; and he did quite wisely. Those few ill-joined beams offered, any way, a solid surface—a support which elsewhere must have utterly failed us.

Towards eight o'clock in the morning a new incident startled us. The ascensional movement suddenly ceased. The raft became still and motionless. " What is the matter now? " I said, querulously, very much startled by this change.

" A simple halt," replied my uncle.

" Is the eruption about to fail? " I asked.

" I hope not."

Without making any reply, I rose. I tried to look around me. Perhaps the raft, checked by some projecting rock, opposed a momentary resistance to the eruptive mass. In this case, it was absolutely necessary to release it as quickly as possible.

Nothing of the kind had occurred. The column of cinders, of scoriæ, of broken rocks and earth, had wholly ceased to ascend. "I tell you, uncle, that the eruption has stopped," was my oracular decision.

"Ah," said my uncle, "you think so, my boy. You are wrong. Do not be in the least alarmed; this sudden moment of calm will not last long, be assured. It has already endured five minutes, and before we are many minutes older we shall be continuing our journey to the mouth of the crater."

All the time he was speaking the Professor continued to consult his chronometer, and he was probably right in his prognostics. Soon the raft resumed its motion, in a very rapid and disorderly way, which lasted two minutes or thereabout; and then again it stopped as suddenly as before. "Good," said my uncle, observing the hour, "in ten minutes we shall start again."

"In ten minutes?"

"Yes—precisely. We have to do with a volcano, the eruption of which is intermittent. We are compelled to breathe just as it does."

Nothing could be more true. At the exact minute he had indicated, we were again launched on high with extreme rapidity. Not to be cast off the raft, it was necessary to hold on to the beams. Then the hoist again ceased. Many times since have I thought of this singular phenomenon without being able to find for it any satisfactory explanation. Nevertheless, it appeared quite clear to me, that we were not in the principal chimney of the volcano, but in an accessory conduit, where we felt the counter shock of the great and principal tunnel filled by burning lava.

It is impossible for me to say how many times this maneuver was repeated. All that I can remember is, that on every ascensional motion, we were hoisted up with ever-increasing velocity, as if we had been launched from a huge projectile. During the sudden halts we were nearly stifled; during the moments of projection the hot air took away our breath.

I thought for a moment of the voluptuous joy of suddenly finding myself in the hyperborean regions with the cold 30 degrees below zero! My exalted imagination pictured to itself the vast snowy plains of the arctic regions, and I was impatient to roll myself on the icy carpet of the north pole. By degrees my head, utterly overcome by a series of violent emotions, began to give way to hallucination. I was delirious. Had it not been for the powerful arms of Hans the guide, I should have broken my head against the granite masses of the shaft.

I have, in consequence, kept no account of what followed for many hours. I have a vague and confused remembrance of continual detonations, of the shaking of the huge granitic mass, and of the raft going round like a spinning top. It floated on the stream of hot lava, amidst a falling cloud of cinders. The huge flames roaring, wrapped us around.

A storm of wind which appeared to be cast forth from an immense ventilator roused up the interior fires of the earth. It was a hot incandescent blast!

At last I saw the figure of Hans as if enveloped in the huge halo of burning blaze, and no other sense remained to me but that sinister dread which the condemned victim may be supposed to feel when led to the mouth of a cannon, at the supreme moment when the shot is fired and his limbs are dispersed into empty space.

CHAPTER XLIII
DAYLIGHT AT LAST

When I opened my eyes I felt the hand of the guide clutching me firmly by the belt. With his other hand he supported my uncle. I was not grievously wounded, but bruised all over in the most remarkable manner. After a moment I looked around, and found that I was lying down on the slope of a mountain not two yards from a yawning gulf into which I should have fallen had I made the slightest false step. Hans had saved me from death, while I rolled insensible on the flanks of the crater.

" Where are we? " dreamily asked my uncle, who literally appeared to be disgusted at having returned to earth. The eider-down hunter simply shrugged his shoulders as a mark of total ignorance.

" In Iceland? " I replied, not positively but interrogatively.

"*Nej,*" said Hans.

" How do you mean? " cried the Professor; " no—what are your reasons? "

" Hans is wrong," said I, rising.

After all the innumerable surprises of this journey, a yet more singular one was reserved to us. I expected to see a cone covered by snow, by extensive and wide-spread glaciers, in the midst of the arid deserts of the extreme northern regions, beneath the full rays of a polar sky, beyond the highest latitudes. But contrary to all our expectations, I, my uncle, and the Icelander, were cast upon the slope of a mountain calcined by the burning rays of a sun which was literally baking us with its fires. I could not believe my eyes, but the actual heat which affected my body allowed me no chance of doubting. We came out of the crater half naked, and the radiant star from which we had asked nothing for two months, was good enough to be prodigal to us of light and warmth—a light and warmth we could easily have dispensed with.

When our eyes were accustomed to the light we had lost sight of so long, I used them to rectify the errors of my imagination. Whatever happened, we should have been at Spitzbergen, and I was in no humor to yield to anything but the most absolute proof.

After some delay, the Professor spoke. " Hem! " he said, in a hesitating kind of way, " it really does not look like Iceland."

" But supposing it were the island of Jean Mayen? " I ventured to observe.

" Not in the least, my boy. This is not one of the volcanoes of the north, with its hills of granite and its crown of snow."

" Nevertheless——"

" Look, look, my boy," said the Professor, as dogmatically as usual. Right above our heads, at a great height, opened the crater of a volcano from which escaped, from one quarter of an hour to the other, with a very loud explosion, a lofty jet of flame mingled with pumice stone, cinders, and lava. I could feel the convulsions of nature in the mountain, which breathed like a huge whale, throwing up from time to time fire and air through its enormous vents.

Below, and floating along a slope of considerable angularity, the stream of eruptive matter spread away to a depth which did not give the volcano a height of three hundred fathoms. Its base disappeared in a perfect forest of green trees, among which I perceived olives, fig trees, and vines loaded with rich grapes. Certainly this was not the ordinary aspect of the Arctic regions. About that there could not be the slightest doubt.

When the eye was satisfied at its glimpse of this verdant expanse it fell upon the waters of a lovely sea or beautiful lake, which made of this enchanted land an island of not many leagues in extent. Towards the setting sun, some distant shores were to be made out on the edge of the horizon. In one place appeared a prodigiously lofty cone, above the summit of which hung dark and heavy clouds.

"Where can we be?" I asked, speaking in a low and solemn voice.

Hans shut his eyes with an air of indifference, and my uncle looked on without clearly understanding. "Whatever this mountain may be," he said, at last, "I must confess it is rather warm. The explosions do not leave off, and I do not think it is worth while to have left the interior of a volcano and remain here to receive a huge piece of rock upon one's head. Let us carefully descend the mountain and discover the real state of the case. To confess the truth, I am dying of hunger and thirst."

Decidedly the Professor had ceased to be a truly reflective character. For myself, forgetting all my necessities, ignoring my fatigues and sufferings, I should have remained still for several hours longer—but it was necessary to follow my companions.

The slope of the volcano was very steep and slippery; we slid over piles of ashes, avoiding the streams of hot lava which glided about like fiery serpents. Still, while we were advancing, I spoke with extreme volubility, for my imagination was too full not to explode in words. "We are in Asia!" I exclaimed; "we are on the coast of India, in the great Malay islands, in the center of Oceana. We have crossed the one half of the globe to come out right at the antipodes of Europe!"

"But the compass!" exclaimed my uncle; "explain that to me!"

"Yes—the compass," I said, with considerable hesitation. "I grant that is a difficulty. According to it, we have always been going northward."

"Then it lied."

"Hem—to say it lied is rather a harsh word," was my answer.

"Then we are at the north pole——"

"The pole—no—well—well, I give it up," was my reply. The plain truth was, that there was no explanation possible. I could make nothing of it.

All the while we were approaching this beautiful verdure, hunger and thirst tormented me fearfully. Happily, after two long hours' march, a beautiful country spread out before us, covered by olives, pomegranates, and vines, which appeared to belong to anybody and everybody. In the state of destitution into which we had fallen, we were not particular to a grape.

What delight it was to press these delicious fruits to our lips, and to bite at grapes and pomegranates fresh from the vine. Not far off, near some fresh and mossy grass, under the delicious shade of some trees, I discovered a spring of fresh water, into which we voluptuously laved our faces, hands, and feet.

While we were all giving way to the delights of new-found pleasures, a little child appeared between two tufted olive trees. "Ah," cried I, "an inhabitant of this happy country."

The little fellow was poorly dressed, weak and suffering, and appeared terribly alarmed at our appearance. Half-naked, with tangled, matted and ragged beards, we did look supremely ill-favored; and unless the country was a bandit land, we were not unlikely to alarm the inhabitants!

Just as the boy was about to take to his heels, Hans ran after him, and brought him back, despite his cries and kicks. My uncle tried to look as gentle as possible, and then spoke in German. "What is the name of this mountain, my friend?"

The child made no reply.

"Good," said my uncle, with a very positive air of conviction, "we are not in Germany." He then made the same demand in English, of which language he was an excellent scholar.

The child shook its head and made no reply.

"Is he dumb?" cried the Professor, who was rather proud of his polyglot knowledge of languages, and making the same demand in French. The boy only stared in his face.

"I must perforce try him in Italian," said my uncle, with a shrug. "*Dove noi siamo?*"

"Yes, tell me where we are?" I added, impatiently and eagerly.

Again the boy remained silent.

"My fine fellow, do you or do you not mean to speak?" cried my uncle, who began to get angry. He shook him and spoke another dialect of the Italian language. "*Come si noma questa isola?*"—what is the name of this island?

"Stromboli," replied the rickety little shepherd, dashing away from Hans and disappearing in the olive groves.

Stromboli! What effect on the imagination did these few words produce! We were in the center of the Mediterranean; amid the Eastern archipelago of mythological memory; in the ancient Strongylos, where Æolus kept the wind and the tempest chained up. And those blue mountains, which rose towards the rising of the sun, were the mountains of Calabria. And that mighty volcano which rose on the southern horizon was Etna, the fierce and celebrated Etna!

"Stromboli! Stromboli!" I repeated to myself. My uncle played a regular accompaniment to my gestures and words. We were singing together like an ancient chorus. Ah—what a journey—what a marvelous and extraordinary journey! Here we had entered the earth by one volcano, and we had come out by another. And this other was situated more than twelve hundred leagues from Sneffels, from that drear country of Iceland cast away on the confines of the earth. The wondrous chances of this expedition had transported us to the most harmonious and beautiful of earthly lands.

After a delicious repast of fruits and fresh water, we again continued our journey in order to reach the port of Stromboli. To say how we had reached the island would scarcely have been prudent. The superstitious character of the Italians would have been at work, and we should have been called demons vomited from the infernal regions. It was therefore necessary to pass for humble and unfor-

tunate shipwrecked travelers. It was certainly less striking and romantic, but it was decidedly safer.

As we advanced, I could hear my worthy uncle muttering to himself—"But the compass. The compass most
certainly marked north. This is a fact I cannot explain
in any way."

"Well, the fact is," said I, with an air of disdain, " we
must not explain anything. It will be much more easy."

" I should like to see a professor of the Johanneum Institution, who is unable to explain a cosmic phenomenon—it
would indeed be strange." And speaking thus; my uncle,
half-naked, his leathern purse round his loins, and his spectacles upon his nose, became once more the terrible Professor of Mineralogy.

An hour after leaving the wood of olives, we reached
the fort of San Vicenza, where Hans demanded the price
of his thirteenth week of service. My uncle paid him, with
many warm shakes of the hand.

At that moment, if he did not indeed quite share our
natural emotion, he allowed his feelings so far to give way
as to indulge in an extraordinary expression for him.
With the tips of two fingers he gently pressed our hands
and smiled.

CHAPTER XLIV
THE JOURNEY ENDED

THIS is the final conclusion of a narrative which will be
probably disbelieved even by people who are astonished at
nothing. I am, however, armed at all points against human incredulity.

We were kindly received by the Strombolite fishermen,
who treated us as shipwrecked travelers. They gave us
clothes and food. After a delay of forty-eight hours, on
the 31st of September a little vessel took us to Messina,
where a few days of delightful and complete repose restored us to ourselves.

On Friday, the 4th of October, we embarked in the *Vol-
turus,* one of the postal packets of the Imperial Messagerie
of France; and three days later we landed at Marseilles,
having no other care on our minds but that of our precious

but erratic compass. This inexplicable circumstance tormented me terribly. On the 9th of October, in the evening, we reached Hamburg.

What was the astonishment of Martha, what the joy of Gretchen! I will not attempt to define it. "Now, then, Harry, that you really are a hero," she said, "there is no reason why you should ever leave me again." I looked at her. She was weeping tears of joy.

I leave it to be imagined if the return of Professor Hardwigg made or did not make a sensation in Hamburg. Thanks to the indiscretion of Martha, the news of his departure for the Interior of the Earth had been spread over the whole world.

No one would believe it—and when they saw him come back in safety they believed it all the less. But the presence of Hans and many stray scraps of information by degrees modified public opinion. Then my uncle became a great man, and I the nephew of a great man; which, at all events, is something. Hamburg gave a festival in our honor. A public meeting of the Johanneum Institution was held, at which the Professor related the whole story of his adventures, omitting only the facts in connection with the compass.

That same day he deposited in the archives of the town the document he had found, written by Saknussemm, and he expressed his great regret that circumstances, stronger than his will, did not allow him to follow the Icelandic traveler's track into the very Center of the Earth. He was modest in his glory, but his reputation only increased.

So much honor necessarily created for him many envious enemies. Of course they existed, and as his theories, supported by certain facts, contradicted the system of science upon the question of central heat, he maintained his own views both with pen and speech against the learned of every country. Although I still believe in the theory of central heat, I confess that certain circumstances, hitherto very ill defined, may modify the laws of such natural phenomena.

At the moment when these questions were being discussed with interest, my uncle received a rude shock—one that he felt very much. Hans, despite everything he could say to the contrary, quitted Hamburg; the man to whom we owed so much would not allow us to pay our deep debt of gratitude. He was taken with nostalgia; a love for his Icelandic home. " *Farvel*," said he, one day, and with this one short word of adieu, he started for Reykjawik, which he soon reached in safety.

We were deeply attached to our brave eider-duck hunter. His absence will never cause him to be forgotten by those whose lives he saved, and I hope, at some not distant day, to see him again.

To conclude, I may say that our Journey into the Interior of the Earth created an enormous sensation throughout the civilized world. It was translated and printed in many languages. All the leading journals published extracts from it, which were commentated, discussed, attacked, and supported with equal animation by those who believed in its episodes, and by those who were utterly incredulous. Wonderful! My uncle enjoyed during his lifetime all the glory he deserved; and he was even offered a large sum of money, by Mr. Barnum, to exhibit himself in the United States; while I am credibly informed by a traveler that he is to be seen in waxwork at Madame Tussaud's!

But one care preyed upon his mind, a care which rendered him very unhappy. One fact remained inexplicable —that of the compass. For a learned man to be baffled by such an inexplicable phenomenon was very aggravating. But heaven was merciful, and in the end my uncle was happy. One day, while he put some minerals belonging to his collection in order, I fell upon the famous compass and examined it keenly. For six months it had lain unnoticed and untouched. I looked at it with curiosity, which soon became surprise. I gave a loud cry. The Professor, who was at hand, soon joined me.

" What is the matter? " he cried.

" The compass! "

" What then? "

" Why, its needle points to the south and not to the north."

" My dear boy, you must be dreaming."

" I am not dreaming. See the poles are changed."

" Changed! "

My uncle put on his spectacles, examined the instrument, and leaped with joy, shaking the whole house. A clear light fell upon our minds.

" Here it is! " he cried, as soon as he had recovered the use of his speech. " Our error is now easily explained. But to what phenomenon do we owe this alteration in the needle! "

" Nothing more simple."

" Explain yourself, my boy. I am on thorns."

" During the storm, upon the Central Sea, the ball of fire which made a magnet of the iron in our raft, turned our compass topsy-turvy."

" Ah! " cried the Professor, with a loud and ringing laugh, " it was a trick of that inexplicable electricity."

From that hour my uncle was the happiest of learned men, and I the happiest of ordinary mortals. For my pretty Virland girl, abdicating her position as ward, took her place in the house in Königstrasse in the double quality of niece and wife. We need scarcely mention that her uncle was the illustrious Professor Hardwigg, corresponding member of all the scientific, geographical, mineralogical and geological societies of the five quarters of the globe.

THE END

Round the world
in eighty days

Round the World in Eighty Days

CHAPTER I

IN WHICH PHILEAS FOGG AND PASSEPARTOUT ACCEPT EACH OTHER AS MASTER AND SERVANT

N the year 1872, the house No. 7, Saville Row, Burlington Gardens—the house in which Sheridan died, in 1814—was inhabited by Phileas Fogg, Esq., one of the most singular and most noticed members of the Reform Club of London, although he seemed to take care to do nothing which might attract attention.

This Phileas Fogg, then, an enigmatic personage, of whom nothing was known but that he was a very polite man, and one of the most perfect gentlemen of good English society, succeeded one of the greatest orators that honor England.

An Englishman Phileas Fogg was surely, but perhaps not a Londoner. He was never seen on 'Change, at the bank, or in any of the counting-rooms of the " City." The docks of London had never received a vessel fitted out by Phileas Fogg. This gentleman did not figure in any public body. His name had never sounded in any Inns of Court. He never pleaded in the Court of Chancery, nor the Queen's Bench. He was neither a manufacturer, nor a merchant, nor a gentleman farmer. He was not a member of the Royal Institution of Great Britain, or the London Institution, or the Literary Institution of the West, or the Law Institute, or that Institute of the Arts and Sciences, placed under the direct patronage of her gracious majesty. In fact, he belonged to none of the numerous societies that swarm in the capital of England, from the Harmonic to the Entomological Society, founded principally for the purpose of destroying hurtful insects. Phileas Fogg was a member of the Reform Club, and that was all.

Should anyone be astonished that such a mysterious gentleman should be among the members of this honorable institution, we will reply that he obtained admission on the recommendation of Baring Brothers, with whom he had an open credit. Was this Phileas Fogg rich? Undoubtedly. But the best informed could not say how he had made his money, and Mr. Fogg was the last person to whom it would have been proper to go for information. He was by no means extravagant in anything, neither was he avaricious, for when money was needed for a noble, useful, or benevolent purpose, he gave it quietly, and even anonymously. In short, no one was less communicative than this gentleman. He talked as little as possible, and seemed much more mysterious than silent. His life was open to the light, but what he did was always so mathematically the same thing, that the imagination, unsatisfied, sought further.

Had he traveled? It was probable, for none knew the world better than he; there was no spot so secluded that he did not appear to have a special acquaintance with it. Sometimes, in a few brief, clear words, he would correct the thousand suppositions circulating in the club with reference to travelers lost or strayed; he pointed out the true probabilities, and so often did events justify his predictions, that he seemed as if gifted with a sort of second sight. He was a man who must have traveled everywhere, in spirit at least.

One thing was certain, that for many years Phileas Fogg had not been from London. Those who had the honor of knowing him more intimately than others, affirmed that no one could pretend to have seen him elsewhere than upon this direct route, which he traversed every day to go from his house to the club. His only pastime was reading the papers and playing whist. He frequently won at this quiet game, so very appropriate to his nature; but his winnings never went into his purse, and made an important item in his charity fund. Besides, it must be remarked, that Mr. Fogg evidently played for the sake of playing, not to win. The game was for him a contest, a struggle against a difficulty; but a motionless, unwearying struggle, and that suited his character.

Phileas Fogg was not known to have either wife or children—which may happen to the most respectable people—neither relatives nor friends—which is more rare, truly. Phileas Fogg lived alone in his house in Saville Row, where nobody entered. There was never a question as to its interior. A single servant sufficed to serve him. Break-fasting and dining at the club, at hours fixed with the utmost exactness, in the same hall, at the same table, not entertaining his colleagues nor inviting a stranger, he returned home only to go to bed, exactly at midnight, without ever making use of the comfortable chambers which the Reform Club puts at the disposal of its favored members. Of the twenty-four hours he passed ten at his residence either sleeping or busying himself at his toilet. If he walked, it was invariably with a regular step in the entrance hall, with its mosaic floor, or in the circular gallery, above which rose a dome with blue painted windows, supported by twenty Ionic columns of red porphyry. If he dined or breakfasted, the kitchens of the club furnished his table their succulent stores; the waiters of the club, grave personages in dress-coats and shoes with swan-skin soles, served him in a special porcelain and on fine Saxon linen; the club decanters of a lost mold contained his sherry, his port, and his claret, flavored with orange-flower water and cinnamon; and finally the ice of the club, brought at great expense from the American lakes, kept his drinks in a satisfactory condition of freshness.

If to live in such conditions is eccentric, it must be granted that eccentricity has something good in it!

The mansion on Saville Row, without being sumptuous, recommended itself by its extreme comfort. Phileas Fogg demanded from his only servant an extraordinary and regular punctuality. This very day, the second of October, Phileas Fogg had dismissed James Forster—this youth having incurred his displeasure by bringing him shaving water at eighty-four degrees Fahrenheit, instead of eighty-six—and he was waiting for his successor, who was to make his appearance between eleven and half past eleven.

Phileas Fogg, squarely seated in his armchair, his feet close together like those of a soldier on parade, his hands resting on his knees, his body straight, his head erect, was watching the hand of the clock move—a complicated mechanism which indicated the hours, the minutes, the seconds, the days, the days of the month, and the year. At the stroke of half past eleven, Mr. Fogg would, according to his daily habit, leave his house and repair to the Reform Club.

At this moment there was a knock at the door of the small parlor in which was Phileas Fogg. James Forster, the dismissed servant, appeared. "The new servant," said he.

A young man, aged thirty, came forward and bowed. "You are a Frenchman, and your name is John?" Phileas Fogg asked him.

"Jean, if it does not displease monsieur," replied the newcomer. "Jean Passepartout, a surname which has clung to me and which my natural aptitude for withdrawing from a business has justified. I believe, sir, that I am an honest fellow; but to be frank, I have had several trades. I have been a traveling singer; a circus rider, vaulting like Leotard, and dancing on the rope like Blondin; then I became professor of gymnastics, in order to render my talents more useful; and in the last place, I was a sergeant fireman at Paris. I have among my papers notes of remarkable fires. But five years have passed since I left France, and wishing to have a taste of family life, I have been a valet in England. Now, finding myself out of a situation, and having learned that Monsieur Phileas Fogg was the most exact and the most settled gentleman in the United Kingdom, I have presented myself to monsieur with the hope of living tranquilly with him, and of forgetting even the name of Passepartout."

"Passepartout suits me," replied the gentleman. "You are recommended to me. I have good reports concerning you. You know my conditions?"

"Yes, sir."

"Well, what time have you?"

"Twenty-four minutes after eleven," replied Passepartout, drawing from the depths of his pocket an enormous silver watch.

"You are slow," said Mr. Fogg.

"Pardon me, monsieur, but it is impossible."

"You are four minutes too slow. It does not matter. It suffices to state the difference. Then, from this moment twenty-nine minutes after eleven o'clock A. M., this Wednesday, October 2, 1872, you are in my service." That said, Phileas Fogg rose, took his hat in his left hand, placed it upon his head with an automatic movement, and disappeared without another word.

216

Passepartout heard the street door close once; it was his new master going out; then a second time; it was his predecessor, James Forster, departing in his turn. Passepartout remained alone in the house in Saville Row.

CHAPTER II
IN WHICH PASSEPARTOUT IS CONVINCED THAT HE HAS FOUND HIS IDEAL

"Upon my word," said Passepartout to himself, first, "I have known at Madame Tussaud's good people as lively as my new master!" Madame Tussaud's "good people" are wax figures, much visited in London, who, indeed, are only wanting in speech.

During the few minutes that he had interviewed Phileas Fogg, Passepartout had examined his future master, rapidly but carefully. He was a man that might be forty years old, of fine handsome face, of tall figure, which a slight corpulence did not misbecome, his hair and whiskers light, his forehead compact, without appearance of wrinkles at the temples, his face rather pale than flushed, his teeth magnificent. He appeared to possess in the highest degree what physiognomists call "repose in action," a quality common to those who do more work than talking. Calm, phlegmatic, with a clear eye and immovable eyelid, he was the finished type of those cool-blooded Englishmen so frequently met in the United Kingdom, and whose somewhat academic posture Angelica Kauffman has marvelously reproduced under her pencil. Seen in the various acts of his existence, this gentleman gave the idea of a well-balanced being in all his parts, evenly hung, as perfect as a chronometer. Indeed, Phileas Fogg was exactness personified, which was seen clearly from "the expression of his feet and his hands," for with man, as well as with the animals, the limbs themselves are organs expressive of the passions.

Phileas Fogg was one of those mathematically exact people, who, never hurried and always ready, are economical of the steps and their motions. He never made one stride too many, always going by the shortest route. He did not give an idle look. He did not allow himself a superfluous gesture. He had never been seen moved or troubled. He

217

was a man of the least possible haste, but he always arrived on time. However, it will be understood that he lived alone, and, so to speak, outside of every social relation. He knew that in life one must take his share of friction, and as frictions retard, he never rubbed against anyone.

As for Jean, called Passepartout, a true Parisian of Paris, he had sought vainly for a master to whom he could attach himself, in the five years that he had lived in England and served as a valet in London. Passepartout was not one of those Frontins or Mascarilles, who, with high shoulders, nose high in air, a look of assurance, and staring eye, are only impudent dunces. No, Passepartout was a good fellow, of amiable physiognomy, his lips a little prominent, always ready to taste or caress, a mild and serviceable being, with one of those good round heads that we like to see on the shoulders of a friend. His eyes were blue, his complexion rosy, his face fat enough for him to see his cheek bones, his chest broad, his form full, his muscles vigorous, and he possessed a herculean strength which his youthful exercise had splendidly developed. His brown hair was somewhat tumbled. If the ancient sculptors knew eighteen ways of arranging Minerva's hair, Passepartout knew of but one for fixing his own: three strokes of a large comb, and it was dressed.

The most meager stock of prudence would not permit of saying that the expansive character of this young man would agree with that of Phileas Fogg. Would Passepartout be in all respects exactly the servant that his master needed? That would only be seen by using him. After having had, as we have seen, quite a wandering youth, he longed for repose. Having heard the exactness and proverbial coolness of the English gentlemen praised, he came to seek his fortune in England. But until the present, fate had treated him badly. He had not been able to take root anywhere. He had served in ten different houses. In every one the people were capricious and irregular, running after adventures or about the country—which no longer suited Passepartout. His last master, young Lord Longsferry, member of Parliament, after having passed his nights in the Haymarket oyster-rooms, returned home too frequently on the shoulders of policemen. Passepartout wishing, above all things, to be able to respect his master, ventured some mild remarks, which were badly received, and he quit. In the meantime, he learned that Phileas Fogg, Esq., was hunting a servant. He made some inquiry about this gentleman. A person whose existence was so regular, who never slept in a strange bed, who did not travel, who was never absent, not even for a day, could not but suit him. He presented himself, and was accepted under the circumstances that we already know.

At half-past eleven, Passepartout found himself alone in the Saville Row mansion. He immediately commenced his inspection, going over it from cellar to garret. This clean, well-ordered, austere, Puritan house, well organized for servants, pleased him. It produced the effect upon him of a fine snail-shell, but one lighted and heated by gas, for carburetted hydrogen answered both purposes here. Passepartout found without difficulty, in the second-story, the room designed for him. It suited him. Electric bells and speaking tubes put it in communication with the lower stories. On the mantel an electric clock corresponded with the one in Phileas Fogg's bed-chamber, both beating the same second at the same instant. " That suits me, that suits me! " said Passepartout.

He observed also in his room a notice fastened above the clock. It was the programme for the daily service. It comprised—from eight o'clock in the morning, the regular hour at which Phileas Fogg, rose, until half-past eleven, the hour at which he left his house to breakfast at the Reform Club—all the details of the service, the tea and toast at twenty-three minutes after eight, the shaving water at thirty-seven minutes after nine, the toilet at twenty minutes before ten, etc. Then from half-past eleven in the morning until midnight, the hour at which the methodical gentleman retired—everything was noted down, foreseen, and regulated. Passepartout took a pleasure in contemplating this programme, and impressing upon his mind its various directions.

As to the gentleman's wardrobe, it was in very good taste and wonderfully complete. Each pair of pantaloons, coat, or vest bore a regular number, which was also entered upon a register, indicating the date at which, according to the season, these garments were to be worn in their turn. The same rule applied to his shoes.

In short, in this house in Saville Row—which in the time of the illustrious but dissipated Sheridan, must have been the temple of disorder—its comfortable furniture indicated a delightful ease. There was no study, there were no books, which would have been of no use to Mr. Fogg, since the Reform Club placed at his disposal two libraries, the one devoted to literature, the other to law and politics. In his bed-chamber there was a medium-sized safe whose construction protected it from fire as well as from burglars. There were no weapons in the house, neither for the chase, nor for war. Everything there denoted the most peaceful habits.

After having minutely examined the dwelling, Passepartout rubbed his hands, his broad face brightened, and he repeated cheerfully: " This suits me! This is the place for me! Mr. Fogg and I will understand each other perfectly! A homebody, and so methodical! A genuine automaton! Well, I am not sorry to serve under an automaton!"

CHAPTER III

IN WHICH A CONVERSATION TAKES PLACE WHICH MAY COST PHILEAS FOGG DEARLY

PHILEAS FOGG had left his house in Saville Row at half-past eleven, and after having put his right foot before his left foot five hundred and seventy-five times, and his left foot before his right foot five hundred and seventy-six times, he arrived at the Reform Club, a spacious and lofty building in Pall Mall, which cost not less than three millions to build.

Phileas Fogg repaired immediately to the dining-room, whose nine windows opened upon a fine garden with trees already gilded by autumn. There, he took his seat at his regular table where his plate was awaiting him. His breakfast consisted of a side dish, a boiled fish with Reading sauce of first quality, a scarlet slice of roast beef garnished with mushrooms, a rhubarb and gooseberry tart, and a bit of Chester cheese, the whole washed down with a few cups of that excellent tea, specially gathered for the stores of the Reform Club.

At forty-seven minutes past noon, this gentleman rose and turned his steps towards the large hall, a sumptuous apartment adorned with paintings in elegant frames. There a servant handed him the *Times* uncut, the tiresome cutting of which he managed with a steadiness of hand which denoted great practice in this difficult operation. The reading of this journal occupied Phileas Fogg until a quarter before four, and that of the *Standard,* which succeeded it, lasted until dinner. This repast passed off in the same way as the breakfast, with the addition of " Royal British Sauce."

At twenty minutes before six the gentleman reappeared in the large hall, and was absorbed in the reading of the *Morning Chronicle.*

Half an hour later various members of the Reform Club entered and came near the fire-place, in which a coal fire was burning. They were the usual partners of Phileas Fogg, like himself passionate players of whist; the engineer Andrew Stuart, the bankers John Sullivan and Samuel Fallentin, the brewer Thomas Flanagan, Gauthier Ralph, one of the directors of the Bank of England—rich and respected personages, even in this club counting among its members the *elite* of trade and finance.

" Well, Ralph," asked Thomas Flanagan, " how about that robbery? "

" Why," replied Andrew Stuart, " the bank will lose the money."

" I hope, on the contrary," said Gauthier Ralph, " that we shall put our hands on the robber. Detectives, very skillful fellows, have been sent to America and the Continent, to all the principal ports of embarkation and debarkation, and it will be difficult for this fellow to escape."

" But you have the description of the robber? " asked Andrew Stuart.

" In the first place, he is not a robber," replied Gauthier Ralph, seriously.

" How, he is not a robber, this fellow who has abstracted fifty-five thousand pounds in bank-notes? "

" No," replied Gauthier Ralph.

" Is he then a manufacturer? " said John Sullivan.

" The *Morning Chronicle* assures us that he is a gentleman."

The party that made this reply was no other than Phileas Fogg, whose head then emerged from the mass of papers heaped around him. At the same time, he greeted his colleagues, who returned his salutation. The matter under discussion, which the various journals of the United Kingdom were discussing ardently, had occurred three days before, on the 29th of September. A package of bank-notes, making the enormous sum of fifty-five thousand pounds, had been taken from the counter of the principal cashier of the Bank of England. The Under-Governor, Gauthier Ralph, only replied to anyone who was astonished that such a robbery could have been so easily accomplished, that at this very moment the cashier was occupied with registering a receipt of three shillings six pence, and that he could not have his eyes everywhere.

But it is proper to be remarked here—which makes the robbery less mysterious—that this admirable establishment, the Bank of England, seems to care very much for the dignity of the public. There are neither guards nor gratings; gold, silver, and bank-notes being freely exposed, and, so to speak, at the mercy of the first comer. They would not suspect the honor of anyone passing by. One of the best observers of English customs relates the following: He had the curiosity to examine closely, in one of the rooms of the bank, where he was one day, an ingot of gold weighing seven to eight pounds, which was lying exposed on the cashier's table; he picked up this ingot, examined it, passed it to his neighbor, and he to another, so that the ingot, passing from hand to hand, went as far as the end of a dark entry, and did not return to its place for half an hour, and the cashier had not once raised his head.

But on the twenty-ninth of September, matters did not turn out quite in this way. The package of bank-notes did not return, and when the magnificent clock, hung above the "drawing office," announced at five o'clock the closing of the office, the Bank of England had only to pass fifty-five thousand pounds to the account of profit and loss.

The robbery being duly known, agents, detectives, selected from the most skillful, were sent to the principal ports, Liverpool, Glasgow, Havre, Suez, Brindisi, New York, etc., with the promise in case of success, of a reward of two thousand pounds and five per cent. of the amount recovered. Whilst waiting for the information which the investigation, commenced immediately, ought to furnish, the detectives were charged with watching carefully all arriving and departing travelers.

As the *Morning Chronicle* said, there was good reason for supposing that the robber was not a member of any of the robber bands of England. During this day, the twenty-ninth of September, a well-dressed gentleman, of good manners, of a distinguished air, had been noticed going in and out of the paying room, the scene of the robbery. The investigation allowed a pretty accurate description of the gentleman to be made out, which was at once sent to all the detectives of the United Kingdom and of the continent. Some hopeful minds, and Gauthier Ralph was one of the number, believed that they had good reason to expect that the robber would not escape.

As may be supposed, this affair was the talk of all London. It was discussed, and sides were taken vehemently for or against the probabilities of success of the city police. It will not be surprising then to hear the members of the Reform Club treating the same subject, all the more that one of the Under-Governors of the Bank was among them.

The Honorable Gauthier Ralph was not willing to doubt the result of the search, considering that the reward offered ought to sharpen peculiarly the zeal and intelligence of the agents. But his colleague, Andrew Stuart, was far from sharing this confidence. The discussion continued then between the gentlemen, who were seated at a whist table, Stuart having Flanagan as a partner, and Fallentin, Phileas Fogg. During the playing the parties did not speak, but, between the rubbers, the interrupted conversation was fully revived.

" I maintain," said Andrew Stuart, " that the chances are in favor of the robber, who must be a skillful fellow ! "

" Well," replied Ralph, " there is not a single country where he can take refuge."

" Pshaw ! "

" Where do you suppose he might go ? "

" I don't know about that," replied Andrew Stuart, " but after all, the world is big enough."

" It was formerly," said Phileas Fogg in a low tone. Then he added, " It is your turn to cut, sir," presenting the cards to Thomas Flanagan.

The discussion was suspended during the rubber. But Andrew Stuart soon resumed it, saying, "How, formerly! Has the world grown smaller perchance?"

"Without doubt," replied Gauthier Ralph. "I am of the opinion of Mr. Fogg. The world has grown smaller, since we can go round it now ten times quicker than one hundred years ago. And, in the case with which we are now occupied, this is what will render the search more rapid."

"And will render more easy the flight of the robber!"

"It is your turn to play, Mr. Stuart!" said Phileas Fogg.

But the incredulous Stuart was not convinced, and when the hand was finished, he replied: "It must be confessed, Mr. Ralph, that you have found a funny way of saying that the world has grown smaller! Because the tour of it is now made in three months——"

"In eighty days only," said Phileas Fogg.

"Yes, gentlemen," added John Sullivan, "eighty days, since the section between Rothal and Allahabad, on the Great Indian Peninsular Railway, has been opened. Here is the calculation made by the *Morning Chronicle:*

From London to Suez via Mont Cenis and Brindisi, by rail and steamers..................	7 days
From Suez to Bombay, steamer................13	days
From Bombay to Calcutta, rail.................. 3	days
From Calcutta to Hong Kong (China) steamer..13	days
From Hong Kong to Yokohama (Japan) steamer. 6	days
From Yokohama to San Francisco, steamer......22	days
From San Francisco to New York, rail........ 7	days
From New York to London, steamer and rail.... 9	days

80 days

"Yes, eighty days!" exclaimed Andrew Stuart, who, by inattention, made a wrong deal, "but not including bad weather, contrary winds, shipwrecks, running off the track, etc."

"Everything included," replied Phileas Fogg, continuing to play, for this time the discussion no longer respected the game.

"Even if the Hindoos or the Indians tear up the rails!"

exclaimed Andrew Stuart, "if they stop the trains, plunder the cars, and scalp the passengers!"

"All included," replied Phileas Fogg, who, throwing down his cards, added, "two trumps."

Andrew Stuart, whose turn it was to deal, gathered up the cards, saying:

"Theoretically, you are right, Mr. Fogg, but practically——"

"Practically also, Mr. Stuart."

"I would like very much to see you do it."

"It depends only upon you. Let us start together."

"Heaven preserve me!" exclaimed Stuart, "but I would willingly wager four thousand pounds that such a journey, made under these conditions, is impossible."

"On the contrary, quite possible," replied Mr. Fogg.

"Well, make it then!"

"The tour of the world in eighty days!"

"Yes!"

"I am willing."

"When?"

"At once. Only I warn you that I shall do it at your expense."

"It is folly!" cried Stuart, who was beginning to be vexed at the persistence of his partner. "Stop! let us play rather."

"Deal again then," replied Phileas Fogg, "for there is a false deal."

Andrew Stuart took up the cards again with a feverish hand; then suddenly, placing them upon the table, he said: "Well, Mr. Fogg, yes, and I bet four thousand pounds!"

"My dear Stuart," said Fallentin, "compose yourself. It is not serious."

"When I say—'I bet,'" replied Andrew Stuart, "it is always serious."

"So be it," said Mr. Fogg, and then, turning to his companions, continued: "I have twenty thousand pounds deposited at Baring Brothers. I will willingly risk them——"

"Twenty thousand pounds!" cried John Sullivan. "Twenty thousand pounds which an unforeseen delay may make you lose!"

"The unforeseen does not exist," replied Phileas Fogg quietly.

"But, Mr. Fogg, this period of eighty days is calculated only as a minimum of time?"

"A minimum well employed suffices for everything," replied Mr. Fogg.

"But in order not to exceed it, you must jump mathematically from the trains into the steamers, and from the steamers upon the trains!"

"I will jump mathematically."

"That is a joke!"

"A good Englishman never jokes, when so serious a matter as a wager is in question," replied Phileas Fogg. "I bet twenty thousand pounds against who will that I will make the tour of the world in eighty days or less— that is, nineteen hundred and twenty hours or one hundred and fifteen thousand two hundred minutes. Do you accept?"

"We accept," replied Messrs. Stuart, Fallentin, Sullivan, Flanagan, and Ralph, after having consulted.

"Very well," said Mr. Fogg. "The Dover train starts at eight forty-five. I shall take it."

"This very evening?" asked Stuart.

"This very evening," replied Phileas Fogg. Then he added, consulting a pocket almanac, "Since to-day is Wednesday, the second of October, I ought to be back in London, in this very saloon of the Reform Club, on Saturday, the twenty-first of December, at eight forty-five in the evening, in default of which the twenty thousand pounds at present deposited to my credit with Baring Brothers will belong to you, gentlemen, in fact and by right. Here is a check of like amount."

A memorandum of the wager was made and signed on the spot by the six parties in interest. Phileas Fogg had remained cool. He had certainly not bet to win, and had risked only these twenty thousand pounds—the half of his fortune—because he foresaw that he might have to expend the other half to carry out this difficult, not to say impracticable, project. As for his opponents they seemed affected, not on account of the stake, but because they had a sort of scruple against a contest under these conditions.

Seven o'clock then struck. They offered to Mr. Fogg to stop playing, so that he could make his preparations for departure.

" I am always ready! " replied this tranquil gentleman, and dealing the cards, he said—" Diamonds are trumps. It is your turn to play, Mr. Stuart."

CHAPTER IV
IN WHICH PHILEAS FOGG SURPRISES PASSEPARTOUT, HIS SERVANT, BEYOND MEASURE

AT twenty-five minutes after seven, Phileas Fogg having gained twenty guineas at whist, took leave of his honorable colleagues, and left the Reform Club. At ten minutes of eight, he opened the door of his house and entered.

Passepartout, who had conscientiously studied his programme, was quite surprised at seeing Mr. Fogg guilty of the inexactness of appearing at this unusual hour. According to the notice, the occupant of Saville Row ought not to return before midnight, precisely.

Phileas Fogg first went to his bed-room. Then he called " Passepartout! "

Passepartout could not reply, for this call could not be addressed to him, as it was not the hour.

" Passepartout," Mr. Fogg called again without raising his voice much.

Passepartout presented himself.

" It is the second time that I have called you," said Mr. Fogg.

" But it is not midnight," replied Passepartout.

" I know it," continued Phileas Fogg, " and I do not find fault with you. We leave in ten minutes for Dover and Calais."

A sort of faint grimace appeared on the round face of the Frenchman. It was evident that he had not fully understood. " Monsieur is going to leave home? " he asked.

" Yes," replied Phileas Fogg. " We are going to make the tour of the world."

Passepartout, with his eyes wide open, his eyebrows raised, his arms extended, and his body collapsed, presented all the symptoms of an astonishment amounting to stupor. " The tour of the world! " he murmured.

" In eighty days," replied Mr. Fogg. " So we have not a moment to lose."

"But the trunks?" said Passepartout, who was unconsciously swinging his head from right to left.

"No trunks necessary. Only a carpet-bag. In it two woolen shirts and three pairs of stockings. The same for you. We will purchase on the way. You may bring down my mackintosh and traveling cloak, also stout shoes, although we will walk but little or not at all. Go."

Passepartout would have liked to make reply. He could not. He left Mr. Fogg's room, went up to his own, fell back into a chair, and making use of a common phrase in his country, he said: "Well, well, that's pretty tough. I who wanted to remain quiet!"

And mechanically he made his preparations for departure. The tour of the world in eighty days! Was he doing business with a madman? No. It was a joke, perhaps? They were going to Dover. Good. To Calais, let it be so. After all, it could not cross the grain of the good fellow very much, who had not trod the soil of his native country for five years. Perhaps they would go as far as Paris, and, indeed, it would give him pleasure to see the great capital again. But, surely, a gentleman so careful of his steps would stop there. Yes, doubtless; but it was not less true that he was starting out, that he was leaving home, this gentleman who until this time had been such a homebody!

By eight o'clock Passepartout had put in order the modest bag which contained his wardrobe and that of his master; then, his mind still disturbed, he left his room, the door of which he closed carefully, and he rejoined Mr. Fogg.

Mr. Fogg was ready. He carried under his arm *Bradshaw's Continental Railway Steam Transit and General Guide* which was to furnish him all the necessary directions for his journey. He took the bag from Passepartout's hands, opened it, and slipped into it a heavy package of those fine bank-notes which are current in all countries. "You have forgotten nothing?" he asked.

"Nothing, monsieur."

"My mackintosh and cloak?"

"Here they are."

"Good, take this bag," and Mr. Fogg handed it to Passepartout. "And take good care of it," he added, "there are twenty thousand pounds in it." The bag nearly slipped out of Passepartout's hands, as if the twenty thousand pounds had been in gold and weighed very heavy.

The master and servant then descended and the street door was double locked. At the end of Saville Row there was a carriage stand. Phileas Fogg and his servant got into a cab which was rapidly driven towards Charing Cross station, at which one of the branches of the Southeastern Railway touches. At twenty minutes after eight the cab stopped before the gate of the station. Passepartout jumped out. His master followed him and paid the driver. At this moment a poor beggar woman, holding a child in her arms, her bare feet all muddy, her head covered with a wretched bonnet from which hung a tattered feather, and a ragged shawl over her other torn garments, approached Mr. Fogg, and asked him for help.

Mr. Fogg drew from his pocket the twenty guineas which he had just won at whist, and giving them to the woman, said, "Here, my good woman, I'm glad to have met you." Then he passed on.

Passepartout had something like a sensation of moisture about his eyes. His master had made an impression upon his heart.

Mr. Fogg and he went immediately into the large sitting-room of the station. There Phileas Fogg gave Passepartout the order to get two first-class tickets for Paris. Then returning, he noticed his five colleagues of the Reform Club.

"Gentlemen, I am going," he said, "and the various *vises* put upon a passport which I take for that purpose will enable you, on my return, to verify my journey."

"Oh! Mr. Fogg," replied Gauthier Ralph, "that is useless. We will depend upon your honor as a gentleman!"

"It is better so," said Mr. Fogg.

"You do not forget that you ought to be back——?" remarked Andrew Stuart.

"In eighty days," replied Mr. Fogg. "Saturday, December 21, 1872, at a quarter before nine P. M. *Au revoir*, gentlemen."

At forty minutes after eight, Phileas Fogg and his servant took their seats in the same compartment. At eight forty-five the whistle sounded, and the train started.

The night was dark. A fine rain was falling. Phileas

Fogg, leaning back in his corner, did not speak. Passepartout, still stupefied, mechanically hugged up the bag with the bank-notes. But the train had not passed Sydenham, when Passepartout uttered a real cry of despair!

"What is the matter?" asked Mr. Fogg.

"Why—in—in my haste—my disturbed state of mind, I forgot——"

"Forgot what?"

"To turn off the gas in my room."

"Very well, young man," replied Mr. Fogg, coolly, "it will burn at your expense."

CHAPTER V
IN WHICH A NEW SECURITY APPEARS ON THE LONDON EXCHANGE

PHILEAS FOGG, in leaving London, doubtless did not suspect the great excitement which his departure was going to create. The news of the wager spread first in the Reform Club, and produced quite a stir among the members of the honorable circle. Then from the club it went into the papers through the medium of the reporters, and from the papers to the public of London and the entire United Kingdom. The question of "the tour of the world" was commented upon, discussed, dissected, with as much passion and warmth, as if it were a new Alabama affair. Some took sides with Phileas Fogg, others—and they soon formed a considerable majority—declared against him. To accomplish this tour of the world, otherwise than in theory and upon paper, in this minimum of time, with the means of communication employed at present, it was not only impossible, it was visionary. The *Times,* the *Standard,* the *Evening Star,* the *Morning Chronicle,* and twenty other papers of large circulation, declared against Mr. Fogg. The *Daily Telegraph* alone sustained him to a certain extent. Phileas Fogg was generally treated as a maniac, as a fool, and his colleagues were blamed for having taken up this wager, which impeached the soundness of the mental faculties of its originator. Extremely passionate, but very logical, articles appeared upon the subject. The interest felt in England for everything concerning geography is well known. So there was not a reader, to whatever class he belonged, who did not devour the columns devoted to Phileas Fogg.

During the first few days, a few bold spirits, principally ladies, were in favor of him, especially after the *Illustrated London News* had published his picture, copied from his photograph deposited in the archives of the Reform Club. Certain gentlemen dared to say, " Humph! why not, after all? More extraordinary things have been seen!" These were particularly the readers of the *Daily Telegraph*. But it was soon felt that this journal commenced to be weaker in its support.

In fact, a long article appeared on the seventh of October, in the *Bulletin* of the Royal Geographical Society. It treated the question from all points of view, and demonstrated clearly the folly of the enterprise. According to this article, everything was against the traveler, the obstacles of man, and the obstacles of nature. To succeed in this project, it was necessary to admit a miraculous agreement of the hours of arrival and departure, an agreement which did not exist, and which could not exist. The arrival of trains at a fixed hour could be counted upon strictly, and in Europe, where relatively short distances are in question; but when three days are employed to cross India, and seven days to cross the United States, could the elements of such a problem be established to a nicety? The accidents to machinery, running of trains off the track, collisions, bad weather, and the accumulation of snows, were they not all against Phileas Fogg? Would he not find himself in winter on the steamers at the mercy of the winds or the fogs? Is it then so rare that the best steamers of the ocean lines experience delays of two or three days? But one delay was sufficient to break irreparably the chain of communication. If Phileas Fogg missed only by a few hours the departure of a steamer, he would be compelled to wait for the next steamer, and in this way his journey would be irrevocably compromised. The article made a great sensation. Nearly all the papers copied it, and the stock in Phileas Fogg went down in a marked degree.

During the first few days which followed the departure of the gentleman, important business transactions had been made on the strength of his undertaking. The world of betters in England is a more intelligent and elevated world than that of gamblers. To bet is according to the English temperament; so that not only the various members of the Reform Club made heavy bets for or against Phileas Fogg, but the mass of the public entered into the movement. Phileas Fogg was entered like a race horse in a sort of stud book. A bond was issued which was immediately quoted upon the London Exchange. "Phileas Fogg," was "bid" or "asked" firm or above par, and enormous transactions were made. But five days after his departure, after the appearance of the article in the *Bulletin* of the Geographical Society, the offerings commenced to come in plentifully. "Phileas Fogg" declined. It was offered in bundles. Taken first at five, then at ten, it was finally taken only at twenty, at fifty, at one hundred!

Only one adherent remained steadfast to him. It was the old paralytic, Lord Albemarle. This honorable gentleman, confined to his arm chair, would have given his fortune to be able to make the tour of the world, even in ten years. He bet five thousand pounds in favor of Phileas Fogg, and even when the folly as well as the uselessness of the project was demonstrated to him, he contented himself with replying: "If the thing is feasible, it is well that an Englishman should be the first to do it!"

The adherents of Phileas Fogg became fewer and fewer; everybody, and not without reason, was putting himself against him; bets were taken at one hundred and fifty and two hundred against one, when, seven days after his departure, an entirely unexpected incident caused them not to be taken at all.

At nine o'clock in the evening of this day, the Commissioner of the Metropolitan Police received a telegraphic dispatch in the following words:

"SUEZ TO LONDON.

"Rowan, Commissioner of Police, Scotland Yard: I have the bank robber, Phileas Fogg. Send without delay warrant of arrest to Bombay (British India).

"FIX, *Detective.*"

The effect of this dispatch was immediate. The honorable gentleman disappeared to make room for the bank-note robber. His photograph, deposited at the Reform Club with those of his colleagues, was examined. It reproduced, feature by feature, the man whose description had been furnished by the commission of inquiry. They recalled how mysterious Phileas Fogg's life had been, his isolation, his sudden departure; and it appeared evident that this person, under the pretext of a journey round the world, and supporting it by a senseless bet, had had no other aim than to mislead the agents of the English police.

CHAPTER VI
IN WHICH THE AGENT FIX SHOWS A VERY PROPER IMPATIENCE

THESE are the circumstances under which the dispatch concerning Mr. Phileas Fogg had been sent.

On Wednesday the ninth of October, there was expected at Suez, at eleven o'clock, A. M., the iron steamer *Mongolia,* of the Peninsular and Oriental Company. The *Mongolia* made regular trips from Brindisi to Bombay by the Suez canal. It was one of the fastest sailers of the line, and had always exceeded the regular rate of speed, that is ten miles an hour between Brindisi and Suez, and nine and fifty-three hundredths miles between Suez and Bombay.

Whilst waiting for the arrival of the *Mongolia,* two men were walking up and down the wharf, in the midst of the crowd of natives and foreigners who come together in this town, no longer a small one, to which the great work of M. Lesseps assures a great future.

One of these men was the Consular agent of the United Kingdom, settled at Suez, who, in spite of the doleful prognostications of the British Government and the sinister predictions of Stephenson, the engineer, saw English ships passing through this canal every day, thus cutting off one-half the old route from England to the East Indies around the Cape of Good Hope.

The other was a small, spare man, of a quite intelligent, nervous face, who was contracting his eyebrows with remarkable persistence. Under his long eyelashes there shone very bright eyes, but whose brilliancy he could suppress at will. At this moment he showed some signs of impatience, going, coming, unable to remain in one spot.

The name of this man was Fix, and he was one of the detectives, or agents of the English police, who had been sent to the various seaports after the robbery committed upon the Bank of England. This Fix was to watch, with the greatest care, all travelers taking the Suez route, and if one of them seemed suspicious to him, to follow him up whilst waiting for a warrant of arrest. Just two days before Fix had received from the Commissioner of the Metropolitan Police the description of the supposed robber. The detective, evidently much excited by the large reward promised in case of success, was waiting then with an impatience easy to understand, the arrival of the *Mongolia.* " And you say, Consul," he asked, for the tenth time, " that this vessel cannot be behind time? "

" No, Mr. Fix," replied the Consul. " She was signaled yesterday off Port Said, and the one hundred and sixty kilometers of the canal are of no moment for such a sailer. I repeat to you that the *Mongolia* has always obtained the reward of twenty-five pounds given by the Government for every gain of twenty-four hours over the regulation time."

" This steamer comes directly from Brindisi? " asked Mr. Fix.

" Directly from Brindisi, where it took on the India mail; from Brindisi, which it left on Saturday, at five o'clock P. M. So have patience; it cannot be behindhand in arriving. But really I do not see how, with the description you have received, you could recognize your man, if he is on board the *Mongolia.*"

" Consul," replied Fix, " we feel these people rather than know them. You must have a scent for them, and the scent is like a special sense in which are united hearing, sight and smell. I have in my life arrested more than one of these gentlemen, and, provided that my robber is on board, I will venture that he will not slip from my hands."

" I hope so, Mr. Fix, for it is a very heavy robbery."

" A magnificent robbery," replied the enthusiastic detective. " Fifty-five thousand pounds! We don't often have such windfalls! The robbers are becoming mean fellows. The race of Jack Sheppard is dying out! They are hung now for a few shillings."

" Mr. Fix," replied the Consul, " you speak in such a way

that I earnestly wish you to succeed; but I repeat to you that, from the circumstances in which you find yourself, I fear that it will be difficult. Do you not know that, according to the description you have received, this robber resembles an honest man exactly?"

"Consul," replied the detective dogmatically, " great robbers always resemble honest people. You understand that those who have rogues' faces have but one course to take, to remain honest, otherwise they would be arrested. Honest physiognomies are the very ones that must be unmasked. It is a difficult task, I admit; and it is not a trade so much as an art."

Fix was not wanting in a certain amount of self-conceit.

In the meantime the wharf was becoming lively little by little. Sailors of various nationalities, merchants, shipbrokers, porters, and fellahs were coming together in large numbers. The arrival of the steamer was evidently near. The weather was quite fine, but the atmosphere was cold from the east wind. A few minarets towered above the town in the pale rays of the sun. Towards the south, a jetty of about two thousand yards long extended like an arm into the Suez roadstead. Several fishing and coasting vessels were tossing upon the surface of the Red Sea, some of which preserved in their style the elegant shape of the ancient galley.

Moving among this crowd, Fix, from the habit of his profession, was carefully examining the passers-by with a rapid glance. It was then half-past ten. " But this steamer will never arrive!" he exclaimed on hearing the port clock strike.

"She cannot be far off," replied the Consul.

"How long will she stop at Suez?" asked Fix.

"Four hours. Time enough to take in coal. From Suez to Aden at the other end of the Red Sea, is reckoned thirteen hundred and ten miles, and it is necessary to lay in fuel."

"And from Suez this vessel goes directly to Bombay?"

"Directly, without breaking bulk."

"Well, then," said Fix, "if the robber has taken this route and this vessel, it must be in his plan to disembark at Suez, in order to reach by another route the Dutch or French possessions of Asia. He must know very well that he would not be safe in India, which is an English country."

"Unless he is a very shrewd man," replied the Consul. "You know that an English criminal is always better concealed in London than he would be abroad."

After this idea, which gave the detective much food for reflection, the Consul returned to his office, situated at a short distance. The detective remained alone, affected by a certain nervous impatience, having the rather singular presentiment that his robber was to be found aboard the *Mongolia*—and truly, if this rascal had left England with the intention of reaching the New World, the East India route, being watched less, or more difficult to watch than that of the Atlantic, ought to have had his preference.

Fix was not long left to his reflections. Sharp whistles announced the arrival of the steamer. Soon was seen the enormous hull of the *Mongolia* passing between the shores of the canal, and eleven o'clock was striking when the steamer came to anchor in the roadstead, while the escaping of the steam made a great noise. There were quite a number of passengers aboard. Some remained on the spar-deck, contemplating the picturesque panorama of the town; but the most of them came ashore in the boats which had gone to hail the *Mongolia*.

Fix was examining carefully all those that landed, when one of them approached him, after having vigorously pushed back the fellahs who overwhelmed him with their offers of service, and asked him very politely if he could show him the office of the English consular agent. And at the same time this passenger presented a passport upon which he doubtless desired to have the British *vise*. Fix instinctively took the passport, and at a glance read the description in it. An involuntary movement almost escaped him. The sheet trembled in his hand. The description contained in the passport was identical with that which he had received from the Commissioner of the Metropolitan Police.

"This passport is not yours?" he said to the passenger.

"No," replied the latter, "it is my master's passport."

"And your master?"

"Remained on board."

"But," continued the detective, "he must present himself in person at the Consul's office to establish his identity."

" What, is that necessary? "

" Indispensable."

" And where is the office? "

" There at the corner of the square," replied the detective pointing out a house two hundred paces off.

" Then I must go for my master, who will not be pleased to have his plans deranged!" Thereupon, the passenger bowed to Fix and returned aboard the steamer.

CHAPTER VII
WHICH SHOWS ONCE MORE THE USELESSNESS OF PASSPORTS IN POLICE MATTERS

THE detective left the wharf and turned quickly towards the Consul's office. Immediately upon his pressing demand he was ushered into the presence of that official.

" Consul," he said, without any other preamble, " I have strong reasons for believing that our man has taken passage aboard the *Mongolia.*" And Fix related what had passed between the servant and himself with reference to the passport.

" Well, Mr. Fix," replied the Consul, " I would not be sorry to see the face of this rogue. But perhaps he will not present himself at my office if he is what you suppose. A robber does not like to leave behind him the tracks of his passage, and besides the formality of passports is no longer obligatory."

" Consul," replied the detective, " if he is a shrewd man, as we think, he will come."

" To have his passport *vised?* "

" Yes. Passports never serve but to incommode honest people and to aid the flight of rogues. I warrant you that his will be all regular, but I hope certainly that you will not *vise* it."

" And why not? If his passport is regular I have no right to refuse my *vise.*"

" But, Consul, I must retain this man until I have received from London a warrant of arrest."

" Ah, Mr. Fix, that is your business," replied the Consul, " but I—I cannot——"

The Consul did not finish his phrase. At this moment there was a knock at the door of his private office, and the office boy brought in two foreigners, one of whom was the very servant who had been talking with the detective. They were, indeed, the master and servant. The master presented his passport, asking the Consul briefly to be kind enough to *vise* it. The latter took the passport and read it carefully, while Fix, in one corner of the room, was observing or rather devouring the stranger with his eyes.

When the Consul had finished reading, he asked, " You are Phileas Fogg, Esq. ? "

" Yes, sir," replied the gentleman.

" And this man is your servant? "

" Yes, a Frenchman named Passepartout."

" You come from London? "

" Yes."

" And you are going? "

" To Bombay."

" Well, sir, you know that this formality of the *vise* is useless, and that we no longer demand the presentation of the passport? "

" I know it, sir," replied Phileas Fogg, " but I wish to prove by your *vise* my trip to Suez."

" Very well, sir." And the Consul having signed and dated the passport, affixed his seal, Mr. Fogg settled the fee, and having bowed coldly, he went out, followed by his servant.

" Well? " asked the detective.

" Well," replied the Consul, " he has the appearance of a perfectly honest man! "

" Possibly," replied Fix; " but that is not the question with us. Do you find, Consul, that this phlegmatic gentleman resembles, feature for feature, the robber whose description I have received? "

" I agree with you, but you know that all descriptions——"

" I shall have a clear conscience about it," replied Fix. "The servant appears to me less of a riddle than the master. Moreover, he is a Frenchman, who cannot keep from talking. I will see you soon again, Consul." The detective then went out, intent upon the search for Passepartout.

In the meantime Mr. Fogg, after leaving the Consul's house, had gone towards the wharf. There he gave some orders to his servant; then he got into a boat, returned on

238

board the *Mongolia,* and went into his cabin. He then took out his memorandum book, in which were the following notes:

"Left London, Wednesday, October 2, 8:45 P. M.

"Arrived at Paris, Thursday, October 3, 7:20 A. M.

"Left Paris, Thursday, 8:40 A. M.

"Arrived at Turin via Mont Cenis, Friday, October 4, 6:35 A. M.

"Left Turin, Friday, 7:20 A. M.

"Arrived at Brindisi, Saturday, October 5, 4 P. M.

"Set sail on the *Mongolia,* Saturday 5 P. M.

"Arrived at Suez, Wednesday, October 9, 11 A. M.

"Total of hours consumed, 158 1-2: or in days, 6 1-2 days."

Mr. Fogg wrote down these dates in a guide-book arranged by columns, which indicated, from the 2d of October to the 21st of December—the month, the day of the month, the day of the week, the stipulated and actual arrivals at each principal point, Paris, Brindisi, Suez, Bombay, Calcutta, Singapore, Hong-Kong, Yokohama, San Francisco, New York, Liverpool, London, and which allowed him to figure the gain made or the loss experienced at each place on the route. In this methodical book he thus kept an account of everything, and Mr. Fogg knew always whether he was ahead of time or behind.

He noted down then this day, Wednesday, October 9, his arrival at Suez, which agreeing with the stipulated arrival, neither made a gain nor a loss. Then he had his breakfast served up in his cabin. As to seeing the town, he did not even think of it, being of that race of Englishmen who have their servants visit the countries they pass through.

CHAPTER VIII
IN WHICH PASSEPARTOUT PERHAPS TALKS A LITTLE MORE THAN IS PROPER

FIX had in a few moments rejoined Passepartout on the wharf, who was loitering and looking about, not believing that he was obliged not to see anything.

"Well, my friend," said Fix, coming up to him, "is your passport *vised?*"

"Ah! it is you, monsieur," replied the Frenchman. "Much obliged. It is all in order."

"And you are looking at the country?"

"Yes, but we go so quickly that it seems to me as if I am traveling in a dream. And so we are in Suez?"

"Yes, in Suez."

"In Egypt?"

"You are quite right, in Egypt."

"And in Africa?"

"Yes, in Africa."

"In Africa!" repeated Passepartout. "I cannot believe it. Just, fancy, sir, that I imagined we would not go further than Paris, and I saw this famous capital again between twenty minutes after seven and twenty minutes of nine in the morning, between the Northern station and the Lyons station, through the windows of a cab in a driving rain! I regret it! I would have so much liked to see again Pere La Chaise and the Circus of the Champs-Elysées!"

"You are then in a great hurry?" asked the detective.

"No, I am not, but my master is. By-the-by, I must buy some shirts and shoes! We came away without trunks, with a carpet bag only."

"I am going to take you to a shop where you will find everything you want."

"Monsieur," replied Passepartout, "you are really very kind!"

And both started off. Passepartout talked incessantly. "Above all," he said, "I must take care not to miss the steamer!"

"You have the time," replied Fix, "it is only noon!"

Passepartout pulled out his large watch. "Noon. Pshaw! It is eight minutes of ten!"

"Your watch is slow!" replied Fix.

"My watch! A family watch that has come down from my great-grandfather! It don't vary five minutes in the year. It is a genuine chronometer."

"I see what is the matter," replied Fix. "You have kept London time, which is about two hours slower than Suez. You must set your watch at noon in each country."

"What! I touch my watch!" cried Passepartout. "Never."

" Well then, it will not agree with the sun."

" So much the worse for the sun, monsieur! The sun will be wrong then!" And the good fellow put his watch back in his fob with a magnificent gesture.

A few moments after Fix said to him: " You left London very hurriedly then? "

" I should think so! Last Wednesday, at eight o'clock in the evening, contrary to all his habits, Monsieur Fogg returned from his club, and in three-quarters of an hour afterward we were off."

" But where is your master going, then? "

" Right straight ahead! He is making the tour of the world!"

" The tour of the world? " cried Fix.

" Yes in eighty days! On a wager, he says; but, between ourselves, I do not believe it. There is no common sense in it. There must be something else."

" This Mr. Fogg is an original genius? "

" I should think so."

" Is he rich? "

" Evidently and he carries such a fine sum with him in fresh, new bank notes! And he doesn't spare his money on the route! Oh! but he has promised a splendid reward to the engineer of the *Mongolia,* if we arrive at Bombay considerably in advance!"

" And you have known him for a long time, this master of yours? "

" I," replied Passepartout, " I entered his service the very day of our departure."

The effect which these answers naturally produced upon the mind of the detective, already strained with excitement, may easily be imagined. This hurried departure from London so short a time after the robbery, this large sum carried away, this haste to arrive in distant countries, this pretext of an eccentric wager, all could have no other effect than to confirm Fix in his ideas. He kept the Frenchman talking, and learned to a certainty that this fellow did not know his master at all, that he lived isolated in London, that he was called rich without the source of his fortune being known, that he was a mysterious man, etc. But at the same time Fix was certain that Phileas Fogg would not get off at Suez, but that he was really going to Bombay.

" Is Bombay far from here? " asked Passepartout.

" Pretty far," replied the detective. " It will take you ten days more by sea."

" And where do you locate Bombay? "

" In India."

" In Asia! The deuce! I must tell you—there is one thing that bothers me—it is my burner."

" What burner? "

" My gas-burner, which I forgot to turn off, and which is burning at my expense. Now, I have calculated that it will cost me two shillings each twenty-four hours, exactly sixpence more than I earn, and you understand that, however little our journey may be prolonged——"

Did Fix understand the matter of the gas? It is improbable. He did not listen any longer, and was coming to a determination. The Frenchman and he had arrived at the shop. Fix left his companion there making his purchases, recommending him not to miss the departure of the *Mongolia,* and he returned in great haste to the Consul's office. Fix had regained his coolness completely, now that he was fully convinced.

" Monsieur," said he to the Consul, " I have my man. He is passing himself off as an oddity, who wishes to make the tour of the world in eighty days."

" Then he is a rogue," replied the Consul, " and he counts on returning to London after having deceived all the police of the two continents."

" We will see," replied Fix.

"" But are you not mistaken? " asked the Consul once more.

" I am not mistaken."

" Why, then, has this robber insisted upon having his stopping at Suez confirmed by a *vise?* "

" Why? I do not know, Consul," replied the detective; "but listen to me." And in a few words he related the salient points of his conversation with the servant of the said Fogg.

" Indeed," said the Consul, " all the presumptions are against this man. And what are you going to do? "

"Send a dispatch to London with the urgent request to send to me at once at Bombay a warrant of arrest, set sail upon the *Mongolia,* follow my robber to the Indies, and there, on English soil, accost him politely, with the warrant in one hand, and the other hand upon his shoulder."

Having uttered these words, the detective took leave of the Consul, and repaired to the telegraph office. Thence he telegraphed to the commissioner of the metropolitan police, as we have already seen. A quarter of an hour later Fix, with his light baggage in his hand, and well supplied with money, went on board the *Mongolia*. Soon the swift steamer was threading its way under full head of steam on the waters of the Red Sea.

CHAPTER IX
IN WHICH THE RED SEA AND THE INDIAN OCEAN SHOW THEMSELVES PROPITIOUS TO PHILEAS FOGG'S DESIGNS

THE distance between Suez and Aden is exactly thirteen hundred and ten miles, and the time-table of the company allows its steamers a period of one hundred and thirty-eight hours to make the distance. The *Mongolia*, whose fires were well kept up, moved along rapidly enough to anticipate her stipulated arrival. Nearly all the passengers who came aboard at Brindisi had India for their destination. Some were going to Bombay, others to Calcutta, but via Bombay, for since a railway crosses the entire breadth of the Indian peninsula, it is no longer necessary to double the island of Ceylon.

There was good living on board the *Mongolia*, in this company of officials, to which were added some young Englishmen, who, with a million in their pockets, were going to establish commercial houses abroad. The purser, the confidential man of the company, the equal of the captain on board the ship, did things elegantly. At the breakfast, at the lunch at two o'clock, at the dinner at half past five, at the supper at eight o'clock, the tables groaned under the dishes of fresh meat and the relishes, furnished by the refrigerator, and the pantries of the steamer. The ladies, of whom there were a few, changed their toilet twice a day. There was music, and there was dancing also when the sea allowed it.

But the Red Sea is very capricious and too frequently rough, like all long, narrow bodies of water. When the wind blew either from the coast of Asia, or from the coast of Africa, the *Mongolia,* being very long and sharp built, and struck amidships, rolled fearfully. The ladies then disappeared; the pianos were silent; songs and dances ceased at once. And yet, notwithstanding the squall and the agitated waters, the steamer, driven by its powerful engine, pursued its course without delay to the straits of Bab-el-Mandeb.

What was Phileas Fogg doing all this time? It might be supposed that, always uneasy and anxious, his mind would be occupied with the changes of the wind interfering with the progress of the vessel, the irregular movements of the squall threatening an accident to the engine, and in short all the possible injuries, which, compelling the *Mongolia* to put into some port, would have interrupted his journey.

By no means, or, at least, if this gentleman thought of these probabilities, he did not let it appear as if he did. He was the same impassible man, the imperturbable member of the Reform Club, whom no incident or accident could surprise. He did not appear more affected than the ship's chronometers. He was seldom seen upon the deck. He troubled himself very little about looking at this Red Sea, so fruitful in recollections, the spot where the first historic scenes of mankind were enacted. He did not recognize the curious towns scattered upon its shores, whose picturesque outlines stood out sometimes against the horizon. He did not even dream of the dangers of the Gulf of Arabia, of which the ancient historians, Strabo, Arrius, Artemidorus, and others, always spoke with dread, and upon which the navigators never ventured in former times without having consecrated their voyage by propitiatory sacrifices.

What was this queer fellow, imprisoned upon the *Mongolia,* doing? At first he took his four meals a day, the rolling and pitching of the ship not putting out of order his mechanism, so wonderfully organized. Then he played at whist. For he found companions as devoted to it as himself: a collector of taxes, who was going to his post at Goa; a minister, the Rev. Decimus Smith, returning to Bombay; and a brigadier general of the English army, who was rejoining his corps at Benares. These three passengers had the same passion for whist as Mr. Fogg, and they played for entire hours, not less quietly than he.

As for Passepartout, sea sickness had taken no hold on

him. He occupied a forward cabin, and ate conscientiously. It must be said that the voyage made under these circumstances was decidedly not unpleasant to him. He rather liked his share of it. Well fed and well lodged, he was seeing the country, and besides he asserted to himself that all this whim would end at Bombay. The next day after leaving Suez it was not without a certain pleasure that he met on deck the obliging person whom he had addressed on landing in Egypt. " I am not mistaken," he said, approaching him with his most amiable smile, " you are the very gentleman that so kindly served as my guide in Suez? "

" Indeed," replied the detective, " I recognize you! You are the servant of that odd Englishman——"

" Just so, Monsieur——? "

" Fix."

" Monsieur Fix," replied Passepartout. " Delighted to meet you again on board this vessel. And where are you going? "

" Why, to the same place as yourself, Bombay."

" That is first rate! Have you already made this trip? "

" Several times," replied Fix. " I am an agent of the Peninsular Company."

" Then you know India? "

" Why—yes," replied Fix, who did not wish to commit himself too far.

" And this India is a curious place? "

" Very curious! Mosques, minarets, temples, fakirs, pagodas, tigers, serpents, dancing girls! But it is to be hoped that you will have time to visit the country? "

" I hope so, Monsieur Fix. You understand very well that it is not permitted to a man of sound mind to pass his life in jumping from a steamer into a railway car and from a railway car into a steamer, under the pretext of making the tour of the world in eighty days! No. All these gymnastics will cease at Bombay, don't doubt it."

" And Mr. Fogg is well? " asked Fix in the most natural tone.

" Very well, Monsieur Fix, and I am too. I eat like an ogre that has been fasting. It is the sea air."

" I never see your master on deck."

" Never. He is not inquisitive."

" Do you know, Mr. Passepartout, that this pretended

tour in eighty days might very well be the cover for some secret mission—a diplomatic mission, for example!"

"Upon my word, Monsieur Fix, I don't know anything about it, I confess, and really I wouldn't give a half crown to know."

After this meeting, Passepartout and Fix frequently talked together. The detective thought he ought to have close relations with the servant of this gentleman Fogg. There might be an occasion when he could serve him. He frequently offered him, in the barroom of the *Mongolia,* a few glasses of whisky or pale ale, which the good fellow accepted without reluctance, and returned even so as not to be behind him—finding this Fix to be a very honest gentleman.

In the meantime the steamer was rapidly getting on. On the 13th they sighted Mocha, which appeared in its enclosure of ruined walls, above which were hanging green date trees. At a distance, in the mountains, there were seen immense fields of coffee trees. Passepartout was delighted to behold this celebrated place, and he found, with its circular walls and a dismantled fort in the shape of a handle, it looked like an enormous cup and saucer.

During the following night the *Mongolia* passed through the Straits of Bab-el-Mandeb, the Arabic name of which signifies "The Gate of Tears," and the next day, the 14th, she put in at Steamer Point, to the northwest of Aden harbor. The *Mongolia* had still sixteen hundred and fifty miles to make before reaching Bombay, and she had to remain four hours at Steamer Point, to lay in her coal. But this delay could not in any way be prejudicial to Phileas Fogg's programme. It was foreseen. Besides, the *Mongolia,* instead of not arriving at Aden until the morning of the 15th, put in there the evening of the 14th, a gain of fifteen hours.

Mr. Fogg and his servant landed. The gentleman wished to have his passport *vised.* Fix followed him without being noticed. The formality of the *vise* through with, Phileas Fogg returned on board to resume his interrupted play. Passepartout, according to his custom, loitered about in the midst of the population of Somanlis, Banyans, Parsees, Jews, 'Arabs, Europeans, making up the twenty-five thousand inhabitants of Aden. He admired the fortifications which make of this town the Gibraltar of the Indian Ocean, and some splendid cisterns, at which the English engineers were still working, two thousand years after the engineers of King Solomon. "Very singular, *very* singular!" said Passepartout to himself on returning aboard. "I see that it is not useless to travel, if we wish to see anything new."

At six o'clock P. M. the *Mongolia* was plowing the waters of the Aden harbor, and soon reached the Indian Ocean. She had one hundred and sixty-eight hours to make the distance between Aden and Bombay. The Indian Ocean was favorable to her, the wind kept in the northwest, and the sails came to the aid of the steam. The ship, well balanced, rolled less. The ladies, in fresh toilets, reappeared upon the deck. The singing and dancing recommenced. Their voyage was then progressing under the most favorable circumstances. Passepartout was delighted with the agreeable companion whom chance had procured for him in the person of Fix.

On Sunday, the 20th of October, toward noon, they sighted the Indian coast. Two hours later, the pilot came aboard the *Mongolia*. The outlines of the hills blended with the sky. Soon the rows of palm trees which abound in the place came into distinct view. The steamer entered the harbor formed by the islands of Salcette, Colaba, Elephanta, and Butcher, and at half past four she put in at the wharves of Bombay. Phileas Fogg was then finishing the thirty-third rubber of the day, and his partner and himself, thanks to a bold maneuver, having made thirteen tricks, wound up this fine trip by a splendid victory. The *Mongolia* was not due at Bombay until the 22d of October. She arrived on the 20th. This was a gain of two days, then, since his departure from London, and Phileas Fogg methodically noted it down in his memorandum book in the column of gains.

No one is ignorant of the fact that India, the great reversed triangle whose base is to the north and its apex to the south, comprises a superficial area of fourteen hundred thousand square miles, over which is unequally scattered a population of one hundred and eighty millions of inhabitants. The British government exercises a real dominion over a certain portion of this vast country. It maintains a Governor-General at Calcutta, Governors at Madras, Bombay, and Bengal, and a Lieutenant-Governor at Agra.

But English India, properly so-called, counts only a superficial area of seven hundred thousand square miles, and a population of one hundred to one hundred and ten millions of inhabitants. It is sufficient to say that a prominent part of the territory is still free from the authority of the Queen; and, indeed, with some of the rajahs of the interior, fierce and terrible, Hindoo independence is still absolute. Since 1756—the period at which was founded the first English establishment on the spot to-day occupied by the city of Madras—until the year in which broke out the great Sepoy insurrection, the celebrated East India Company was all-powerful. It annexed little by little the various provinces, bought from the rajahs at the price of annual rents, which it paid in part or not at all; it named its Governor-General and all its civil or military employes; but now it no longer exists, and the English possessions in India are directly under the Crown. Thus the aspect, the manners, and the distinctions of race of the peninsula are being changed every day. Formerly they traveled by all the old means of conveyance, on foot, on horseback, in carts, in small vehicles drawn by men, in palanquins, on men's backs, in coaches, etc. Now, steamboats traverse with great rapidity the Indus and the Ganges, and a railway crossing the entire breadth of India, and branching in various directions, puts Bombay at only three days from Calcutta.

The route of this railway does not follow a straight line across India. The air line distance is only one thousand to eleven hundred miles, and trains, going at only an average rapidity, would not take three days to make it; but this distance is increased at least one-third by the arc described by the railway rising to Allahabad, in the northern part of the peninsula. In short, these are the principal points of the route of the Great Indian Peninsular Railway. Leaving the island of Bombay, it crosses Salcette, touches the mainland opposite Tannah, crosses the chain of the Western Ghauts, runs to the northeast as far as Burhampour, goes through the nearly independent territory of Bundelkund, rises as far as Allahabad, turns towards the east, meets the Ganges at Benares, turns slightly aside, and descending again to the southeast by Burdivan and the French town of Chandernagor, it reaches the end of the route at Calcutta.

It was at half past four P. M. that the passengers of the *Mongolia* had landed in Bombay, and the train for Calcutta would leave at precisely eight o'clock. Mr. Fogg then took leave of his partners, left the steamer, gave his servant directions for some purchases, recommended him expressly to be at the station before eight o'clock, and with his regular step, which beat the second-like pendulum of an astronomical clock, he turned his steps towards the passport office. He did not think of looking at any of the wonders of Bombay, neither the city hall, nor the magnificent library, nor the forts, nor the docks, nor the cotton market, nor the shops, nor the mosques, nor the synagogues, nor the Armenian churches, nor the splendid pagoda of Malebar Hill, adorned with two polygonal towers. He would not contemplate either the masterpieces of Elephanta, or its mysterious hypogea, concealed in the southeast of the harbor, or the Kanherian grottoes of the Island of Salcette, those splendid remains of Buddhist architecture! No, nothing of that for him. After leaving the passport office, Phileas Fogg quietly repaired to the station, and there had dinner served. Among other dishes, the landlord thought he ought to recommend to him a certain giblet of " native rabbit," of which he spoke in the highest terms. Phileas Fogg accepted the giblet and tasted it conscientiously; but in spite of the spiced sauce, he found it detestable. He rang for the landlord.

" Sir," he said, looking at him steadily, " is that rabbit? "

" Yes, my lord," replied the rogue boldly, " the rabbit of the jungles."

" And that rabbit did not mew when it was killed? "

"Mew! oh, my lord! a rabbit! I swear to you——"

"Landlord," replied Mr. Fogg coolly, "don't swear, and recollect this: in former times, in India, cats were considered sacred animals. That was a good time."

"For the cats, my lord?"

"And perhaps also for the travelers!"

After this observation Mr. Fogg went on quietly with his dinner.

A few minutes after Mr. Fogg, the detective Fix also landed from the *Mongolia,* and hastened to the Commissioner of Police in Bombay. He made himself known in his capacity as detective, the mission with which he was charged, his position towards the robber. Had a warrant of arrest been received from London? They had received nothing. And, in fact, the warrant, leaving after Fogg, could not have arrived yet.

Fix was very much out of countenance. He wished to obtain from the Commissioner an order for the arrest of this gentleman Fogg. The director refused. The affair concerned the metropolitan government, and it alone could legally deliver a warrant. This strictness of principles, this rigorous observance of legality is easily explained with the English manners, which, in the matter of personal liberty, does not allow anything arbitrary. Fix did not persist, and understood that he would have to be resigned to waiting for his warrant. But he resolved not to lose sight of his mysterious rogue, whilst he remained in Bombay. He did not doubt that Phileas Fogg would stop there—and as we know, it was also Passepartout's conviction—which would give the warrant of arrest time to arrive.

But after the last orders which his master had given him on leaving the *Mongolia,* Passepartout had understood very well that it would be the same with Bombay as with Suez and Paris, that the journey would not stop here, that it would be continued at least as far as Calcutta, and perhaps further. And he began to ask himself if, after all, this bet of Mr. Fogg's was not really serious, and if a fatality was not dragging him, he who wished to live at rest, to accomplish the tour of the world in eighty days! Whilst waiting, and after having obtained some shirts and shoes, he took a walk through the streets of Bombay. There was a great crowd of people there. and among the Europeans of all nationalities, Persians with pointed caps, Bunyas with round turbans, Sindes with square caps, Armenians in long robes, Parsees in black mitres. A festival was just being held by the Parsees, the direct descendants of the followers of Zoroaster, who are the most industrious, the most civilized, the most intelligent, the most austere of the Hindoos—a race to which now belong the rich native merchants of Bombay. Upon this day they were celebrating a sort of religious carnival, with processions and amusements, in which figured dancing girls dressed in rose-colored gauze embroidered with gold and silver, who danced wonderfully and with perfect decency to the sound of viols and tam-tams.

It is superfluous to insist here whether Passepartout looked at these curious ceremonies, whether his eyes and ears were stretched wide open to see and hear, whether his entire appearance was that of the freshest greenhorn that can be imagined. Unfortunately for himself and his master, whose journey he ran the risk of interrupting, his curiosity dragged him further than was proper.

In fact, after having looked at this Parsee carnival, Passepartout turned towards the station, when, passing the splendid pagoda on Malebar Hill, he took the unfortunate notion to visit its interior. He was ignorant of two things: First, that the entrance into certain Hindoo pagodas is formally forbidden to Christians, and next, that the believers themselves cannot enter there without having left their shoes at the door. It must be remarked here that the English government, for sound political reasons, respecting and causing to be respected in its most insignificant details the religion of the country, punishes severely whoever violates its practices. Passepartout having gone in, without thinking of doing wrong, like a simple traveler, was admiring in the interior the dazzling glare of the Brahmin ornamentation, when he was suddenly thrown down on the sacred floor. Three priests, with furious looks, rushed upon him, tore off his shoes and stockings, and commenced to beat him, uttering savage cries. The Frenchman, vigorous and agile, rose again quickly. With a blow of his fist and a kick he upset two of his adversaries, very much hampered by their long robes, and rushing out of the pagoda with all the quickness of his legs, he had soon distanced the third Hindoo, who had followed him closely, by mingling with the crowd.

At five minutes of eight, just a few minutes before the leaving of the train, hatless and barefoot, having lost in the scuffle the bundle containing his purchase, Passepartout arrived at the railway station. Fix was on the wharf. Having followed Mr. Fogg to the station, he understood that the rogue was going to leave Bombay. His mind was immediately made up to accompany him to Calcutta, and further, if it was necessary. Passepartout did not see Fix, who was standing in a dark place, but Fix heard him tell his adventures in a few words to his master.

" I hope it will not happen to you again," was all Phileas Fogg replied, taking a seat in one of the cars of the train. The poor fellow, barefoot and quite discomfited, followed his master without saying a word.

Fix was going to get in another car, when a thought stopped him, and suddenly modified his plan of departure. " No, I will remain," he said to himself. " A transgression committed upon Indian territory. I have my man."

'At this moment the locomotive gave a vigorous whistle, and the train disappeared in the darkness.

CHAPTER XI
IN WHICH PHILEAS FOGG BUYS A CONVEYANCE AT A FABULOUS PRICE

THE train had started on time. It carried a certain number of travelers, some officers, civil officials, and opium and indigo merchants, whose business called them to the eastern part of the peninsula.

Passepartout occupied the same compartment as his master. A third traveler was in the opposite corner. It was the Brigadier-General, Sir Francis Cromarty, one of the partners of Mr. Fogg during the trip from Suez to Bombay, who was rejoining his troops, stationed near Benares.

Sir Francis Cromarty, tall, fair, about fifty years old, who had distinguished himself highly during the last revolt of the Sepoys, truly deserved to be called a native. From his youth he had lived in India, and had only been occasionally in the country of his birth. He was a well-posted man, who would have been glad to give information as to the manners, the history, the organization of this Indian country, if Phileas Fogg had been the man to ask for such things. But this gentleman was not asking anything. He was not traveling, he was describing a circumference. He was a heavy body, traversing an orbit around the terrestrial globe, according to the laws of rational mechanics. At this moment he was going over in his mind the calculations of the hours consumed since his departure from London, and he would have rubbed his hands, if it had been in his nature to make a useless movement.

Sir Francis Cromarty had recognized the originality of his traveling companion, although he had only studied him with his cards in his hands, and between two rubbers. He was ready to ask whether a human heart beat beneath this cold exterior, whether Phileas Fogg had a soul alive to the beauties of nature and to moral aspirations. That was the question for him. Of all the oddities the general had met, none were to be compared to this product of the exact sciences. Phileas Fogg had not kept secret from Sir Francis Cromarty his plan for a tour around the world, nor the conditions under which he was carrying it out. The general saw in this bet only an eccentricity without a useful aim, and which was wanting necessarily in the *transire bene-faciendo* which ought to guide every reasonable man. In the manner in which this singular gentleman was moving on, he would evidently be doing nothing, either for himself or for others.

An hour after having left Bombay, the train, crossing the viaducts, had left behind the Island of Salcette and reached the mainland. At the station Callyan, it left to the right the branch which, via Kandallah and Pounah descends towards the southeast of India, and reaches the station Panwell. At this point, it became entangled in the defiles of the Western Ghaut mountains, with bases of trappe and basalt, whose highest summits are covered with thick woods.

From time to time, Sir Francis Cromarty and Phileas Fogg exchanged a few words, and at this moment the general, recommencing a conversation which frequently lagged, said, " A few years ago, Mr. Fogg, you would have experienced at this point a delay which would have probably interrupted your journey."

" Why so, Sir Francis? "

" Because the railway stopped at the base of these mountains, which had to be crossed in a palanquin or on a pony's back as far as the station of Kandallah, on the opposite slope."

" That delay would not have deranged my programme," replied Mr. Fogg. " I would have foreseen the probability of certain obstacles."

" But, Mr. Fogg," replied the general, " you are in danger of having a bad business on your hands with this young man's adventure."

Passepartout, with his feet wrapped up in his cloak, was sleeping soundly, and did not dream that they were talking about him. " The English government is extremely severe, and rightly, for this kind of trespass," continued Sir Francis. " It insists, above all things, that the religious customs of the Hindoos shall be respected, and if your servant had been taken——"

" Yes, *if* he had been taken, Sir Francis," replied Mr. Fogg, " he would have been sentenced, he would have undergone his punishment, and then he would have quietly returned to Europe. I do not see how this matter could have delayed his master!"

And, thereupon, the conversation stopped again. During the night, the train crossed the Ghauts, passed on to Nassik, and the next day, the 21st of October, it was hurrying across a comparatively flat country, formed by the Khandeish territory. The country, well cultivated, was strewn with small villages, above which the minaret of the pagoda took the place of the steeple of the European church. Numerous small streams, principally tributaries of the Godavery, irrigated this fertile country.

Passepartout having waked up, looked around, and could not believe that he was crossing the country of the Hindoos in a train of the Great Peninsular Railway. It appeared improbable to him. And yet there was nothing more real! The locomotive, guided by the arm of an English engineer and heated with English coal, was puffing out its smoke over plantations of cotton trees, coffee, nutmeg, clove, and red pepper. The steam twisted itself into spirals about groups of palms, between which appeared picturesque bungalows, a few viharis (a sort of abandoned monasteries), and wonderful temples enriched by the inexhaustible ornament of Indian architecture. Then immense reaches of country stretched out of sight, jungles, in which were not wanting snakes and tigers whom the noise of the train did not frighten, and finally forests cut through by the route of the road, still the haunts of elephants, which, with a pensive eye, looked at the train as it passed so rapidly.

During the morning, beyond the station of Malligaum, the travelers traversed that fatal territory, which was so frequently drenched with blood by the sectaries of the goddess Kali. Not far off rose Ellora and its splendid pagodas, and the celebrated Aurungabad, the capital of the ferocious Aureng-Zeb, now simply the principal place of one of the provinces detached from the kingdom of Nizam. It was over this country that Feringhea, the chief of the Thugs, the king of stranglers, exercised his dominion. These assassins, united in an association that could not be reached, strangled, in honor of the goddess of death, victims of every age, without ever shedding blood, and there was a time when the ground could not be dug up anywhere in this neighborhood without finding a corpse. The English government has been able, in great part, to prevent these murders, but the horrible organization exists yet, and carries on its operations.

At half past twelve, the train stopped at the station at Burhampour, and Passepartout was able to obtain for gold a pair of Indian slippers, ornamented with false pearls, which he put on with an evident show of vanity. The travelers took a hasty breakfast, and started again for Assurghur, after having for a moment stopped upon the shore of the Tapty, a small river emptying into the Gulf of Cambay, near Surat.

It is opportune to mention the thoughts with which Passepartout was busied. Until his arrival at Bombay, he had thought that matters would go no farther. But now that he was hurrying at full speed across India, his mind had undergone a change. His natural feelings came back to him with a rush. He felt again the fanciful ideas of his youth, he took seriously his master's plans, he believed in the reality of the bet, and consequently in this tour of the world, and in this maximum of time which could not be exceeded. Already he was disturbed at the possible delays, the accidents which might occur upon the route. He felt interested in the wager, and trembled at the thought that he might have compromised it the evening before by his un-pardonable foolishness, so that, much less phlegmatic than Mr. Fogg, he was much more uneasy. He counted and recounted the days that had passed, cursed the stopping of the train, accused it of slowness, and blamed Mr. Fogg *in petto* for not having promised a reward to the engineer. The good fellow did not know that what was possible upon a steamer was not on a railway train, whose speed is regulated.

Towards evening they entered the defiles of the mountains of Sutpour, which separate the territory of Khandeish from that of Bundelcund.

The next day, the 22nd of October, Passepartout, having consulted his watch, replied to a question of Sir Francis Cromarty that it was three o'clock in the morning. In fact, this famous watch, always regulated by the meridian of Greenwich, which is nearly seventy-seven degrees west, ought to be and was four hours slow.

Sir Francis then corrected the hour given by Passepartout, and added the same remark that the latter had already heard from Fix. He tried to make him understand that he ought to regulate his watch on each new meridian, and that since he was constantly going towards the east, that is, in the face of the sun, the days were shorter by as many times four minutes as he had crossed degrees. It was useless. Whether the stubborn fellow had understood the remarks of the general or not, he persisted in not putting his watch ahead, which he kept always at London time. An innocent madness at any rate, which could hurt no one.

At eight o'clock in the morning, and fifteen miles before they reached Rothal, the train stopped in the midst of an immense opening, on the edge of which were some bungalows and workmen's huts. The conductor of the train passed along the cars calling out, " The passengers will get out here! "

Phileas Fogg looked at Sir Francis Cromarty, who appeared not to understand this stop in the midst of a forest of tamarinds and acacias. Passepartout not less surprised, rushed onto the track and returned almost immediately, crying: " Monsieur, no more railway! "

" What do you mean? " asked Sir Francis Cromarty.

" I mean that the train goes no farther! "

The brigadier general immediately got out of the car. Phileas Fogg, in no hurry, followed him. Both spoke to the conductor.

" Where are we? " asked Sir Francis Cromarty.

" At the hamlet of Kholby," replied the conductor.

" We stop here? "

" Without doubt. The railway is not finished——"

" How! It is not finished? "

" No! There is still a section of fifty miles to construct between this point and Allahabad, where the track commences again."

" But the papers have announced the opening of the entire line."

" But, general, the papers were mistaken."

" And you give tickets from Bombay to Calcutta! " replied Sir Francis Cromarty, who was beginning to be excited.

" Of course," replied the conductor; " but travelers know very well that they have to be otherwise transported from Kholby to Allahabad."

Sir Franics Cromarty was furious. Passepartout would have willingly knocked the conductor down who could not help himself. He did not dare look at his master.

" Sir Francis," said Mr. Fogg simply, " we will go, if you will be kind enough, to see about some way of reaching Allahabad."

" Mr. Fogg, this is a delay absolutely prejudicial to your interests! "

" No, Sir Francis, it was provided for."

" What, did you know that the railway——"

" By no means, but I knew that some obstacle or other would occur sooner or later upon my route. Now, nothing is interfered with. I have gained two days which I can afford to lose. A steamer leaves Calcutta for Hong Kong at noon on the 25th. This is only the 23d, and we shall arrive at Calcutta in time."

Nothing could be said in reply to such complete certainty as this.

It was only too true that the finished portion of the railway stopped at this point. The newspapers are like certain watches which have a mania for getting ahead of time, and they had announced the finishing of the line prematurely.

The most of the passengers knew of this break in the line, and descending from the train, they examined the vehicles of all sorts in the village, four-wheeled palkigharis, carts drawn by zebus, a sort of ox with humps, traveling cars resembling walking pagodas, palanquins, ponies, etc. Mr. Fogg and Sir Francis Cromarty, after having hunted through the entire village, returned without having found anything.

"I shall go on foot," said Mr. Fogg.

Passepartout, who had then rejoined his master, made a significant grimace, looking down at his magnificent but delicate slippers. Very fortunately, he had also been hunting for something, and hesitating a little, he said:

"Monsieur, I believe I have found a means of conveyance."

"What?"

"An elephant, belonging to an Indian living a hundred steps from here."

"Let us go to see the elephant," replied Mr. Fogg. Five minutes later, Phileas Fogg, Sir Francis Cromarty, and Passepartout arrived at a hut which was against an enclosure of high palisades. In the hut there was an Indian, and in the enclosure an elephant. Upon their demand, the Indian took Mr. Fogg and his two companions into the enclosure.

They found there a half-tamed animal, which his owner was raising, not to hire out, but as a beast of combat. To this end he had commenced to modify the naturally mild character of the animal in a manner to lead him gradually to that paroxysm of rage called "mutsh" in the Hindoo language, and that by feeding him for three months with sugar and butter. This treatment may not seem the proper one to obtain such a result, but it is none the less employed with success by their keepers.

Kiouni, the animal's name, could, like all his fellows, go rapidly on a long march, and in default of other conveyance, Phileas Fogg determined to employ him. But elephants are very expensive in India, where they are beginning to get scarce. The males, which alone are fit for circus feats, are very much sought for. These animals are rarely reproduced when they are reduced to the tame state, so that they can be obtained only by hunting. So they are the object of extreme care, and when Mr Fogg asked the Indian if he would hire him his elephant he flatly refused.

Fogg persisted and offered an excessive price for the animal, ten pounds per hour. Refused. Twenty pounds. Still refused. Forty pounds. Refused again. Passepartout jumped at every advance in price. But the Indian would not be tempted. The sum was a handsome one, however. Admitting the elephant to be employed fifteen hours to reach Allahabad, it was six hundred pounds earned for his owner.

Phileas Fogg, without being at all excited, proposed then to the Indian to buy his animal, and offered him at first one thousand pounds. The Indian would not sell! Perhaps the rogue scented a large transaction.

Sir Francis Cromarty took Mr. Fogg aside and begged him to reflect before going further. Phileas Fogg replied to his companion that he was not in the habit of acting without reflection, that a bet of twenty thousand pounds was at stake, that this elephant was necessary to him, and that, should he pay twenty times his value, he would have this elephant.

Mr. Fogg went again for the Indian, whose small eyes, lit up with greed, showed that with him it was only a question of price. Phileas Fogg offered successively twelve hundred, fifteen hundred, eighteen hundred, and finally two thousand pounds. Passepartout, so rosy oridnarily, was pale with emotion.

At two thousand pounds the Indian gave up.

" By my slippers," cried Passepartout, " here is a magnificent price for elephant meat! "

The business concluded, all that was necessary was to find a guide. That was easier. A young Parsee, with an intelligent face, offered his services. Mr. Fogg accepted him, and offered him a large reward to sharpen his wits. The elephant was brought out and equipped without delay. The Parsee understood perfectly the business of " mahout," or elephant driver. He covered with a sort of saddle cloth the back of the elephant, and put on each flank two kinds of rather uncomfortable howdahs.

Phileas Fogg paid the Indian in bank notes taken from the famous carpet bag. It seemed as if they were taken from Passepartout's very vitals. Then Mr. Fogg offered to Sir Francis Cromarty to convey him to Allahabad. The general accepted; one passenger more was not enough to tire this enormous animal. Some provisions were bought at Kholby. Sir Francis Cromarty took a seat in one of the howdahs, Phileas Fogg in the other. Passepartout got astride the animal, between his master and the brigadier general. The Parsee perched upon the elephant's neck, and at nine o'clock the animal, leaving the village, penetrated the thick forest of palm trees.

CHAPTER XII
IN WHICH PHILEAS FOGG AND HIS COMPANIONS VENTURE THROUGH THE FORESTS OF INDIA, AND WHAT FOLLOWS

THE guide, in order to shorten the distance to be gone over, left to his right the line of the road, the construction of which was still in process. This line, very crooked, owing to the capricious ramifications of the Vindhia mountains, did not follow the shortest route, which it was Phileas Fogg's interest to take. The Parsee, very familiar with the roads and paths of the country, thought to gain twenty miles by cutting through the forest, and they submitted to him.

Phileas Fogg and Sir Francis Cromarty, plunged to their necks in their howdahs, were much shaken up by the rough trot of the elephant, whom his mahout urged into a rapid gait. But they bore it with the peculiar British apathy, talking very little, and scarcely seeing each other.

As for Passepartout, perched upon the animal's back, and directly subjected to the swaying from side to side, he took care, upon his master's recommendation, not to keep his tongue between his teeth, as it would have been cut short off. The good fellow, at one time thrown forward on the elephant's neck, at another thrown back upon his rump, was making leaps like a clown on a spring-board. But he joked and laughed in the midst of his somersaults, and from time to time he would take from his bag a lump of sugar, which the intelligent Kiouni took with the end of his trunk, without interrupting for an instant his regular trot.

After two hours' march the guide stopped the elephant

and gave him an hour's rest. The animal devoured branches of trees and shrubs, first having quenched his thirst at a neighboring pond. Sir Francis Cromarty did not complain of this halt. He was worn out. Mr. Fogg appeared as if he had just got out of bed.

"But he is made of iron!" said the brigadier general, looking at him with admiration.

"Of wrought iron," replied Passepartout, who was busy preparing a hasty breakfast.

At noon, the guide gave the signal for starting. The country soon assumed a very wild aspect. To the large forests there succeeded copses of tamarinds and dwarf palms, then vast, arid plains, bristling with scanty shrubs, and strewn with large blocks of syenites. All this part of upper Bundelcund, very little visited by travelers, is inhabited by a fanatical population, hardened in the most terrible practices of the Hindoo religion. The government of the English could not have been regularly established over a territory subject to the influence of the rajahs, whom it would have been difficult to reach in their inaccessible retreats in the Vindhias.

They were descending the last declivities of the Vindhias. Kiouni had resumed his rapid gait. Towards noon, the guide went round the village of Kallenger, situated on the Cani, one of the tributaries of the Ganges. He always avoided inhabited places, feeling himself safer in those desert, open stretches of country which mark the first depressions of the basin of the great river. Allahabad was not twelve miles to the northeast. Halt was made under a clump of banana trees, whose fruit, as healthy as bread, "as succulent as cream," travelers say, was very much appreciated.

At two o'clock, the guide entered the shelter of a thick forest, which he had to traverse for a space of several miles. He preferred to travel thus under cover of the woods. At all events, up to this moment there had been no unpleasant meeting, and it seemed as if the journey would be accomplished without accident, when the elephant, showing some signs of uneasiness, suddenly stopped.

It was then four o'clock.

"What is the matter?" asked Sir Francis Cromarty, raising his head above his howdah.

"I do not know, officer," replied the Parsee, listening to a confused murmur which came through the thick branches.

A few moments after, this murmur became more defined. It might have been called a concert, still very distant, of human voices and brass instruments.

Passepartout was all eyes, all ears. Mr. Fogg waited patiently, without uttering a word.

The Parsee jumped down, fastened the elephant to a tree, and plunged into the thickest of the undergrowth. A few minutes later he returned, saying:

"A Brahmin procession is coming this way. If it is possible, let us avoid being seen."

The guide unfastened the elephant, and led him into a thicket, recommending the travelers not to descend. He held himself ready to mount the elephant quickly, should flight become necessary. But he thought that the troop of the faithful would pass without noticing him, for the thickness of the foliage entirely concealed him.

The discordant noise of voices and instruments approached. Monotonous chants were mingled with the sound of the drums and cymbals. Soon the head of the procession appeared from under the trees, at fifty paces from the spot occupied by Mr. Fogg and his companions. Through the branches they readily distinguished the curious *personnel* of this religious ceremony.

In the first line were the priests, with miters upon their heads and attired in long robes adorned with gold and silver lace. They were surrounded by men, women, and children, who were singing a sort of funeral psalmody, interrupted at regular intervals by the beating of tam-tams and cymbals. Behind them on a car with large wheels, whose spokes and felloes represented serpents intertwined, appeared a hideous statue, drawn by two pairs of richly caparisoned zebus. This statue had four arms, its body colored with dark red, its eyes haggard, its hair tangled, its tongue hanging out, its lips colored with henna and betel. Its neck was encircled by a collar of skulls, around its waist a girdle of human hands. It was erect upon a prostrate giant, whose head was missing.

Sir Francis Cromarty recognized this statue.

"The goddess Kali," he murmured; "the goddess of love and death."

" Of death, I grant, but of love, never!" said Passepartout. " The ugly old woman!"

The Parsee made him a sign to keep quiet.

Around the statue there was a group of old fakirs jumping and tossing themselves about convulsively. Smeared with bands of ochre, covered with cross-like cuts, whence their blood escaped drop by drop—stupid fanatics, who, in the great Hindoo ceremonies, precipitated themselves under the wheels of the car of Juggernaut.

Behind them, some Brahmins in all the magnificence of their Oriental costume, were dragging a woman who could hardly hold herself erect.

This woman was young, and as fair as a European. Her head, her neck, her shoulders, her ears, her arms, her hands, and her toes were loaded down with jewels, necklaces, bracelets, earrings, and finger rings. A tunic, embroidered with gold, covered with a light muslin, displayed the outlines of her form.

Behind this young woman—a violent contrast for the eyes—were guards, armed with naked sabers fastened to their girdles and long damaskeened pistols, carrying a corpse upon a palanquin.

It was the body of an old man, dressed in the rich garments of a rajah, having, as in life, his turban embroidered with pearls, his robe woven of silk and gold, his sash of cashmere ornamented with diamonds, and his magnificent arms as an Indian prince.

Then, musicians and a rear guard of fanatics, whose cries sometimes drowned the deafening noise of the instruments, closed up the cortege.

Sir Francis Cromarty looked at all this pomp with a singularly sad air, and turning to the guide, he said: " A suttee?"

The Parsee made an affirmative sign and put his fingers on his lips. The long procession slowly came out from the trees, and soon the last of it disappeared in the depths of the forest.

Little by little the chanting died out. There were still the sounds of distant cries, and finally a profound silence.

Phileas Fogg had heard the word uttered by Sir Francis Cromarty, and as soon as the procession had disappeared, he asked, " What is a suttee?"

" A suttee, Mr. Fogg," replied the brigadier general, " is a human sacrifice, but a voluntary sacrifice. The woman that you have just seen will be burned to-morrow in the early part of the day."

" Oh, the villains! " cried Passepartout, who could not prevent this cry of indignation.

" And this corpse? " asked Mr. Fogg.

" It is that of the prince, her husband," replied the guide, " an independent rajah of Bundelcund."

" How," replied Phileas Fogg, without his voice betraying the least emotion, " do these barbarous customs still exist in India, and have not the English been able to extirpate them? "

" In the largest part of India," replied Sir Francis Cromarty, " these sacrifices do not come to pass; but we have no influence over these wild countries, and particularly over this territory of Bundelcund. All the northern slope of the Vindhias is the scene of murders and incessant robberies."

" The unfortunate woman," murmured Passepartout, " burned alive! "

" Yes," replied the general, " burned, and if she was not you would not believe to what a miserable condition she would be reduced by her near relatives. They would shave her hair; they would scarcely feed her with a few handfuls of rice; they would repulse her; she would be considered as an unclean creature, and would die in some corner like a sick dog. So that the prospect of this frightful existence frequently drives these unfortunates to the sacrifice much more than love or religious fanaticism. Sometimes, however, the sacrifice is really voluntary and the energetic intervention of the government is necessary to prevent it. Some years ago, I was living at Bombay, when a young widow came to the governor to ask his authority for her to be burned with the body of her husband. As you may think, the governor refused. Then the widow left the city, took refuge with an independent rajah, and there she accomplished the sacrifice."

During the narrative of the general, the guide shook his head, and when he was through, said : " The sacrifice which takes place to-morrow is not voluntary."

" How do you know? "

"It is a story which everybody in Bundelcund knows," replied the guide.

"But this unfortunate did not seem to make any resistance," remarked Sir Francis Cromarty.

"Because she was intoxicated with the fumes of hemp and opium."

"But where are they taking her?"

"To the pagoda of Pillaji, two miles from here. There she will pass the night in waiting for the sacrifice."

"And this sacrifice will take place——?"

"At the first appearánce of day."

After this answer, the guide brought the elephant out of the dense thicket, and jumped on his neck. But at the moment that he was going to start him off by a peculiar whistle, Mr. Fogg stopped him and addressing Sir Francis Cromarty, said: "If we could save this woman!"

"Save this woman, Mr. Fogg!" cried the brigadier general.

"I have still twelve hours to spare. I can devote them to her."

"Why, you are a man of heart!" said Sir Francis Cromarty.

"Sometimes," replied Phileas Fogg simply, "when I have time."

CHAPTER XIII
IN WHICH PASSEPARTOUT PROVES AGAIN THAT FORTUNE SMILES UPON THE BOLD

THE design was bold, full of difficulties, perhaps impracticable. Mr. Fogg was going to risk his life, or at least his liberty, and consequently the success of his plans, but he did not hesitate. He found, besides, a decided ally in Sir Francis Cromarty. As to Passepartout, he was ready and could be depended upon. His master's idea excited him. He felt that there was a heart and soul under this icy covering. He almost loved Phileas Fogg.

Then there was the guide. What part would he take in the matter? Would he not be with the Indians? In default of his aid, it was at least necessary to be sure of his neutrality. Sir Francis Cromarty put the question to him frankly.

"Officer," replied the guide, "I am a Parsee, and that women is a Parsee. Make use of me."

"Very well, guide," replied Mr. Fogg.

"However, do you know," replied the Parsee, "that we not only risk our lives, but horrible punishments if we are taken. So see."

"That is seen," replied Mr. Fogg. "I think that we shall have to wait for night to act?"

"I think so too," replied the guide. The brave Hindoo then gave some details as to the victim. She was an Indian of celebrated beauty, of the Parsee race, the daughter of a rich merchant of Bombay. She had received in that city an absolutely English education, and from her manners and cultivation she would have been thought a European. Her name was Aouda.

An orphan, she was married against her will to this old rajah of Bundelcund. Three months after she was a widow. Knowing the fate that awaited her, she fled, was retaken immediately, and the relatives of the rajah, who had an interest in her death, devoted her to this sacrifice from which it seemed that she could not escape.

This narrative could only strengthen Mr. Fogg and his companions in their generous resolution. It was decided that the guide should turn the elephant towards the pagoda of Pillaji, which he should approach as near as possible. A half hour afterwards a halt was made under a thick clump of trees, five hundred paces from the pagoda, which they could not see, but they heard distinctly the yellings of the fanatics.

The means of reaching the victim were then discussed. The guide was acquainted with the pagoda, in which he asserted that the young woman was imprisoned. Could they enter by one of the doors, when the whole band was plunged in the sleep of drunkenness, or would they have to make a hole through the wall? This could be decided only at the moment and the place. But there could be no doubt that the abduction must be accomplished this very night, and not when, daylight arrived, the victim would be led to the sacrifice. Then no human intervention could save her.

Mr. Fogg and his companions waited for night. As soon as the shadows fell, towards six o'clock in the evening, they determined to make a reconnoissance around the pagoda.

The last cries of the fakirs had died out. According to their customs, these Indians were plunged in the heavy intoxication of " hang," liquid opium mixed with an infusion of hemp, and it would perhaps be possible to slip in between them to the temple.

The Parsee guiding, Mr. Fogg, Sir Francis Cromarty, and Passepartout advanced noiselessly through the forest. After ten minutes' creeping under the branches, they arrived on the edge of a small river, and there by the light of iron torches at the end of which was burning pitch, they saw a pile of wood. It was the funeral pile, made of costly sandal wood, and already saturated with perfumed oil. On its upper part the embalmed body of the rajah was resting, which was to be burned at the same time as his widow. At one hundred paces from this pile rose the pagoda whose minarets in the darkness pierced the tops of the trees. " Come! " said the guide in a low voice.

Soon the guide stopped at the end of a clearing, lit up by a few torches. The ground was covered with groups of sleepers, heavy with drunkenness.

In the background, among the trees, the temple of Pillaji stood out indistinctly. But to the great disappointment of the guide, the guards of the rajahs lighted by smoky torches, were watching at the doors, and pacing up and down with drawn sabers. Phileas Fogg and Sir Francis Cromarty understood as well as himself that they could attempt nothing on this side. They stopped and talked together in a low tone.

" Let us wait," said the brigadier general, " it is not eight o'clock yet, and it is possible that these guards may succumb to sleep."

" That is possible, indeed," replied the Parsee.

Phileas Fogg and his companions stretched themselves out at the foot of a tree and waited. They waited thus until midnight. The situation did not change. The same watching outside. It was evident that they could not count on the drowsiness of the guards.

After a final conversation, the guide said he was ready to start. Mr. Fogg, Sir Francis, and Passepartout followed him. They made a pretty long detour, so as to reach the pagoda by the rear. About a half hour past midnight they arrived at the foot of the walls.

But it was not sufficient to reach the foot of the walls, it was necessary to make an opening there. For this operation Phileas Fogg and his companions had nothing at all but their pocket-knives. Fortunately, the temple walls were composed of a mixture of bricks and wood, which could not be difficult to make a hole through. The first brick once taken out, the others would easily follow. They went at it, making as little noise as possible. The Parsee, from one side, and Passepartout, from the other, worked to unfasten the bricks, so as to get an opening two feet wide.

The work was progressing, but—unfortunate mischance—some guards showed themselves at the rear of the pagoda, and established themselves there so as to hinder an approach.

It would be difficult to describe the disappointment of these four men, stopped in their work. "What can we do but leave?" asked the general in a low voice.

"We can only leave," replied the guide.

"Wait," said Fogg. "It will do if I reach Allahabad to-morrow before noon."

"But what hope have you?" replied Sir Francis Cromarty. "It will soon be daylight, and——"

"The chances which escape us now may return at the last moment."

The general would have liked to read Phileas Fogg's eyes. What was this cold-blooded Englishman counting on? Would he, at the moment of the sacrifice, rush towards the young woman, and openly tear her from her murderers?

That would have been madness, and how could it be admitted that this man was mad to this degree? Nevertheless, Sir Francis Cromarty consented to wait until the denouement of this terrible scene. The guide did not leave his companions at the spot where they had hid, but took them back to the foreground of the clearing. There, sheltered by a clump of trees, they could watch the sleeping groups.

In the meantime Passepartout, perched upon the lower branches of a tree, was meditating an idea which had first crossed his mind like a flash, and which finally imbedded itself in his brain. He had commenced by saying to himself, "What madness!" and now he repeated, "Why not, after all? It is a chance, perhaps the only one, and with such brutes——"

At all events, Passepartout did not put his thought into any other shape, but he was not slow in sliding down, with the ease of a snake, on the lower branches of the tree, the end of which bent toward the ground.

The hours were passing, and soon a few less somber shades announced the approach of day. It was like a resurrection in this slumbering crowd. The groups wakened up. The beating of tam-tams sounded, songs and cries burst out anew. The hour had come in which the unfortunate was to die.

The doors of the pagoda were now opened. A more intense light came from the interior. Mr. Fogg and Sir Francis could see the victim, all lighted up, whom two priests were dragging to the outside. It seemed to them that, shaking off the drowsiness of intoxication by the highest instinct of self-preservation, the unfortunate woman was trying to escape from her executioners. Sir Francis's heart throbbed violently, and with a convulsive movement seizing Phileas Fogg's hand, he felt that it held an open knife.

The young woman had fallen again into the stupor produced by the fumes of the hemp. She passed between the fakirs, who escorted her with their religious cries. Phileas Fogg and his companions followed her, mingling with the rear ranks of the crowd.

Two minutes after, they arrived at the edge of the river, and stopped less than fifty paces from the funeral pile, upon which was lying the rajah's body. In the semi-obscurity, they saw the victim, motionless, stretched near her husband's corpse. Then a torch was brought, and the wood, impregnated with oil, soon took fire.

At this moment, Sir Francis Cromarty and the guide held back Phileas Fogg, who in an impulse of generous madness, was going to rush toward the pile.

But Phileas Fogg had already pushed them back, when the scene changed suddenly. A cry of terror arose. The whole crowd, frightened, cast themselves upon the ground.

The old rajah was not dead, then; he was seen suddenly rising upright, like a phantom, raising the young woman in his arms, descending from the pile in the midst of the clouds of smoke which gave him a spectral appearance.

The fakirs, the priests, overwhelmed with a sudden fear, were prostrate, their faces to the ground, not daring to raise their eyes, and look at such a miracle! The inanimate victim was held by the vigorous arms carrying her, without seeming to be much of a weight. Mr. Fogg and Sir Francis had remained standing. The Parsee had bowed his head, and Passepartout, without doubt, was not less stupefied.

The resuscitated man came near the spot where Mr. Fogg and Sir Francis Cromarty were, and said shortly, "Let us be off!"

It was Passepartout himself who had slipped to the pile in the midst of the thick smoke! It was Passepartout who, profiting by the great darkness still prevailing, had rescued the young woman from death! It was Passepartout who, playing his part with the boldest good-luck, passed out in the midst of the general fright!

An instant after the four disappeared in the woods, and the elephant took them onwards with a rapid trot. Cries, shouts, and even a bullet, piercing Phileas Fogg's hat, apprised them that the stratagem had been discovered.

Indeed, on the burning pile still lay the body of the old rajah. The priests, recovered from their fright, learned that the abduction had taken place. They immediately rushed into the forest. The guards followed them. Shots were fired; but the abductors fled rapidly, and, in a few moments they were out of range of balls or arrows.

CHAPTER XIV

IN WHICH PHILEAS FOGG DESCENDS THE ENTIRE SPLENDID VALLEY OF THE GANGES WITHOUT EVER THINKING OF LOOKING AT IT

THE bold abduction had succeeded. An hour after Passepartout was still laughing at his success. Sir Francis Cromarty grasped the hand of the brave fellow. His master said to him, " Good," which in that gentleman's mouth was equivalent to high praise. To which Passepartout replied that all the honor of the affair belonged to his master. As for himself he had only had a " droll " idea, and he laughed in thinking that for a few moments he, Passepartout, the former gymnast, the ex-sergeant of firemen, had been the widower of a charming woman, an old embalmed rajah!

As for the young Indian widow, she had no knowledge of

what had passed. Wrapped up in traveling cloaks, she was resting in one of the howdahs.

Meanwhile the elephant, guided with the greatest certainty by the Parsee, moved on rapidly through the still dark forest. One hour after having left the pagoda of Pillaji, he shot across an immense plain. At seven o'clock they halted. The young woman was still in a state of complete prostration. The guide made her drink a few swallows of water and brandy, but the stupefying influence which overwhelmed her continued for some time longer. Sir Francis Cromarty, who knew the effects of intoxication produced by inhalation of the fumes of hemp, had no uneasiness on her account.

But if the restoration of the young woman was not a question in the general's mind, he was not less assured for the future. He did not hesitate to say to Phileas Fogg that if Aouda remained in India, she would inevitably fall again into the hands of her executioners. These fanatics were scattered throughout the entire peninsula, and notwithstanding the English police, they would certainly be able to recapture their victim, whether at Madras, at Bombay, or at Calcutta. And in support of this remark, Sir Francis quoted a fact of the same nature which had recently transpired. According to his view, the young woman would really not be safe until after leaving India. Phileas Fogg replied that he would note these remarks and think them over.

Towards ten o'clock the guide announced the station of Allahabad. The interrupted line of the railway recommenced there, whence trains traverse, in less than a day and a night, the distance separating Allahabad from Calcutta.

Phileas Fogg ought then to arrive in time to take a steamer which would not leave until the next day, October 25, at noon, for Hong Kong.

The young woman was placed in a waiting-room of the station. Passepartout was directed to purchase for her various articles of dress, such as a robe, shawl, furs, etc., whatever he could find. His master opened an unlimited credit for him.

Passepartout went out immediately and ran through the streets of the city. Allahabad, that is, the " City of God," is one of the most venerated of India, on account of its be-

271

ing built at the junction of two sacred rivers, the Ganges and the Jumna, whose waters attract pilgrims from the whole peninsula. It is said also that, according to the legends of the Ramayana, the Ganges takes its source in heaven, whence, thanks to Brahma, it descends upon the earth.

In making his purchases, Passepartout had soon seen the city, at one time defended by a magnificent fort, which has become a State prison. There are no more commerce and no more manufactures in this city, formerly a manufacturing and commercial point. Passepartout, who vainly sought a variety shop, such as there was in Regent street, a few steps off from Farmer & Co., found only at a second-hand dealer's, an old whimsical Jew, the objects which he needed —a dress of Scotch stuff, a large mantle, and a magnificent otter-skin pelisse, for which he did not hesitate to pay seventy-five pounds. Then, quite triumphant, he returned to the station.

Aouda commenced to revive. The influence to which the priests of Pillaji had subjected her, disappeared by degrees, and her beautiful eyes resumed all their Indian softness.

When the poet-king, Ucaf Uddaul celebrates the charms of the Queen of Ahemhnagara, he thus expresses himself, " Her shining tresses, regularly divided into two parts, encircle the harmonious outlines of her delicate and white cheeks, brilliant with their glow and freshness. Her ebony eyebrows have the form and strength of the bow of Kama, god of love; and under her long silken lashes, in the black pupil of her large limpid eyes, there float, as in the sacred lakes of the Himalaya, the purest reflections of the celestial light. Fine, regular, and white, her teeth shine out between her smiling lips, like dew-drops in the half-closed bosom of the pomegranate blossom. Her ears, types of the symmetric curves, her rosy hands, her little feet, curved and tender as lotus buds, shine with the splendor of the finest pearls of Ceylon, the most beautiful diamonds of Golconda. Her delicate and supple waist, which a hand can clasp, heightens the elegant outline of her rounded figure, and the wealth of her bosom, where youth in its prime displays its most perfect treasures, and under the silken folds of her tunic she seems to have been modeled in pure silver by the divine hand of Vicvarcarma, the immortal sculptor."

But, without all this poetic amplification, it is sufficient to say that Aouda, the widow of the rajah of Bundelcund, was a charming woman in the entire European acceptation of the phrase. She spoke English fluently and with great purity, and the guide had not exaggerated in asserting that this young Parsee woman had been transformed by education.

Meanwhile the train was about to leave Allahabad. The Parsee was waiting. Mr. Fogg paid him the compensation agreed upon, without exceeding it a farthing. This astonished Passepartout a little, who knew everything that his master owed to the devotion of the guide. The Parsee, in fact, had risked his life voluntarily in the affair at Pillaji; and if, later, the Hindoos should learn it, he would hardly escape their vengeance.

The question of Kiouni also remained. What would be done with an elephant bought so dearly?

But Phileas Fogg had already taken a resolution upon this point.

"Parsee," he said to the guide, "you have been serviceable and devoted. I have paid for your service, but not for your devotion. Do you wish this elephant? It is yours."

The eyes of the guide sparkled.

"Your honor is giving me a fortune!" he cried.

"Accept, guide," replied Mr. Fogg, "and I will be yet your debtor."

"Good!" cried Passepartout. "Take him, friend! Kiouni is a brave and courageous animal." And going to the brave he gave him some lumps of sugar, saying, "Here, Kiouni, here, here!"

The elephant uttered some grunts of satisfaction. Then taking Passepartout by the waist, and encircling him with his trunk, he raised him as high as his head. Passepartout, not at all frightened, caressed the animal, who replaced him gently on the ground, and to the shaking of the honest Kiouni's trunk there answered a vigorous shaking of the good fellow's hand.

A few moments after, Phileas Fogg, Sir Francis Cromarty, and Passepartout, seated in a comfortable car, the best seat in which Aouda occupied, were running at full speed towards Benares. Eighty miles at the most separate this place from Allahabad, and they were passed over in two hours.

During this passage the young woman completely revived; the drowsy fumes of the "hang" disappeared. What was her astonishment to find herself on this railway, in this compartment clothed in European habiliments, in the midst of travelers entirely unknown to her. At first her companions gave her the greatest care, and revived her with a few drops of liquor; then the brigadier general told the story. He dwelt upon the devotion of Phileas Fogg, who had not hesitated to stake his life to save her, and upon the denouement of the adventure, due to the bold imagination of Passepartout.

Mr. Fogg let him go on without saying a word. Passepartout, quite ashamed, repeated that "it was not worth while."

Aouda thanked her deliverers profusely, by her tears more than by her words. Her beautiful eyes, rather than her lips, were the interpreters of her gratitude. Then, her thoughts carrying her back to the scenes of the suttee, seeing again the Indian country where so many dangers still awaited her, she shuddered with terror.

Phileas Fogg understood what was passing in Aouda's mind, and, to reassure her, offered, very coolly, to take her to Hong Kong, where she might remain until this affair had died out. Aouda accepted the offer gratefully. At Hong Kong there resided one of her relatives, a Parsee like herself, and one of the principal merchants of that city, which is entirely English, though occupying a point on the Chinese coast.

At half-past twelve, noon, the train stopped at the Benares station. The Brahmin legends assert that this place occupies the site of the ancient Casi, which was formerly suspended in space, between the zenith and the nadir, like Mahomet's tomb. But at this more material period Benares, the Athens of India, was prosaically resting on the earth, and Passepartout could for an instant see its brick houses, its clay huts, which gave it a very desolate appearance, without any local color.

Here was where Sir Francis Cromarty was going to stop. The troops which he was rejoining were camping a few miles to the north of the city. The brigadier general then made his adieus to Phileas Fogg, wishing him all possible success, and expressing the wish that he would recommence the journey in a less original, but more profitable manner. Mr. Fogg pressed lightly his companion's fingers. The parting greetings of Aouda were more demonstrative. She would never forget what she owed Sir Francis Cromarty. As for Passepartout he was honored with a hearty shake of the hand by the general. Quite affected, he asked where and when he could be of service to him. Then they parted.

Leaving Benares, the railway followed in part the valley of the Ganges. Through the windows of the car, the weather being quite clear, appeared the varied country of Behar, mountains covered with verdure, fields of barley, corn, and wheat, jungles full of green alligators, villages well kept, forests yet green. A few elephants, and zebus with large humps, came to bathe in the waters of the sacred river, and also notwithstanding the advanced season and the already cold temperature, bands of Hindoos of both sexes, who were piously performing their holy ablutions.

All this panorama passed like a flash, and frequently a cloud of steam concealed its details from them. The travelers could scarcely see the fort of Chunar, twenty miles to the southeast of Benares, the old stronghold of the rajahs of Behar, Ghazepour, and its large rose-water manufactories; the tomb of Lord Cornwallis rising on the left bank of the Ganges; the fortified town of Buxar; Patna, the great manufacturing and commercial city, where the principal opium market in India is held; Monghir, a more than European town, as English as Manchester or Birmingham, famous for its iron foundries, its manufactories of cutlery, and whose high chimneys cover with a black smoke the heavens of Brahma—a real fist-blow in the country of dreams!

Then night came, and in the midst of the howlings of the tigers, the bears, and the wolves, which fled before the locomotive, the train passed on at full speed, and they saw nothing of the wonders of Bengal, or Golconda, or Gour in ruins, or Mourshedabad, the former capital, or Burdwan, or Hougly, or Chandernagar, that French point in the Indian territory, on which Passepartout would have been proud to see his native flag floating.

Finally, at seven o'clock A. M., Calcutta was reached.

The steamer to leave for Hong Kong did not weigh anchor until noon. Phileas Fogg had then five hours before him.

According to his journal, this gentleman should arrive in the capital of India, October 25, twenty-three days after leaving London, and he arrived there on the stipulated day. He was neither behind nor ahead of time. Unfortunately the two days gained by him between London and Bombay had been lost, we know how, in this trip across the Indian peninsula, but it is to be supposed that Phileas Fogg did not regret them.

CHAPTER XV

IN WHICH THE BAG WITH THE BANK-NOTES IS RELIEVED OF A FEW THOUSANDS POUNDS MORE!

THE train stopped at the station. Passepartout first got out of the car, and was followed by Mr. Fogg, who aided his young companion to descend. Phileas Fogg counted on going directly to the Hong Kong steamer, in order to fix Aouda there comfortably. He did not wish to leave her as long as she was in this country, so dangerous for her.

At the moment that Mr. Fogg was going out of the station a policeman approached him and said, " Mr. Phileas Fogg? "

" I am he."

" Is this man your servant? " added the policeman, pointing to Passepartout.

" Yes."

" You will both be so kind as to follow me."

Mr. Fogg made no movement indicating any surprise. This agent was a representative of the law, and for every Englishman the law is sacred. Passepartout, with his French habits, wanted to discuss the matter, but the policeman touched him with his stick, and Phileas Fogg made him a sign to obey.

" This young lady can accompany us? " asked Mr. Fogg.

" She can," replied the policeman.

The policeman conducted Mr. Fogg, Aouda, and Passepartout to a palki-ghari, a sort of four-wheeled vehicle with four seats, drawn by two horses. They started. No one spoke during the twenty-minutes' ride.

The vehicle first crossed the " black town," with its narrow

streets, its huts in which groveled a miscellaneous population, dirty and ragged; then they passed through the European town, adorned with brick houses, shaded by cocoa-nut
trees, bristling with masts, through which, notwithstanding
the early hour, were driving handsomely dressed gentlemen,
in elegant turn-outs.

The palki-ghari stopped before a dwelling of plain appearance, but not used for private purposes. The policeman let
his prisoners out, for they could, indeed, be called thus, and
he led them into a room with grated windows, saying to
them, "At half-past eight you will appear before Judge
Obadiah."

Then he left, and closed the door.

"See! we are prisoners!" cried Passepartout, dropping
into a chair.

Aouda, addressing Mr. Fogg immediately, said in a voice
whose emotion she sought in vain to disguise, " Sir you must
leave me! It is on my account that you are pursued! It is
because you have rescued me!"

Phileas Fogg contented himself with saying that that
could not be possible. Pursued on account of this suttee
affair! Inadmissible! How would the complainants dare
present themselves? There was a mistake. Mr. Fogg
added that, in any event, he would not abandon the young
woman, and that he would take her to Hong Kong.

"But the steamer leaves at noon!" remarked Passepartout.

"Before noon we shall be on board," was the simple reply
of the impassible gentleman.

This was so flatly asserted that Passepartout could not
help saying to himself, "Parbleu! that is certain! before
noon we will be on board!" But he was not at all re-
assured.

At half-past eight the door of the room was opened. The
policeman reappeared, and he led the prisoners into the next
room. It was a court-room, and quite a large crowd, composed of Europeans and natives, already occupied the rear
of the room.

Mr. Fogg, Aouda, and Passepartout were seated on a
bench in front of the seats reserved for the magistrate and
the clerk.

This magistrate, Judge Obadiah, entered almost immediately, followed by the clerk. He was a large, fat man. He took down a wig hung on a nail and hastily put it on his head. "The first case," he said.

But putting his hand to his head, he added, "Humph! this is not my wig!"

"That's a fact, Mr. Obadiah, it is mine," replied the clerk.

"My dear Mr. Oysterpuff, how do you think that a judge can give a wise sentence with a clerk's wig?"

An exchange of wigs had been made. During these preliminaries, Passepartout was boiling over with impatience, for the hands appeared to him to move terribly fast over the face of the large clock in the court-room.

"The first case," said Judge Obadiah again.

"Phileas Fogg?" said Clerk Oysterpuff.

"Here I am," replied Mr. Fogg.

"Passepartout?"

"Present!" replied Passepartout.

"Good!" said Judge Obadiah. "For two days, prisoners, you have been looked for upon the arrival of all the trains from Bombay."

"But of what are we accused?" cried Passepartout impatiently.

"You shall know now," replied the judge.

"Sir," said Mr. Fogg then, "I am an English citizen, and have the right——"

"Have you been treated disrespectfully," asked Mr. Obadiah.

"Not at all."

"Very well, let the complainants come in."

Upon the order of the judge a door was opened, and three Hindoo priests were led in by a tipstaff.

"Well, well!" murmured Passepartout, "they are the rascals who were going to burn our young lady!"

The priests stood up before the judge, and the clerk read in a loud voice a complaint of sacrilege, preferred against Mr. Phileas Fogg and his servant, accused of having violated a place consecrated by the Brahmin religion.

"You have heard the charge?" the judge asked Phileas Fogg.

"Yes, sir," replied Mr. Fogg, consulting his watch, "and I confess it."

"Ah! You confess?"

" I confess and expect these three priests to confess in their turn what they were going to do at the pagoda of Pillaji."

The priests looked at each other. They did not seem to understand the words of the accused.

" Truly! " cried Passepartout impetuously, " at the pagoda of Pillaji, where they were going to burn their victim! "

More stupefaction of the priests, and profound astonishment of Judge Obadiah.

" What victim? " he answered. " Burn whom? In the heart of the city of Bombay? "

" Bombay? " cried Passepartout.

" Certainly. We are not speaking of the pagoda of Pillaji, but of the pagoda of Malebar in Bombay."

" And as a proof here are the desecrator's shoes," added the clerk, putting a pair on his desk.

" Those are my shoes! " cried Passepartout, who, surprised at the last charge, could not prevent this involuntary exclamation.

The confusion in the minds of the master and servant may be imagined. They had forgotten the incident of the pagoda of Bombay, and that was the very thing which had brought them before the magistrate in Calcutta.

In fact, Fix understood the advantage that he might get from this unfortunate affair. Delaying his departure twelve hours, he had taken counsel with the priests of Malebar Hill, and had promised them large damages, knowing very well that the English Government was very severe upon this kind of trespass; then by the following train he had sent them forward on the track of the perpetrator. But, in consequence of the time employed in the deliverance of the young widow, Fix and the Hindoos arrived at Calcutta before Phileas Fogg and his servant, whom the authorities, warned by telegraph, were to arrest as they got out of the train. The disappointment of Fix may be judged of, when he learned that Phileas Fogg had not yet arrived in the capital of India. He was compelled to think that his robber, stopping at one of the stations of the Peninsular Railway, had taken refuge in the northern provinces. For twenty-four hours, in the greatest uneasiness, Fix watched for him at the station. What was his joy then when, this very morning, he saw him get out of the car, accompanied, it is true, by a young woman whose presence he could not explain. He immediately sent a policeman after him; and this is how Mr. Fogg, Passepartout, and the widow of the rajah of Bundelcund were taken before Judge Obadiah.

And if Passepartout had been less preoccupied with his affair, he would have perceived in a corner of the room the detective, who followed the discussion with an interest easy to understand, for at Calcutta, as at Bombay, and as at Suez, the warrant of arrest was still not at hand!

But Judge Obadiah had taken a note of the confession escaped from Passepartout, who would have given all he possessed to recall his imprudent words.

"The facts are admitted?" said the judge.

"Admitted," replied Mr. Fogg coldly.

"Inasmuch," continued the judge, "as the English law intends to protect equally and rigorously all the religions of the people of India the trespass being admitted by this man Passepartout, convicted of having violated with sacrilegious feet the pavement of the pagoda of Malebar Hill in Bombay, on the 20th day of October, I sentence the said Passepartout to fifteen days' imprisonment, and a fine of three hundred pounds."

"Three hundred pounds!" cried Passepartout, who was really only alive to the fine.

"Silence!" said the tipstaff in a shrill voice.

"And," added Judge Obadiah, "inasmuch as it is not materially proved that there was not a connivance between the servant and the master, the latter of whom ought to be held responsible for the acts and gestures of a servant in his employ, I detain the said Phileas Fogg and sentence him to eight days' imprisonment and one hundred and fifty pounds fine. Clerk, call another case!"

Fix, in his corner, experienced an unspeakable satisfaction. Phileas Fogg, detained eight days in Calcutta! It would be more than time enough for the warrant to arrive.

Passepartout was crushed. This sentence would ruin his master. A wager of twenty thousand pounds lost, and all because, in the height of folly, he had gone into that cursed pagoda!

Phileas Fogg, as much master of himself as if this sentence did not concern him, did not even knit his eyebrows.

THE BAG WITH THE BANK-NOTES

But at the moment that the clerk was calling another case, he rose and said, " I offer bail."

" It is your right," replied the judge.

Fix felt a cold shudder down his back, but he recovered himself again, when he heard the judge, " in consideration of the fact of Phileas Fogg and his servant both being strangers," fix the bail for each at the enormous sum of one thousand pounds.

It would cost Mr. Fogg two thousand pounds, unless he was cleared from his sentence.

" I will pay it," said that gentleman.

And he took from the bag which Passepartout carried a bundle of bank-notes, which he placed on the clerk's desk.

" This sum will be returned to you on coming out of prison," said the judge. " In the meantime, you are free under bail."

" Come," said Phileas Fogg to his servant.

" But they should at least return me my shoes," cried Passepartout, with an angry movement.

They returned him his shoes.

" These are dear! " he murmued; " more than a thousand pounds apiece! Without counting that they pinch me! "

Passepartout, with a very pitiful look, followed Mr. Fogg, who had offered his arm to the young woman. Fix still hoped that his robber would not decide to surrender this sum of two thousand pounds, and that he would serve out his eight days in prison. He put himself, then, on Fogg's tracks.

Mr. Fogg took a carriage, into which Aouda, Passepartout, and he got out immediately. Fix ran behind the carriage, which soon stopped on one of the wharves of the city.

Half a mile out in the harbor the *Rangoon* was anchored, her sailing flag hoisted to the top of the mast. Eleven o'clock struck. Mr. Fogg was one hour ahead. Fix saw him get out of the carriage, and embark in a boat with Aouda and his servant. The detective stamped his foot.

" The rascal! " he cried: " he is going off! Two thousand pounds sacrificed! Prodigal as a robber! Ah! I will follow him to the end of the world, if it is necessary;

but, at the rate at which he is going, all the stolen money will be gone!"

The detective had good reason for making this remark. In fact, since he left London, what with traveling expenses, rewards, the elephant purchase, bail, and fines, Phileas Fogg had already scattered more than five thousand pounds on his route, and the percentage of the sum recovered, promised to the detectives, was constantly diminishing.

CHAPTER XVI

IN WHICH FIX HAS NOT THE APPEARANCE OF KNOWING ANYTHING ABOUT THE MATTERS CONCERNING WHICH THEY TALK TO HIM

THE *Rangoon,* one of the vessels employed by the Peninsular and Oriental Company in the Chinese and Japanese seas, was an iron screw steamer, of seventeen hundred and seventy tons, and nominally of four hundred horse-power. She was equally swift, but not so comfortable as the *Mongolia.* Aouda was not as well fixed in her as Phileas Fogg would have desired. But, after all, it was only a distance of three thousand five hundred miles, and the young woman did not show herself a troublesome passenger.

During the first few days of the passage Aouda became better acquainted with Phileas Fogg. On every occasion she showed him the liveliest gratitude. The phlegmatic gentleman listened to her, at least in appearance, with the most extreme indifference, not one tone of his voice or gesture betraying in him the slightest emotion. He saw that she was wanting in nothing. At certain hours he came regularly, if not to talk with her, at least to listen to her. He fulfilled toward her the duties of the strictest politeness, but with the grace and startling effects of an automaton whose movements had been put together for that purpose. Aouda did not know what to think of him, but Passepartout had explained to her a little the eccentric character of his master. He had told her what sort of a wager was taking him round the world. Aouda had smiled; but, after all, she owed her life to him, and her deliverer could not lose, because she saw him through her gratitude.

Aouda confirmed the narrative of the guide in reference

to her affecting history. She belonged, in fact, to the race which occupies the first rank among the natives. Several Parsee merchants have made large fortunes in India in the cotton trade. One of them, Sir James Jejeebhoy, was raised to the nobility by the English Government, and Aouda was a relative of this rich person, who lived in Bombay. It was indeed a cousin of Sir Jejeebhoy, the honorable Jejeeh, whom she counted on joining at Hong Kong. Would she find a refuge with him and assistance? She could not say so positively. To which Mr. Fogg replied that she should not be uneasy, and everything would be mathematically arranged. That was the phrase he used.

Did the young woman understand this horrible adverb? We do not know. However, her large eyes were fixed upon those of Mr. Fogg—her large eyes " clear as the sacred lakes of the Himalaya! " But the intractable Fogg, as reserved as ever, did not seem to be the man to throw himself into this lake.

The first part of the *Rangoon's* voyage was accomplished under excellent conditions. The weather was moderate. All the lower portion of the immense Bay of Bengal was favorable to the steamer's progress. The *Rangoon* soon sighted the great Andaman, the principal one of the group of islands, which is distinguished by navigators at a great distance by the picturesque Saddle Peak mountain, two thousand four hundred feet high.

The panoramic development of this island was superb. Immense forests of palm trees, arecas, bamboo, nutmeg trees, teak-wood, giant mimosas, and tree-like ferns covered the country in the foreground, and in the background there stood out in relief the graceful outline of the mountains. Along the shore there swarmed by thousands those precious swallows whose eatable nests form a dish much sought for in the celestial empire. But all this varied spectacle offered to the eyes by the Andaman group passed quickly, and the *Rangoon* swiftly pursued her way towards the straits of Malacca, which were to give her access to the Chinese seas.

During this trip what was detective Fix doing, so unluckily dragged into a voyage round the world? On leaving Calcutta, after having left instructions to forward the warrant to him at Hong Kong, if it should arrive, he succeeded in getting aboard the *Rangoon* without being perceived by

Passepartout, and he hoped that he might conceal his presence until the arrival of the steamer. In fact, it would have been difficult for him to explain how he was on board without awaking the suspicions of Passepartout, who thought he was in Bombay. But he was led to renew his acquaintance with the good fellow by the very logic of circumstances. How? We shall see.

All the hopes, all the desires of the detective were now concentrated on a single point in the world, Hong Kong—for the steamer would stop too short a time in Singapore for him to operate in that city. The arrest of the robber must then be made in Hong Kong, or he would escape irrecoverably.

In fact, Hong Kong was still English soil, but the last he would find on the road. Beyond, China, Japan, America would offer a pretty certain refuge to Mr. Fogg. At Hong Kong, if he should finally find there the warrant of arrest, which was evidently running after him, Fix would arrest Fogg, and put him in the hands of the local police. No difficulty there. But after Hong Kong a simple warrant of arrest would not be sufficient. An extradition order would be necessary. Thence delays and obstacles of every kind, of which the rogue would take advantage to escape finally. If he failed at Hong Kong, it would be, if not impossible, at least very difficult to attempt it again with any chance of success.

" Then," repeated Fix during the long hours that he passed in his cabin, " then, either the warrant will be at Hong Kong and I will arrest my man, or it will not be there, and this time I must, at all hazards, delay his departure! I have failed at Bombay, I have failed at Calcutta! If I miss at Hong Kong, I shall lose my reputation! Cost what it may, I *must* succeed. But what means shall I employ to delay, if it is necessary, the departure of this accursed Phileas Fogg? "

As a last resort, Fix had decided to tell everything to Passepartout, to let him know who the master was that he was serving, and whose accomplice he certainly was not. Passepartout, enlightened by this revelation, fearing to be compromised, would without doubt take sides with him, Fix. But it was a very hazardous means, which could only be employed in default of any other. One word from Passepartout to his master would have been sufficient to compromise the affair irrevocably.

The detective was then extremely embarrassed when the presence of Aouda on board of the *Rangoon,* in company with Phileas Fogg, opened new perspectives to him.

Who was this woman? What combination of circumstances had made her Fogg's companion? The meeting had evidently taken place between Bombay and Calcutta. But at what point of the peninsula? Was it chance which had brought together Phileas Fogg and the young traveler? Had not this journey across India, on the contrary, been undertaken by this gentleman with the aim of joining this charming person? For she was charming! Fix had had a good view of her in the audience hall of the Calcutta tribunal.

It may be comprehended to what a point the detective would be entangled. He asked himself if there was not a criminal abduction in this affair. Yes! that must be it! This idea once fastened in the mind of Fix, and he recognized all the advantage that he could get from this circumstance. Whether this young woman was married or not, there was an abduction, and it was possible to put the ravisher in such embarrassment in Hong Kong that he could not extricate himself by paying money.

But it was not necessary to await the arrival of the *Rangoon* at Hong Kong. This Fogg had the detestable habit of jumping from one vessel into another and before the affair was entered upon he might be far enough off.

The important thing was to warn the English authorities, and to signal the *Rangoon* before her arrival. Now, nothing would be easier to accomplish, as the steamer would put in at Singapore, which is connected with the Chinese coast by a telegraph line.

But, before acting, and to be more certain, Fix determined to question Passepartout. He knew it was not very difficult to start the young man talking, and he decided to throw off the incognito that he had maintained until that time. Now there was no time to lose. It was October 31, and the next day the *Rangoon* would drop anchor at Singapore.

This very day, October 30, Fix, leaving his cabin, went upon deck, with the intention of meeting Passepartout first, with signs of the greatest surprise. Passepartout was walking in the forward part of the vessel when the detective rushed toward him exclaiming, " Is this you, on the *Rangoon?* "

" Monsieur Fix aboard! " replied Passepartout, very much surprised, recognizing his old acquaintance of the *Mongolia.*

" What! I left you at Bombay, and I meet you again on the route to Hong Kong! Are you making also the tour of the world? "

" No, no," replied Fix. " I expect to stop at Hong Kong, at least for a few days."

" Ah! " said Passepartout, who seemed astonished for a moment. " But why have I not seen you aboard since we left Calcutta? "

" Indeed, I was sick—a little sea-sickness—I remained lying down in my cabin—I did not get along as well in the Bay of Bengal as in the Indian Ocean. And your master, Phileas Fogg? "

" Is in perfect health, and as punctual as his diary! Not one day behind! Ah! Monsieur Fix, you do not know it, but we have a young lady with us also."

" A young lady? " replied the detective, who acted exactly as if he did not understand what his companion was saying.

But Passepartout soon gave him the thread of the whole story. He related the incident of the pagoda in Bombay, the purchase of the elephant at the cost of two thousand pounds, the suttee affair, the abduction of Aouda, the sentence of the Calcutta court, and their freedom under bail. Fix, who knew the last portion of these incidents, seemed not to know any of them, and Passepartout gave himself up to the pleasure of telling his adventures to a hearer who showed so much interest.

" But," asked Fix at the end of the story, " does your master intend to take this young woman to Europe? "

" Not at all, Monsieur Fix; not at all! We are simply going to put her in charge of one of her relatives, a rich merchant of Hong Kong."

" Nothing to be done there," said the detective to himself, concealing his disappointment. " Take a glass of gin, Mr. Passepartout."

" With pleasure, Monsieur Fix. It is the least that we should drink to our meeting aboard the *Rangoon.*"

AFTER this day, Passepartout and the detective met frequently, but the latter maintained a very great reserve towards his companion, and he did not try to make him talk. Once or twice only he had a glimpse of Mr. Fogg, who was glad to remain in the grand saloon of the *Rangoon,* either keeping company with Aouda, or playing at whist, according to his invariable habit.

As for Passepartout, he thought very seriously over the singular chance which had once more put Fix on his master's route. And in fact, it was a little surprising. This gentleman, very amiable and very complacent, certainly, whom they met first at Suez, who embarked upon the *Mongolia,* who landed at Bombay, where he said that he would stop, whom they meet again on the *Rangoon, en route* for Hong Kong—in a word, following step by step the route marked out by Mr. Fogg—he was worth the trouble of being thought about. There was at least a singular coincidence in it all. What interest had Fix in it? Passepartout was ready to bet his slippers—he had carefully preserved them—that Fix would leave Hong Kong at the same time as they, and probably on the same steamer.

If Passepartout had thought for a century, he would never have guessed the detective's mission. He would never have imagined that Phileas Fogg was being " followed," after the fashion of a robber, around the terrestrial globe. But as it is in human nature to give an explanation for everything, Passepartout, suddenly enlightened, interpreted in his way the permanent presence of Fix, and, indeed, his interpretation was very plausible. According to him Fix was, and could be, only a detective sent upon Mr. Fogg's tracks by his colleagues of the Reform Club, to prove that this tour around the world was accomplished regularly, according to the time agreed upon.

" That is plain! that is plain! " repeated the honest fellow to himself, quite proud of his clearsightedness. " He is a spy whom these gentlemen have put upon our heels. This is undignified! To have Mr. Fogg, a man so honorable and just, tracked by a detective! Ah! gentlemen of the Reform Club, that will cost you dearly! "

Passepartout, delighted with his discovery, resolved, however, to say nothing of it to his master, fearing that he would be justly wounded at this mistrust which his opponents showed. But he promised himself to banter Fix, as opportunity offered, with covert allusions, and without committing himself.

On Wednesday, October 30, in the afternoon, the *Rangoon* entered the Straits of Malacca, separating the peninsula of that name from Sumatra. Mountainous, craggy, and very picturesque islets concealed from the passenger the view of this large island.

At four o'clock the next morning, the *Rangoon,* having gained a half day on its time table, put in at Singapore, to take in a new supply of coal.

Phileas Fogg noted this gain in the proper column, and this time he landed, accompanying Aouda, who had expressed a desire to walk about for a few hours. Fix, to whom every act of Fogg seemed suspicious, followed him without letting himself be noticed. Passepartout, who was going to make his ordinary purchases, laughed *in petto* seeing Fix's maneuver.

The island of Singapore is neither large nor of an imposing aspect. It is wanting in mountains, that is to say, in profiles. However, it is charming even in its meagerness. It is a park laid out with fine roads. An elegant carriage, drawn by handsome horses, such as have been imported from New Holland, took Aouda and Phileas Fogg into the midst of massive groups of palm trees, of brilliant foliage, and clove trees, the cloves of which are formed from the very bud of the half opened flower. Bands of monkeys, lively and grimacing, were not wanting in the woods, nor perhaps tigers in the jungles. Should anyone be astonished to learn that in this island, comparatively so small, these terrible carnivorous animals were not destroyed to the very last one, we may reply that they come from Malacca, swimming across the straits.

After having driven about the country for two hours, Aouda and her companion—who looked a little without seeing anything—returned into the town, a vast collection of heavy, flat looking houses, surrounded by delightful gardens, in which grow mangoes, pineapples, and all the best fruits in the world. At ten o'clock they returned to the steamer, having been followed, without suspecting it, by the detective, who had also gone to the expense of a carriage.

Passepartout was waiting for them on the deck of the *Rangoon.* The good fellow had bought a few dozen of mangoes, as large as ordinary apples—dark brown outside, brilliant red inside—and whose white pulp, melting in the mouth, gives the true gourmand an unexcelled enjoyment. Passepartout was only too happy to offer them to Aouda, who thanked him very gracefully.

About thirteen hundred miles separate Singapore from the island of Hong Kong, a small English territory, detached from the Chinese coast. It was Phileas Fogg's interest to accomplish this in six days at the most, in order to take at Hong Kong the steamer leaving on the 6th of November for Yokohama, one of the principal ports of Japan.

The *Rangoon* was heavily laden. Many passengers had come aboard at Singapore—Hindoos, Ceylonese, Chinamen, Malays and Portuguese—mostly second class. The weather, which had been quite fine until this time, changed with the last quarter of the moon. The sea was high. The wind sometimes blew a gale, but fortunately from the southeast, which favored the movement of the steamer. When it was practicable, the captain had the sails unfurled. The *Rangoon,* brig-rigged, sailed frequently with its two topsails and foresail, and its speed increased under the double impetus of steam and sail. The vessel thus made her way over a short and sometimes fatiguing sea, along the shores of Anam and Cochin China.

But the passengers would have to blame the *Rangoon* rather than the ocean for their sickness and fatigue. In fact, the ships of the Peninsular Company, in the China service, are seriously defective in their construction. The proportion of their draught, when loaded, to their depth of hold, has been badly calculated, and consequently they stand the sea but poorly. Their bulk, closed, impenetrable to the water, is insufficient. They are "drowned," to use a maritime expression, and, in consequence, it does not take very many waves thrown upon the deck to slacken their speed.

Great precautions had to be taken then in bad weather. It was sometimes necessary to sail under a small head of steam. This loss of time did not seem to affect Phileas Fogg at all, but Passepartout was much put out about it. He blamed the captain, the engineer, and the company, and sent to old Nick all those who had anything to do with the transportation of the passengers. Perhaps, also, the thought of the gas burner still burning at his expense in the house in Saville Row had a large share in his impatience.

"Are you in a very great hurry to arrive at Hong Kong?" the detective asked him one day.

"In a very great hurry!" replied Passepartout.

"You think that Mr. Fogg is in a hurry to take the Yokohama steamer?"

"In a dreadful hurry."

"Then you believe now in this singular voyage around the world?"

"Absolutely. And you, Monsieur Fix?"

"I? I don't believe in it."

"You're a sly fellow," replied Passepartout, winking at him.

This expression left the detective in a reverie. The epithet disturbed him without his knowing very well why. Had the Frenchman guessed his purpose? He did not know what to think. But how had Passepartout been able to discover his capacity as a detective, the secret of which he alone knew. And yet, in speaking thus to him Passepartout certainly had an after thought.

It happened another day that the good fellow went a little further. It was too much for him; he could no longer hold his tongue. "Let us see, Monsieur Fix," he asked his companion in a roguish tone, "when we have arrived at Hong Kong, shall we be so unfortunate as to leave you there?"

"Oh!" replied Fix, quite embarrassed, "I do not know! Perhaps——"

"Ah!" said Passepartout, "if you accompany us, I would be so happy! Let us see! An agent of the Peninsular Company could not stop on the route! You were only going to Bombay, and now you will soon be in China. America is not far off, and from America to Europe it is only a step!"

Fix looked attentively at his companion, who showed the pleasantest face in the world, and he decided to laugh with him. But the latter, who was in the humor, asked him if his business brought him in much?

"Yes and no," replied Fix without frowning. "There are fortunate and unfortunate business enterprises. But you understand of course that I don't travel at my own expense!"

"Oh! I am very sure of that," replied Passepartout, laughing still louder.

The conversation finished, Fix returned to his cabin, and sat down to think. He was evidently suspected. In one way or another the Frenchman had recognized his capacity as a detective. But had he warned his master? What *role* would he play in all this? Was he an accomplice or not? Had they got wind of the matter, and was it consequently all up? The detective passed some perplexing hours there, at one time believing everything lost; at one time hoping that Fogg was ignorant of the situation; and, finally, not knowing what course to pursue.

Meanwhile his brain became calmer, and he resolved to act frankly with Passepartout. If matters were not in the proper shape to arrest Fogg at Hong Kong, and if Fogg was then prepared to leave finally the English territory, he (Fix) would tell Passepartout everything. Either the servant was the accomplice of his master, and the latter knew everything, and in this case the affair was definitely compromised, or the servant had no part in the robbery, and then his interest would be to abandon the robber.

Such was the respective situation of these two men, and above them Phileas Fogg was hovering in his majestic indifference. He was accomplishing rationally his orbit around the world, without being troubled by the asteroids gravitating around him.

And yet, in the vicinity, there was—according to the expression of astronomers—a disturbing star which ought to have produced a certain agitation in this gentleman's heart. But no! The charm Aouda did not act, to the great surprise of Passepartout, and the disturbances, if they existed, would have been more difficult to calculate than those of Uranus, which led to the discovery of Neptune. Yes! it was a surprise every day for Passepartout, who read in the eyes of the young woman so much gratitude to his master! Phileas Fogg had decidedly heart enough for heroic actions, but for love, none at all! As for the thoughts which the chances of the journey might have produced in him, there was not a trace.

Passepartout was living in a continual trance. One day, leaning on the railing of the engine-room, he was looking at the powerful engine which sometimes moved very violently, when, with the pitching of the vessel the screw would fly out of the water. The steam then escaped from the valves, which provoked the anger of the worthy fellow. "These valves are not charged enough!" he cried. "We are not going! Oh, these Englishmen! If we were only in an American vessel, we would blow up, perhaps, but we would go more swiftly!"

CHAPTER XVIII
IN WHICH PHILEAS FOGG, PASSEPARTOUT, AND FIX, EACH GOES ABOUT HIS OWN BUSINESS

DURING the last few days of the voyage the weather was pretty bad. The wind became very boisterous. Remaining in the northwest quarter, it impeded the progress of the steamer. The *Rangoon,* too unsteady already, rolled heavily, and the passengers quite lost their temper over the long, tiresome waves which the wind raised at a distance.

During the days of the 3d and 4th of November it was a sort of tempest. The squall struck the sea with violence. The *Rangoon* had to go slowly for half a day, keeping herself in motion with only ten revolutions of the screw, so as to lean with the waves. All the sails had been reefed and there was still too much rigging whistling in the squall.

The rapidity of the steamer, it may be imagined, was very much diminished, and it was estimated that she would arrive at Hong Kong twenty hours behind time, and perhaps more, if the tempest did not cease.

Phileas Fogg looked intently at this spectacle of a raging sea, which seemed to struggle directly against him, with his customary impassibility. His brow did not darken an instant, and yet a delay of twenty hours might seriously interfere with his voyage by making him miss the departure of the Yokohama steamer. But this man without nerves felt neither impatience nor annoyance. It seemed truly as if this tempest formed a part of his programme, and was foreseen. Aouda, who talked with her companion about this mishap, found him as calm as in the past.

Fix did not look at these things in the same light. On the contrary, this tempest pleased him very much. His satisfaction would have known no bounds, if the *Rangoon* had been obliged to fly before the violent storm. All these delays suited him, for they would oblige this man Fogg to remain some days at Hong Kong. Finally the skies with their squalls and tempests became his ally. He was a little sick, it is true, but what did that matter? He did not count his nausea, and when his body was writhing under the sea-sickness, his spirit was merry with the height of its satisfaction.

As for Passepartout, it may be guessed how illy concealed his anger was during this time of trial. Until then, everything had moved on so well! Land and sea seemed to be devoted to his master. Steamers and railways obeyed him. Wind and steam combined to favor his journey. Had the hour of mistakes finally sounded? Passepartout, as if the twenty thousand pounds of the wager had to come out of his purse, was no longer happy. This tempest exasperated him, this squall put him in a rage, and he would have gladly whipped the disobedient sea! Poor fellow! Fix carefully concealed from him his personal satisfaction, and it was well, for if Passepartout had guessed the secret delight of Fix, Fix would have been roughly used.

Passepartout remained on the *Rangoon's* deck during the entire continuance of the blow. He could not remain below; he climbed up in the masts; he astonished the crew and helped at everything with the agility of a monkey. A hundred times he questioned the captain, the officers, the sailors, who could not help laughing at seeing him so much out of countenance. Passepartout wanted to know positively how long the storm would last. They sent him to the barometer, which would not decide to ascend. Passepartout shook the barometer, but nothing came of it, neither the shaking nor the insults that he heaped upon the irresponsible instrument.

Finally the tempest subsided. The sea became calmer on the 4th of November. The wind veered two points to the south and again became favorable. Passepartout cleared up with the weather. The top sails and lower sails could be unfurled, and the *Rangoon* resumed her route with marvelous swiftness.

But all the time lost could not be regained. They could only submit, and land was not signaled until the 6th at five o'clock A. M. The diary of Phileas Fogg put down the arrival of the steamer on the 5th, and she did not arrive until the 6th, which was a loss of twenty-four hours, and of course they would miss the Yokohama steamer.

At six o'clock the pilot came aboard the *Rangoon* and took his place on the bridge to guide the vessel through the channels into the port of Hong Kong.

Passepartout was dying to ask this man whether the Yokohama steamer had left Hong Kong. But he did not dare, preferring to preserve a little hope until the last moment. He had confided his anxiety to Fix, who—the cunning fox—tried to console him by saying that Mr. Fogg would be in time to take the next boat. This put Passepartout in a towering rage.

But if Passepartout did not venture to ask the pilot, Mr. Fogg, after consulting his *Bradshaw,* asked in his quiet manner of the said pilot if he knew when a vessel would leave Hong Kong for Yokohama. "To-morrow morning, at high tide," replied the pilot.

"Ah," said Mr. Fogg, without showing any astonishment.

Passepartout, who was present, would have liked to hug the pilot, whose neck Fix would have wrung with pleasure.

"What is the name of the steamer," asked Mr. Fogg.

"The *Carnatic,*" replied the pilot.

"Was she not to leave yesterday?"

"Yes, sir, but they had to repair one of her boilers, and her departure has been put off until to-morrow."

"Thank you," replied Mr. Fogg, who, with his automatic step, went down again into the saloon of the *Rangoon.*

Passepartout caught the pilot's hand, and, pressing it warmly, said, "Pilot, you are a good fellow!"

The pilot doubtless never knew why his answers had procured him this friendly expression. A whistle blew, and he went again upon the bridge of the steamer and guided her through the flotilla of junks, tankas, fishing-boats, and vessels of all kinds which crowded the channels of Hong

Kong. In an hour the *Rangoon* was at the wharf, and the passengers landed.

It must be confessed that in this circumstance chance had singularly served Phileas Fogg. Without the necessity of repairing her boilers, the *Carnatic* would have left on the 5th of November, and the passengers for Japan would have had to wait a week for the departure of the next steamer. Mr. Fogg, it is true, was twenty-four hours behind time, but this delay could not have any evil consequences for the rest of the journey.

In fact, the steamer which crosses the Pacific from Yokohama to San Francisco was in direct connection with the Hong Kong steamer, and the former could not leave before the latter had arrived. Evidently they would be twenty-four hours behind time at Yokohama, but it would be easy to make them up during the voyage across the Pacific, lasting twenty-two days. Phileas Fogg found himself, then, within about twenty-four hours of the conditions of his programme thirty-five days after leaving London.

The *Carnatic* not leaving until five o'clock the next morning, Mr. Fogg had sixteen hours to attend to his business— that is, that which concerned Aouda. On landing from the vessel, he offered his arm to the young woman and led her to a palanquin. He asked the men who carried it to point him out a hotel, and they named the Club Hotel. The palanquin started, followed by Passepartout, and twenty minutes after they arrived at their destination.

An apartment was secured for the young woman, and Phileas Fogg saw that she was made comfortable. Then he told Aouda that he was going immediately to look for the relative in whose care he was to leave her at Hong Kong. At the same time he ordered Passepartout to remain at the hotel until his return, so that the young woman should not be left alone.

The gentleman was shown the way to the Exchange. There, they would unquestionably know a personage, such as the honorable Jejeeh, who was reckoned among the richest merchants of the city.

The broker whom Mr. Fogg addressed did indeed know the Parsee merchant. But for two years he had not lived in China. Having made his fortune, he had gone to live in

Europe—in Holland, it was believed, which was explained by the extensive correspondence which he had had with that country during his life as a merchant.

Phileas Fogg returned to the Club Hotel. He immediately asked permission to see Aouda, and without any other preamble, told her that the honorable Jejeeh was no longer living in Hong Kong, but probably was living in Holland.

Aouda did not reply at first. Passing her hand over her forehead, she thought for a few moments, and then said in her sweet voice, " What ought I to do, Mr. Fogg?"

" It is very simple," replied the gentleman. " Go on to Europe."

" But I cannot abuse——"

" You do not abuse, and your presence does not at all embarrass my programme. Passepartout!"

" Monsieur," replied Passepartout.

" Go to the *Carnatic* and engage three cabins."

Passepartout, delighted with continuing his voyage in the company of the young woman, who was very gracious to him, immediately left the Club Hotel.

CHAPTER XIX

IN WHICH PASSEPARTOUT TAKES A LITTLE TOO LIVELY IN-TEREST IN HIS MASTER, AND WHAT FOLLOWS

HONG KONG is only a small island secured to England by the treaty of Nanking, after the war of 1842. In a few years, the colonizing genius of Great Britain had established there an important city, and created the port Victoria. This island is situated at the mouth of the Canton river, and sixty miles only separate it from the Portuguese city of Macao, built on the other shore. Hong Kong must necessarily vanquish Macao in a commercial struggle, and now the greatest part of the Chinese transportation is done through the English city. Docks, hospitals, wharves, warehouses, a Gothic cathedral, a Government House, macadamized streets, all would lead one to believe that one of the commercial cities of the counties of Kent or Surrey, traversing the terrestrial sphere, had found a place at this point in China, nearly at its antipodes.

Passepartout, with his hands in his pockets, sauntered to-wards the port Victoria, looking at the palanquins, the curtained carriages still in favor in the Celestial Empire, and all the crowd of Chinese, Japanese, and Europeans hurrying along in the streets. In some things, it was like Bombay, Calcutta, or Singapore that the worthy fellow was finding again on his route. There is thus a track of English towns all around the world.

Passepartout arrived at Victoria port. There, at the mouth of Canton river, was a perfect swarm of the ships of all nations, English, French, American, Dutch, war and merchant vessels, Japanese or Chinese craft, junks, sempas, tankas, and even flower-boats, which formed so many parterres floating on the waters. Walking along, Passepartout noticed a certain number of natives dressed in yellow, all of quite advanced age. Having gone into a Chinese barber's to be shaved " a la Chinese," he learned from Figaro in the shop, who spoke pretty good English, that these ancient men were at least eighty years old, and that at this age they had the privilege of wearing yellow, the Imperial color. Passepartout found this very funny, without knowing exactly why.

His beard shaved, he repaired to the wharf from which the *Carnatic* would leave, and there he perceived Fix walking up and down, at which he was not at all astonished. But the detective showed upon his face marks of great disappointment.

" Good! " said Passepartout to himself; " that will be bad for the gentlemen of the Reform Club! "

And he accosted Fix with his merry smile, without seeming to notice the vexed air of his companion.

Now, the detective had good reasons to fret about the infernal luck which was pursuing him. No warrant! It was evident that the warrant was running after him, and that it could reach him only if he stopped some days in this city. Now, Hong Kong being the last English territory on the route, this Mr. Fogg would escape him finally, if he did not succeed in detaining him there.

" Well, Monsieur Fix, have you decided to come with us as far as America? " asked Passepartout.

" Yes," replied Fix between his closed teeth.

" Well then! " cried Passepartout, shouting with

laughter. " I knew very well that you could not separate yourself from us. Come and engage your berth, come!"

And both entered the ticket office and engaged cabins for four persons. But the clerk told them that the repairs of the *Carnatic* being completed, the steamer would leave at eight o'clock in the evening, and not the next morning, as had been announced.

" Very good!" replied Passepartout, " that will suit my master. I am going to inform him."

At this moment Fix took an extreme step. He determined to tell Passepartout everything. It was the only means, perhaps, that he had of retaining Phileas Fogg for a few days in Hong Kong.

Leaving the office, Fix offered to treat his companion in a tavern. Passepartout had the time. He accepted Fix's invitation.

A tavern opened on the quay. It had an inviting appearance. Both entered. It was a large room, finely decorated, at the back of which was stretched a camp bed, furnished with cushions. Upon this bed were lying a certain number of sleepers.

Some thirty customers in the large room occupied small tables of plaited rushes. Some emptied pints of English beer, ale or porter, others jugs of alcoholic liquors, gin, or brandy. Besides, the most of them were smoking long, red-clay pipes, stuffed with little balls of opium mixed with essence of rose. Then, from time to time, some smoker overcome would fall down under the table, and the waiters of the establishment, taking him by the head and feet, carried him onto the camp-bed, alongside of another. Twenty of these sots were thus laid side by side, in the last stage of brutishness.

Fix and Passepartout understood that they had entered a smoking-house haunted by those wretched, stupefied, lean, idiotic creatures, to whom mercantile England sells annually ten million four hundred thousand pounds' worth of the fatal drug called opium. Sad millions are these, levied on one of the most destructive vices of human nature.

The Chinese Government has tried hard to remedy such an abuse by severe laws, but in vain. From the rich class, to whom the use of opium was at first formally reserved, it has descended to the lower classes, and its ravages can no longer be arrested. Opium is smoked everywhere and always in the Middle Empire. Men and women give themselves up to this deplorable passion, and when they are accustomed to inhaling the fumes they can no longer do without it, except by suffering terrible cramps in the stomach. A great smoker can smoke as many as eight pipes a day, but he dies in five years.

Now it was in one of the numerous smoking-houses of this kind, which swarm even in Hong Kong, that Fix and Passepartout had entered with the intention of refreshing themselves. Passepartout had no money, but he accepted willingly the "politeness" of his companion, ready to return it to him at the proper time and place.

They called for two bottles of port, to which the Frenchman did full justice, whilst Fix, more reserved, observed his companion with the closest attention. They talked of one thing and another, and especially of the excellent idea that Fix had of taking passage on the *Carnatic*. The bottles now being empty, Passepartout rose to inform his master that the steamer would leave several hours in advance of the time announced.

Fix detained him.

"One moment," he said.

"What do you wish, Monsieur Fix?"

"I have some serious matters to talk to you about."

"Serious matters?" cried Passepartout, emptying the few drops of wine remaining in the bottom of his glass. "Very well, we will talk about them to-morrow. I have not the time to-day."

"Remain," replied Fix. "It concerns your master, Phileas Fogg."

Passepartout, at this phrase, looked attentively at his questioner. The expression of Fix's face seemed singular to him. He took a seat again. "What have you to say to me?" he asked.

Fix placed his hand upon his companion's arm, and lowering his voice, he asked him, "You have guessed who I am."

"Parbleu!" said Passepartout smiling.

"Then I am going to tell you everything."

"Now that I know everything, my friend. Ah! that's pretty tough! But go on. But first let me tell you that these gentlemen have put themselves to very useless expense."

"Useless," said Fix. "You speak confidently! It may be seen that you do not know the size of the sum!"

"But I do know it," said Passepartout. "Twenty thousand pounds!"

"Fifty-five thousand!" replied Fix, grasping the Frenchman's hand.

"What!" cried Passepartout, "Monsieur Fogg would have dared—Fifty-five thousand pounds! Well, well! All the more reason that I should not lose an instant," he added rising again.

"Fifty-five thousand pounds!" replied Fix, who forced Passepartout to sit down again, after having ordered a decanter of brandy,—"and if I succeed, I get a reward of two thousand pounds. Do you wish five hundred of them on condition that you help me?"

"Help you!" cried Passepartout, whose eyes were opened very wide.

"Yes, help me to detain Mr. Fogg in Hong Kong for a few days!"

"Phew!" said Passepartout, "what are you saying? How, not satisfied with having my master followed, with suspecting his faithfulness, do these gentlemen wish to throw new obstacles in his way. I am ashamed for them."

"Ah! what do you mean by that?" asked Fix.

"I mean that it is simple indelicacy. It is about the same as stripping Monsieur Fogg and putting his money in their pockets."

"Ah! that is the very thing we are coming to!"

"But it is a trap!" cried Passepartout—who was getting lively under the influence of the brandy with which Fix was plying him, and which he drank without noticing it—"a real trap! Gentlemen! Colleagues!"

Fix began to be puzzled.

"Colleagues!" cried Passepartout, "members of the Reform Club! You must know, Monsieur Fix, that my master is an honest man, and that, when he has made a bet, he intends to win it fairly."

"But who do you think I am?" asked Fix, fastening his look upon Passepartout.

"Parbleu! an agent of the members of the Reform Club

with the mission to interfere with my master's journey, which is singularly humiliating. So, although it has been some time already since I guessed your business, I have taken good care not to disclose it to Monsieur Fogg."

"He knows nothing?" asked Fix quickly.

"Nothing," answer Passepartout, emptying his glass once more.

The agent passed his hand over his forehead. He hesitated before continuing the conversation. What ought he to do? The error of Passepartout seemed sincere, but it rendered his plan more difficult. It was evident that this young man was speaking with perfect good faith, and that he was not his master's accomplice—which Fix had feared. "Well," he said to himself, "since he is not his accomplice, he will aid me."

The detective had the advantage a second time. Besides, he had no more time to wait. At any cost Fogg must be arrested at Hong Kong.

"Listen," said Fix, in an abrupt tone, "listen carefully to me. I am not what you think, that is, an agent of the members of the Reform Club——"

"Bah!" said Passepartout, looking at him in a jocose way.

"I am a police detective, charged with a mission by the Metropolitan Government.

"You—a detective!"

"Yes, and I will prove it," replied Fix. "Here is my commission."

And the agent, taking a paper from his pocket-book, showed his companion a commission signed by the Commissioner of the Central Police. Passepartout stunned, unable to articulate a word, looked at Fix.

"The bet of Mr. Fogg," continued Fix, "is only a pretext of which you are the dupes, you and his colleagues of the Reform Club, for he had an interest in assuring himself of your unconscious complicity."

"But why?" cried Passepartout.

"Listen. The 28th of September, ultimo, a robbery of fifty-five thousand pounds was committed at the Bank of England, by an individual whose description they were able to obtain. Now, look at this description, and it is feature for feature that of Mr. Fogg."

"Humbug!" cried Passepartout, striking the table with his clenched fist. "My master is the most honest man in the world!"

"How do you know?" replied Fix. "You are not even acquainted with him. You entered his service the day of his departure, and he left precipitately under a senseless pretext, without trunks, and carrying with him a large sum in bank notes! And you dare to maintain that he is an honest man?"

"Yes, yes!" repeated the poor fellow mechanically.

"Do you wish, then, to be arrested as his accomplice?"

Passepartout dropped his head in his hands. He could no longer be recognized. He did not look at the detective. Phileas Fogg, the deliverer of Aouda, the brave and generous man, a robber! And yet how many presumptions there were against him. Passepartout tried to force back the suspicions which would slip into his mind. He would never believe in his master's guilt.

"To conclude, what do you want of me?" said he to the detective by a strong effort.

"See here," replied Fix, "I have tracked Mr. Fogg to this point, but I have not yet received the warrant of arrest, for which I asked, from London. You must help me, then, to keep him in Hong Kong——"

"I! Help you!"

"And I will share with you the reward of two thousand pounds promised by the Bank of England!"

"Never!" replied Passepartout, who wanted to rise and fell back, feeling his reason and his strength at once escaping him.

"Monsieur Fix," he said, stammering, "even if everything you have told me should be true—if my master should be the robber whom you seek—which I deny—I have been —I am in his service—I have seen him kind and generous— betray him—never—no, not for all the gold in the world— I am from a village where they don't eat that kind of bread!"

"You refuse?"

"I refuse."

"Treat it as if I had said nothing," replied Fix, "and let's take a drink."

"All right, let's take a drink!"

Passepartout felt himself more and more overcome by intoxication. Fix, understanding that he must at all hazards separate him from his master, wanted to finish him. On the table were a few pipes filled with opium. Fix slipped one into Passepartout's hand, who took it, lifted it to his lips, lighted it, took a few puffs, and fell over, his head stupefied under the influence of the narcotic.

" At least," said Fix, seeing Passepartout out of the way, " Mr. Fogg will not be informed in time of the departure of the *Carnatic,* and if he leaves he will at least be without this cursed Frenchman ! "

Then he left, after paying his bill.

CHAPTER XX
IN WHICH FIX COMES IN DIRECT CONTACT WITH PHILEAS FOGG

DURING this scene, which might perhaps seriously interfere with his future, Mr. Fogg, accompanying Aouda, was taking a walk through the streets of the English town. Since Aouda accepted his offer to take her to Europe, he had to think of all the details necessary for so long a journey. That an Englishman like him should make the tour of the world with a carpet-bag in his hand, might pass; but a lady could not undertake such a journey under the same conditions. Hence, the necessity of buying clothing and articles necessary for the voyage. Mr. Fogg acquitted himself of his task with the quiet characteristic of him, and he invariably replied to all the excuses and objections of the young woman, confused by so much kindness. " It is the interest of my journey; it is in my programme."

The purchases made, Mr. Fogg and the young woman returned to the hotel and dined at the *table d'hôte,* which was sumptuously served. Then Aouda, a little tired, went up into her room after having shaken hands English fashion with her imperturbable deliverer.

He, Fogg, was absorbed all the evening in reading the *Times* and the *Illustrated London News.* If he had been a man to be astonished at anything it would have been not to have seen his servant at the hour for retiring. But knowing that the Yokohama steamer was not to leave Hong

Kong before the next morning, he did not otherwise bother himself about it. The next morning Passepartout did not come at Mr. Fogg's ring.

What the honorable gentleman thought on learning that his servant had not returned to the hotel, no one could have said. Mr. Fogg contented himself with taking his carpet-bag, calling for Aouda and sending for a palanquin. It was then eight o'clock, and high tide, of which the *Carnatic* was to take advantage to go out through the passes, was put down at half-past nine.

When the palanquin arrived at the door of the hotel, Mr. Fogg and Aouda got into the comfortable vehicle, and their baggage followed them on a wheelbarrow. Half an hour later the travelers dismounted on the wharf and there Phileas Fogg learned that the *Carnatic* had left the evening before.

Mr. Fogg, who counted on finding at the same time both the steamer and his servant, was compelled to do without both. But not a sign of disappointment appeared upon his face; and, when Aouda looked at him with uneasiness, he contented himself with replying, " It is an incident, Madame, nothing more."

At this moment a person who had been watching him closely came up to him. It was the detective, Fix, who turned to him and said, " Are you not like myself, sir, one of the passengers of the *Rangoon,* who arrived yesterday? "

" Yes, sir," replied Mr. Fogg coldly, " but I have not the honor——"

" Pardon me, but I thought I would find your servant here."

" Do you know where he is, sir? " asked the young woman quickly.

" What! " replied Fix, feigning surprise, " is he not with you? "

" No," replied Aouda. " He has not returned since yesterday. Has he perhaps embarked without us aboard the *Carnatic?* "

" Without you, madame? " replied Fix. " But, excuse my question, you expected then to leave by that steamer? "

" Yes, sir."

" I too, madame, and I am much disappointed. The *Carnatic,* having completed her repairs, left Hong Kong twelve hours sooner without warning anyone, and we must now wait a week for another steamer!"

Fix felt his heart jump for joy in pronouncing these words, "a week." A week! Fogg detained a week at Hong Kong! There would be time to receive the warrant of arrest. Chance would at last declare for the representative of the law.

It may be judged then what a stunning blow he received, when he heard Phileas Fogg say in his calm voice. "But there are other vessels than the *Carnatic,* it seems to me, in the port of Hong Kong."

And Mr. Fogg, offering his arm to Aouda, turned towards the docks in search of a vessel leaving. Fix, stupefied, followed. It might have been said that a thread attached him to this man.

However, chance seemed really to abandon him whom it had served so well up to that time. Phileas Fogg, for three hours, traversed the port in every direction, decided, if it was necessary, to charter a vessel to take him to Yokohama; but he saw only vessels loading or unloading, which consequently could not set sail. Fix began to hope again.

But Mr. Fogg was not disconcerted, and he was going to continue his search, if he had to go as far as Macao, when he was accosted by a sailor on the end of the pier. "Your honor is looking for a boat?" said the sailor to him, taking off his hat.

"You have a boat ready to sail?" asked Mr. Fogg.

"Yes, your honor, a pilot-boat, the best in the flotilla."

"She goes fast?"

"Between eight and nine knots an hour, nearly the latter. Will you look at her?"

"Yes."

"Your honor will be satisfied. Is it for an excursion?"

"No; for a voyage."

"A voyage?"

"You will undertake to convey me to Yokohama?"

The sailor, at these words, stood with arms extended and eyes starting from his head. "Your honor is joking?" he said.

"No, I have missed the sailing of the *Carnatic,* and I must be at Yokohama on the 14th, at the latest, to take the steamer for San Francisco."

"I regret it," replied the pilot, "but it is impossible."

"I offer you one hundred pounds per day, and a reward of two hundred pounds if I arrive in time."

"You are in earnest?" asked the pilot.

"Very much in earnest," replied Mr. Fogg.

The pilot withdrew to one side. He looked at the sea, evidently struggling between the desire to gain an enormous sum and the fear of venturing so far. Fix was in mortal suspense.

During this time, Mr. Fogg had returned to Aouda. "You will not be afraid, madame?" he asked.

"With you—no, Mr. Fogg," replied the young woman.

The pilot had come towards the gentleman again, and was twisting his hat in his hands.

"Well, pilot?" said Mr. Fogg.

"Well, your honor," replied the pilot, "I can risk neither my men, nor myself, nor yourself, in so long a voyage on a boat scarcely twenty tons, at this time of the year. Besides, we would not arrive in time, for it is sixteen hundred and fifty miles from Hong Kong to Yokohama."

"Only sixteen hundred," said Mr. Fogg.

"It is the same thing."

Fix took a good long breath.

"But," added the pilot, "there might perhaps be a means to arrange it otherwise."

Fix did not breathe any more.

"How?" asked Phileas Fogg.

"By going to Nagasaki, the southern extremity of Japan, eleven hundred miles, or only to Shanghai, eight hundred miles from Hong Kong. In this last journey, we would not be at any distance from the Chinese coast, which would be a great advantage, all the more so that the currents run to the north."

"Pilot," replied Phileas Fogg, "I must take the American mail steamer at Yokohama, and not at Shanghai or Nagasaki."

"Why not?" replied the pilot. "The San Francisco steamer does not start from Yokohama. She stops there and at Nagasaki, but her port of departure is Shanghai."

"You are certain of what you are saying?"

"Certain."

"And when does the steamer leave Shanghai?"

" On the 11th, at seven o'clock in the evening. We have then four days before us. Four days, that is ninety-six hours, and with an average of eight knots an hour, if we have good luck, if the wind keeps to the southeast, if the sea is calm, we can make the eight hundred miles which separate us from Shanghai."

" And you can leave——"

" In an hour, time enough to buy my provisions and hoist sail."

" It is a bargain—you are the master of the boat? "

" Yes, John Bunsby, master of the *Tankadere.*"

" Do you wish some earnest money? "

" If it does not inconvenience your honor."

" Here are two hundred pounds on account—Sir," added Phileas Fogg turning towards Fix, " if you wish to take advantage——"

" Sir," answered Fix resolutely, " I was going to ask this favor of you."

" Well. In half an hour we will be on board."

" But this poor fellow—" said Aouda, whom Passepartout's disappearance worried very much.

" I am going to do all I can to find him," replied Phileas Fogg.

And while Fix, nervous, feverish, angry, repaired to the pilot boat, the two others went to the police station at Hong Kong. Phileas Fogg gave there Passepartout's description, and left a sufficient sum to find him.· The same formality was carried out at the French consular agent's, and the palanquin having stopped at the hotel where the baggage had been taken took the travelers back to the outer pier.

Three o'clock struck. The pilot-boat, No. 43, her crew on board, and her provisions stowed away, was ready to set sail. She was a charming little schooner of twenty tons —this *Tankadere*—with a sharp cut-water, very graceful shape, and long water lines. She might have been called a racing yacht. Her shining copper sheathing, her galvanized iron work, her deck white as ivory, showed that Master John Bunsby knew how to keep her in good condition. Her two masts leaned a little to the rear. She carried brigantine-foresail, storm-jib, and standing-jib, and could rig up splendidly for a rear wind. She ought to sail wonderfully well, and in fact she had won several prizes in pilot-boat matches.

The crew of the *Tankadere* was composed of the master, John Bunsby, and four men. They were of that class of hardy sailors who, in all weathers, venture out in search of vessels, and are thoroughly acquainted with these seasons. John Bunsby, a man about forty-five years, vigorous, well sunburnt, of a lively expression, of an energetic face, self-reliant, well posted in his business, would have inspired confidence in the most timorous.

Phileas Fogg and Aouda went on board. Fix was already there. They went down by steps in the rear of the schooner into a square cabin, whose walls bulged out in the form of cots, above a circular divan. In the middle, there was a table lighted by a hanging lamp. It was small, but neat.

" I regret having nothing better to offer you," said Mr. Fogg to Fix, who bowed without replying.

The detective felt somewhat humiliated by thus taking advantage of Mr. Fogg's kindnesses. " Surely," he thought, " he is a very polite rogue, but he is a rogue!"

At ten minutes after three the sails were hoisted. The English flag was flying at the gaff of the schooner. The passengers were seated on deck. Mr. Fogg and Aouda cast a last look at the wharf, in hopes of seeing Passepartout.

Fix was not without apprehension, for chance might have brought to this place the unfortunate young man whom he had so indignantly treated, and then an explanation would have taken place, from which the detective would not have got out to advantage. But the Frenchman did not show himself, and doubtless the stupefying narcotic still held him under its influence.

Finally, Master John Bunsby ordered a start, and the *Tankadere,* taking the wind under her brigantine, foresail, and standing jib, flew out in the sea.

IN WHICH THE MASTER OF THE " TANKADERE " RUNS GREAT RISK OF LOSING A REWARD OF TWO HUNDRED POUNDS

THIS voyage of eight hundred miles, undertaken in a craft of twenty tons, and especially in that season of the year, was venturesome. The Chinese seas are generally rough, exposed to terrible blows, principally during the equinoxes, and this was in the first days of November.

It would have very evidently been to the advantage of the pilot to take his passengers as far as Yokohama, as he was paid so much per day. But it would have been great imprudence on his part to attempt such a voyage under such conditions, and it was a bold act, if not a rash one, to go as far as Shanghai. But John Bunsby had confidence in his *Tankadere,* which rode the waves like a gull, and perhaps he was not wrong.

During the later hours of this day the *Tankadere* sailed through the capricious channels of Hong Kong, and, in all her movements, from whatever quarter the wind came, she behaved handsomely.

" I do not need, pilot," said Phileas Fogg, the moment the schooner touched the open sea, " to recommend to you all possible diligence."

" Your honor may depend upon me," replied John Bunsby. " In the matter of sails, we are carrying all that the wind will allow us to carry. Our poles would add nothing, and would only interfere with the sailing of our craft."

" It is your trade, and not mine, pilot, and I trust to you."

Phileas Fogg, his body erect, and legs wide apart, standing straight as a sailor, looked at the surging sea without staggering. The young woman seated aft, felt quite affected looking at the ocean, already darkened by the twilight, which she was braving upon so frail a craft. Above her head were unfurled the white sails, looking in space like immense wings. The schooner, impelled by the wind, seemed to fly through the air.

Night set in. The moon was entering her first quarter, and her scanty light was soon extinguished in the haze of the horizon. Clouds were rising from the east, and already covered a portion of the heavens.

The pilot had put his lights in position—an indispensable

precaution to take in these seas, so much frequented by vessels bound landward. Collisions were not rare, and at the rate she was going, the schooner would be shattered by the least shock.

Fix was dreaming forward on the vessel. He kept himself apart, knowing Fogg naturally to be not much of a talker. Besides, he hated to speak to this man, whose accommodations he had accepted. He·was thinking thus of the future. It appeared certain to him that Mr. Fogg would not stop at Yokohama, that he would immediately take the San Francisco steamer to reach America, whose vast extent would assure him impunity with security. It seemed to him that Phileas Fogg's plan could not be simpler.

Instead of embarking in England for the United States, like a common rogue, this Fogg had made the grand rounds, and traversed three-quarters of the globe, in order to gain more surely the American continent, where he would quietly consume the large sum stolen from the bank, after having thrown the police off his track. But, once upon the soil of the United States, what would Fix do? Abandon this man? No, a hundred times no! And until he had obtained an extradition order he would not leave him for an instant. It was his duty, and he would fulfill it to the end. In any event one happy result had been obtained. Passepartout was no longer with his master; and, especially after the confidence Fix had reposed in him, it was important that the master and servant should never see each other again.

Phileas Fogg was constantly thinking of his servant, who had disappeared so singularly. After having thought over everything, it seemed not impossible to him that, in consequence of a misunderstanding, the poor fellow had set sail upon the *Carnatic* at the last moment. It was the opinion of Aouda also, who regretted very much this good servant, to whom she owed so much. It might be that they would find him again at Yokohama, and if the *Carnatic* had taken him thither, it would be easy to find it out.

Towards ten o'clock the breeze began to freshen. Perhaps it would have been prudent to take in a reef, but the pilot, having carefully examined the state of the heavens, left the rigging as it was. Besides, the *Tankadere* carried sail admirably, having a deep draft of water, and everything was prepared to go rapidly, in case of a gale.

At midnight Phileas Fogg and Aouda descended into the cabin. Fix had preceded them, and was stretched on one of the cots. As for the pilot and his men, they remained on deck all night.

The next day, the 8th of November, at sunrise, the schooner had made more than one hundred miles. Her course, frequently tried, showed that the average of her speed was between eight and nine knots an hour. The *Tankadere* carried full sail, and in this rig she obtained the maximum of rapidity. If the wind kept the same, the chances were in her favor.

The *Tankadere*, during the whole day, did not go far from the coast, whose currents were favorable to her, and which was five miles off at the most from her larboard quarter, and irregularly outlined appeared sometimes across the clearings. The wind coming from the land was, on that account, not quite so strong, a fortunate circumstance for the schooner, for vessels of a small tonnage suffer above all from the roll of the sea which interferes with their speed, "killing" them, to use the sailors' expression.

Towards noon the breeze abated a little and set in from the southeast. The pilot put up his poles; but at the end of two hours it was necessary to take them down, as the wind freshened up again.

Mr. Fogg and the young woman, very fortunately unaffected by seasickness, ate with a good appetite the preserves and ship biscuit. Fix was invited to share their repast, and was compelled to accept, knowing very well that it is as necessary to ballast stomachs as vessels, but it vexed him! To travel at this man's expense, to be fed from his provisions, was rather against his grain. He ate, daintily, it is true, but finally he ate.

However, this repast finished, he took Mr. Fogg aside and said to him: "Sir——"

This "sir" scorched his lips, and he controlled himself so as not to collar this "gentleman"! "Sir, you have been very kind to offer me a passage on your vessel. But, although my resources do not permit me to expend as freely as you, I intend to pay my share——"

"Let us not speak of that, sir," replied Mr. Fogg.

"But, if I insist——"

"No, sir," repeated Fogg, in a tone which did not admit of reply. "That will enter into the general expenses."

Fix bowed; he had a stifling feeling, and going forward, he lay down, and did not say a word more during the day.

In the meantime they were moving on rapidly. John Bunsby had high hopes. He said to Mr. Fogg several times that they would arrive at Shanghai at the desired time. Mr. Fogg simply replied that he counted on it. The whole crew went to work in earnest. The reward enticed these good people. So there was not a sheet which was not conscientiously tightened! Not a sail which was not vigorously hoisted! Not a lurch for which the man at the helm could be blamed. They would not have maneuvered more rigorously in a regatta of the Royal Yacht Club.

In the evening, the pilot marked on the log a distance of two hundred and twenty miles from Hong Kong, and Phileas Fogg might hope that on arriving at Yokohama he would not have to note any delay in his journal. Thus, the first serious mischance that he had suffered since his departure from London would probably not affect his journey worth mentioning.

During the night, towards the early morning hours, the *Tankadere* entered, without difficulty, the Straits of Fo Kien, which separate the large Island of Formosa from the Chinese coast, and she crossed the Tropic of Cancer. The sea was very rough in these straits, full of eddies formed by counter-currents. The schooner labored heavily. The short waves broke her course. It became very difficult to stand upon the deck.

With daybreak, the wind became fresher. There was the appearance of a squall in the heavens. Besides, the barometer announced a speedy change of the atmosphere; its daily movement was irregular, and the mercury oscillated capriciously. The sea was seen rising towards the southeast in long swells, betokening a tempest. The evening before the sun had set in a red haze, amid the phosphorescent scintillations of the ocean.

The pilot examined the threatening aspect of the sky for a long time, and muttered between his teeth indistinctly. At a certain moment, finding himself near his passenger, he said in a low voice: "Can I speak freely to your honor?"

"You can," replied Phileas Fogg.

"Well, we are going to have a squall."

"Will it come from the north or the south," asked Mr. Fogg simply.

"From the south. See. A typhoon is coming up."

"Good for the typhoon from the south, since it will send us in the right direction," replied Mr. Fogg.

"If you take it so," replied the pilot, "I have nothing more to say."

John Bunsby's presentiments did not deceive him. At a less advanced season of the year, the typhoon, according to the expression of a celebrated meteorologist, would have passed off like a luminous cascade of electric flames, but in November it was to be feared that it would burst with violence.

The pilot took his precautions in advance. He had all the schooner's sails reefed, and the yards brought on deck. The pole-masts were dispensed with. All hands went forward. The hatches were carefully fastened. Not a drop of water could then enter the hull of the vessel. A single triangular sail, a foresail of strong canvas, was hoisted as a storm-jib, so as to hold the schooner to the wind behind. And they waited.

John Bunsby had begged his passengers to go down into the cabin; but in the narrow space, almost deprived of air, and knocked about by the waves, this imprisonment had in it nothing agreeable. Neither Mr. Fogg, nor Aouda, nor even Fix was contented to leave the deck.

Towards eight o'clock the storm of rain and wind struck the deck. With nothing but her little bit of sail, the *Tankadere* was raised like a feather by the wind, the violence of which could not well be described in words. Compare her speed to quadruple that of a locomotive rushing along under full head of steam, and it would still be below the truth.

During the whole day the vessel ran on thus towards the north, carried by the tremendous waves, preserving, fortunately, a rapidity equal to theirs. Twenty times she was almost submerged by these mountains of water which rose upon her from the rear, but an adroit turn of the helm by the pilot warded off the catastrophe. The passengers were sometimes covered all over by the showers of spray, which they received philosophically. Fix did not like it, doubtless, but the intrepid Aouda, with her eyes fixed upon her companion, whose coolness she could only admire, showed herself worthy of him, and braved the storm at his side. As for Phileas Fogg, it seemed as if this typhoon formed a part of his programme.

Up to this time the *Tankadere* had always held her course towards the north; but, toward evening, as might have been feared, the wind, shifting three-quarters, blew from the northwest. The schooner, now having her side to the waves, was terribly shaken. The sea struck her with a violence well calculated to terrify anyone who does not know how solidly every part of a vessel is fastened together.

With nightfall the tempest grew wilder. Seeing darkness come on, and with it the increase of the storm, John Bunsby felt great uneasiness. He asked himself if it would not be time to put in somewhere, and he consulted his crew.

His men consulted, John Bunsby approached Mr. Fogg, and said to him: " I belive, your honor, that we would do well to make one of the ports of the coast."

" I believe so, also," replied Phileas Fogg.

" Ah!" said the pilot, " but which one?"

" I only know one," replied Mr. Fogg quietly.

" And that is——?"

" Shanghai!"

The pilot could not at first comprehend for a few moments what this answer meant; how much obstinacy and tenacity it comprised. Then he cried: " Ah, well, yes! your honor is right. On to Shanghai!"

And the direction of the *Tankadere* was unwaveringly kept to the north.

It was truly a terrible night! It was a miracle that the little craft did not capsize. Twice she was submerged, and everything would have been carried off the deck, if the fastening of the ropes had given way. Aouda was worn out, but she did not utter a complaint. More than once Mr. Fogg had to rush towards her to protect her from the violence of the waves.

Daylight reappeared. The tempest was still raging with the greatest fury. However, the wind fell again into the southeast. It was a favorable change, and the *Tankadere* resumed her way on this high sea, whose waves then struck

314

those produced by the new direction of the wind. Thence a shock of counter-rolling waves, which would have crushed a less solidly built bark.

From time to time through the broken mist the coast could be perceived, but not a ship in sight. The *Tankadere* was the only one keeping the sea.

At noon there were some signs of a calm, which, with the sinking of the sun towards the horizon, were more distinct. The short duration of the tempest was owing to its very violence. The passengers, completely worn out, could eat a little and take some rest.

The night was comparatively quiet. The pilot had the sails again hoisted at a low reef. The speed of the vessel was considerable. The next day, the 11th, at day-dawn, the coast being sighted, John Bunsby was able to assert that they were not one hundred miles from the wharfs at Shanghai.

One hundred miles, and only this day left to make the distance! That very evening Mr. Fogg ought to arrive at Shanghai, if he did not wish to miss the departure of the Yokohama steamer. Without this storm, during which he lost several hours, he would not, at this moment, have been thirty miles from port.

The breeze sensibly slackened, but fortunately the sea fell with it. The schooner was covered with canvas. Poles, stay-sails, counter-jibs, all were carried, and the sea foamed under her keel.

At noon, the *Tankadere* was not more than forty-five miles from Shanghai. She had six hours more to make that port before the departure of the steamer for Yokohama.

The fears of all were great; they wanted to arrive at any cost. All felt their hearts impatiently beating—Phileas Fogg doubtless excepted. The little schooner must keep up an average of nine knots an hour, and the wind was constantly going down! It was an irregular breeze, with capricious puffs coming from the coast. They passed, and the sea became more smooth immediately after.

But the vessel was so light, and her high sails, of a fine material, caught the capricious breeze so well that, with the current in their favor, at six o'clock John Bunsby counted only ten miles to Shanghai river, for the city itself is situated at a distance of twelve miles at least above the mouth. At seven o'clock they were still three miles from Shanghai. A formidable oath escaped from the pilot's lips. It was evident that the reward of two hundred pounds was going to slip from him. He looked at Mr. Fogg. Mr. Fogg was impassible, and yet his whole fortune was at stake at this moment.

At this moment, too, a long, black funnel, crowned with a wreath of smoke, appeared on the edge of the water. It was the American steamer going at the regular hour. "Maledictions on her!" cried John Bunsby, who pushed back the rudder desperately.

"Signal her!" said Phileas Fogg, simply.

A small brass cannon stood on the forward deck of the *Tankadere*. It served to make signals in hazy weather.

The cannon was loaded to the muzzle, but at the moment that the pilot was going to apply a red-hot coal to the touchhole, Mr. Fogg said: "Hoist your flag."

The flag was hoisted half-mast. It was a signal of distress, and it was to be hoped that the American steamer, perceiving it, would change her course for a moment to assist the little craft.

"Fire!" said Mr. Fogg. And the booming of the little cannon sounded through the air.

CHAPTER XXII

IN WHICH PASSEPARTOUT SEES VERY WELL THAT, EVEN AT THE ANTIPODES, IT IS PRUDENT TO HAVE SOME MONEY IN ONE'S POCKET

THE *Carnatic*, having left Hong Kong on the 6th of November, at half past six P. M., turned under full head of steam towards the Japanese shores. She carried a full load of freight and passengers. Two cabins aft were unoccupied. They were the ones retained for Mr. Phileas Fogg.

The next morning the men in the forward part of the vessel saw, not without some surprise, a passenger, with half-stupefied eyes and disordered head, coming out of the second cabin, and with tottering steps taking a seat on deck.

This passenger was Passepartout himself. This is what

had happened: Some minutes after Fix left the smoking-house two waiters raised Passepartout, who was in a deep sleep, and laid him on the bed reserved for the smokers. But, three hours later, Passepartout, pursued even in his bad dreams by a fixed idea, woke again and struggled against the stupefying action of the narcotic. The thought of unaccomplished duty shook off his torpor. He left this drunkard's bed, reeling, supporting himself by the wall, falling and rising, but always and irresistibly urged on by a sort of instinct. He finally went out of the smoking-house, crying in a dream, " The *Carnatic!* the *Carnatic!* "

The steamer was there, steam up, ready to leave. Passepartout had only a few steps to go. He rushed upon the plank, crossed it, and fell unconscious on the forward deck at the very moment that the *Carnatic* was slipping her moorings.

Some of the sailors, as men accustomed to this kind of scenes, took the poor fellow down into a second cabin, and Passepartout only waked the next morning, one hundred and fifty miles from the Chinese coast.

This is then why Passepartout found himself this morning on the *Carnatic's* deck, taking full draughts of the fresh sea breezes. The pure air sobered him. He commenced to collect his ideas, but he did not succeed without difficulty. But, finally, he recalled the scenes of the day before, the confidences of Fix, the smoking-house, etc.

" It is evident," he said to himself, " that I have been abominably drunk! What will Mr. Fogg say? In any event I have not missed the steamer, and this is the principal thing."

Then, thinking of Fix, he said to himself: " As for him, I hope we are now rid of him, and that he has not dared, after what he proposed to me, to follow us on the *Carnatic*. A police detective on my master's heels, accused of the robbery committed upon the Bank of England! Pshaw! Mr. Fogg is as much a robber as I am a murderer! "

Ought Passepartout to tell these things to his master? Would it be proper to inform him of the part played by Fix in this affair? Would it not be better to wait until his return to London, to tell him that an agent of the Metropolitan Police had followed him, and then have a laugh with him? Yes, doubtless. In any event, it was a matter to be looked into. The most pressing thing was to rejoin Mr. Fogg and beg him to pardon him for his inexcusable conduct.

Passepartout then rose. The sea was rough, and the ship rolled heavily. The worthy fellow—his legs not very steady yet—reached as well as he could the after-deck of the ship. He saw no one on the deck that resembled either his master or Aouda.

"Good," said he. "Aouda is still abed at this hour. As for Mr. Fogg, he has probably found some whist player, and according to his habit——"

So saying, Passepartout descended to the saloon. Mr. Fogg was not there. Passepartout had but one thing to do: to ask the purser which cabin Mr. Fogg occupied. The purser replied that he did not know any passenger of that name.

"Pardon me," said Passepartout, persisting. "The gentleman in question is tall, cold, non-communicative, accompanied by a young lady——"

"We have no young lady on board," replied the purser. " To convince you, here is the list of passengers. You can examine it."

Passepartout looked over the list. His master's name did not appear. He felt bewildered. Then an idea struck him. "Ah! but see! Am I on the *Carnatic?*" he cried.

"Yes," replied the purser.

"*En route* for Yokohama?"

"Exactly so."

Passepartout had for a moment feared that he had mistaken the vessel! But though he was on the *Carnatic,* he was certain that his master was not there for he had not seen him.

Passepartout dropped into an arm-chair. It was a thunder stroke for him. And suddenly, there was a gleam of light. He recollected that the hour of departure for the *Carnatic* had been anticipated, that he was to notify his master, and that he had not done it! It was his fault, then, if Mr. Fogg and Aouda had missed this steamer!

His fault, yes, but still more that of the traitor who, to separate him from his master, to keep the latter in Hong Kong, had made him drunk! For at last he understood the detective's maneuver. And now Mr. Fogg surely ruined, his bet lost, arrested, perhaps imprisoned! Passepartout at this thought tore his hair. Ah! if Fix ever fell into his hands, what a settlement of accounts there would be!

Finally, after the first moment of bewilderment, Passepartout recovered his coolness and studied the situation. It was not enviable. The Frenchman was on the road to Japan. Certain of arriving there, how was he to get away? His pocket was empty. Not a shilling, not a penny in it! However, his passage and meals on board were paid in advance. He had then five or six days to come to a decision. It could not be described how he ate and drank during the voyage. He ate for his master, for Aouda, and for himself. He ate as if Japan, where he was going to land, was a desert country, bare of every eatable substance.

At high tide on the morning of the 13th, the *Carnatic* entered the port of Yokohama. This place is an important stopping point in the Pacific, where all the mail and passenger steamers between North America, China, Japan, and the Malay Islands put in. Yokohama is situated on the Bay of Yeddo, at a short distance from that immense city, the second capital of the Japanese empire, formerly the residence of the Tycoon, at the time that civil emperor existed, and the rival of Miako, the largest city in which the Mikado, the ecclesiastical emperor, the descendant of the gods, lives.

The *Carnatic* came alongside the wharf at Yokohama near the jetties of the port and the custom house, in the midst of the numerous vessels belonging to all nations.

Passepartout set foot, without any enthusiasm, on this so curious soil of the Sons of the Sun. He had nothing better to do than to take chance for his guide, and to go at a venture through the streets of the city.

He found himself at first in an absolutely European city, with its low front houses, ornamented with verandas, under which showed elegant peristyles. This city, covered with its streets, its squares, its docks, its warehouses, the entire space comprised between "Treaty Promontory" and the river. There, as at Hong Kong, and as at Calcutta, there was a confused swarm of people of all races, Americans, English, Chinese, Dutch, merchants ready to sell everything and to buy everything, in the midst of whom the Frenchman found himself as strange as if he had been cast into the Hottentot country.

Passepartout had, it is true, one resource; it was to make himself known at the French or English Consular Agent's established at Yokohama; but he hated to tell his story, so intimately connected with that of his master, and before coming to that, he wished to exhaust all other chances.

Then, having gone through the European quarter of the city, without chance having served him in anything, he entered the Japanese quarter, decided, if it was necessary, to push on to Yeddo.

This native portion of Yokohama is called Benten, from the name of a goddess of the sea, worshiped in the neighboring islands. There were to be seen splendid avenues of firs and cedars; the sacred gates of a strange architecture; bridges half hid in the midst of bamboos and reeds; temples sheltered under the immense and melancholy shade of aged cedars, retreats in the depths of which vegetated the priests of Buddhism and the sectaries of the religion of Confucius; interminable streets in which could have been gathered a whole crop of children, rose-tinted and red-cheeked, good little people who might have been cut out of some native screen, and who were playing in the midst of short-legged poodles, and yellowish, tailless cats, very indolent, and very affectionate.

In the streets there was a constant swarm, going and coming incessantly; priests passing in procession, beating their monotonous tambourines; patrolmen, custom house or police officers, with pointed hats incrusted with lace, and carrying two sabers in their belts; soldiers dressed in blue cotton, with white stripes, and armed with percussion muskets; guards of the Mikado, enveloped in their silken doublets, with hauberk and coat of mail, and a number of other military men of all ranks—for in Japan the profession of a soldier is as much esteemed as it is despised in China. Then, mendicant friars, pilgrims in long robes, simple civilians, with their glossy and jet-black hair, large heads, long bust, slender legs, short stature, and complexions from the dark shades of copper to dead white, but never yellow like that of the Chinese, from whom the Japanese differ essentially. Finally, between the carriages, the palanquins, the horses, the porters, the curtained wheelbarrows, and bamboo litters, were seen moving some homely women, with tightly-drawn eyes, sunken chests, and teeth blackened according to the

IT IS PRUDENT TO HAVE MONEY

fashion of the time, taking short steps with their little feet,
upon which were canvas shoes, straw sandals, or clogs of
worked wood. They also wore with elegance the national
garment, the "kiri mon," a sort of dressing-gown, crossed
with a silk scarf, whose broad girdle expanded behind into
an extravagant knot, which the modern Parisian ladies
seem to have borrowed from the Japanese.

Then Passepartout found himself in the fields, in the
midst of immense rice fields. There were expanding, with
flowers which threw out their last perfumes, dazzling ca-
melias, not borne upon shrubs, but upon trees; and in the
bamboo enclosures, cherry, plum, and apple trees, which
the natives cultivate rather for their blossoms than for their
fruit, and which grinning scarecrows protect from the
beaks of the sparrows, the pigeons, the crows, and other
voracious birds. There was not a majestic cedar which
did not shelter some large eagle; not a weeping willow
which did not cover with its foliage some heron, sadly
perched on one foot; while, finally, in all directions there
were rooks, ducks, hawks, wild geese, and a large number
of those cranes which the Japanese treat as "lords," and
which symbolize for them long life and good fortune.

Wandering thus, Passepartout saw some violets among
the grass, and said: "Good! there is my supper."

But having smelt them, he found no odor in them.

"No chance there!" he thought.

The good fellow had certainly had the foresight to breakfast as heartily as possible before he left the *Carnatic;* but
after walking around for a day he felt that his stomach was
very empty. He had noticed that sheep, goats, or pigs were
entirely wanting at the stalls of the native butchers; and as
he knew that it is a sacrilege to kill beeves, kept only for the
needs of agriculture, he concluded that meat was scarce in
Japan. He was not mistaken; but in default of butcher's
meat, his stomach would have accommodated itself very
well to quarters of deer or wild boar, some partridges or
quails, some poultry or fish, with which the Japanese feed
themselves almost exclusively, with the product of the rice
fields. But he had to put a brave heart against ill luck, and
postponed to the next day the care of providing for his
nourishment.

Night came on. Passepartout returned to the native

quarter, and wandered in the streets in the midst of the many-colored lanterns, looking at the groups of dancers, executing their feats of agility, and the astrologers in the open air gathering the crowd around their telescopes. Then he saw again the harbor, relieved by the fires of many fishermen who were catching fish by the light of their torches.

Finally, the streets became empty. To the crowd succeeded the rounds of the patrolmen. These officers, in their magnificent costumes and in the midst of their suite, resembled ambassadors, and Passepartout repeated pleasantly, each time that he met some dazzling patrol, " Good, good! Another Japanese embassy starting for Europe!"

CHAPTER XXIII
IN WHICH PASSEPARTOUT'S NOSE IS LENGTHENED ENORMOUSLY

THE next day Passepartout, tired out and hungry, said to himself that he must eat at any cost, and the sooner the better. He had this resource, to sell his watch, but he would rather die of hunger. Now was the time, or never, for this good fellow to utilize the strong, if not melodious, voice with which nature had favored him.

He knew a few French and English airs, and he determined to try them. The Japanese ought certainly to be lovers of music, since everything with them was done to the sound of the cymbals, the tam-tams, and drums, and they could not but appreciate the talents of a European amateur.

But, perhaps, he was a little early to organize a concert, and the *dilettanti,* unexpectedly wakened, would, perhaps, not have paid the singer in money with the Mikado's likeness.

Passepartout decided, then, to wait a few hours; but in sauntering along the thought came to him that he would look too well dressed for a wandering artist, and the idea struck him to exchange his clothing for a suit more in harmony with his position. This exchange would besides produce a sum which he could immediately apply to satisfying his appetite.

322

This resolution taken, it only remained to execute it. It was only after a long search that Passepartout found a native clothes dealer, to whom he told his want. The European garments pleased the man, and soon Passepartout came out wrapped in an old Japanese robe, and on his head a sort of one-sided turban, discolored by the action of the weather. But in return, a few small pieces of money jingled in his pocket.

"Good!" he thought, "I will fancy that we are in the carnival!"

Passepartout's first care, thus "Japanesed," was to enter a tea house of modest appearance, and there, with some remains of poultry and a few handfuls of rice, he breakfasted like a man for whom dinner would be still a problem to be solved.

"Now," he said to himself, when he had taken hearty refreshment, "the question is not to lose my head. I have no longer the resource of selling this garment for another still more Japanese. I must then consider the means of getting away as promptly as possible from this country of the sun, of which I shall preserve but a sorry recollection."

Passepartout then thought of visiting the steamers about to set sail for America. He counted on offering himself in the capacity of cook or servant, asking only his passage and his meals as his entire compensation. Once at San Francisco, he would see how he would get out of his scrape. The important thing was to traverse these four thousand, seven hundred miles of the Pacific stretching between Japan and the new world.

Passepartout, not being a man to let an idea languish, turned towards the port of Yokohama. But as he approached the docks, his plans, which had appeared so simple to him at the moment when he had the idea, seemed more and more difficult of execution. Why should they need a cook or servant aboard an American steamer, and what confidence would he inspire, muffled up in this manner? What recommendations would be of any service? What references could he give?

As he was thus reflecting, his eyes fell upon an immense placard which a sort of clown was carrying through the streets of Yokohama. This programme was thus worded in English:

ACROBATIC JAPANESE TROUPE OF THE
HONORABLE WILLIAM BATULCAR.
LAST REPRESENTATIONS, BEFORE DEPARTURE FOR THE
UNITED STATES OF AMERICA
LONG NOSES! LONG NOSES!
UNDER THE DIRECT PROTECTION OF THE GOD TINGOU!
GREAT ATTRACTION!

" The United States of America," cried Passepartout,
" that's just what I want! "

He followed the man with his placard, and thus soon re-
entered the Japanese quarter. A quarter of an hour later,
he stopped before a large house surrounded by clusters of
streamers, and whose exterior walls represented, without
perspective, but in violent colors, a whole company of jugglers.

It was the Honorable Batulcar's establishment, who was
a sort of American Barnum, director of a troupe of mounte-
banks, jugglers, clowns, acrobats, equilibrists, gymnasts,
which, according to the placard, was giving its last performance before leaving the Empire of the Sun for the
States of the Union.

Passepartout entered under the porch in front of the
house, and asked for Honorable Mr. Batulcar. He appeared in person.

" What do you wish? " he said to Passepartout, taking
him at first for a native.

" Do you need a servant? " asked Passepartout.

" A servant," cried the Barnum, stroking his thick gray
beard hanging heavily under his chin. " I have two, obedi-
ent and faithful, who have never left me, and who serve
me for nothing, on condition that I feed them. And here
they are," he added, showing his two robust arms, furrowed
with veins as large as the strings of a bass viol.

" So I can be of no good to you? "

" None."

" The devil! It would have suited me so well to leave
with you."

" Ah, I see! " said the Honorable Batulcar. " You are
as much a Japanese as I am a monkey! Why are you
dressed in this way? "

" One dresses as one can."

" Very true. You are a Frenchman? "

" Yes, a Parisian from Paris."

" Then you ought to know how to make grimaces? "

" Indeed," replied Passepartout, vexed at seeing his nationality call forth this question, " we Frenchmen know how to make grimaces, it is true, but not better than the Americans."

" Just so. Well, if I do not take you as a servant I can take you as a clown. You understand, my good fellow? In France, they exhibit foreign clowns, and abroad, French clowns."

" Ah! "

" You are strong, are you not? "

" Particularly when I have been at the table."

" And you know how to sing? "

" Yes," replied Passepartout, who had formerly taken part in street concerts.

" But do you know how to sing on your head, with a top spinning on the sole of your left foot, and a saber balanced on the sole of your right? "

" Parbleu! " replied Passepartout, who recalled the first exercises of his youth.

" Then, you see, all is right! " replied the Honorable Batulcar.

The engagement was concluded there and then.

At last Passepartout had found a position. He was engaged to do everything in the celebrated Japanese troupe. It was not very flattering, but within a week he would be on his way to San Francisco.

The performance, so noisily announced by the Honorable Batulcar, was to commence at three o'clock, and soon the formidable instruments of a Japanese orchestra, drums and tam-tams, sounded at the door. We understand very well that Passepartout could not have studied a part, but he was to give the support of his solid shoulders in the grand feat of the " human pyramid," executed by the Long Noses of the god Tingou. This great attraction of the performance was to close the series.

Before three o'clock, the spectators had crowded the large building. Europeans and natives, Chinese and Japanese, men, women, and children, rushed upon the narrow benches, and into the boxes opposite the stage. The musicians had entered, and the full orchestra, with gongs, tam-

tams, bones, flutes, tambourines, and large drums went to work furiously.

The performance was what all these acrobatic exhibitions are. But it must be confessed that the Japanese are the best equilibrists in the world. One, with his fan and small bits of paper, executed the graceful trick of the butterflies and flowers. Another, with the odorous smoke of his pipe, traced rapidly in the air a series of bluish words, which formed a compliment addressed to the audience. The latter juggled with lit candles, which he blew out in succession as they passed before his lips, and which he lit again, one after the other, without interrupting, for a single moment, his wonderful jugglery. The former produced, by means of spinning tops, the most improbable combinations. Under his hand these humming machines seemed to be gifted with a life of their own in their interminable whirling; they ran over pipe stems, over the edges of sabers, over wires as thin as hair, stretched from one side of the stage to the other; they went round large glass vases, they went up and down bamboo ladders, and scattered into all the corners, and produced harmonic effects of a strange character by combining their various tones. The jugglers tossed them up, and they turned in the air; they threw them like shuttle-cocks with wooden battledores, and they kept on turning; they thrust them into their pockets, and when they borught them out they were still spinning—until the moment when a relaxed spring made them bud out into a Chinese tree!

It is useless to describe here the wonderful feats of the acrobats and gymnasts of the troupe. The turning on ladders, poles, balls, barrels, etc., was executed with remarkable precision. But the principal attraction of the performance was the exhibition of the Long Noses, astonishing equilibrists, with whom Europe is not yet acquainted.

These Long Noses form a special company placed under the direct patronage of the god Tingou. Dressed like heroes of the middle ages, they bore a splendid pair of wings on their shoulders. But what distinguished them more particularly was the long nose with which their faces were ornamented, and, above all, the use they made of them. These noses were nothing less than bamboos, five, six, ten feet long; some straight, others curved; the latter smooth, the former with warts on them. It was on these appendages, fastened firmly, that all their balancing feats were performed. A dozen of these sectaries of the god Tingou lay upon their backs, and their comrades came, dressed like lightning rods, to make sport on their noses, jumping, leaping from one to the other, executing the most incredible somersaults.

To close, they had specially announced to the public the " human pyramid," in which fifty Long Noses were to represent the car of Juggernaut. But instead of forming this pyramid by taking their shoulders for a point of support, the artists of the Honorable Batulcar made it with their noses. Now, the one of them who usually formed the base of the car had left the troupe, and as all that was necessary was to be strong and agile, Passepartout was chosen to take his place.

The good fellow felt quite melancholy, when—sad recollection of his youth—he had put on this costume of the middle ages, adorned with parti-colored wings, and when a nose six feet long had been put on his face. But this nose was to earn his bread for him, and he took his part.

Passepartout went upon the stage and took his place with those of his colleagues who were to form the base of the Car of Juggernaut. All stretched themselves on the floor, their noses turned towards the ceiling. A second section of equilibrists placed themselves upon these long appendages, a third formed a story above, then a fourth, and on these noses which only touched at the point, a human monument soon rose to the height of the cornices of the theater.

Now, the applause was redoubled, and the instruments in the orchestra crashed like so much thunder, when the pyramid shook, the equilibrium was broken, one of the noses of the base was missing, and the monument fell like a house of cards.

It was Passepartout's fault, who, leaving his post, clearing the footlights without the aid of his wings, and climbing up to the right-hand gallery, fell at the feet of a spectator, crying: " Ah! my master! my master!"

" You here? "

" Myself! "

" Well then, in that case, to the steamer, young man! "

Mr. Fogg, Aouda, who accompanied him, and Passepar-

tout rushed through the lobbies to the outside of the building. There they found the Honorable Batulcar, furious,
claiming damages for the "breakage." Phileas Fogg appeased his anger by throwing him a handful of bank notes.
Mr. Fogg and Aouda set foot on the American steamer,
followed by Passepartout, with his wings on his back, and
on his face the nose six feet long which he had not yet been
able to tear off!

CHAPTER XXIV
DURING WHICH IS ACCOMPLISHED THE VOYAGE ACROSS THE
PACIFIC OCEAN

WHAT had happened in sight of Shanghai is understood.
The signals made by the *Tankadere* had been observed by
the Yokohama steamer. The captain, seeing a flag at half-
mast, had turned his vessel towards the little schooner. A
few minutes after, Phileas Fogg, paying for his passage at
the price agreed upon, put in the pocket of John Bunsby,
master, five hundred and fifty pounds. Then the honorable
gentleman, Aouda, and Fix ascended to the deck of
the steamer, which immediately took its course for Nagasaki
and Yokohama.

Having arrived on the morning of the 14th of November,
on time, Phileas Fogg, letting Fix go about his business, had
gone aboard the *Carnatic,* and there he learned, to the great
joy of Aouda—and perhaps to his own, but he did not let
it appear—that the Frenchman, Passepartout, had really
arrived the day before at Yokohama.

Phileas Fogg, who was to start again the same evening
for San Francisco, sent immediately in search of his servant.
He inquired in vain of the French and English consular
agents, and after uselessly running through the streets of
Yokohama, he despaired of finding Passepartout again,
when chance, or perhaps a sort of presentiment, made him
enter the theater of the Honorable Batulcar. He would
certainly not have recognized his servant under this eccentric mountebank dress; but the latter, lying on his back,
saw his master in the gallery. He could not restrain a
movement of his nose. Thence a breaking of the equilibrium and what followed.

This is what Passepartout learned from Aouda's mouth,

who told him then how the voyage had been made from Hong Kong to Yokohama, in company of a Mr. Fix, on the schooner *Tankadere*.

At the name of Fix, Passepartout did not change countenance. He thought that the time had not come to tell his master what had passed between the detective and himself. Thus, in the story which Passepartout told of his adventures, he only accused and excused himself of having been overcome by the intoxication of opium in a smoking house in Hong Kong.

Mr. Fogg listened coldly to this narrative, without replying; then he opened for his servant a credit sufficient for him to procure on board more suitable garments. And, indeed, an hour had not passed, when the good fellow, having cut off his nose and shed his wings, had nothing more about him which recalled the sectary of the god Tingou.

The steamer making the voyage from Yokohama to San Francisco belonged to the Pacific Mail Steamship Company, and was named the *General Grant*. She was a large side-wheel steamer of two thousand five hundred tons, well equipped and of great speed. The *General Grant* was rigged as a three-masted schooner, and she had a large surface of sails, which aided her steam power materially. By making twelve miles an hour the steamer would only need twenty days to cross the Pacific. Phileas Fogg then had good reasons for believing that, landed at San Francisco on the 3d of December, he would be in New York on the 11th, and in London on the 20th, thus gaining some hours on the fatal date of the 21st of December.

The passengers aboard the steamer were quite numerous —some Englishmen, many Americans, a genuine emigration of coolies to America, and a certain number of officers of the Indian army, who made use of their leave of absence by making the tour of the world.

During this voyage there was no nautical incident. The steamer, borne up on its large wheels, supported by its large amount of canvas, rolled but little. The Pacific Ocean justified its name sufficiently. Mr. Fogg was as calm and non-communicative as usual. His young companion felt herself more and more attached to this man by other ties than those of gratitude. This silent nature, so generous in short, made a greater impression upon her than she thought, and almost unknown to herself she allowed herself to have feelings which did not seem to affect in any way the enigmatic Fogg.

Besides, Aouda was very much interested in the gentleman's plans. She was uneasy at the retarding circumstances which might prevent the success of the tour. She frequently talked with Passepartout, who readily detected the feelings of Aouda's heart. This good fellow had the most implicit faith with regard to his master; he did not exhaust his praises of the honesty, the generosity, the devotion of Phileas Fogg; then he reassured Aouda as to the issue of the voyage, repeating that the most difficult part was done, that they had left the fantastic countries of China and Japan, that they were returning to civilized countries, and finally, that a train from San Francisco to New York, and a transatlantic steamer from New York to Liverpool, would be sufficient, doubtless, to finish this impossible tour of the world in the time agreed upon.

Nine days after leaving Yokohama, Phileas Fogg had traversed exactly the half of the terrestrial globe.

In fact, the *General Grant,* on the 23d of November, passed the one hundred and eightieth meridian, upon which in the southern hemisphere are to be found the antipodes of London. It is true that of the eighty days at his disposal he had used fifty-two, and there only remained to him twenty-eight to be consumed. But we must notice that if the gentleman only found himself half way round by the difference of meridians, he had really accomplished more than two-thirds of its entire course. Indeed, what forced detours from London to Aden, from Aden to Bombay, from Calcutta to Singapore, from Singapore to Yokohama! By following around the fiftieth parallel, which is that of London, the distance would have been but about twelve thousand miles, whilst Phileas Fogg was compelled, by the caprices of the means of locomotion, to travel over twenty-six thousand, of which he had already made about seventeen thousand five hundred, at this date, the 23d of November. But now the route was a straight one, and Fix was no longer there to accumulate obstacles.

It happened also that on this 23d of November, Passepartout made quite a joyful discovery. It will be recollected that the obstinate fellow had insisted on keeping London time with his famous family watch, deeming incorrect the time of the various countries that he traversed. Now this day, although he had neither put his watch forward or back, it agreed with the ship's chronometers.

The triumph of Passepartout may be comprehended. He would have liked to know what Fix would have said if he had been present.

" The rogue who told me a heap of stories about the meridians, the sun and the moon! " said Passepartout. " Pshaw! if one listened to that sort of people, we would have a nice sort of clocks and watches! I was very sure that one day or another, the sun would decide to regulate itself by my watch! "

Passepartout was ignorant of this: that if the face of his watch had been divided into twenty-four hours like the *Italian* clocks, he would have had no reason for triumph, for the hands of his watch, when it was 9 o'clock in the morning on the vessel, would have indicated 9 o'clock in the evening, that is, the twenty-first hour after midnight—a difference precisely equal to that which exists between London and the one hundred and eightieth meridian.

But if Fix had been capable of explaining this purely physical effect, Passepartout, doubtless, would have been incapable, if not of understanding it, at least of admitting it. And in any event, if the impossible thing should occur that the detective would unexpectedly show himself aboard at this moment, it is probable that Passepartout would have spitefully talked with him on quite a different subject, and in quite a different manner.

Now, where was Fix at this moment?

He was actually on board the *General Grant*. In fact, on arriving at Yokohama the detective, leaving Mr. Fogg, whom he thought he would see again during the day, had immediately gone to the English Consul's. There he finally found the warrant of arrest, which, running after him from Bombay, was already forty days old, which had been sent to him from Hong Kong on the very *Carnatic* on board of which he was supposed to be. The detective's disappointment may be imagined! The warrant was useless! Mr. Fogg had left the English possessions! An order of extradition was now necessary to arrest him!

" Let it be so! " said Fix to himself, after the first moment of anger. " My warrant is no longer good here; it will be in England. This rogue has the appearance of returning to his native country believing that he has thrown the police off their guard. Well, I will follow him there. As for the money, heaven grant there may be some left! But what with traveling, rewards, trials, fines, elephants, expenses of every kind, my man has already left more than five thousand pounds on his route. After all, the Bank is rich!"

His decision taken, he immediately went on board the *General Grant,* and was there when Mr. Fogg and Aouda arrived. To his extreme surprise, he recognized Passepartout under his fantastic costume. He concealed himself immediately in his cabin, to avoid an explanation which might damage everything—and, thanks to the number of the passengers, he counted on not being seen by his enemy, when this very day he found himself face to face with him on the forward part of the ship.

Passepartout jumped at Fix's throat, without any other explanation, and to the great delight of certain Americans, who immediately bet for him, he gave the unfortunate detective a superb volley of blows, showing the great superiority of French over English boxing.

When Passepartout had finished he found himself calmer and comforted. Fix rose in pretty bad condition, and, looking at his adversary, he said to him coldly, " Is it finished?"

" Yes, for the moment."

" Then I want a word with you."

" But I——"

" In your master's interest."

Passepartout, as if conquered by this coolness, followed the detective, and they both sat down in the forward part of the steamer. " You have thrashed me," said Fix. " Good; I expected it. Now, listen to me. Until the present I have been Mr. Fogg's adversary, but now I am with him."

" At last!" cried Passepartout, " you believe him to be an honest man?"

" No," replied Fix coldly. " I believe him to be a rogue. Sh! Don't stir, and let me talk. As long as Mr. Fogg was in the English possessions, I had an interest in retaining him whilst waiting for a warrant of arrest. I did everything I could for that. I sent against him the priests of

Bombay, I made you drunk at Hong Kong, I separated you from your master, I made him miss the Yokohama steamer."

Passepartout listened with clenched fists.

"Now," continued Fix, "Mr. Fogg seems to be returning to England? Well, I will follow him there. But henceforth it shall be my aim to clear the obstacles from his path as zealously and carefully as before I took pains to accumulate them. You see, my game is changed, and it is changed because my interest desires it. I add, that your interest is similar to mine, for you will only know in England whether you are in the service of a criminal or an honest man!"

Passepartout listened to Fix very attentively and he was convinced that the latter spoke with entire good faith.

"Are we friends?" asked Fix.

"Friends, no," replied Passepartout; "allies, yes; and under this condition that, at the least appearance of treason, I will twist your neck."

"Agreed," said the detective, quietly.

Eleven days after, on the 3d of December, the *General Grant* entered the bay of the Golden Gate, and arrived at San Francisco. Mr. Fogg had neither gained nor lost a single day.

CHAPTER XXV

IN WHICH A SLIGHT GLIMPSE OF SAN FRANCISCO IS HAD— A POLITICAL MEETING

It was seven o'clock in the morning when Phileas Fogg, Aouda and Passepartout set foot on the American continent, if this name can be given to the floating wharf on which they landed. These wharves, rising and falling with the tide, facilitate the loading and unloading of vessels. Clippers of all sizes were moored there, steamers of all nationalities, and those steamboats with several decks, which ply on the Sacramento and its tributaries. There were accumulated also the products of a commerce which extends to Mexico, Peru, Chili, Brazil, Europe, Asia and all the islands of the Pacific Ocean.

Passepartout, in his joy at finally touching American soil, thought in landing he would execute a perilous leap in his finest style. But when he fell upon the wharf, the planks of which were worm-eaten, he almost fell through. Quite put out by the manner in which he had " set foot " on the new continent, the good fellow uttered a terrible cry, which sent flying an innumerable flock of cormorants and pelicans, the customary inhabitants of the movable wharves.

Mr. Fogg, as soon as he landed, ascertained the hour at which the first train left for New York. It was at six o'clock in the evening. He had, then, an entire day to spend in the California capital. He ordered a carriage for Aouda and himself. Passepartout mounted the box, and the vehicle, at three dollars for the trip, turned towards the International Hotel.

From the elevated position that he occupied, Passepartout observed with curiosity the great American city, the broad streets, low, evenly-ranged houses, the Anglo-Saxon Gothic churches and temples, the immense docks, the palatial warehouses, some of wood and some of brick; the numerous vehicles in the streets, omnibuses and horse-cars, and on the crowded sidewalks not only American and Europeans, but also Chinese and Indians—the component parts of a population of more than two hundred thousand inhabitants.

Passepartout was quite surprised at all he saw. He was not in the city of 1849, in the city of bandits, incendiaries, and assassins, running after the native gold, an immense concourse of all the outlaws, who gambled with gold dust, a revolver in one hand and a knife in the other. This " good time " had passed away. San Francisco presented the aspect of a large commercial city. The high tower of the City Hall overlooked all these streets and avenues, crossing each other at right angles, between which were spread out verdant squares, then a Chinese quarter, which seemed to have been imported from the Celestial Empire in a toy-box. No more sombreros, or red shirts after the fashion of the miners, or Indians with feathers, but silk hats and black clothes worn by a large number of gentlemen of absorbing activity. Certain streets, among others Montgomery street, the Regent street of London, the Boulevard des Italiens of Paris, the Broadway of New York, the State street of Chicago were lined with splendid stores, in whose windows were displayed the products of the entire world.

When Passepartout arrived at the International Hotel, it seemed to him that he had not left England. The ground floor of the hotel was occupied by an immense bar, a sort of sideboard opened gratis to every passer-by. Dried beef, oyster soup, biscuit, and cheese were dealt out without the customer having to take out his purse. He only paid for his drink—ale, porter, or sherry, if he fancied refreshment. That appeared "very American" to Passepartout. The hotel restaurant was comfortable. Mr. Fogg and Aouda took seats at a table and were abundantly served in very small dishes by negroes of darkest hue.

After breakfast, Phileas Fogg, accompanied by Aouda, left the hotel to go to the office of the English consul to have his passport *vised* there. On the pavement, he found his servant, who asked him if it would not be prudent, before starting on the Pacific railroad, to buy a few dozen Enfield rifles or Colt's revolvers. Passepartout had heard so much talk of the Sioux and Pawnees stopping trains like ordinary Spanish brigands. Mr. Fogg replied that it was a useless precaution, but he left him free to act as he thought best. Then he went to the office of the consul.

Phileas Fogg had not gone two hundred steps, when, "by the greatest accident," he met Fix, who manifested very great surprise! How! Mr. Fogg and he had taken together the voyage across the Pacific, and they had not met on board the vessel! At all events, Fix could only be honored by seeing again the gentleman to whom he owed so much; and his business calling him to Europe, he would be delighted to continue his journey in such agreeable company.

Mr. Fogg replied that the honor would be his, and Fix—who made it a point not to lose sight of him—asked his permission to visit with him this curious city of San Francisco, which was granted.

Aouda, Phileas Fogg, and Fix sauntered through the streets. They soon found themselves in Montgomery street, where the crowd of people was enormous. On the sidewalks, in the middle of the street, on the horse-car rails, notwithstanding the incessant passage of the coaches and omnibuses, on the steps of the stores, in the windows of all the houses, and even up to the roofs, there was an innumerable crowd. Men with placards circulated among the groups. Banners and steamers floated in the wind. There were shouts in every direction.

" Hurrah for Camerfield! "

" Hurrah for Mandiboy! "

It was a political meeting. At least so Fix thought, and he communicated his ideas to Mr. Fogg, adding, " We will perhaps do well, sir, not to mingle in this crowd. Only hard blows will be got here."

" In fact," replied Phileas Fogg, " blows, if they are political, are not less blows."

Fix could not help smiling at this remark, and in order to see, without being caught in the crowd, Aouda, Phileas Fogg and he secured a place upon the upper landing of a flight of steps reaching to the top of a terrace, situated in the upper end of Montgomery street. Before them, on the other side of the street, between the wharf of a coal merchant and the warehouse of a petroleum dealer, there was a large platform in the open air, towards which the various currents of the crowd seemed to be tending.

Why this meeting? What was the occasion of its being held? Phileas Fogg did not know at all. Was it for the nomination of some high military or civil official, a State Governor, or a member of Congress? It might readily be supposed so, seeing the great excitement that was agitating the city.

At this moment there was quite a movement in the crowd. Every hand was thrown in the air. Some, tightly closed, seemed to rise and fall rapidly in the midst of the cries— an energetic manner, no doubt, of casting a vote. The crowd fell back. The banners wavered, disappeared for an instant, and reappeared in tatters. The surging of the crowd extended to the steps, whilst every head moved up and down on the surface like a sea suddenly agitated by a squall. The number of black hats diminished perceptibly, and the most of them seemed to have lost their normal height.

" It is evidently a meeting," said Fix; " and the question which has excited it must be a stirring one. I would not be astonished if they were still discussing the Alabama affair, although it has been settled."

" Perhaps," simply replied Mr. Fogg.

" In any event," replied Fix, " two champions are in each

other's presence, the Hon. Mr. Camerfield and the Hon. Mr. Mandiboy."

Aouda, leaning on Phileas Fogg's arm, looked with surprise at this noisy scene, and Fix was going to ask one of his neighbors the reason of this popular effervescence, when a more violent movement broke out. The hurrahs, interspersed with insults, redoubled. The staffs of the banners were transformed into offensive arms. Instead of hands, there were fists everywhere. From the top of carriages and omnibuses blocked in their course, formidable blows were exchanged. Everything was made use of as projectiles. Boots and shoes described extended curves in the air, and it seemed even as if some revolvers mingled their national sounds with the loud cries of the crowd.

The crowd approached the flight of stairs, and swept over onto the lower steps. One of the parties had evidently been repulsed without disinterested spectators knowing whether the advantage was with Mandiboy or Camerfield.

" I believe that it is prudent for us to retire," said Fix, who did not want his " man " to get hurt or mixed up in a bad business. " If this is an English question, and we are recognized, we will be treated roughly in this mixed crowd."

" An English citizen——" replied Phileas Fogg.

But the gentleman could not finish his sentence. Behind him, on the terrace above the stairs, there were frightful yells. They cried, " Hip! hip! hurrah for Mandiboy! " It was a party of voters coming to the rescue, flanking the Camerfield party.

Mr. Fogg, Aouda, and Fix found themselves between two fires. It was too late to escape. This torrent of men, armed with loaded canes and bludgeons, was irresistible. Phileas Fogg and Fix, in protecting the young woman, were very roughly treated. Mr. Fogg, not less phlegmatic than usual, tried to defend himself with the natural weapons placed at the end of the arms of every Englishman, but in vain. A large rough fellow, with a red beard, flushed face, and broad shoulders, who seemed to be the chief of the band, raised his formidable fist to strike Mr. Fogg, and he would have damaged that gentleman very much, if Fix, throwing himself in the way, had not received the blow in his place. An enormous bump rose at once under the detective's silk hat, transformed into a simple cap.

"Yankee!" said Mr. Fogg, casting at his adversary a look of deep scorn.

"Englishman!" replied the other. "We will see each other again."

"When you please."

"Your name?"

"Phileas Fogg. And yours?"

"Colonel Stamp Proctor."

Then the crowd passed on, throwing Fix down. He rose with his clothes torn, but without serious hurt. His traveling overcoat was torn in two unequal parts, and his pantaloons resembled those of certain Indians, who, as a fashion, put them on only after first taking out the seat. But to sum up, Aouda had been spared, and Fix alone had been harmed by the fist-blow.

"Thanks," said Mr. Fogg to the detective, as soon as they were out of the crowd.

"No thanks necessary;" replied Fix, "but come with me."

"Where?"

"To a tailor's."

In fact, this visit was opportune. The garments of Phileas Fogg and Fix were in tatters, as if these two gentlemen had fought for Hon. Messrs. Camerfield and Mandiboy.

An hour afterwards they had respectable clothes and hats. Then they returned to the International Hotel.

Passepartout was waiting there for his master, armed with a half-dozen sharp-shooting, six-barreled, breech-loading revolvers. When he perceived Fix in company with Mr. Fogg, his brow darkened. Aouda, however, having told in a few words what had happened, Passepartout became calm again. Fix was evidently no longer an enemy, but an ally. He was keeping his word.

Dinner over, a coach drove up to take the passengers and their baggage to the station. As they were getting into the coach Mr. Fogg said to Fix, "Did you see Colonel Proctor again?"

"No," replied Fix.

"I shall return to America to find him again," said Mr. Fogg coldly. "It would not be proper for an English citzen to allow himself to be treated in this way."

A GLIMPSE OF SAN FRANCISCO

The detective smiled and did not answer him. But it is seen that Mr. Fogg was one of those Englishmen, who, while they do not tolerate dueling at home, will fight abroad, when it is necessary to maintain their honor.

At a quarter before six the travelers reached the station and found the train ready to start. At the moment that Mr. Fogg was going to get into the cars, he called a porter and asked him, "Was there not some disturbance in San Francisco to-day?"

"It was a political meeting, sir," replied the porter.

"But I thought I noticed some excitement in the streets."

"It was simply a meeting for an election."

"The election of a general-in-chief, doubtless?" asked Mr. Fogg.

"No, sir, of a justice of the peace."

Upon this reply, Phileas Fogg jumped aboard the car, and the train started at full speed.

CHAPTER XXVI
IN WHICH OUR PARTY TAKE THE EXPRESS TRAIN ON THE PACIFIC RAILROAD

"From Ocean to Ocean"—so say the Americans, and these four words ought to be the general name of the "grand trunk," which traverses the United States in their greatest breadth. But, in reality, the Pacific Railroad is divided into two distinct parts; the Central Pacific from San Francisco to Ogden, and the Union Pacific from Ogden to Omaha. At that point five distinct lines meet, which place Omaha in frequent communication with New York.

New York and San Francisco are therefore now united by an uninterrupted metal ribbon, measuring not less than three thousand seven hundred and eighty-six miles. Between Omaha and the Pacific, the railroad traverses a country still frequented by the Indians and wild animals—a vast extent of territory which the Mormons commenced to colonize about 1845, after they were driven out of Illinois.

Formerly, under the most favorable circumstances, it took six months to go from New York to San Francisco. Now it is done in seven days. It was in 1862, notwithstanding the opposition of the Southern Congressmen, who wished a

339

more southerly line, that the route of the railroad was fixed between the forty-first and the forty-second parallel. President Lincoln, of so lamented memory, himself fixed in the State of Nebraska, at the city of Omaha, the beginning of the new network. Work was commenced immediately, and prosecuted with that American activity, which is neither slow nor routine-like. The rapidity of the construction did not in any way injure its thoroughness. On the prairies the road progressed at the rate of a mile and a half per day. A locomotive, moving over the rails laid yesterday, carried the rails for the next day, and ran upon them in proportion as they were laid.

Such was this long artery which the trains would pass over in seven days, and which would permit the Honorable Phileas Fogg—at least he hoped so—to take the Liverpool steamer, on the 11th, at New York.

The car occupied by Phileas Fogg was a sort of long omnibus, resting on two trucks, each with four wheels, whose ease of motion permits of going round short curves. There were no compartments inside; two rows of seats placed on each side, perpendicularly to the axle, and between which was reserved an aisle, leading to the dressing-rooms and others, with which each car is provided. Through the whole length of the train the cars communicated by platforms, and the passengers could move about from one end to the other of the train, which placed at their disposal palace, balcony, restaurant, and smoking cars. All that is wanting is a theater car. But there will be one, some day.

On the platforms book and newsdealers were constantly circulating, dealing out their merchandise; and vendors of liquors, eatables and cigars, were not wanting in customers.

The travelers left Oakland Station at six o'clock. It was already night, cold and dreary, with an overcast sky, threatening snow. The train did not move with great rapidity. Counting the stops, it did not run more than twenty miles an hour, a speed which ought, however, to enable it to cross the United States in the fixed time.

They talked but little in the car. Sleep soon overcame the passengers. Passepartout sat near the detective, but he did not speak to him. Since the late events, their relations had become somewhat cold. No more sympathy or intimacy. Fix had not changed his manner, but Passepartout retained an extreme reserve, ready at the least suspicion to choke his old friend.

An hour after the starting of the train a fine snow commenced to fall, which fortunately could not delay the progress of the train. Through the windows nothing was seen but an immense white sheet, against which the clouds of steam from the locomotive looked grayish.

At eight o'clock a steward entered the car, and announced to the passengers that the hour for retiring had come. This was a sleeping car, which in a few minutes was transformed into a dormitory. The backs of the seats unfolded, beds carefully packed away were unrolled by an ingenious system, berths were improvised in a few moments, and each passenger had soon at his disposal a comfortable bed, which thick curtains protected from all indiscreet looks. The sheets were clean and the pillows soft. Nothing more to be done but to lie down and sleep—which everyone did, as if he had been in the comfortable cabin of a steamer—while the train moved on under full head of steam across the State of California.

In that portion of the country between San Francisco and Sacramento the ground is not very hilly. This portion of the railroad, under the name of the Central Pacific, originally had Sacramento for its starting point, and went towards the east to meet that starting from Omaha. From San Francisco to the capital of California, the line ran directly to the northeast, along American river, which empties into San Pablo Bay. The one hundred and twenty miles included between these two important cities were accomplished in six hours, and towards midnight, while they were getting their first sleep, the travelers passed through Sacramento.

It was seven o'clock in the morning when Cisco Station was passed. An hour afterwards the dormitory had become an ordinary car, and the passengers could get through the windows a glimpse of the picturesque views of this mountainous country. The route of the train followed the windings of the Sierra, here clinging to the sides of the mountains, there suspended above precipices, avoiding sharp angles by bold curves, plunging into narrow gorges from which there seemed to be no exit. The locomotive, flashing fire like a chased animal, its large smoke-pipe throwing out lurid lights, its sharp bell, its cow-catcher, extending out like a spur, mingled its shrieks and bellowings with the noise of the torrents and cascades, and twined its smoke in the dark branches of the firs.

There were few or no tunnels or bridges on the route. The railroad turned the flank of the mountains, not seeking in a straight line the shortest route from one point to another, and not doing violence to nature. About nine o'clock, the train entered the State of Nevada, through the Carson Valley, always following a northeasterly direction. At noon it left Reno, where the passengers had twenty minutes for breakfast. From this point, the iron road, skirting Humboldt river, passed a few miles to the north. Then it bent to the east, and did not leave the stream until it reached the Humboldt range, where the river takes its source, nearly in the eastern end of the State of Nevada.

After breakfasting, Mr. Fogg, Aouda and their companions took their seats again in the car. Phileas Fogg, the young woman, Fix, and Passepartout, comfortably seated, looked at the varied country passing before their sight, vast prairies, mountains whose profiles were shown upon the horizon, and creeks tumbling down, a foaming mass of water. Sometimes, a large herd of bisons, gathering in the distance, appeared like a moving dam. These innumerable armies of grazing animals frequently oppose an insurmountable obstacle to the passage of trains. Thousands of these animals have been seen moving on for several hours in close ranks across the railroad. The locomotive is then forced to stop and wait until the path is clear again.

The same thing happened on this occasion. About three o'clock in the afternoon a herd of ten or twelve thousand blocked the railroad. The engine, having slackened its speed, tried to plunge its spur into the flank of the immense column, but it had to stop before the impenetrable mass.

They saw these buffaloes, as the Americans improperly call them, moving with their steady gait, frequently bellowing terribly. They had a larger body than those of the bulls of Europe, short legs and tail, a projecting saddle forming a muscular bump, horns separated at the base, their heads, neck, and shoulders covered with long, shaggy hair. They could not think of stopping this moving mass.

When the bisons have adopted a course, nothing could swerve them from it or modify it. They are a torrent of living flesh which no dam could hold.

The travelers, scattered on the platforms, looked at this curious spectacle. But Phileas Fogg, who ought to be the most in a hurry, had remained in his seat, and was waiting philosophically until it should please the buffaloes to open a passage. Passepartout was furious at the delay caused by this mass of animals. He wanted to fire all his revolvers at them.

" What a country!" he cried. " Mere cattle stop trains, and move along in procession without hurrying, as if they did not impede travel! Parbleu! I would like to know if Mr. Fogg had foreseen this mischance in his programme! And what an engineer, who does not dare to rush his engine through this impeding mass of beasts!"

The engineer had not attempted to overcome the obstacle, and he acted wisely. He would undoubtedly have crushed the first buffaloes struck by the cow-catcher; but, powerful as it was, the engine would have soon been stopped, and the train thrown off the track and wrecked.

The best course, then, was to wait patiently, ready to make up the lost time by an increase of the speed of the train. The passage of the bisons lasted three full hours, and the road was not clear again until night-fall. At this moment the last ranks of the herd crossed the rails, whilst the first were disappearing below the southern horizon.

It was then eight o'clock, when the train passed through the defiles of the Humboldt range, and half-past nine when it entered Utah Territory, the region of the **Great Salt Lake**, the curious Mormon country.

CHAPTER XXVII
IN WHICH PASSEPARTOUT FOLLOWS, WITH A SPEED OF TWENTY MILES AN HOUR, A COURSE OF MORMON HISTORY

DURING the night of the 5th to the 6th of December, the train went for fifty miles to the southeast, then it ran up-wards about as far northerly, approaching the **Great Salt Lake**.

Passepartout, about nine o'clock in the morning, went on the platform to take the air. The weather was cold, the sky gray, but it had stopped snowing. The disc of the sun, enlarged by the mist, looked like an enormous piece of gold, and Passepartout was busy calculating its value in pounds sterling, when his attention was taken from this useful work by the appearance of a very strange personage.

This personage, who took the train at Elko Station, was tall, very brown, had black mustache, black stockings, a black silk hat, black waistcoat, black pantaloons, white cravat, and black dog-skin gloves. He might have been taken for a clergyman. He went from one end of the train to the other, and on the door of each car fastened with wafers a written notice.

Passepartout approached and read on one of these notices that Elder William Hitch, taking advantage of his presence on train No. 48, would, from eleven to twelve o'clock, deliver an address on Mormonism in car No. 117—inviting to hear him all desirous of being instructed concerning the mysteries of the religion of the " Latter Day Saints."

" Certainly, I will go," said Passepartout to himself, who knew nothing of Mormonism but its custom of polygamy, the base of Mormon society.

The news spread rapidly through the train, which carried about one hundred passengers. Of this number thirty at most, attracted by the notice of the meeting, occupied at eleven o'clock the seats in car No. 117. Passepartout was prominent in the front rank of the faithful. Neither his master nor Fix thought it worth while to take the trouble.

At the appointed hour Elder William Hitch rose, and in quite an irritated voice, as if he had been contradicted in advance, he cried, " I tell you that Joe Smith is a martyr, that his brother Hiram is a martyr, and that the persecution by the United States Government of the prophets will also make a martyr of Brigham Young. Who dares to maintain the contrary? "

No one ventured to contradict the missionary, whose excitement contrasted with his naturally calm physiognomy. But, without doubt, his anger was explained by the fact that Mormonism was now subjected to severe trials. The United States Government had, not without difficulty, just reduced these independent fanatics. It had made itself

master of Utah, and had subjected it to the laws of the
Union, after imprisoning Brigham Young, accused of rebellion and polygamy. Since that period, the disciples of
the prophet redoubled their efforts, and whilst not coming
to acts, resisted in words the demands of Congress.

We see that Elder William Hitch was trying to proselyte
even on the trains. And then he related, emphasizing his
narrative by his loud voice and the violence of his gestures,
the history of Mormonism from *Bible* times, how in Israel,
a Mormon prophet of the tribe of Joseph, published the
annals of the new religion and bequeathed them to his son
Morom; how, many centuries later, a translation of this
precious book, written in Egyptian characters, was made
by Joseph Smith, Jr., a farmer in the State of Vermont,
who revealed himself as a mystical prophet in 1825; how,
finally, a celestial messenger appeared to him in an illuminated forest and gave him the annals of the Lord.

At this moment, some of his hearers, not much interested
in the retrospective narrative of the missionary, left the
car; but William Hitch, continuing, related how Smith,
Jr., with his father, his two brothers, and a few disciples,
founded the religion of the Latter Day Saints—a religon
which, adopted not only in America, but in England, in
Scandinavia, and in Germany, counts among its faithful,
artisans and also a number of people engaged in the liberal
professions; how a colony was founded in Ohio; how a
temple was built at a cost of two hundred thousand dollars,
and a city built at Kirkland; how Smith became an enterprising banker and received from a simple mummy showman a papyrus scroll containing a narrative written by
Abraham and other celebrated Egyptians.

This narrative becoming a little long, the ranks of his
hearers thinned out still more, and the audience only consisted of twenty persons. But the Elder, undisturbed by
this desertion, related the details of how Joe Smith became
bankrupt in 1837; how his ruined stockholders gave him
a coat of tar and feathers; how he appeared again, more
honorable and more honored than ever, a few years after,
at Independence, in Missouri, at the head of a flourishing
community, which counted not less than three thousand
disciples; and that then, pursued by the hatred of the Gen-
tiles, he had to fly to the far West.

Ten hearers were still there, and among them the honest Passepartout, who listened with all his ears. Thus he learned how, after long persecutions, Smith reappeared in Illinois, and in 1839 founded, on the banks of the Mississippi, Nauvoo the beautiful, whose population rose to twenty-five thousand souls; how Smith became the Mayor, Chief Justice, and General-in-Chief; how in 1843 he announced himself as candidate for the Presidency of the United States; and how finally, he was drawn into an ambuscade at Carthage, thrown into prison, and assassinated by a band of masked men.

At this moment Passepartout was the only hearer in the car, and the Elder, looking him in the face, fascinating him by the words, recalled to his mind that, two years after the assassination of Smith, his successor, the inspired prophet Brigham Young, leaving Nauvoo, established himself on the banks of Salt Lake, and that there, in that splendid Territory, in the midst of that fertile country, on the road which the emigrants take in crossing Utah to reach California, the new colony, thanks to the Mormon principles of polygamy, had increased enormously.

"And this," added William Hitch, "is why the jealousy of Congress has been aroused against us! why the United States soldiers have invaded the soil of Utah! why our chief, the prophet Brigham Young, has been imprisoned in defiance of all justice. Shall we give up to force? Never! Driven from Vermont, driven from Illinois, driven from Ohio, driven from Missouri, driven from Utah, we shall find some independent territory yet where we shall pitch our tents. And you my brother," added the Elder, fixing his angry look on his single hearer, "will you plant yours in the shadow of our flag?"

"No," replied Passepartout bravely, flying in his turn, leaving the fanatic to preach in the desert.

But, during this discourse, the train had advanced rapidly, and about half-past twelve it touched the northwest corner of the Great Salt Lake. Thence could be embraced in a vast circumference the aspect of this inland lake, which also bears the name of the Dead Sea, and into which empties an American Jordan. A beautiful lake, hemmed in by craggy rocks of broad surface, encrusted with white salt, a superb sheet of water which formerly covered a larger space; but in time, its shores, rising by degrees, reduced its superficial area and increased its depth.

The Salt Lake, about seventy miles long, and thirty-five wide, is situated three thousand eight hundred feet above the level of the sea. It holds considerable salt in solution, and one-fourth the weight of the water is solid matter. Its specific gravity is 1,170, that of distilled water being 1,000. Fishes cannot live in it. Those that the Jordan, Weber, and other creeks, carry into it soon perish; but it is not true that the density of its waters is such that a man cannot dive into it.

Around the lake the country was admirably tilled; for the Mormons understand agricultural pursuits; ranches and corrals for domestic animals; fields of wheat, corn, sorghum, luxuriant prairies, and everywhere hedges of wild roses, clumps of acacias and euphorbias, such would have been the appearance of this country six months later; but at this moment the ground was covered with a thin sheet of snow, descending lightly upon it.

At two o'clock the travelers got out at Ogden. The train stopping for six hours, Mr. Fogg, Aouda, and their two companions had time to repair to the City of the Saints by the short branch from Ogden. Two hours were sufficient to visit this absolutely American town, and as such, built after the pattern of all the cities of the Union, vast checker-boards with long cold lines, " with the somber sadness of right angles," according to Victor Hugo's expression. The founder of the City of the Saints could not escape from the need of symmetry which distinguishes the Anglo-Saxons. In this singular country, where the men are certainly not up to the level of their institutions, everything is done " squarely," cities, houses, and follies.

At three o'clock, the travelers were promenading through the streets of the town, built between the banks of the Jordon and the first rise of the Wahsatch Mountains. They noticed there few or no churches, but as monuments, the prophet's house, the court-house, and the arsenal; then houses of bluish bricks with verandas and porches, surrounded by gardens bordered with acacias, palms and locusts. A wall of clay and pebbles, built in 1853, surrounded the town. In the principal street, where the market is, were some hotels adorned with pavilions, and among others Salt Lake House.

Mr. Fogg and his companions did not find the town thickly peopled. The streets were almost deserted, save perhaps the part where the Temple was, which they reached only after having traversed several quarters surrounded by palisades. The women were pretty numerous, which was explained by the singular composition of Mormon households. It must not be supposed, however, that all Mormons are polygamists. They are free, but it is well to remark that all the females in Utah are anxious to be married; for, according to the religion of the country, the Mormon heaven does not admit to the possession of its beatitudes the unmarried of the feminine sex. These poor creatures neither seemed well off, nor happy. Some, the richer ones, doubtless, wore a short, low-cut, black silk dress, under a hood or a very modest shawl. The others were dressed in Indian fashion.

Passepartout, in his position as one convinced, did not regard without a certain fright these Mormon women, charged, in groups, with making a single Mormon happy. With his good sense, it was the husband whom he specially pitied. It seemed to him terrible to have to guide so many wives at once through the vicissitudes of life, conduct them, as it were, in a body to the Mormon paradise, with the prospect of finding them to all eternity in the company of the glorious Smith, who was to be the ornament of this place of delights. Certainly, he did not feel called, and he thought—perhaps he was mistaken—that the women of Salt Lake City cast rather embarrassing looks at his person.

Very fortunately, his stay in the City of the Saints was not prolonged. At a few minutes past four o'clock the travelers were again at the station, and took their seats in the cars.

The whistle sounded; but at the moment that the driving-wheels of the locomotive, slipping upon the rails, commenced to impart some movement to the train, the cry, " Stop! stop! " was heard.

They do not stop trains just started. The gentleman who uttered the cry was evidently a Mormon behind time. He was breathless from running. Fortunately for him the station had neither gates nor barriers. He rushed, then, on the track, jumped upon the steps of the last car, and fell, out of breath, on one of the seats.

Passepartout, who had followed with emotion the incidents of this gymnastic feat, went to look at the tardy one, in whom he took a lively interest, when he learned that this citizen of Utah had thus taken flight in consequence of a household scene.

When the Mormon had recovered his breath, Passepartout ventured to ask him politely how many wives he had to himself—and from the manner in which he had just run away he would suppose that he had at least twenty of them.

" One, sir ! " replied the Mormon, raising his arms heavenward—" One, and that was enough ! "

CHAPTER XXVIII
IN WHICH PASSEPARTOUT COULD NOT SUCCEED IN MAKING ANYONE LISTEN TO REASON

THE train leaving Great Salt Lake and the station at Ogden, ran for an hour towards the north, as far as Weber River, having accomplished about nine hundred miles from San Francisco. Leaving this point, it resumed the easterly direction across the rocky hills of the Wahsatch Mountains. It is in this part of the territory, comprised between these mountains and the Rock Mountains properly so called, that the American engineers were confronted with the greatest difficulties. On this portion of the route the subsidy of the United States Government was raised to forty-eight thousand dollars per mile, whilst on the plains it was only sixteen thousand dollars; but the engineers, as has already been said, have not done violence to nature—they have played with her, going round the difficulties. To reach the great basin, only one tunnel, fourteen thousand feet long, was bored in the entire route of the railroad.

At Salt Lake the road had up to this time reached its greatest altitude. From this point its profile described a very long curve, descending towards Bitter Creek Valley, then re-ascending to the dividing ridge of the waters between the Atlantic and the Pacific. The creeks were numerous in this mountainous region. It was necessary to cross the Muddy, the Green, and others, on culverts.

Passepartout became more impatient in proportion as he approached the end of his journey. Fix in his turn would have been very glad to get out of this rough country. He feared delays, he dreaded accidents, and was more in a hurry than Phileas Fogg himself to set foot upon English soil!

At ten o'clock at night the train stopped at Fort Bridger station, which it left almost immediately, and twenty miles further on it entered Wyoming Territory—following the entire valley of the Bitter Creek, whence flow a portion of the streams forming the water system of Colorado.

The next day, the 7th of December, there was a stop of a quarter hour at Green River station. The snow had fallen quite heavily through the night, but mingled with rain and half melted it could not interfere with the progress of the train. But this bad weather kept Passepartout in constant uneasiness, for the accumulation of the snow clogging the car wheels would certainly endanger the journey.

" What an idea," he said to himself, " for my master to travel during the winter! Could he not wait for the fine season of the year to increase his chances? "

But at this moment, while the good fellow was busy only with the condition of the sky and the lowering of the temperature, Aouda was experiencing more serious fears, which proceeded from quite another cause.

Some of the passengers had got out of the cars, and were walking on the platform of the Green River Station, waiting for the train to leave. The young woman, looking through the window pane, recognized among them Colonel Stamp Proctor, the American who had behaved so rudely to Phileas Fogg at the time of the political meeting in San Francisco. Aouda, not wishing to be seen, drew back from the window.

This circumstance made a lively impression upon the young woman. She was attached to the man who, however coldly, gave her every day tokens of the most absolute devotion. She doubtless did not comprehend the entire depth of the sentiment which her deliverer inspired in her, and to this sentiment she gave as yet only the name of gratitude; but unknown to herself, it was more than that. Her heart was therefore wrung at the sight of the rough fellow of whom Mr. Fogg would, sooner or later, demand satisfaction. Evidently, it was chance alone that had brought Colonel Proctor into this train; but he was there, and Phileas Fogg must be prevented at any cost from seeing his adversary.

When the train had started again, Aouda took advantage of a moment, when Mr. Fogg was sleeping, to post Fix and Passepartout as to the situation.

"That Proctor is on the train!" cried Fix. "Well, compose yourself, madame; before dealing with the gentleman—with Mr. Fogg—he will have to deal with me! It seems to me that in all this business I have received the greatest insults!"

"And moreover," added Passepartout, "I will take care of him, Colonel as he is."

"Mr. Fix," continued Aouda, "Mr. Fogg will allow no one to avenge him. He has said that he will return to America to find this ruffian. If, then, he sees Colonel Proctor, we cannot prevent an encounter, which may lead to deplorable results. He must therefore not see him."

"You are right, madame," replied Fix; "an encounter might ruin everything. Conqueror or conquered, Mr. Fogg would be delayed, and——"

"And," added Passepartout, "that would win the bet of the gentlemen of the Reform Club. In four days we shall be in New York! Well, then, if my master does not leave his car for four days, we may hope that chance will not put him face to face with this cursed American, confound him! Now, we can easily prevent him——"

The conversation was interrupted. Mr. Fogg had waked up, and was looking at the country through the window pane obscured by the snow. But later, and without being heard by his master or Aouda, Passepartout said to the detective: "Would you truly fight for him?"

"I would do anything to take him back to Europe alive!" simply replied Fix, in a tone which indicated an unbroken will.

Passepartout felt a shudder over him, but his convictions as to the honesty of his master were not weakened.

And now, were there any means by which Mr. Fogg could be detained in this car, so as to prevent any encounter between him and the colonel? That could not be difficult, as the gentleman was naturally not excitable or inquisitive.

At all events, the detective thought he had found this means, for a few moments later he said to Phileas Fogg:

" These are long and slow hours that we pass thus on the railway."

" Indeed they are," replied the gentleman, " but they pass."

" On board the steamers," continued the detective, " you used to take a turn at whist?"

" Yes," replied Phileas Fogg, " but here it would be difficult. I have neither cards nor partners."

" Oh! as for the cards, we will find it easy to buy them. They are sold on all trains in America. As for partners, if, perchance, madame——"

" Certainly, sir," replied the young woman quickly, " I understand whist. That is part of the English education."

" And I," continued Fix, " have some pretensions to playing a good game. Now, with us three and a dummy——"

" As you please, sir," replied Phileas Fogg, delighted at resuming his favorite game, even on the railroad.

Passepartout was dispatched in search of the steward, and he soon returned with two complete decks of cards, counters, and a shelf covered with cloth. Nothing was wanting. The game commenced. Aouda understood whist well enough, and she even was complimented sometimes by the severe Phileas Fogg. As for the detective, he was simply an adept, and worthy of holding his head up with this gentleman.

" Now," said Passepartout to himself, " we will keep him. He will not budge any more!"

At eleven o'clock in the morning, the train had reached the dividing ridge of the waters of the two oceans. It was at Bridger Pass, at a height of seven thousand five hundred and twenty-four English feet above the level of the sea, one of the highest points touched by the profile of the route in this passage across the Rocky Mountains. After going about two hundred miles, the travelers finally found themselves on the vast plains extending as far as the Atlantic, and which nature made so propitious for laying a railroad.

On the slopes of the Atlantic basin already appeared the first streams, tributaries of the North Platte river. The entire northern and eastern horizon was covered by the immense semi-circular curtain, which forms the southern portion of the Rocky Mountains, the hightest being Laramie's Peak. Between this curve and the line of the road extended vast and plentifully watered plains. On the right of the road rose the first spurs of the mountainous mass, rounding off to the south as far as the sources of the Arkansas river, one of the large tributaries of the Mississippi.

At half past twelve, the travelers caught sight for an instant of Fort Halleck, which commands this country. A few hours more, and the crossing of the Rocky Mountains would be accomplished. It was to be hoped, then, that no accident would mark the passage of the train through this difficult region. The snow had stopped falling. The weather became cold and dry. Large birds, frightened by the locomotive, were flying in the distance. Not a deer, a bear, or a wolf, showed itself on the plain. It was the desert in all its barrenness.

After a very comfortable breakfast, served up in the car, Mr. Fogg and his partners had just resumed their interminable whist, when sharp whistles were heard. The train stopped.

Passepartout put his head out of the door, and saw nothing which could explain this stop. No station was in sight.

Aouda and Fix feared for an instant that Mr. Fogg would think of going out on the track. But the gentleman contented himself with saying to his servant, " See then what it is."

Passepartout rushed out of the car. About forty passengers had left their seats, and among them Colonel Stamp Proctor.

The train had stopped in front of a red signal which blocked the way. The engineer and conductor, having got out, discussed quite excitedly with a signal man, whom the station master at Medicine Bow, the next station, had sent in advance of the train. Some of the passengers approached and took part in the discussion, among others the aforesaid Colonel Proctor, with his loud voice and imperious gestures.

Passepartout, having rejoined the group, heard the signal man say, " No! there is no means of passing. The bridge at Medicine Bow is shaky and will not bear the weight of the train."

The bridge in question was a suspension bridge over a rapids, about a mile from the place where the train had stopped. According to the signalman, it threatened to fall, several of the wires having snapped, and it was impossible to risk its passage. He did not exaggerate in any way, then, in asserting that they could not pass over the bridge. And besides, with the careless habits of the Americans, we may say that when they are prudent, we would be very foolish not to be so.

Passepartout, not daring to go to inform his master, listened with set teeth, immovable as a statue.

"Ah, indeed!" cried Colonel Proctor, "we are not going, I imagine, to remain here, and take root in the snow!"

"Colonel," replied the conductor, "we have telegraphed to Omaha for a train, but it is not probable that it will arrive at Medicine Bow before six hours."

"Six hours!" cried Passepartout.

"Without doubt," replied the conductor. "Besides, that time will be necessary for us to reach the station on foot."

"But it is only a mile from here," said one of the passengers.

"A mile, in fact, but on the other side of the river."

"And cannot the river be crossed in a boat?" asked the colonel.

"Impossible. The creek is swollen with the rains. It is a torrent, and we will be compelled to make a detour of ten miles to the north to find a ford."

The colonel launched a volley of oaths, blaming the company, and the conductor. Passepartout furious, was not far from joining with him. Here was a material obstacle against which, this time, all his master's bank-notes would be of no avail.

The disappointment was general among the passengers, who, without counting the delay, saw themselves obliged to foot it fifteen miles across the plain covered with snow. There was a hubbub, exclamations, loud and deep, which would certainly have attracted Phileas Fogg's attention, if that gentleman had not been absorbed in his game.

But Passepartout found himself compelled to inform

him, and with drooping head, he turned towards the car, when the engineer of the train, a genuine Yankee, named Forster, raising his voice, said, " Gentlemen, there might be a way of passing."

" On the bridge? " asked a passenger.

" On the bridge."

" With our train? " asked the colonel.

" With our train."

Passepartout stopped, and devoured the engineer's words.

" But the bridge threatens to fall! " continued the conductor.

" It doesn't matter," replied Forster. " I believe that by rushing the train over at its maximum speed we would have some chances of passing."

" The devil! " exclaimed Passepartout.

But a certain number of the passengers were immediately carried away by the proposition. It pleased Colonel Proctor particularly. That hot-head found the thing very feasible. He recalled, even, that engineers had had the idea of passing rivers without bridges, with trains closely coupled, rushing at the height of their speed, etc. And, finally, all those interested took sides with the engineer's views.

" We have fifty chances for passing," said one.

" Sixty," said another.

" Eighty! Ninety out of one hundred! "

Passepartout was perplexed, although he was willing to try anything to accomplish the passage of Medicine creek, but the attempt seemed to him a little too " American."

" Besides," he thought, " there is a much simpler thing to do, and these people don't even think of it." " Monsieur," he said to one of the passengers, " the way proposed by the engineer seems a little hazardous to me, but——"

" Eighty chances! " replied the passenger, turning his back to him.

" I know very well," replied Passepartout, addressing another gentleman, " but a simple reflection——"

" No reflection, it is useless! " replied the American addressed, shrugging his shoulders, " since the engineer assures us that we will pass! "

" Without doubt," continued Passepartout, " we will pass, but it would perhaps be more prudent——"

"What prudent!" cried Colonel Proctor, jumping at this word, heard by chance. "At full speed, you have been told! Don't you understand? At full speed!"

"I know—I understand," repeated Passepartout, whom no one would allow to finish his phrase; "but it would be, if not more prudent, since the word offends you, at least more natural——"

"Who? What? How? What is the matter with this fellow?" was heard from all directions.

The poor fellow did not know whom to address.

"Are you afraid?" Colonel Proctor asked him.

"I, afraid?" cried Passepartout. "Well, so be it! I will show these people that a Frenchman can be as American as they!"

".All aboard! All aboard!" cried the conductor.

"Yes, all aboard," repeated Passepartout; "all aboard! and right away! But they can't prevent me from thinking that it would have been more natural for us to have gone over the bridge afoot, and then brought the train afterwards!"

But no one heard this sage reflection, and no one would have acknowledged its justness.

The passengers took their seats again in the cars. Passepartout resumed his, without saying anything of what had occurred. The players were entirely .absorbed in their game.

The locomotive whistled vigorously. The engineer reversed his engine, and backed for about a mile—returned like a jumper who is going to take a leap. Then, at a second whistle, they commenced to move forwards, the speed increased; it soon became frightful; but a single puffing was heard from the locomotive; the pistons worked twenty strokes to the second; the axles smoked in the journals. They felt, so to speak, that the entire train, moving at the rate of one hundred miles to the hour, did not bear upon the rails. The speed destroyed the weight.

And they passed! And it was like a flash of lightning. They saw nothing of the bridge. The train leaped, it might be said, from one bank to the other, and the engineer could not stop his train for five miles beyond the station.

But the train had scarcely crossed the river than the bridge, already about to fall, went down with a crash into the rapids of Medicine Bow.

CHAPTER XXIX

THAT same evening the train continued its course without obstructions, passed Fort Sanders, crossed the Cheyenne Pass and arrived at Evans Pass. At this point, the railroad reached the highest point on the route, *i e.,* eight thousand and ninety-one feet above the level of the ocean. The travelers now only had to descend to the Atlantic over those boundless plains, leveled by nature.

There was the branch from the " grand trunk " to Denver City, the principal town of Colorado. This territory is rich in gold and silver mines, and more than fifty thousand inhabitants have already settled there.

At this moment thirteen hundred and eighty-two miles had been made from San Francisco in three days and three nights. Four nights and four days, if nothing interfered, ought to be sufficient to reach New York. Phileas Fogg was then still within his time.

During the night they passed to the left of Camp Walbach. Lodge Pole Creek ran parallel to the road, following the straight boundary between the Territories of Wyoming and Colorado. At eleven o'clock they entered Nebraska, passing near Sedgwick, and they touched at Julesburg, on the South Fork of the Platte River.

It was at this point that the Union Pacific Road was inaugurated on the 23d of October, 1867, by its chief engineer, General G. M. Dodge. There stopped the two powerful locomotives, drawing the nine cars of invited guests, prominent among whom was the Vice-President of the road, Thomas C. Durant; three cheers were given; there the Sioux and Pawnees gave an imitation Indian battle; there the fireworks were set off; there, finally, was struck off by means of a portable printing press the first number of the *Railway Pioneer.* Thus was celebrated the inauguration of this great railroad, an instrument of progress and civilization, thrown across the desert, and destined to bind together towns and cities not yet in existence. The whistle of the locomotive, more powerful than the lyre of Amphion, was soon to make them rise from the American soil.

At eight o'clock in the morning Fort McPherson was left

357

behind. Three hundred and fifty-seven miles separate this point from Omaha. The railroad followed, on its left bank, the capricious windings of the South Fork of Platte river. At nine o'clock they arrived at the important town of North Platte, built between the two arms of the main stream, which join each other around it, forming a single artery—a large tributary—whose waters mingle with those of the Missouri a little above Omaha.

The one hundred and first meridian was passed.

Mr. Fogg and his partner had resumed their play. Neither of them complained of the length of the route—not even the dummy. Mr. Fix had won a few guineas at first, which he was in a fair way to lose, but he was not less deeply interested than Mr. Fogg. During this morning chance singularly favored this gentleman. Trumps and honors were showered into his hands. At a certain moment, after having made a bold combination, he was about to play a spade, when behind the seat a voice was heard, saying, " I should play a diamond."

Mr. Fogg, Aouda, and Fix raised their heads. Colonel Proctor was near them.

Stamp Proctor and Phileas Fogg recognized each other at once.

" Ah, it is you, Englishman," cried the colonel: " it's you who is going to play a spade."

" And who plays it," replied Phileas Fogg coldly, laying down a ten of that color.

" Well, it suits me to have it diamonds," replied Colonel Proctor, in an irritated voice.

And he made a motion as if to pick up the card played, adding, " You don't understand anything of this game."

" Perhaps I will be more skillful at another," said Phileas Fogg, rising.

" You have only to try it, son of John Bull! " replied the coarse fellow.

Aouda became pale. All the blood went to her heart. She seized Phileas Fogg's arm, and he gently repulsed her. Passepartout was ready to throw himself on, looking at his adversary with the most insulting air. But Fix had risen, and going to Colonel Proctor, said to him, " You forget that you have me to deal with; me whom you have not only insulted, but struck! "

"Mr. Fix," said Mr. Fogg, "I beg your pardon, but it concerns me alone. In insisting that I was wrong in playing a spade, the colonel has insulted me anew, and he shall give me satisfaction."

"When you will, and where you will," replied the American, "and with whatever weapon you please!"

Aouda tried in vain to restrain Mr. Fogg. The detective uselessly endeavored to take up the quarrel on his own account. Passepartout wanted to throw the colonel out of the door, but a sign from his master stopped him. Phileas Fogg went out of the car, and the American followed him on the platform.

"Sir," said Mr. Fogg to his adversary, "I am very much in a hurry to return to Europe, and any delay whatever would be very prejudicial to my interests."

"Well! what does that concern me?" replied Colonel Proctor.

"Sir," replied Mr. Fogg, very politely, "after our meeting in San Francisco, I formed the plan to come back to America to find you, as soon as I had completed the business which calls me to the Old World."

"Truly!"

"Will you appoint a meeting with me in six months?"

"Why not in six years?"

"I say six months," replied Mr. Fogg, "and I will be prompt to meet you."

"All evasions!" cried Stamp Proctor. "Immediately, or not at all."

"All right," replied Mr. Fogg. "You are going to New York?"

"No."

"To Chicago?"

"No."

"To Omaha?"

"It concerns you very little! Do you know Plum Creek station?"

"No," replied Mr. Fogg.

"It is the next station. The train will be there in an hour. It will stop ten minutes. In ten minutes we can exchange a few shots with our revolvers."

"Let it be so," replied Mr. Fogg. "I will stop at Plum Creek."

" And I believe that you will remain there!" added the American with unparalleled insolence.

" Who knows, sir?" replied Mr. Fogg, and he re-entered the car as coolly as usual.

That gentleman commenced to reassure Aouda, saying to her that blusterers were never to be feared. Then he begged Fix to act as his second in the encounter which was going to take place. Fix could not refuse, and Phileas Fogg resumed quietly his interrupted game, playing a spade with perfect serenity.

At eleven o'clock the whistle of the locomotive announced that they were near Plum Creek station. Mr. Fogg rose, and followed by Fix, he went out on the platform. Passepartout accompanied him, carrying a pair of revolvers. Aouda remained in the car, as pale as death.

At this moment the door of the next car opened, and Colonel Proctor appeared likewise upon the platform, followed by his second, a Yankee of his own stamp. But at the moment that the two adversaries were going to step off the train, the conductor ran up to them and cried :

" You can't get off, gentlemen."

" Why not?" asked the Colonel.

" We are twenty minutes behind time, and the train does not stop."

" But I am going to fight a duel with this gentleman."

" I regret it," replied the conductor, " but we are going to start again immediately. Hear the bell ringing!"

The bell was ringing, and the train moved on.

" I am really very sorry, gentlemen," said the conductor. " Under any other circumstances, I could have obliged you. But, after all, since you had not the time to fight here, who hinders you from fighting while the train is in motion?"

" Perhaps that will not suit the gentleman!" said Colonel Proctor with a jeering air.

" That suits me perfectly," replied Phileas Fogg.

" Well, we are decidedly in America!" thought Passepartout, " and the conductor is a gentleman of the first order."

Having said this, he followed his master.

The two combatants and their seconds, preceded by the conductor, repaired to the rear of the train, passing through the cars. The last car was only occupied by about ten or a dozen passengers. The conductor asked them if they would be kind enough to vacate for a few moments for two gentlemen who had an affair of honor to settle.

Why not? The passengers were only too happy to be able to accommodate the two gentlemen, and they retired on the platforms. The car, fifty feet long, accommodated itself very conveniently to the purpose. The two adversaries might march on each other in the aisle, and fire at their ease. There never was a duel easier to arrange. Mr. Fogg and Colonel Proctor, each furnished with two six barreled revolvers, entered the car. Their seconds, remaining outside, shut them in. At the first whistle of the locomotive, they were to commence firing. Then after a lapse of two minutes what remained of the two gentlemen would be taken out of the car Truly, there could be nothing simpler. It was even so simple that Fix and Passepartout felt their hearts beating almost as if they would break.

They were waiting for the whistle agreed upon, when suddenly savage cries resounded. Reports accompanied them, but they did not come from the car reserved for the duelists. These reports continued, on the contrary, as far as the front, and along the whole line of the train. Cries of fright made themselves heard from the inside of the cars.

Colonel Proctor and Mr. Fogg, with their revolvers in hand, went out of the car immediately, and rushed forward where the reports and cries resounded more noisily. They understood that the train had been attacked by a band of Sioux.

It was not the first attempt of these daring Indians. More than once already they had stopped the trains. According to their habit, without waiting for the stopping of the train, rushing upon the steps to the number of a hundred, they had scaled the cars like a clown does a horse at full gallop.

These Sioux were provided with guns. Thence the reports, to which the passengers, nearly all armed, replied sharply by shots from their revolvers. At first the Indians rushed upon the engine. The engineer and fireman were half stunned with blows from their muskets. A Sioux chief, wishing to stop the train, but not knowing how to maneuver the handle of the regulator, had opened wide the steam valve instead of closing it, and the locomotive, beyond control, ran on with frightful rapidity.

At the same time, the Sioux entered the cars, they ran like enraged monkeys over the roofs, they drove in the doors and fought hand to hand with the passengers. The trunks, broken open and robbed, were thrown out of the baggage car on the road. Cries and shots did not cease.

But the passengers defended themselves courageously. Some of the cars, barricaded, sustained a siege, like real moving forts, borne on at a speed of one hundred miles an hour.

From the commencement of the attack Aouda had behaved courageously. With revolver in hand, she defended herself heroically, firing through the broken panes when some savage presented himself. About twenty Sioux, mortally wounded, fell upon the track, and the car wheels crushed like worms those that slipped onto the rails from the top of the platforms. Several passengers, severely wounded by bullets or clubs, lay upon the seats.

But an end must be put to this. This combat had lasted already for ten minutes, and could only end to the advantage of the Sioux, if the train was not stopped. In fact, Fort Kearney station was not two miles distant. There was a military post, but that passed, between Fort Kearney and the next station the Sioux would be masters of the train.

The conductor was fighting at Mr. Fogg's side, when a ball struck him and he fell. As he fell, he cried, " We are lost if the train is not stopped inside of five minutes! "

" It shall be stopped! " said Phileas Fogg, who was about to rush out of the car.

" Remain, monsieur," Passepartout cried to him. " That is my business."

Phileas Fogg had not the time to stop the courageous young man, who, opening a door without being seen by the Indians, succeeded in slipping under the car. Whilst the struggle continued, and whilst the balls were crossing each other above his head recovering his agility, his suppleness as a clown he made his way under the cars. Clinging to the chains, assisting himself by the lever of the brakes and the edges of the window sashes, climbing from one car to another with marvelous skill, he thus reached the front of the train. He had not been seen; he could not have been.

There, suspended by one hand between the baggage car and the tender, with the other he loosened the couplings; but in consequence of the traction, he would never have been able to pull out the yoking-bar if a sudden jolt of the engine had not made the bar jump out, and the train, detached, was left farther and farther behind, while the locomotive flew on with new speed.

Carried on by the force acquired, the train still rolled on for a few minutes, but the brakes were maneuvered from the inside of the cars, and the train finally stopped less than one hundred paces from Kearney Station.

The soldiers of the fort, attracted by the firing, ran hastily to the train. The Sioux did not wait for them, and before the train stopped entirely the whole band had decamped.

But when the passengers counted each other on the platform of the station, they noticed that several were missing, and among others the courageous Frenchman, whose devotion had just saved them.

CHAPTER XXX
IN WHICH PHILEAS FOGG SIMPLY DOES HIS DUTY

THREE passengers, including Passepartout, had disappeared. Had they been killed in the fight? Were they taken prisoners by the Sioux? As yet it could not be told.

The wounded were quite numerous, but none mortally. The one most seriously hurt was Colonel Proctor, who had fought bravely, and who fell struck by a ball in the groin. He was carried to the station with the other passengers, whose condition demanded immediate care.

Aouda was safe. Phileas Fogg, who had not spared himself, had not a scratch. Fix was wounded in the arm— but it was an unimportant wound. But poor Passepartout was missing, and tears flowed from the young woman's eyes.

Meanwhile, all the passengers had left the train. The wheels of the cars were stained with blood. To the hubs and spokes hung ragged pieces of flesh. As far as the eye could reach long red trails were seen on the white plain.

The last Indians were then disappearing in the south, along the banks of Republican river.

Mr. Fogg, with folded arms, stood motionless. He had a serious decision to make. Aouda, near him, looked at him without uttering a word. He understood her look. If his servant was a prisoner ought he not to risk everything to rescue him from the Indians?

"I will find him dead or alive," he said simply to Aouda.

"Ah! Mr. Fogg—Mr. Fogg!" cried the young woman, seizing her companion's hands and covering them with tears.

"Alive!" added Mr. Fogg, "if we do not lose a minute!"

With this resolution Phileas Fogg sacrificed himself entirely. He had just pronounced his ruin. A single day's delay would make him miss the steamer from New York. His bet would be irrevocably lost. But in the face of the thought, "It is my duty!" he did not hestitate.

The captain commanding Fort Kearney was there. His soldiers—about a hundred men—had put themselves on the defensive in the event of the Sioux making a direct attack upon the station.

"Sir," said Mr. Fogg to the captain, "three passengers have disappeared."

"Killed?" asked the captain.

"Killed or prisoners," replied Mr. Fogg. "That is an uncertainty which we must bring to an end. It is your intention to pursue the Sioux?"

"It is a grave matter, sir," said the captain. "These Indians may fly beyond the Arkansas! I could not abandon the fort entrusted to me."

"Sir," replied Phileas Fogg, "it is a question of the life of three men."

"Doubtless—but can I risk the life of fifty to save three?"

"I do not know whether you can, but you ought."

"Sir," replied the captain, "no one here has the right to tell me what my duty is."

"Let it be so!" said Phileas Fogg coldly, "I will go alone!"

"You, sir!" cried Fix, who approached, "go alone in pursuit of the Indians!"

" Do you wish me then to allow to perish the unfortunate man to whom everyone of us that is living owes his life? I shall go."

" Well, no, you shall not go alone!" cried the captain, moved in spite of himself. " No! You are a brave heart! Thirty volunteers!" he added, turning to his soldiers.

The whole company advanced in a body. The captain had to select from these brave fellows. Thirty soldiers were picked out, and an old sergeant put at their head.

" Thanks, captain!" said Mr. Fogg.

" You will permit me to accompany you?" Fix asked the gentleman.

" You will do as you please," replied Phileas Fogg. " But if you wish to do me a service, you will remain by Aouda. In case anything should happen to me——"

A sudden paleness overcast the detective's face. To separate himself from the man whom he had followed step by step and with so much persistence! To let him venture so much in the desert. Fix looked closely at the gentleman, and whatver he may have thought, in spite of his prejudices, in spite of his inward struggle, he dropped his eyes before that quiet, frank look.

" I will remain," he said.

A few moments after, Mr. Fogg pressed the young woman's hand; then, having placed in her care his precious traveling bag, he set out with the sergeant and his little band.

But before starting, he said to the soldiers, " My friends, there are five thousand dollars for you if you save the prisoners!"

It was then a few minutes past noon.

Aouda retired into a sitting room of the station, and there, alone, she waited, thinking of Phileas Fogg, his simple and grand generosity, his quiet courage. Mr. Fogg had sacrificed his fortune, and now he was staking his life—and all this without hesitation from a sense of duty, without words. Phileas Fogg was a hero in her eyes.

The detective was not thinking thus, and he could not restrain his agitation. He walked feverishly up and down the platform of the station, one moment vanquished, he became himself again. Fogg having gone, he comprehended his foolishness in letting him go. What! Had he consented to be separated from the man that he had just been following around the world! His natural disposition got the upper hand; he criminated and accused himself; he treated himself as if he had been the director of the Metropolitan Police reproving an agent caught at a very green trick.

"I have been a silly fellow!" he thought. "The other fellow will have told him who I was! He has gone; he will not return! Where can I capture him now? But how have I so allowed myself to be fascinated when I have a warrant for his arrest in my pocket! I am decidedly only an ass!"

Thus reasoned the detective, while the hours slipped on too slowly for his liking. He did not know what to do. Sometimes, he felt like telling Aouda everything. But he understood how he would be received by the young woman. What course should he take? He was tempted to go in pursuit of this Fogg across the immense white plains. It did not seem impossible for him to find him. The footprints of the detachment were still imprinted upon the snow! But under a fresh covering every track would soon be effaced.

Fix was discouraged. He felt an almost insurmountable desire to abandon the party. This very occasion of leaving Kearney station and of prosecuting the journey, so fruitful in mishaps, was opened to him.

About two o'clock in the afternoon, while the snow was falling in large flakes, long whistles were heard coming from the east. An enormous shadow, preceded by a lurid light, slowly advanced, considerably increased by the mist, which gave it a fantastic appearance.

But no train was expected yet from the east. The help asked for by telegraph could not arrive so soon and the train from Omaha to San Francisco would not pass until the next day. They were soon enlightened.

This locomotive, moving under a small head of steam, and whistling very loud, was the one which, after being detached from the train, had continued its course with such frightful speed, carrying the unconscious fireman and engineer. It had run on for several miles; then the fire had gone down for want of fuel; the steam had slackened, and an hour afterwards, relaxing its speed by degrees, the engine finally stopped twenty miles beyond Kearney station.

Neither the engineer nor the fireman was dead, and after a very long swoon they revived. The engine had stopped. When he saw himself in the desert, and the locomotive without cars attached to it, the engineer understood what had happened. He could not guess how the locomotive had been detached from the train, but he did not doubt that the train, left behind, was in distress.

The engineer did not hesitate as to what he ought to do. To continue his course in the direction of Omaha was prudent, to return towards the train, which the Indians were perhaps yet robbing, was dangerous. No matter! Coal and wood were thrown into the furnace, the fire started up again, the head of steam increased again, and about two o'clock in the afternoon the engine returned, running backwards to Kearney station. This was the whistling they heard in the mist.

It was a great satisfaction for the travelers, when they saw the locomotive put at the head of the train. They were going to be able to continue their journey so unfortunately interrupted.

On the arrival of the engine, Aouda came out of the station, and addressing the conductor she asked:

" You are going to start? "

" This very instant, madame."

" But the prisoners—our unfortunate companions——"

" I cannot interrupt the trip," replied the conductor. " We are already three hours behind time."

" And when will the next train coming from San Francisco pass? "

" To-morrow evening, madame."

" To-morrow evning! But it will be too late. We must wait——"

" Impossible," replied the conductor. " If you are going, get aboard the car."

" I will not go," replied the young woman.

Fix heard this conversation. A few moments before, when every means of locomotion failed him, he had decided to quit Kearney, and now that the train was there ready to continue its course, and he only had to seat himself again in the car, an irresistible force fixed him to the ground. The platform of the station burned his feet, and he could not tear himself away from it. The conflict within himself recommenced. His anger at his want of success choked him. He was going to struggle on to the end.

Meanwhile the passengers and some of the wounded— among others Colonel Proctor, whose condition was very serious—had taken seats in the cars. The buzzing of the overheated boiler was heard; the steam escaped through the valves; the engine whistled, the train started, and soon disappeared, mingling its white smoke with the whirling of the snow.

The detective Fix had remained.

Some hours passed. The weather was very bad, the cold very keen. Fix, seated on a bench in the station, was motionless. It might have been supposed that he was sleeping. Notwithstanding the storm, Aouda left every moment the room which had been placed at her disposal. She went to the end of the platform, trying to look through the tempest of snow, wishing to pierce the mist which narrowed the horizon around her, listening if she could hear any sound. But there was nothing. She went in then, chilled through, to return a few moments later, and always in vain.

Evening came. The little detachment had not returned. Where was it at this moment? Had it been able to overtake the Indians? Had there been a fight, or were these soldiers, lost in the mist, wandering at a venture? The captain of Fort Kearney was very uneasy, although he did not wish to let his uneasiness appear.

Night came; the snow fell less heavily, but the intensity of the cold increased. The most intrepid glance would not have looked at this vast, obscure space without terror. An absolute silence prevailed over the plain. Neither the flight of a bird nor the passage of a wild beast disturbed the unbroken quiet.

During the whole night Aouda, her mind full of dark presentiments, her heart filled with anguish, wandered on the border of the prairie. Her imagination carried her afar off and showed her a thousand dangers. What she suffered during those long hours could not be expressed. Fix, still immovable in the same spot, did not sleep. Once a man approached and spoke to him, but the detective sent him away, after replying to him by a negative sign.

Thus the night passed. At dawn, the half-concealed disk of the sun rose from a misty horizon. Still the eye might reach as far as two miles. Phileas Fogg and the detachment had gone to the south. The south was entirely deserted. It was then seven o'clock in the morning.

The captain, extremely anxious, did not know what course to take. Ought he to send a second detachment to help the first? Ought he to sacrifice fresh men with so few chances of saving those who were sacrificed at first? But his hesitation did not last, and with a gesture calling one of his lieutenants, he gave him the order to throw out a reconnoissance to the south, when shots were heard. Was it a signal? The soldiers rushed out of the fort, and half a mile distant they perceived a small band returning in good order.

Phileas Fogg marched at the head, and near him Passepartout and the two passengers, rescued from the hands of the Sioux.

There was a fight ten miles south of Fort Kearney. Passepartout and his two companions were already struggling against their captors, and the Frenchman had knocked down three of them with his fist, when his master and the soldiers rushed to their rescue.

All—the deliverers and the delivered—were received with cries of joy, and Phileas Fogg divided among the soldiers the reward he had promised them, whilst Passepartout repeated to himself, not without reason, "I must confess that I am certainly costing my master very dearly."

Fix, without uttering a word, looked at Mr. Fogg, and it would have been difficult to analyze the impressions struggling within him. As for Aouda, she took the gentleman's hand, and pressed it in hers, without being able to utter a word!

In the meantime Passepartout, upon his arrival, was looking for the train at the station. He thought he would find it there, ready to start for Omaha, and he hoped they could still make up the lost time. "The train, the train!" he cried.

"Gone," replied Fix.

"And when will the next train pass?" asked Fogg.

"Not until this evening."

"Ah!" simply replied the impassible gentleman.

369

PHILEAS FOGG found himself twenty hours behind time. Passepartout, the involuntary cause of this delay, was desperate. He had certainly ruined his master!

At this moment the detective approached Mr. Fogg, and looking closely in his face, asked: " Very seriously, sir, you are in a hurry? "

" Very seriously," replied Phileas Fogg.

" I insist," continued Fix. " It is very much to your interest to be in New York on the 11th, before nine o'clock in the evening, the time of departure of the Liverpool steamer."

" I have a very great interest."

" And if your journey had not been interrupted by this Indian attack, you would have arrived in New York on the morning of the 11th? "

" Yes, twelve hours before the departure of the steamer."

" Well, you are now twenty hours behind time. The difference between twenty and twelve is eight. Eight hours are to be made up. Do you wish to try to do it? "

" On foot? " asked Mr. Fogg.

" No, on a sledge," replied Fix, " on a sledge with sails. A man has proposed this means of conveyance to me."

It was the man who had spoken to the detective during the night, and whose offer he had refused.

Phileas Fogg did not reply to Fix; but Fix having shown him the man in question, who was walking up and down before the station, the gentleman went up to him. An instant after, Phileas Fogg and this American, named Mudge, entered a hut built at the foot of Fort Kearney.

There Mr. Fogg examined a very singular vehicle, a sort of frame laid on two long beams, a little raised in front, like the runners of a sledge, and upon which five or six persons could be seated. On the front of the frame was fastened a very high mast, to which an immense brigantine sail was attached. The mast, firmly held by metallic fastenings, held an iron stay, which served to hoist a large jib-sail. At the rear a sort of rudder allowed the apparatus to be steered.

As could be seen, it was a sledge sloop-rigged. During

the winter, on the icy plains, when the trains are blocked up by the snow, these vehicles make extremely rapid trips from one station to another. They carry a tremendous press of sail, far more than a cutter, and, with the wind behind, they glide over the surface of the prairie with a speed equal to, if not greater than, that of an express train.

In a few moments, the bargain was concluded between Mr. Fogg and the owner of this land craft. The wind was good. It blew with a strong breeze from the west. The snow had hardened, and Mudge was certain that he could take Mr. Fogg in a few hours to Omaha. There the trains are frequent, and the routes leading to Chicago and New York are numerous. It was not impossible to make up the time lost. There should be no hesitation in making the attempt.

Mr. Fogg, not wishing to expose Aouda to the discomforts of a trip in the open air, with the cold rendered more unbearable by the speed, proposed to her to remain under Passepartout's care at Kearney station. The honest fellow would undertake to bring her to Europe by a better route and under more acceptable conditions.

Aouda refused to be separated from Mr. Fogg, and Passepartout felt very happy at this determination. Indeed, nothing in the world would have induced him to leave his master, since Fix was to accompany him.

As to what the detective then thought, it would be difficult to say. Had his convictions been shaken by Phileas Fogg's return, or rather did he consider him a very shrewd rogue, who, having accomplished his tour of the world, believed that he would be entirely safe in England? Perhaps Fix's opinion concerning Phileas Fogg was really modified. But he was none the less decided to do his duty, and more impatient than all of them to hasten with all his might the return to England.

At eight o'clock the sledge was ready to start. The travelers—we were tempted to say the passengers—took their places, and wrapped themselves closely in their traveling cloaks. The two immense sails were hoisted, and, under the pressure of the wind, the vehicle slipped over the hardened snow with a speed of forty miles an hour.

The distance between Fort Kearney and Omaha is, in a

straight line—in a bee-line, as the Americans say—two hundred miles at the most. If the wind continued, this distance could be accomplished in five hours. If no accident happened, the sledge ought to reach Omaha at one o'clock in the afternoon.

What a journey! The travelers, huddled up against each other, could not speak. The cold, increased by the speed, cut off their words. The sledge glided as lightly over the surface of the plain as a vessel over the surface of the water—with the swell at least. When the breeze came, skimming the earth, it seemed as if the sledge was lifted from the ground by its sails, which were like huge wings. Mudge, at the rudder, kept the straight line, and with a turn of the tiller he corrected the lurches which the apparatus had a tendency to make. All sail was carried. The jib had been arranged so that it no longer was screened by the brigantine. A top-mast was hoisted, and another jib stretched to the wind added its force to that of the other sails. It could not be exactly estimated, but certainly the speed of the sledge could not be less than forty miles an hour.

"If nothing breaks," said Mudge, "we shall arrive!"

It was Mudge's interest to arrive at the time agreed upon, for Mr. Fogg adhering to his plan, had stimulated him by the promise of a handsome reward.

The prairie, which the sledge was crossing in a straight line, was as flat as a sea. It might have been called a frozen pond. The railroad which ran through this section, ascended from southwest to northwest by Grand Island, Columbus, an important Nebraska town, Schuyler, Fremont, then Omaha. During its entire course, it followed the right bank of Platte river. The sledge, shortening this route, took the cord of the arc described by the railroad. Mudge did not fear being stopped by the Platte river, at the short bend in front of Fremont, as it was frozen over. The way was then entirely free of obstructions, and Phileas Fogg had only two things to fear: an accident to the apparatus, a change or a calm of the wind.

But the breeze did not abate. On the contrary, it blew so hard that it bent the mast, which the iron fastenings kept firm. These metal fastenings, like the chords of an instrument, resounded as if a violin bow had produced their vibrations. The sledge slid along in the midst of a plaintive harmony, of a very perculiar intensity.

" These cords give the fifth and the octave," said Mr. Fogg.

And these were the only words he uttered during this trip. Aouda, carefully wrapped in furs and cloaks, was preserved as much as possible from the attacks of the cold.

Passepartout, his face red as the solar disk when it sets in the mist, drew in the biting air. With the depth of unshaken confidence that he possessed, he was ready to hope again. Instead of arriving in New York in the morning, they would arrive there in the evening, but there might be some chances that it would be before the departure of the Liverpool steamer.

Passepartout even experienced a strong desire to grasp the hand of his ally Fix. He did not forget that it was the detective himself who had procured the sledge with sails, and consequently the only means there was to reach Omaha in good time. But by some unknown presentiment, he kept himself in his accustomed reserve.

At all events, one thing which Passepartout would never forget was the sacrifice which Mr. Fogg had unhesitatingly made to rescue him from the hands of the Sioux. As for that, Mr. Fogg had risked his fortune and his life—— No! his servant would not forget him!

Whilst each one of the travelers allowed himself to wander off in such various reflections the sledge flew over the immense carpet of snow. If it passed over creeks, tributaries, or sub-tributaries of Little Blue river, they did not perceive it. The fields and the streams disappeared under a uniform whiteness.

The plain was absolutely deserted. Comprised between the Union Pacific Road and the branch uniting Kearney to St. Joseph, it formed as it were a large uninhabited island. Not a village, not a station, not even a fort. From time to time they saw passing like a flash some grimacing tree, whose white skeleton was twisted about by the wind. Sometimes flocks of wild birds rose: sometimes, also, prairie wolves in large bands, gaunt, famished, urged on by a ferocious demand of nature, vied with the sledge in swiftness. Then Passepartout, with revolver in hand, held himself ready to fire upon those that came nearest.

If any accident had then stopped the sledge, the travelers, attacked by these ferocious carnivorous beasts, would have run the greatest risks. But the sledge kept on in its course, it was not long in getting ahead, and soon the whole howling band was left behind.

At noon, Mudge recognized by certain landmarks that he was crossing the frozen course of the Platte river. He said nothing, but he was sure that in twenty miles more he would reach Omaha.

And, indeed, one hour afterwards this skillful guide, abandoning the helm, hastened to the halyards of the sails and furled them, whilst the sledge, carried on by its irresistible force, accomplished another half mile under bare poles. Finally it stopped, and Mudge pointing out a mass of roofs white with snow, said: " We have arrived.'"

Arrived! Arrived indeed at the station which, by numerous trains is in daily communication with the eastern part of the United States! Passepartout and Fix jumped to the ground and shook their stiffened limbs. They helped Mr. Fogg and the young woman to descend from the sledge. Phileas Fogg settled generously with Mudge, whose hand Passepartout shook like a friend's, and all hurried towards the depot in Omaha.

The Pacific Railroad, properly so called, has its terminus at this important city in Nebraska, placing the Mississippi basin in connection with the great ocean. To go from Omaha to Chicago, the Chicago, Rock Island and Pacific Road is taken, running directly to the east, and passing fifty stations.

A through train was ready to start. Phileas Fogg and his companions only had time to hurry into a car. They had seen nothing of Omaha; but Passepartout acknowledged to himself that it was not to be regretted, as they were not on a sight-seeing tour. The train passed with very great speed into the state of Iowa, through Council Bluffs, Des Moines, and Iowa City. During the night it crossed the Mississippi at Davenport, and entered Illinois at Rock Island. The next day, the 10th, at four o'clock in the afternoon, they arrived at Chicago, already risen from its ruins, and sitting more proudly than ever on the shores of the beautiful Lake Michigan.

Nine hundred miles separate Chicago from New York.

Trains are not wanting at Chicago. Mr. Fogg passed immediately from one to the other. The nimble locomotive of the Pittsburg, Fort Wayne, and Chicago Railway started at full speed, as if it understood that the honorable gentleman "had no time to lose." It traversed Indiana and Ohio, passing by populous cities and over wide expanses of agricultural land, with but few pauses; and, sixteen hours after leaving Chicago, the Ohio was reached.

At thirty-five minutes after nine, on the evening of the 11th, the train entered the great depot at Jersey City, the walls of which are washed by the Hudson river. From this station, the eastern terminus of a railroad system of great magnitude, fifty-one passenger and eighty-one freight trains depart every twenty-four hours, and an equal number arrive. Steamers and sailing vessels lined the miles of docks extending on both sides of the station, and the mighty river was filled with craft of all kinds engaged in the commerce of New York, which rose in front of the travelers as they emerged upon the broad, covered way running in front of the depot, where the gigantic ferryboats of the railroad company receive and land their myriads of travelers, pausing not in their work day or night.

At thirty-five minutes after nine at night, the train stopped in the depot, near the very pier of the Cunard line of steamers, otherwise called The British and North American Royal Mail Steam Packet Company.

The *China,* bound for Liverpool, had left thirty-five minutes before!

CHAPTER XXXII
IN WHICH PHILEAS FOGG ENGAGES IN A DIRECT STRUGGLE WITH ILL LUCK

THE *China,* in leaving, seemed to have carried away with her Phileas Fogg's last hope. In fact, none of the other steamers in the direct service between America and Europe, neither the French Transatlantic steamers, nor the ships of the White Star line, nor those of the Inman Company, nor those of the Hamburg line, nor any others, could serve the gentleman's projects.

The *Pereire,* of the French Atlantic Company, would not start until the 14th of December. And besides, like those of the Hamburg Company, she would not go directly to Liverpool or London, but to Havre, and this additional trip from Havre to Southampton, delaying Phileas Fogg, would have rendered his last efforts of no avail.

The gentleman posted himself thoroughly about all this by consulting his Bradshaw, which gave him, day by day, the movements of the transoceanic vessels.

Passepartout was annihilated. It killed him to miss the steamer by thirty-five minutes. It was his fault, he who, instead of aiding his master, had not ceased to scatter obstacles in his way! And when he reviewed in his mind all the incidents of the journey; when he calculated the sums spent, which was pure loss, and for his own interest; when he thought that this enormous bet, added to the heavy expenses of this now useless journey, would completely ruin Mr. Fogg, he overwhelmed himself with opprobrium.

Mr. Fogg did not reproach him at all, and leaving the pier of the ocean steamers, he said only these words: " We will consult to-morrow. Come."

Mr. Fogg, Aouda, Fix, and Passepartout crossed the Hudson from Jersey City in the ferry boat, and got into a carriage, which took them to the St. Nicholas hotel, on Broadway. Rooms were put at their disposal, and the night passed,—a very short one for Phileas Fogg, who slept soundly, but very long for Aouda and her companions, whose agitation did not allow them to rest.

The next day was the 12th of December. From the 12th, at seven in the morning, to the 21st, at eight forty-five in the evening, there remained nine days, thirteen hours, and forty-five minutes. If, then, Phileas Fogg had left the night before in the *China,* one of the best sailers of the Cunard line, he would have arrived at Liverpool, and then in London, in the desired time!

Phileas Fogg left the hotel alone, having recommended his servant to wait for him, and to notify Aouda to hold herself in readiness at any moment.

Mr. Fogg repaired to the banks of the Hudson, and among the ships moored to the wharf, or anchored in the stream, he sought with care those which were about to leave. Several vessels had their signals for departure up and were preparing to put to sea at the morning high tide, for in this immense and admirable port, there is not a day when a hundred vessels do not set sail for every quarter of the globe; but the most of them were sailing vessels, and they would not suit Phileas Fogg.

This gentleman was seeming to fail in his last attempt, when he perceived, moored in front of the battery, at a cable's length at most, a merchantman, with screw, of fine outlines, whose smoke-stack, emitting clouds of smoke, indicated that she was preparing to sail.

Phileas Fogg hailed a boat, got in it, and with a few strokes of the oar, he found himself at the ladder of the *Henrietta,* an iron-hulled steamer, with her upper parts of wood.

The captain of the *Henrietta* was on board. Phileas Fogg went up on deck and asked for the captain, who presented himself immediately.

He was a man fifty years old, a sort of sea wolf, a grumbler who would not be very accommodating. His large eyes, his complexion oxydized copper, his red hair, his large chest and shoulders, indicated nothing of the appearance of a man of the world.

" The captain? " asked Mr. Fogg.

" I am he."

" I am Phileas Fogg, of London."

" And I am Andrew Speedy, of Cardiff."

" You are going to start? "

" In an hour."

" You are loaded for——? "

" Bordeaux."

" And your cargo? "

" Gravel in the hold. I have no freight. I sail in ballast."

" You have passengers? "

" No passengers. Never have passengers. A merchandise that's in the way and reasons."

" Your vessel sails swiftly? "

" Between eleven and twelve knots. The *Henrietta,* well known."

" Do you wish to convey me to Liverpool, myself and three persons? "

" To Liverpool? Why not to China? "

" I said Liverpool."

" No! "

" No? "

" No. I am setting out for Bordeaux, and I shall go to Bordeaux."

" It don't matter what price?"

" It don't matter what price!"

The captain spoke in a tone which did not admit of a reply.

" But the owners of the *Henrietta*——" replied Phileas Fogg.

" The owners of the *Henrietta* are myself," replied the captain. " The vessel belongs to me."

" I will freight it for you."

" No."

" No? "

" I will buy it from you."

Phileas Fogg did not change countenance. But the situation was serious. It was not at New York as at Hong Kong, nor with the captain of the *Henrietta* as with the captain of the *Tankadere*. Until the present the gentleman's money had always overcome obstacles. This time the money failed.

But the means of crossing the Atlantic in a vessel must be found, unless they went across in a balloon, which would have been very venturesome, and which, besides, was not practicable.

Phileas Fogg, however, appeared to have an idea, for he said to the captain: " Well, will you take me to Bordeaux?"

" No, even if you would pay me two hundred dollars."

" I offer you two thousand."

" For each person?"

" For each person."

" And there are four of you?"

" Four."

Captain Speedy commenced to scratch his forehead as if he would tear the skin off. Eight thousand dollars to be made, without changing his course; it was well worth the trouble of putting aside his decided antipathy for every kind of passenger. Passengers at two thousand dollars apiece, besides, are no longer passengers, but valuable merchandise.

"I leave at nine o'clock," said Captain Speedy, simply, "and you and yours will be there?"

"At nine o'clock we will be on board!" simply replied Mr. Fogg.

It was half past eight. To land from the *Henrietta*, get in a carriage, repair to the St. Nicholas Hotel, and take back with him Aouda, Passepartout, and even the inseparable Fix, to whom he graciously offered a passage, this was all done by the gentleman with the quiet which never deserted him under any circumstances. At the moment that the *Henrietta* was ready to sail, all four were aboard.

When Passepartout learned what this last voyage would cost, he uttered one of those prolonged "Oh's!" which run through all the spaces of the descending chromatic scale!

As for Detective Fix, he said to himself that the Bank of England would not come out whole from this affair. In fact, by the time of their arrival, and admitting that this Mr. Fogg would not throw a few handfuls besides into the sea, more than seven thousand pounds would be missing from the bank notes in the traveling bag!

CHAPTER XXXIII
IN WHICH PHILEAS FOGG SHOWS HIMSELF EQUAL TO CIRCUMSTANCES

AN hour afterwards the steamer *Henrietta* passed the light-boat which marks the entrance of the Hudson, turned Sandy Hook Point, and put to sea. During the day she skirted Long Island, in the offing of the Fire Island Light, and rapidly ran towards the east.

At noon of the next day, the 13th of December, a man went upon the bridge to take charge of the vessel. It would certainly be supposed that this man was Captain Speedy! Not at all. It was Phileas Fogg.

As for Captain Speedy, he was very snugly locked up in his cabin, and was howling at a rate that denoted an anger very pardonable, which amounted to a paroxysm.

What had happened was very simple. Phileas Fogg wanted to go to Liverpool; the captain would not take him there. Then Phileas Fogg had agreed to take passage for Bordeaux, and during the thirty hours that he had been on board, he had maneuvered so well with his bank notes, that the crew, sailors and firemen—an occasional crew, on bad terms with the captain—belonged to him. And this is why Phileas Fogg commanded in the place of Captain Speedy, why the captain was shut up in his cabin, and why, finally, the *Henrietta* was steering her course towards Liverpool. It was very clear, seeing Mr. Fogg maneuver, that he had been a sailor.

Now, how the adventure would come out, would be known later. Aouda's uneasiness did not cease, although she said nothing. Fix was stunned at first. Passepartout found the thing simply splendid.

" Between eleven and twelve knots," Captain Speedy had said, and the *Henrietta* did indeed maintain this average of speed.

If then—how many " ifs " yet!—if the sea did not become too rough, if the wind did not rise in the east, if no mishap occurred to the vessel, no accident to the engine, the *Henrietta* in the nine days, counting from the 12th of December to the 21st, could accomplish the three thousand miles separating New York from Liverpool. It is true that once arrived, the *Henrietta* affair on top of the bank affair might take the gentleman a little farther than he would like.

During the first few days they went along under excellent conditions. The wind was not too rough; the sails were hoisted, and with them the *Henrietta* sailed like a genuine transatlantic steamer.

Passepartout was delighted. The last exploit of his master, the consequences of which he preferred not to consider, filled him with enthusiasm. The crew had never seen a gayer, more agile fellow. He made a thousand friendships with the sailors and astonished them by his acrobatic feats. He lavished upon them the best names and the most attractive drinks. He thought that they maneuvered like gentlemen, and that the firemen coaled up like heroes. His good humor was very communicative, and impressed itself upon all. He had forgotten the past, with its annoyances and its perils. He thought only of the end, so nearly reached, and sometimes he boiled over with impatience, as if he had been heated by the furnaces of the *Henrietta*. Frequently, also, the worthy fellow revolved around Fix;

he looked at him with a distrustful eye, but he did not speak to him, for there no longer existed any intimacy between these two old friends.

Besides, Fix, it must be confessed, did not understand this thing at all. The conquest of the *Henrietta,* the purchase of her crew, and Fogg maneuvering like an accomplished seaman—this combination of things confused him. He did not know what to think. But, after all, a man who commenced by stealing fifty-five thousand pounds could finish by stealing a vessel. And Fix was naturally led to believe that the *Henrietta,* directed by Fogg, was not going to Liverpool at all, but into some quarter of the world where the robber, become a pirate, would quietly place himself in safety! This hypothesis, it must be confessed, could not be more plausible, and the detective commenced to regret very seriously having entered upon this affair.

As for Captain Speedy, he continued to howl in his cabin, and Passepartout, whose duty it was to provide his meals, did it only with the greatest precautions, although he was so strong. Phileas Fogg had no longer the appearance of even suspecting that there was a captain on board.

On the 13th, they passed the edge of the Banks of Newfoundland. Those are bad latitudes. During the winter, especially, the fogs are frequent there, the blows dreadful. Since the day before, the barometer, suddenly fallen, indicated an approaching change in the atmosphere. In fact, during the night the temperature varied, the cold became keener, and at the same time the wind shifted into the southeast.

This was a misfortune. Mr. Fogg, in order not to be driven out of his course, had to reef his sails and increase his steam. But the progress of the ship was slackened, owing to the condition of the sea, whose long waves broke against her stern. She was violently tossed about, and to the detriment of her speed. The breeze increased by degrees to a hurricane, and it was already a probable event that the *Henrietta* might not be able to hold herself upright against the waves. Now, if she had to fly before the storm, the unknown, with all its bad chances, threatened them.

Passepartout's face darkened at the same time as the sky, and for two days the good fellow was in mortal dread.

But Phileas Fogg was a bold sailor, who knew how to keep head against the sea, and he kept on his course, without even putting the vessel under a small head of steam. The *Henrietta,* whenever she could rise with the wave, passed over it, but her deck was swept from end to end. Sometimes, too, when a mountain wave raised the stern out of the water, the screw came out of the water, beating the air with its blades, but the ship still moved right on.

Still the wind did not become as severe as might have been feared. It was not one of those hurricanes which sweep on with a velocity of ninety miles an hour. It continued quite fresh, but unfortunately it blew obstinately from the southeast, and did not allow the sails to be hoisted. And yet, as we will see, it would have been very useful if they could have come to the aid of the steam!

The 16th of December was the seventy-fifth day that had elapsed since leaving London. The *Henrietta* had not yet been seriously delayed. The half of the voyage was nearly accomplished, and the worst localities had been passed. In summer, success would have been certain. In winter they were at the mercy of the bad weather. Passepartout did not speak. Secretly he hoped, and if the wind failed them, he counted at least upon the steam.

Now, on this day, the engineer ascended to the deck, met Mr. Fogg, and talked very earnestly with him. Without knowing why—by a presentiment, doubtless—Passepartout felt a sort of vague uneasiness. He would have given one of his ears to have heard with the other what was said. But he could catch a few words, these among others, uttered by his master: " You are certain of what you say? "

" I am certain, sir," replied the engineer. " Do not forget that, since our departure, all our furnaces have been going, and although we had enough coal to go under a small head of steam from New York to Bordeaux, we have not enough for a full head of steam from New York to Liverpool! "

" I will take the matter under consideration," replied Mr. Fogg.

Passepartout understood. A mortal fear took possession of him.

The coal was about to give out.

"Ah! if my master wards that off," he said to himself, "he will certainly be a famous man!"

And having met Fix, he could not help posting him as to the situation.

"Then," replied the detective, with set teeth, "you believe that we are going to Liverpool?"

"I do, indeed!"

"Idiot!" replied the detective, shrugging his shoulders as he turned away.

Passepartout was on the point of sharply resenting the epithet, whose true signification he could not understand; but he said to himself that the unfortunate Fix must be very much disappointed, and humiliated in his self esteem, having so awkwardly followed a false scent around the world, and he refrained from condemning him.

And now what course was Phileas Fogg going to take? It was difficult to guess. But it appeared that the phlegmatic gentleman decided upon one, for that evening he sent for the engineer and said to him: "Keep up your fires and continue on your course until the complete exhaustion of the fuel."

A few moments after, the smoke stack of the *Henrietta* was vomiting torrents of smoke.

The vessel continued, then, to sail under full steam; but, as he had announced, two days later, the 18th, the engineer informed him that the coal would give out during the day.

"Don't let the fires go down," replied Mr. Fogg. "On the contrary, let the valves be charged."

About noon of this day, having taken observations and calculated the position of the vessel, Phileas Fogg sent for Passepartout and ordered him to go for Captain Speedy. This good fellow felt as if he had been commanded to unchain a tiger, and he descended into the poop, saying to himself, "Positively I shall find a madman!"

In fact, a few minutes later a bomb came on the poop deck, in the midst of cries and oaths. This bomb was Captain Speedy. It was evident that it was going to burst.

"Where are we?" were the first words he uttered in the midst of his choking anger, and certainly if the worthy man had been apoplectic, he would never have recovered from it.

"Where are we?" he repeated, his face purple.

" Seven hundred and seventy miles from Liverpool," replied Mr. Fogg, with imperturbable calmness.

" Pirate! " cried Andrew Speedy.

" I have sent for you, sir——"

" Sea-skimmer! "

—" Sir," continued Phileas Fogg, " to ask you to sell me your ship."

" No! by all the devils, no! "

" I shall be obliged to burn her."

" To burn my ship! "

" At least her upper portions, for we are out of fuel."

" Burn my ship! " cried Captain Speedy, who could no longer pronounce his syllables. " A ship that is worth fifty thousand dollars! "

" Here are sixty thousand! " replied Phileas Fogg, offering him a roll of bank notes.

This produced a powerful effect upon Andrew Speedy. No American is without emotion at the sight of sixty thousand dollars. The captain forgot in an instant his anger, his imprisonment, all his grievances from his passenger. His ship was twenty years old. It might be quite a bargain! The bomb could not explode. Mr. Fogg had withdrawn the fuse.

" And the iron hull will be left me," he said in a singularly softened tone.

" The iron hull and the engine, sir. It is a bargain? "

" A bargain."

And Andrew Speedy, snatching the roll of bank notes, counted them and slipped them into his pocket.

During this scene, Passepartout was white as a sheet. As for Fix he narrowly escaped an apoplectic fit. Nearly twenty thousand pounds spent, and yet this Fogg was going to relinquish to the seller the hull and the engine, that is, nearly the entire value of the vessel! It is true that the sum stolen from the bank amounted to fifty-five thousand pounds!

When Andrew Speedy had pocketed his money, Mr. Fogg said to him: " Sir, don't let all this astonish you. Know that I lose twenty thousand pounds if I am not in London on the 21st of December, at a quarter before nine in the evening. Now, I had missed the steamer from New York, and as you refused to take me to Liverpool——"

"And I have done well, by all the imps of the lower regions," cried Andrew Speedy, "since I make by it, at least forty thousand dollars."

Then he added, more calmly: "Do you know one thing, captain——?"

"Fogg."

"Well, Captain Fogg, there is something of the Yankee in you."

And having paid his passenger what he thought to be a compliment, he went away, when Phileas Fogg said to him: "Now this ship belongs to me?"

"Certainly, from the keel to the truck of the masts, all the wood, understand."

"Very well. Cut away the inside arrangements and fire up with the *débris*."

It may be judged how much of this dry wood was necessary to maintain the steam at a sufficient pressure. This day, the poop deck, the cabins, the bunks, and the spare deck all went.

The next day, the 19th of December, they burned the masts, the rafts, and the spars. They cut down the masts, and delivered them to the ax. The crew displayed an incredible zeal. Passepartout, hewing, cutting, sawing, did the work of ten men. It was a perfect fury of demolition.

The next day, the 20th, the railings, the armor, all of the ship above water, the greater part of the deck, were consumed. The *Henrietta* was now a vessel cut down like a pontoon.

But on this day they sighted the coast of Ireland and Fastnet Light.

However, at ten o'clock in the evening, the ship was only passing Queenstown. Phileas Fogg had only twenty-four hours to reach London! Now, this was the time the *Henrietta* needed to reach Liverpool, even under full headway. And the steam was about to fail the bold gentleman!

"Sir," said Captain Speedy to him then, who had come to be interested in his projects, "I really pity you. Everything is against you. We are as yet only in front of Queenstown."

"Ah!" said Mr. Fogg, "that is Queenstown, the place where we perceive the light?"

"Yes."

"Can we enter the harbor?"

"Not for three hours. Only at high tide."

"Let us wait," Phileas Fogg replied çalmly, without letting it be seen on his face that, by a last inspiration, he was going to try to conquer once more his contrary fate!

Queenstown is a port on the coast of Ireland, at which the transatlantic steamers coming from the United States deposit their mail bag. These letters are carried to Dublin by express trains always ready to start. From Dublin they arrive in Liverpool by very swift vessels, thus gaining twelve hours over the most rapid sailers of the ocean.

These twelve hours which the American couriers gained, Phileas Fogg intended to gain, too. Instead of arriving by the *Henrietta* in the evening of the next day, at Liverpool, he would be there by noon, and, consequently, he would have time enough to reach London before a quarter of nine in the evening.

Towards one o'clock in the morning, the *Henrietta* entered Queenstown harbor at high tide, and Phileas Fogg, having received a vigorous shake of the hand from Captain Speedy, left him on the leveled hulk of his vessel, still worth the half of what he had sold it for!

The passengers landed immediately. Fix, at this moment, had a fierce desire to arrest Mr. Fogg. He did not do it, however. Why? What conflict was going on within him? Had he changed his mind with reference to Mr. Fogg? Did he finally perceive that he was mistaken? Fix, however, did not leave Mr. Fogg. With him, Aouda, and Passepartout, who did not take time to breathe, he jumped into the train at Queenstown at half past one in the morning, arrived in Dublin at break of day, and immediately embarked on one of those steamers—regular steel spindles, all engine—which, disdaining to rise with the waves, invariably pass right through them.

At twenty minutes before noon, the 21st of December, Phileas Fogg finally landed on the quay at Liverpool. He was now only six hours from London.

But at this moment Fix approached him, put his hand on his shoulder, and, showing his warrant, said: "You are really Phileas Fogg?"

"Yes, sir."

"I arrest you, in the name of the Queen!"

CHAPTER XXXIV
WHICH GIVES PASSEPARTOUT THE OPPORTUNITY OF LET-
TING OUT SOME ATROCIOUS, BUT PERHAPS UN-
PUBLISHED, WORDS

PHILEAS FOGG was in prison. He had been shut up in the custom house in Liverpool, and was to pass the night there, awaiting his transfer to London.

At the moment of his arrest, Passepartout wished to rush upon the detective. Some policemen held him back. Aouda, frightened by the brutality of the act, and knowing nothing about it, could not understand it. Passepartout explained the situation to her. Mr. Fogg, this honest and courageous gentleman, to whom she owed her life, was arrested as a robber. The young woman protested against such an allegation, her heart rose with indigation, and tears flowed from her eyes when she saw that she could not do anything, or attempt anything to save her deliverer.

As for Fix, he had arrested the gentleman because his duty commanded him to, whether he was guilty or not. The courts would decide the question.

But then a thought came to Passepartout—the terrible thought that he was certainly the cause of all this misfortune! Indeed, why had he concealed this adventure from Mr. Fogg? When Fix had revealed both his capacity as a detective and the mission with which he was charged, why had he decided not to warn his master? The latter, informed, would without doubt have given Fix proofs of his innocence; he would have demonstrated to him his error; at any rate he would not have conveyed at his expense and on his tracks this unfortunate detective, whose first care was to arrest him the moment he set foot on the soil of the United Kingdom. Thinking of his faults and 'is imprudence, the poor fellow was overwhelmed with remorse. He wept, so that it was painful to look at him. He felt like blowing his brains out.

Aouda and he remained, notwithstanding the cold, under the porch of the custom house. Neither of them wished to leave the place. They wanted to see Mr. Fogg once more.

As for that gentleman, he was really ruined, and at the very moment that he was about to reach his end. This arrest would ruin him irrecoverably. Having arrived at

Liverpool at twenty minutes before twelve, noon, on the 21st of December, he had until quarter of nine in the evening to appear at the Reform Club—that is, nine hours and five minutes, and he only needed six to reach London. At this moment, anyone entering the custom house would have found Mr. Fogg seated motionless, on a wooden bench, without anger, imperturbable. He could not have been said to be resigned, but this blow had not been able to move him, in appearance at least. Was he fostering within himself one of those secret spells of anger, terrible because they are pent up, and which break out only at the last moment with irresistible force? We do not know. But Phileas Fogg was there, calm, waiting for—what? Did he cherish some hope? Did he still believe in success, when the door of his prison was closed upon him?

However that may be, Mr. Fogg carefully put his watch on the table, and watched the hands move. Not a word escaped from his lips, but his look had a rather singular fixedness.

In any event the situation was terrible, and for anyone that could read his thoughts, they ran thus:

An honest man, Phileas Fogg was ruined.

A dishonest man, he was caught.

Did he think of escaping? Did he think of looking to see whether there was a practicable outlet from his prison? Did he think of flying? We would be tempted to believe so; for, once he took the tour of the room. But the door was securely locked and the windows had iron bars. He sat down again, and took from his pocket-book the diary of his journey. On the line which bore these words:

" December 21st, Saturday, Liverpool," he added:

" Eightieth day, 11 :40 A. M.," and he waited.

The custom house clock struck one. Mr. Fogg observed that his watch was two hours fast by this clock.

Two hours! Admitting that he should jump aboard an express train at this moment he could still arrive in London and at the Reform Club before quarter of nine in the evening. A light frown passed over his forehead.

At thirty-three minutes after two o'clock, a noise sounded outside, a bustle from the opening of doors. The voice of Passepartout was heard, and also that of Fix.

Phileas Fogg's look brightened up a moment.

The door opened, and he saw Aouda, Passepartout, Fix, rushing towards him.

Fix was out of breath, his hair all disordered, and he could not speak.

"Sir," he stammered, "sir—pardon—an unfortunate resemblance—robber arrested three days ago—you—free——!"

Phileas Fogg was free! He went to the detective, looked him well in the face, and, with the only rapid movement that he ever had made or ever would make in his life, he drew both his arms back, and then, with the precision of an automaton, he struck the unfortunate detective with both his fists.

"Well hit!" cried Passepartout, who, allowing himself an atrocious flow of words, quite worthy of a Frenchman, added: "Zounds! this is what might be called a fine application of English fists!"

Fix, prostrate, did not utter a word. He only got what he deserved. But Mr. Fogg, Aouda, and Passepartout immediately left the custom house. They jumped into a carriage, and in a few minutes arrived at the depot. Phileas Fogg asked if there was an express train ready to start for London.

It was forty minutes past two. The express had left thirty-five minutes before.

Phileas Fogg then ordered a special train. There were several locomotives of great speed with steam up; but, owing to the exigencies of the service, the special train could not leave the depot before three o'clock.

At three o'clock, Phileas Fogg, after saying a few words to the engineer about a certain reward to be won, moved on in the direction of London, in the company of the young woman and his faithful servant.

The distance which separates Liverpool from London must be accomplished in five hours and a half—a very feasible thing when the road is clear on the whole route. But there were compulsory delays, and when the gentleman arrived at the depot all the clocks in London were striking ten minutes of nine.

Phileas Fogg, after having accomplished this tour of the world, arrived five minutes behind time!

He had lost his bet.

IN WHICH PASSEPARTOUT DOES NOT HAVE REPEATED TO HIM TWICE THE ORDER HIS MASTER GIVES HIM

THE next day the residents of Saville Row would have been much surprised, if they had been told that Phileas Fogg had returned to his dwelling. The doors and windows were all closed. No change had taken place outside.

After leaving the depot Phileas Fogg gave Passepartout an order to buy some provisions, and he had gone into his house.

This gentleman received with his habitual impassibility the blow which struck him. Ruined! and by the fault of that awkward detective! After moving on with steady step during this long trip, overturning a thousand obstacles, braving a thousand dangers, and having still found time to do some good on his route, to fail before a brutal act, which he could not foresee, and against which he was defenseless —that was terrible! He had left only an insignificant remnant of the large sum which he had taken away with him when he started on his journey. His fortune now only consisted of the twenty thousand pounds deposited at Baring Brothers, and those twenty thousand pounds he owed to his colleagues of the Reform Club. Having incurred so many expenses, if he had won the bet he would not have been enriched; and, it is probable that he had not sought to enrich himself, being of that class of men who bet for the sake of honor—but this bet lost would ruin him entirely. The gentleman's decision was taken. He knew what remained for him to do.

A room in the house in Saville Row was set apart for Aouda. The young woman was desperate. From certain words which Mr. Fogg let drop, she understood that he contemplated some fatal design.

It is known, indeed, to what lamentable extremities these Englishmen are carried sometimes under the pressure of a fixed idea. Thus, Passepartout, without seeming to do so, was closely watching his master.

But first the good fellow descended to his room and turned off the burner which had been burning for eighty days. He found in the letter box a note from the gas company, and he thought that it was more than time to stop the expenses for which he was responsible.

The night passed. Mr. Fogg had retired; but had he slept? As for Aouda, she could not take a single moment's rest. Passepartout had watched, like a dog, at his master's door.

The next morning Mr. Fogg sent for him, and ordered him very briefly to prepare Aouda's breakfast. As for himself, he would be satisfied with a cup of tea and a piece of toast. Aouda would be kind enough to excuse him from breakfast and dinner, for all his time would be devoted to arranging his affairs. He would not come down, he would only ask Aouda's permission to have a few moment's conversation with her in the evening.

Passepartout, having been given the programme for the day, had nothing to do but to conform to it. He looked at his master, still so impassible, and he could not make up his mind to quit his room. His heart was full, and his conscience weighed down with remorse, for he accused himself more than ever for this irreparable disaster. Yes if he had warned Mr. Fogg, if he had disclosed to him the plans of the detective Fix, Mr. Fogg would certainly not have dragged the detective Fix with him as far as Liverpool, and then——

Passepartout could not hold in any longer. "My master! Monsieur Fogg!" he cried, "curse me. It is through my fault that——"

"I blame no one," replied Phileas Fogg in the calmest tone. "Go."

Passepartout left the room and went to find the young woman to whom he made know his master's intentions. "Madame," he added, "I can do nothing by myself, nothing at all. I have no influence over my master's mind. You, perhaps——"

"What influence would I have," replied Aouda. "Mr. Fogg is subject to none. Has he ever understood that my gratitude for him was overflowing? Has he ever read my heart? My friend you must not leave him for a single instant. You say that he has shown a desire to speak to me this evening?"

"Yes, madame. It is no doubt with reference to making your position in England comfortable."

"Let us wait," replied the young woman, who was quite pensive.

Thus, during this day, Sunday, the house in Saville Row was as if uninhabited, and for the first time since he lived there, Phileas Fogg did not go to his club, when the Parliament House clock struck half past eleven.

And why should this gentleman have presented himself at the Reform Club? His colleagues no longer expected him. Since Phileas Fogg did not appear in the saloon of the Reform Club the evening of the day before, on this fatal date, Saturday, December 21, at quarter before nine, his bet was lost. It was not even necessary that he should go to his banker's to draw this sum of twenty thousand pounds. His opponents had in their hands a check signed by him, and it only needed a simple writing to go to Baring Brothers in order that the twenty thousand pounds might be carried to their credit.

Mr. Fogg had then nothing to take him out, and he did not go out. He remained in his room, putting his affairs in order. Passepartout was continually going up and down stairs. The hours did not move for this poor fellow. He listened at the door of his master's room, and in doing so, did not think he committed the least indiscretion. He looked through the keyhole, and imagined that he had this right. Passepartout feared at every moment some catastrophe. Sometimes he thought of Fix, but a change had taken place in his mind. He no longer blamed the detective. Fix had been deceived, like everybody else, with respect to Philas Fogg, and in following him and arresting him he had only done his duty, while he——. This thought overwhelmed him, and he considered himself the most wretched of human beings.

When, finally, Passepartout would be too unhappy to be alone, he would knock at Aouda's door, enter her room, and sit down in a corner without saying a word, and look at the young woman with a pensive air.

About half-post seven in the evening, Phileas Fogg sent to ask Aouda if she could receive him and in a few moments after the young woman and he were alone in the room.

Phileas Fogg took a chair and sat down near the fireplace opposite Aouda. His face reflected no emotion. Fogg returned was exactly the Fogg who had gone away. The same calmness, the same impassibility.

He remained without speaking for five minutes. Then, raising his eyes to Aouda, he said:

"Madame, will you pardon me for having brought you to England?"

"I, Mr. Fogg!" replied Aouda, suppressing the throbbings of her heart.

"Be kind enough to allow me to finish," continued Mr. Fogg. "When I thought of taking you so far away from that country, become so dangerous for you, I was rich, and I counted on placing a portion of my fortune at your disposal. Your life would have been happy and free. Now, I am ruined."

"I know it, Mr. Fogg," replied the young woman, "and I in turn will ask you:—Will you pardon me for having followed you, and—who knows? for having perhaps assisted in your ruin by delaying you?"

"Madame, you could not remain in India, and your safety was only assured by removing you so far that those fanatics could not retake you."

"So, Mr. Fogg," replied Aouda, "not satisfied with rescuing me from a horrible death, you believed you were obliged to assure my position abroad?"

"Yes, madame," replied Fogg, "but events have turned against me. However, I ask your permission to dispose of the little I have left in your favor."

"But you, Mr. Fogg, what will become of you?" asked Aouda.

"I, madame, replied the gentleman, coldly, "I do not need anything."

"But how, sir, do you look upon the fate that awaits you?"

"As I ought to look at it," replied Mr. Fogg.

"In any event," continued Aouda, "want could not reach such a man as you. Your friends——"

"I have no friends, madame."

"Your relatives——"

"I have no relatives now."

"I pity you then, Mr. Fogg, for solitude is a sad thing. What! have you not one heart into which to pour your troubles? They say, however, that with two misery itself is bearable?"

"They say so, madame."

"Mr. Fogg," then said Aouda, rising and holding out her hand to the gentleman, "do you wish at once a relative and a friend? Will you have me for your wife?"

Mr. Fogg, at this, rose in his turn. There seemed to be an unusual reflection in his eyes, a trembling of his lips. Aouda looked at him. The sincerity, rectitude, firmness, and sweetness of this soft look of a noble woman, who dared everything to save him to whom she owed everything, first astonished him, then penetrated him. He closed his eyes for an instant, as if to prevent this look from penetrating deeper. When he opened them again, he simply said, "I love you. Yes, in truth, by everything most sacred in the world, I love you, and I am entirely yours!"

"Ah," cried Aouda, pressing his hand to her heart.

He rang for Passepartout. He came immediately. Mr. Fogg was still holding Aouda's hand in his. Passepartout understood, and his broad face shone like the sun in the zenith of tropical regions.

Mr. Fogg asked him if he would be too late to notify Rev. Samuel Wilson, of Mary-le-Bone parish.

Passepartout gave his most genial smile.

"Never too late," he said.

It was then five minutes after eight.

"It will be for to-morrow, Monday," he said.

"For to-morrow, Monday?" asked Mr. Fogg looking at the young woman.

"For to-morrow, Monday!" replied Aouda.

Passepartout went out, running as hard as he could.

CHAPTER XXXVI
IN WHICH "PHILEAS FOGG" IS AGAIN AT A PREMIUM IN THE MARKET

IT is time to tell here what a change of opinion was produced in the United Kingdom when they learned of the arrest of the true robber of the bank, a certain James Strand, which took place in Edinburgh on the 17th of December.

Three days before, Phileas Fogg was a criminal whom the police were pursuing to the utmost, and now he was the most honest gentleman, accomplishing mathematically his eccentric tour around the world.

What an effect, what an excitement in the papers! All the betters for or against, who had already forgotten this affair, revived as if by magic. All the transactions became of value. All the engagements were renewed, and it must be said that betting was resumed with new energy. The name of Phileas Fogg was again at a premium on the market.

The five colleagues of the gentleman, at the Reform Club, passed these three days in some uneasiness. Would this Phileas Fogg, whom they had forgotten, reappear before their eyes? Where was he at this moment? On the 17th of December—the day that James Strand was arrested—it was seventy-six days since Phileas Fogg started, and no news from him! Was he dead? Had he given up the effort, or was he continuing his course as agreed upon? And would he appear on Saturday, the 21st of December, at a quarter before nine in the evening, the very impersonation of exactness, on the threshold of the saloon of the Reform Club?

We must give up the effort to depict the anxiety in which for three days all of London society lived. They sent dispatches to America, to Asia, to get news of Phileas Fogg. They sent morning and evening to watch the house in Saville Row. Nothing there. The police themselves did not know what had become of the detective Fix, who had so unfortunately thrown himself on a false scent. This did not prevent bets from being entered into anew on a larger scale. Phileas Fogg, like a race-horse, was coming to the last turn. He was quoted no longer at one hundred, but at twenty, ten, five; and the old paralytic Lord Albemarle bet even in his favor.

So that on Saturday evening there was a crowd in Pall Mall and in the neighboring streets. It might have been supposed that there was an immense crowd of brokers permanently established around the Reform Club. Circulation was impeded. They discussed, disputed, and cried the prices of "Phileas Fogg," like they did those of English Consols. The policemen had much difficulty in keeping the crowd back, and in proportion as the hour approached at which Phileas Fogg ought to arrive, the excitement took incredible proportions.

This evening, the five colleagues of the gentleman were

assembled in the grand saloon of the Reform Club. The two bankers, John Sullivan and Samuel Fallentin, the engineer Andrew Stuart, Gauthier Ralph, the directors of the Bank of England, and the brewer, Thomas Flanagan, all waited with anxiety.

At the moment that the clock in the grand saloon indicated twenty-five minutes past eight, Andrew Stuart, rising, said:

" Gentleman, in twenty minutes the time agreed upon between Mr. Phileas Fogg and ourselves will have expired."

" At what hour did the last train arrive from Liverpool? " asked Thomas Flanagan.

" At twenty-three minutes after seven," replied Gauthier Ralph, " and the next train does not arrive until ten minutes after twelve, midnight."

" Well, gentlemen," continued Andrew Stuart, " if Phileas Fogg had arrived in the train at twenty-three minutes after seven, he would already be here. We can then consider we have won the bet."

" Let us wait before deciding," replied Samuel Fallentin. " You know that our colleague is an oddity of the first order. His exactness in everything is well known. He never arrives too late or too soon, and he will appear here at the very last minute, or I shall be very much surprised."

" And I," said Andrew Stewart, who was, as always, very nervous, " would not believe it was he even if I saw him."

" In fact," replied Thomas Flanagan, " Phileas Fogg's project was a senseless one. However exact he might be, he could not prevent the occurrence of inevitable delays, and a delay of but two or three days would be sufficient to compromise the tour."

" You will notice besides," added John Sullivan, " that we have received no news from our colleague, and yet telegraph lines were not wanting upon his route."

" Gentlemen, he has lost," replied Andrew Stuart, " he has lost a hundred times! You know, besides, that the *China*—the only steamer from New York that he could take for Liverpool to be of any use to him—arrived yesterday. Now, here is the list of passengers, published by the *Shipping Gazette,* and the name of Phileas Fogg is not among them. Admitting the most favorable chances, our colleague has scarcely reached America! I calculate twenty days, at least, as the time that he will be behind, and old Lord Albermarle will be minus his five thousand pounds!"

"It is evident," replied Gauthier Ralph, "and to-morrow we have only to present to Baring Brothers Mr. Fogg's check."

At this moment, the clock in the saloon struck forty minutes after eight.

"Five minutes yet," said Andrew Stuart.

The five colleagues looked at each other. It may be believed that their hearts beat a little more rapidly, for, even for good players, it was a great risk. But they did not betray themselves, for at Samuel Fallentin's suggestion, they seated themselves at a card table.

"I would not give my part of four thousand pounds in the bet," said Andrew Stuart, seating himself, "even if I was offered three thousand nine hundred and ninety-nine!"

At this moment the hands noted forty-two minutes after eight.

The players took up their cards, but their eyes were constantly fixed upon the clock. It may be asserted that, notwithstanding their security, the minutes had never seemed so long to them!

"Forty-three minutes after eight," said Thomas Flanagan, cutting the cards which Gauthier Ralph presented to him.

Then there was a moment's silence. The immense saloon of the club was quiet. But outside they heard the hubbub of the crowd, above which were sometimes heard loud cries. The pendulum of the clock was beating the seconds with mathematical regularity, and every player could count them as they struck his ear.

"Forty-four minutes after eight," said John Sullivan in a voice in which was heard an involuntary emotion.

One more minute and the bet would be won. Andrew Stuart and his colleagues played no longer. They had abandoned their cards! They were eagerly counting the seconds!

At the fortieth second, nothing. At the fiftieth still nothing!

At the fifty-fifth, there was a roaring like that of thunder outside, shouts, hurrahs, and even curses kept up in one

The players rose.

At the fifty-seventh second, the door of the saloon opened, and the pendulum had not beat the sixtieth second, when Phileas Fogg appeared, followed by an excited crowd, who had forced an entrance into the club, and in his calm voice, he said:

"Gentlemen, here I am!"

CHAPTER XXXVII

IN WHICH IT IS PROVED THAT PHILEAS FOGG HAS GAINED NOTHING BY MAKING THIS TOUR OF THE WORLD UNLESS IT BE HAPPINESS

YES! Phileas Fogg in person.

It will be remembered that at five minutes after eight in the evening, about twenty-five hours after the arrival of the travelers in London, Passepartout was charged by his master to inform Rev. Samuel Wilson in reference to a certain marriage which was to take place the next day.

Passepartout went, delighted. He repaired with rapid steps to the residence of Rev. Samuel Wilson, who had not come home. Of course Passepartout waited, but he waited full twenty minutes at least.

In short, it was thirty-five minutes past eight when he left the clergyman's house. But in what a condition! His hair disordered, hatless, running, running as has never been seen in the memory of man, upsetting passers-by, rushing along the sidewalks like a water-spout.

In three minutes, he had returned to the house in Saville Row, and fell, out of breath, in Mr. Fogg's room.

He could not speak.

"What is the matter?" asked Mr. Fogg.

"Master"—stammered Passepartout—"Marriage—impossible!"

"Impossible?"

"Impossible—to-morrow."

"Why?"

"Because to-morrow is—Sunday!"

"Monday," replied Mr. Fogg.

"No—to-day—Saturday."

"Saturday? Impossible!"

"Yes, yes, yes, yes!" cried Passepartout. "You have made a mistake of one day. We arrived twenty-four hours in advance—but there are not ten minutes left!"

Passepartout seized his master by the collar, and dragged him along with irresistible force!

Phileas Fogg, thus taken, without having time to reflect, left his room, went out of his house, jumped into a cab, promised one hundred pounds to the driver, and, after running over two dogs and running into five carriages, arrived at the Reform Club. The clock indicated quarter of nine, when he appeared in the grand saloon.

Phileas Fogg had accomplished this tour of the world in eighty days!

Phileas Fogg had won his bet of twenty thousand pounds!

And now, how could so exact and cautious a man have made this mistake of a day? How did he think that it was the evening of Saturday, December 21, when it was only Friday, December 20, only seventy-nine days after his departure.

This is the reason for this mistake. It is very simple.

Phileas Fogg had, without suspecting it, gained a day on his journey—only because he had made the tour of the world going to the *east*, and on the contrary he would have lost a day going in the contrary direction, that is, towards the *west*.

Indeed, journeying towards the east Phileas Fogg was going towards the sun, and consequently the days became as many times four minutes less for him, as he crossed degrees in that direction. Now there are three hundred and sixty degrees to the earth's circumference, and these three hundred and sixty degrees, multiplied by four minutes, give precisely twenty-four hours—that is to say, the day unconsciously gained. In other words, while Phileas Fogg, traveling towards the east, saw the sun pass the meridian *eighty* times, his colleagues, remaining in London, saw it pass only *seventy-nine times*. Therefore this very day, which was Saturday, and not Sunday, as Mr. Fogg thought, his friends were waiting for him in the saloon of the Reform Club.

And Passepartout's famous watch, which had always kept London time, would have shown this, if it had indicated the days, as well as the minutes and hours!

Phileas Fogg then had won the twenty thousand pounds.

But as he had spent in his journey about nineteen thousand, the pecuniary result was small. However, as has been said, the eccentric gentleman had sought in his bet to gain the victory, and not to make money. And even the thousand pounds remaining he divided between Passepartout and the unfortunate Fix, against whom he could not cherish a grudge. Only for the sake of exactness, he retained from his servant the cost of the gas burned through his fault for nineteen hundred and twenty hours.

This very evening Mr. Fogg, as impassible and as phlegmatic as ever, said to Aouda:

" This marriage is still agreeable to you? "

" Mr. Fogg," replied Aouda ," it is for me to ask you that question. You were ruined; now you are rich——"

" Pardon me, madam; my fortune belongs to you. If you had not thought of the marriage, my servant would not have gone to the house of Rev. Samuel Wilson. I would not have been apprised of my mistake, and——"

" Dear Mr. Fogg——" said the young woman.

" Dear Aouda," replied Phileas Fogg.

It is readily understood that the marriage took place forty-eight hours later, and Passepartout, superb, resplendent, dazzling, was present as the young woman's witness. Had he not saved her, and did they not owe him that honor?

At daylight the next morning, Passepartout knocked noisily at his master's door.

The door opened, and the impassible gentleman appeared.

" What is the matter, Passepartout? "

" What's the matter, sir! I have just found out this moment——"

" What? "

" That we could make the tour of the world in seventy-eight days."

" Doubtless," replied Mr. Fogg, " by not crossing India. But if I had not crossed India, I would not have saved Aouda, she would not be my wife, and——"

And Mr. Fogg quietly shut the door.

Thus Phileas Fogg won his bet. In eighty days he had accomplished the tour around the world! To do this he had employed every means of conveyance, steamers, railways, carriages, yachts, merchant vessels, sledges, elephants.

FOGG HAS GAINED NOTHING

The eccentric gentleman had displayed in this affair his wonderful qualities of coolness and exactness.

But what then? What had he gained by leaving home? what had be brought back from his journey?

Nothing, do you say? Nothing, perhaps, but a charming woman, who—improbable as it may appear—made him the happiest of men!

Truly, would you not, for less than that, make the tour of the world?

THE END

This book designed by
William B. Taylor
is a production of
Heron Books, London

Printed on wood free paper
and bound by Hazell Watson & Viney Ltd,
Aylesbury, Bucks

Printed and bound in England